The Pecci Chronicles

Confessions of a Corsair

The Pecci Chronicles

Confessions of a Corsair

a novel by

p.m. pecci

BraintreeBooks

Mashpee, MA

BraintreeBooks

The Pecci Chronicles:
Confessions of a Corsair

Published by BraintreeBooks
ISBN # 978-1-7341513-0-5

Copyedited by David Aretha

Cover and Title Design: Vladimir Manyukhim

Format Design and Publishing Assistant: Ryan Forsythe

Author photo by Michael Pecci

Image from *Mœurs, usages et costumes au moyen âge et à l'époque de la renaissance* by P. L. Jacob and Franz Kellerhoven (1871). No known copyright restrictions.

First BraintreeBooks edition, December 2019

www.BraintreeBooks.net

To Eileen

My soulmate and my co-pilot
through all of my life journeys

Mortal man, living in the world, is compared to a vessel upon perilous seas, bearing rich merchandise, by which, if it can come to harbour, the merchant will be rendered rich and happy. The ship from the commencement to the end of its voyage is in great peril of being lost or taken by an enemy, for the seas are always beset with perils. So is the body of man during its sojourn in the world. The merchandise he bears is his soul, his virtues, and his good deeds. The harbour is paradise, and he who reaches that haven is made supremely rich. The sea is the world, full of vices and sins, and in which all, during their passage through life, are in peril and danger of losing body and soul and of being drowned in the infernal sea, from which God in His grace keeps us! Amen.

- Nicolas de Rouge
Troyes 1490.

Prologue

Revelation

The snow continued to fall. At times, quite peacefully in the intermittent moments of stillness, and at times, fiercely as the winds from the north roared across the valley and battered against the ancient stone walls of the tower. The cluster of out buildings and factories that had surrounded the tower, encircling the hillock upon which the entire complex had been erected, were covered with a foot of ice and snow. The entire countryside was as frozen as the deepest recesses of Lucifer's prison. The winter winds of 1229 brought the harshest weather in memory. No one had seen such weather this far south of the Alps, and the people working within the complex at the base of the tower were whispering that God, having had enough of the wickedness that had become the custom of mankind, had decided to freeze His children until such time as the children of Noah would come again to rule the land. The Taurisi had been gone for decades, and their roots, which had been replanted with such optimism and at such cost, had withered in the blood-red Tuscan soil. Most of those who should have remembered the ancient people had long been dead or had assimilated so well into their adopted Tuscan culture that their ancient customs and culture had faded into oblivion. All that remained was an aching for something lost and the yearning for something better.

The room was cold even though the tiny windows were fitted with glass to allow the light in and to keep the cold out. Such an extravagance was not common to most of the rooms in the castle but were a welcoming necessity for the master in his bed chamber. The fire in the hearth cracked and spit, the autumn-cut logs not having time to properly age, nor dry thoroughly, after being dug out from the thick covering of snow. Great plumes of smoke billowed as the flames licked the wet wood. Some were drafted up the chimney to the heavens above. The captured smoke had made the chill air thick within the chamber. Giovanni called out to Nikos to bring more wood to warm the cavernous chamber. He needed to warm his weary bones. In earlier days Giovanni would not have minded the cold, but now he was old, and his blood was thin. His bones were brittle, and the weight of ninety years was taking its toll on this body and his mind.

Nikos emerged from behind the heavy velvet drape that covered the entrance to the bed chamber. The covering had kept the warmth within the thick stone walls while keeping the chilling drafts out. His arms were filled with wood, which he lay in a heap before the hearth so that it might dry before being tossed onto the fire. He was thankful there was no lack of chestnut and ash from the forests to the northeast. Great stockpiles had been cut during the summer months and had been stored in the cavernous storerooms, so that the fires of Vol-tuma would be fed throughout the entire year. Giovanni grimaced at the thought that each log burned for his warmth was one less for his blast furnaces that still produced most of the iron and steel used to outfit the finest armies on the continent. But for him to survive the icy cold of this horrendous winter, he would have to divert some of his profits to satisfy his own comfort.

A cast-iron pot hung over the glowing embers and the water within had come to a rolling boil. Carefully, Nikos lifted the pot from its hook and placed it upon a small wooden stool. With exacting care, he measured out the dried marigold petals from a crafted leather satchel and sprinkled them into the boiling water. Quietly, he spoke a prayer for insight. He then drew several dried bay leaves from a second satchel and threw them into the pot, praying for divine guidance. From a third satchel he extracted a quantity of rosemary and added it to the brew, imploring the Holy Spirit to keep his master safe during his mystical journey. Once the herbs had sufficiently rendered their magical properties, he carefully poured the elixir into Giovanni's exquisitely crafted chalice of visions. Nikos knew full well that such a magical potion was not needed for a powerful seer such as Giovanni, but it had brought his master comfort and peace, which would help him to open his mind and accept the visions.

Throughout the old man's life, those visions had brought so much unwanted pain and anguish. For many of his later years, they had simply gone away, causing him to seek every sort of magical remedy to bring them back to him. And in those final years of his life, he had welcomed back the visions that had become a source of hope and comfort and resolution to him. It had frightened Nikos each time Giovanni would fall into one of his trances, and he would lovingly sit by his master's feet, sometimes holding onto Giovanni's trembling legs, as if to hold him steady upon this earth, to prevent him from being pulled into the other world in which the man's spirit would walk. He knew the terrible toll such visionary journeys would take upon the psychic, for he had witnessed many times how close to death his friend had come with the strongest of those visions.

The spirits of the other world are strong indeed, and they long to feast upon the spirits of those who walk upon this earth. Giovanni had always been blessed and cursed with visions of things past, present, and future. Such is the insignificance of time and reckoning when one walks in the spirit world. In the beginning, he was almost destroyed by the power of the visions, but he later learned to control the sight while living among the ancient Taurisi in the Hidden Realm of Curtun. Nikos had never visited the kingdom of the Sons of Noah but had known many of the Taurisi who had once lived in that doomed realm. He had loved and mourned many of those who had managed to escape from destruction, sadly watching them fade into oblivion.

It was plain for all to see that Nikos had truly loved Giovanni, for throughout his entire adult life, he had dedicated his heart and his soul to his friend and his friend's children, unselfishly and with great devotion. He had spent his life serving Giovanni not only as a devoted servant, but as a friend and a confidant, as an agent and a partner in business, and as a counsellor. He was Giovanni's voice of reason and compassion. It was Nikos who had completed Giovanni in more ways than any of the many women whom the master had ever claimed to love. No other knew the true worth of the man known as Giovanni Bartolomeo Pecci da Cortona. Nikos was Greek by birth, the nephew of Niketas Koniates, imperial historian of Constantinople, but due to circumstances, he was forced to leave the Imperial City and had lived the better part of his life in the company of Giovanni and his circle of wealthy Italian bankers and merchants. Despite his effeminate looks and manner so natural to the Greeks of Byzantium, he was never made to suffer the hatred and prejudices that most Italians had held toward the deceitful Byzantines.

And Giovanni had loved Nikos, as much as he could love anyone, for he somehow had filled the void in Giovanni's heart with goodness, which otherwise had been rotting after years of physical and mental abuse at the hands of the most corrupt in the Holy Mother Church. With each transaction and transgression, Giovanni had deposited one or several of the cardinal sins into his soul, leaving no room for anything but the love of power and wealth. For Nikos, his unrequited love was satisfied with his service and loyalty to Giovanni and the very opportunity to be close to the one he truly loved. Their bond was strong and lasting. It was not physical. For that, in youth, they would seek pleasure in the brothels or in the lower courts of the monarchs of Europe.

Nikos had marveled at the life that he had shared with Giovanni, as he ceremoniously presented the chalice to the seer. Giovanni had drawn his chair close to the fire and had wrapped his withering body in a heavy shawl of lambswool. Carefully, Nikos placed a crown of dried mug wort upon his master's head to act as a talisman against an evil possession. Such precautions were always taken, more for Nikos' comfort, for he could not stand to see any evil perpetrated against his master. He always feared for Giovanni's fragile health and the effect these recent visions were having upon the aged man. He could not comprehend a life without his friend, nor a world deprived of the genius that was Giovanni.

He looked lovingly back to the first time he had set his eyes upon the youthful and energetic man from Cortona, blinding his vision of the frail and troubled man sitting before him in the fire's light. No longer did he wonder what his life would have been had he not met the handsome young Italian merchant so many years before. No longer did he have regrets of leaving his homeland and his family or for hitching his wagon to so mighty a steed. His family was all gone. The Constantinople of his youth was in total disarray, conquered by unholy crusaders and turned into a puppet state of Venice, that whore of the Adriatic. How many miles had he traveled in his lifetime with

Giovanni at his side? How many seas did he cross in the service of his master?

Slowly Giovanni emptied the warm contents of the chalice, drinking deeply the soothing potion while drawing the visionary powers from deep within his own being. Sleep lay heavily upon his eyelids, and while consciousness began to slip from his nodding head, Nikos tossed a branch of cypress upon the fire. He sprinkled several pinches of frankincense to enhance the purity of Giovanni's visions, and then quietly positioned himself at his master's feet. Lovingly he wrapped his arms about Giovanni's legs, and then he lay his head against the chair and prepared himself for a long and arduous night.

Darkness enveloped the room. All was quiet but the cracking of the burning logs and the hissing of the glowing embers. A heavy pall of smoke emanated from the hearth and wrapped itself like a serpent around the old man's head, assailing his nostrils with its vision-enhancing scent. Giovanni drew in several deep breaths of the incense, eyes shut tightly, head moving slowly in a circular motion, matching his deep rhythmic breathing. The pounding in his frail chest began to echo in his brain as the sounds from the fire became a redundant chanting and his ears began to detect the low-pitched singing of angels. His mind was filled with a certain ecstasy as he floated in his holy trance. He welcomed his visions in his old age, and yet he feared them also. He held tightly to the sweet angelic sounds, for he knew that the others were sure to come. He had spent his entire life having to deal with these otherworldly visions that came to him unannounced and unexpected, wreaking havoc with his mind and body and causing great anxiety and confusion. He had accepted his role as a vessel into which the Holy Spirit would pour the visions of things to come, both good and evil. He learned to be grateful of the gift that had been passed down to him from generations of seers, and yet he was most fearful of the responsibility that came with such a powerful gift. Though he had tried in early times to bury this precious gift deep within the dungeon of his soul, he would, at times, find himself helpless to its urgency. Never could he tame it, for he had realized it was not his to control, but rather his to accept. He had learned early that though his gift had come at a great price, he was cunning enough to realize the immense benefits brought to him so long as he used his power wisely. It was this very power that enabled him to elevate himself from the humble life of a farm boy to one of the wealthiest men in the land. He was happy with his life as he reflected on his many accomplishments. And yet, he was miserable.

The embers began to pulsate from red to black in a rhythm matching the pulsing in his head. He knew what was to come, for it had happened each time he was visited by the Holy Spirit. Slowly, from the depths of Hell came the pounding voices of the demons who were so familiar to him. They tormented his soul and they attempted with each visitation to steal a piece of his soul for their own. Giovanni had known that these demons had already gained much of their prize, despite the help and guidance of the angels. For in all his actions and deeds, Giovanni had willingly traded away his goodness for the worldly pleasures that come with wealth. The demonic voices were becoming louder in his ears, forcing him to recall each crooked transaction of his life that had depleted his reserve of goodness and enriched Satan's purse of misery. In the darkness of his lonely tower, Giovanni would once again witness the battle between good and evil that had been waged for his eternal spirit.

In the end, as the embers began to cool and the stars began to fade, the battle was put aside. The agonizing shrieks of the demons faded, and the glorious voices of the angels were left to whisper a final warning and plea to Giovanni's soul. For some time, he sat in silence in the gloom of his darkened chamber. His breath was labored, and his heart was heavy. He seemed to be frozen in time, not able to move a muscle, as if trapped within an icy tomb. Throughout that long and cold night, Giovanni was forced to scrutinize the ledger of his miserable life, and to review every entry into that heinous book. Satan had profited greatly during the past night, and yet, the strength and goodness of the Holy Spirit had provided him with a special gift, the chance to redeem himself through the complete and honest confession of his sins, and the absolute acknowledgement of his many evil deeds. For only by laying his soul bare for all to examine could he hope to gain forgiveness from those still living upon this Earth and from those who dwelled in the peace of the Kingdom of Heaven or who toiled optimistically in the caverns of Purgatory awaiting their own chance of redemption.

Suddenly Giovanni had become aware of Nikos, sitting by his side with his arms wrapped tightly around the old man's legs. Nikos was not much younger than Giovanni, and the elder knew his dearest friend had surely spent an agonizing night watching over him as he wrestled with the demons. The cold and dampness of the stone floor must have been a misery to the younger's aging bones. Giovanni lifted the shawl from his shivering shoulders and wrapped it around Nikos, taking care not to wake him. He placed his hand upon his friend's head, and a wave of love began to wash over him. As if by magic, Giovanni was able to finally feel the love and loyalty that Nikos had had for him over so many years, those feelings to which he had been so blind. In the silence of that early winter's morning, Giovanni had received a clear vision of what he needed to do to redeem his soul. God had granted him the time to make his final confession.

Ever so gently Giovanni stroked Nikos' head until his friend shook off the exhaustion of a sleepless night. Softly, he spoke to his companion.

"Dearest Nikos, the fire has gone out and the chill is creeping into our bones. Raise yourself from the cold floor and attend the hearth. Heat some water so that we may warm ourselves and prepare a simple meal so that we may nourish our weary bodies. I have experienced the most incredible vision and my journey has made me hungry."

Nikos rose from the floor and followed his master's instructions without saying a word. He was used to Giovanni's demanding ways and took no offense to his abruptness. His body still ached from sitting on the cold floor, anchored to his friend's mortal body while Giovanni's spirit walked with the angels.

"The Holy Spirit has come back to me and has shown me the path to my salvation," Giovanni continued as Nikos stoked the flames and prepared the breakfast. "The Devil, as usual, has kept a close eye upon his prize, and has tried to counter every move that the Holy Spirit has made during the battle for my soul. Fiercely have they battled, and by dawn's early light, I had lost all hope of redemption. Strong is the Devil, and cunning is he in his deceit. Stronger, yet, is the power of God through the Holy Spirit. Before the last embers had cooled and the visions had faded away, the Holy Spirit gave to me one last gift of hope."

"'Giovanni,' the Holy Spirit said to me. 'Salvation is bought with forgiveness, and forgiveness can only be earned through confession and remorse. For you to be granted any hope of redemption you must fully understand the actions you have taken throughout your life, as well as the repercussions those actions have had upon others. You must totally accept the responsibility for your actions, and truly beg forgiveness from those you have sinned against. Your confession must be honest and complete, and you must make it willingly so that all may see.'"

"'Show me what I must do,' said I. 'Let me know what must be done to alter the fate of my fetid soul. What can I do to rob the Devil of the prize he most eagerly craves? Show me how I may earn the forgiveness of the Lord and return to the good graces of Almighty God.'"

Nikos handed his master a warm cup of chamomile-infused water, a plate of cold meat and cheese, and a small chunk of bread, which the old man accepted most greedily. His strength had been totally depleted during the night, and he knew that he needed to restore his health in order to accomplish the task that had been given to him. He turned to his servant, who had already taken his own nourishment, and said,

"Dearest Nikos. You have known me for most of my life. You have been with me at my best and at my worst times. You have loved me and have been loyal to me, despite my many faults and wicked deeds. You know me, perhaps, better than I know myself. You know the sins I have committed, and I suppose that you know the reasons that drove me to commit such affronts to God. I need you one last time to help me free my soul of the years of filth that encases it. The Holy Spirit has shown me the way. With God's mercy I have been given time to rectify my wrongs and to set my foot once again upon the path of righteousness. I will confess to committing all the seven deadly sins that most displease the Almighty. But mere admission is not enough to earn forgiveness, and there is much that I must learn before I can rid myself of such heavy guilt. The Lord has given me time to accomplish one last task. For seven nights I shall be guided to the root of my evil. One night for each of the deadliest of sins I have committed. With my guide's help, I hope to learn the errors of my ways, and acquire sufficient remorse to earn my way out of Hell."

"How is it that I can help you, Master?" asked Nikos. "I will willingly guide you to wherever you must go. Only tell me what I must do."

Giovanni looked lovingly at his friend, knowing in his heart that Nikos would follow him into Hell if that was what was needed to ease his master's burden.

"Sweet Nikos," he said. "Where I must go, you cannot follow, nor lead the way, for the path does not lie in this world. I must learn what I must learn and seek salvation in the spirit world in which I alone can travel. I need you, my trusted scribe, to remain by my side, physically planted in this mortal world, and with pen and parchment, record all that I shall transmit to you from the other world. I need you to be most diligent and conscientious in capturing every word, sound, or conversation that I can pass through the spectral veil. Through your accurate transcription I will be able to bare my soul to the world and seek forgiveness and prayers of mercy from all who read my confession. The time I have been granted is short, and the task may seem near impossible. Yet I am filled with hope that I may escape the fires of Hell. Strengthen yourself, for the nights may be long and arduous, and the days filled with dictation and transcription. Make certain that the vision potions are prepared properly and bring from the storeroom a great quantity of parchment, ink, and quills to this room in readiness for our journey."

Giovanni wasted no time in beginning his task. Nikos had brought up a large quantity of parchment, which his master had purchased on one of his many trips to Venice. Each sheet was of equal dimension and of the highest quality, capable of holding the ink without running or smudging. The parchment was sturdy and made to last. For years, such parchments had been pressed tightly between the leather binders of Giovanni's journals, used to record all business transacted for the many companies disbursed throughout the world and owned by just one man—Giovanni Bartolomeo Pecci da Cortona. Nikos had been employed as Giovanni's scribe, as well as serving as his partner with a myriad of other duties. He was most proficient in recording, in multiple languages and at varying speed, all that was dictated to him. Legal documents and contracts were his specialty, but he had also extensive experience in recording Giovanni's many travel adventures throughout the years.

"Before I begin to recount my life's story," he said to Nikos, "I must dictate my confession. Prepare this as a separate document to be added to my journal. I shall begin my journey by confessing my sins, though with the guidance of the Holy Spirit I may have to amend such confession over the course of the next seven nights."

The Confession of Giovanni Bartolomeo Pecci da Cortona

"Hear me, O God! How wicked are the sins of men! Men say this, and you pity them, because you made man, but you did not make sin in him."

Oh! Blessed Augustine, you too have recorded such words of wisdom and truth while you confessed your sins to Almighty God, and for all in the world to see. Eight hundred years, and your words, like red hot pokers, still burn deeply into my heart, even as I cause them to be put to parchment. They tear at my heart and my soul as I ponder their heaviness, and their truth. Have pity upon this wretched soul, all wise and merciful God, for I, your aged and humbled servant, Giovanni Bartolomeo Pecci da Cortona, have greatly sinned throughout my entire life, in thought and in deed. From Thee, Dearest Lord, I beg forgiveness for each of my transgressions, for my weaknesses and my failures, the list of which is long, and not unknown to Thee. Thou, who art all-knowing, have followed me throughout my life and have spoken to me in my heart. Yet, through pride and stubbornness, I have heeded not Thy sacred counsel, nor gratefully accepted the comfort of Thy blessed love. Arrogance and greed have led this wicked servant down a perilous path and has allowed me to steel my heart against the wondrous gifts that Thou hath placed within my custody. I have heard Thy voice, and I have seen the visions that The Holy Spirit has writ upon my sullied soul, and yet I have chosen to ignore Thy loving guidance and have caused my soul to wallow in the seduction of the vices—pride and envy, lust and deceit, avarice, anger and greed.

I confess these sins to Thee, and I acknowledge all that I have done. I humbly beg Thee to show mercy upon this repentant fool. Grant me Thy loving forgiveness and lift the burden of these sins from my troubled soul. Grant me Thy blessed peace so that I may be welcomed back into Thy Most Holy Grace. I beg this of Thee, My God and My Father, and of Thy Most Holy Son, Jesus Christ, and of The Holy Spirit. You who have been with me always. I beseech Thee, and Thy

Holy Mother Mary, and all the saints in Heaven, to look favorably upon this humbled servant, and guide me to eternal rest in the light of Thy forgiveness. I ask Thee to look down upon the family of this repentant soul and to grant them Thy mercy and Thy peace and love, and Thy protection, so that they may live good and honest lives, and prove their worthiness of Thy many gifts.

Through Thy Holy Spirit you have shown me the path to salvation, which I promise to follow with complete honesty and remorse. With this confession that I have been commanded to recount, I beg forgiveness from Thee, O God, as well as from those whom I have loved and whom I have wronged in my life. To them, I will freely confess my sins. From them, I beg forgiveness and understanding, just as I hope to gain understanding and remorse through your guidance. Grant me the strength to complete my sacred task and grant me peace in my dying hours. I herewith open my heart and soul so that all may know the true person who is named Giovanni, and so that all may understand the circumstances that have forced this wretched soul to sin.

I shall commit my final days to re-examining my time upon this earth and I will offer up the true worth of my mortal actions to be recorded into this journal so that those who may review the ledger of my life, can tally the debits and the credits of my actions, and hopefully, without bias, calculate the net worth of my life to be good. I ask those who may read this to draw their own conclusions as to the value of my wretched soul, and I ask forgiveness and pity from those who may judge this soul to be debased. I humbly beseech such kind souls to offer prayers to Almighty God for His mercy toward this penitent.

My only wish is that with this confession I may highlight the many shortfalls of my life and offer such example as a guiding light to help the reader to navigate the dangerous waters upon which we all must travel. Hear now, my true confession and share in the visions that I am about to experience.

In the Twelfth Month of the 1229th year of Our Lord, Jesus Christ

Giovanni Bartolomeo Pecci da Cortona

Nikos presented his master with the document and after a careful review, Giovanni signed and affixed his personal seal. He returned the document and said to his scribe, “My life has been long, Nikos, and there is much to tell. Let us begin.”

Chapter One
Pride

I

My Earliest Years

I was born into the family Pecci on a farm in the township of Cortona. My blood is part of this red earth. Deep run the memories. I was told in later years that in ancient times our bloodline was noble, of high rank amongst the Etrusci, The Sons of Noah—those who are no more. Such noble vines are difficult to wipe out completely even though notoriety and wealth, once ours by right of noble birth, was all but obliterated when the mighty Romans came into this fair land and conquered the confederacy of the Etrusci. We repeat, never to forget, the stories of the great battles between the Romans and the Lords of the Hills, and later, of the greatest battle of them all between the Romans and our cousins, the Carthaginians. So many thousands of lifeless bodies lie deep within the marshes and beneath the haunted waves of Lago Trasameno.

From such ancient lineage grew within me a mighty pride, a strong desire to travel and a drive to acquire the wealth that had been taken from my ancestors. In my youth my father was just a farmer on the land that was his father's—or so I had thought. I was given more than most in those times, yet my greed for a better life was strong, even at such a tender age. I was not content to follow in my father's footsteps, to be chained to the land. I had been educated at a young age, by the Benedictine friars at the Abbey of Sant' Antimo where I had learned to read and write and to recite Scripture, and where I had whetted my appetite for places beyond the hills and fields of Cortona. I was taught by my father and my father's father the cultivation of grapes and the ancient secrets of producing a fine wine. I herded the goats and sheep on the slopes of Cortona and I wallowed with the pigs and the chickens. And I also grew up enjoying the best cheese, the sweetest figs, and the tastiest olives. In truth, I had wanted for nothing, and yet my soul was always hungry for more.

My mother had weaned me on the stories of the privileged life she had once known, prior to her dreary life as the wife of a freeman. Many a night she would comfort me and sing to me and tell me stories of life in the great estates of her kin folk, in the early days of her youth. O, how I marveled at the excesses to which she was accustomed, and the life that she was forced to give up, all for the love of a simple farmer. My father was a noble man, if not by title but through his demeanor. My mother was a duchess, if only through the eyes of a loving child and a devoted husband.

In those early years, my greed was strong, my desire to venture afar was forever burning, my lust for life beyond my limited existence was insatiable. At such a tender age I had already begun to sin. I had also learned to hide my feelings. So young, the walls of my prison were being constructed.

I was born in the 1135th year of Our Lord, to Beatrice Manenti and Vincenzo Pecci da Cortona. Though the household into which I was born was simple as compared to what it has become over these many years, it was, through my father's hard work and industrious planning, a sizable farm at the foothills of Cortona. Even though my father's lineage had once been considered noble, such hereditary titles were kept hidden from me—lost in antiquity. Father had carved out his own position in the community of small hamlets and villages in and around the larger town of Cortona. He was looked upon by most in the area as a leading voice, a wise and gentle man, a trusted compatriot and friend. He tamed the land with the bent of his back and the sweat of his brow, and the cunning of his brain.

Life in those early times had been much harder than it is today. The land was an unforgiving mistress who required much care and attention while remaining fickle and ever reluctant to easily yield her bounty. Freemen were only beginning to harness the means to claim small patches of earth as their own, a sometimes-perilous gift that came with a high price to those peasants who struggled to sustain the most meager semblance of life. In previous generations, when most men belonged to the lord, and tilled his fields and sowed his crops, the peasants might rely upon their masters for protection in times of war and for sustenance during times of want. During my father's early years, freemen such as he were able, through prudent stewardship of their paltry holdings, to acquire additional holdings from those less fortunate who ran afoul of the fates.

Unlike most of those in his position, my father would acquire small farms or plots of land but would retain the ill-fated owners as his tenants and allow them to share in the bounty of their piece of land. In this way, he was able to increase his holdings, maintain a higher level of productivity, and increase the number of clients who were beholding to him for his generosity. He had begun early enough in his life to accumulate fertile lands throughout the Val d' Chiana, so that when it was time for him to take a wife, his reputation had spread across the hills and vales as far as Siena.

As it happened in those days, my father had become acquainted with a certain Giancarlo Manenti, a Sienese merchant who had traveled through the Val d' Chiana on many occasions, as he made his way home from trading in the East. Through shared business dealings, the two had become close friends. It was during one of my father's visits to Siena that he was introduced to, and fell in love with, my mother, the beautiful and noble Beatrice Manenti, youngest sister of Giancarlo. The Manenti were of noble lineage, a distant branch of the powerful counts of Orvieto who controlled a vast area between Siena and Arezzo. In later years, Uncle Giancarlo married Donata Soarzi, widow of Provenzano Soarzi. The Soarzi too were a great and noble family who ruled over all the peoples west of Siena to the slope of Monte Maggio and the headwaters of the Elsa. Through the Manenti-Soarzi marriage, Giancarlo had gained a young wife, who was heavy with child, and the possibility to control Provenzano's estate until such time as the child had reached maturity and inherited the estate.

Unfortunately for Giancarlo, Provenzano's land and the castle that had been known as Stigliano were placed in trust with the Bishop of Siena until reclaimed by the returning Crusader or his rightful heir. Like many on that Holy Crusade, he lost his life upon the shores of Asia Minor, never to gain the glory of Heaven nor the salvation of his soul. The child born to Donata, a daughter named Anna, along with her rightful inheritance including the castle of Stigliano, would many years later be woven into the fabric of my own life. These connections, with much regret and a heavy heart, I lay before you in part, to show how fortunes have been made through the misfortune of others, and how status could be gained through fortuitous unions of families and commerce. The times were ripe for successful enterprise of those with brains and strong ambition.

The union of Vincenzo Pecci and Beatrice Manenti, celebrated in Siena in the spring of the year 1134, would increase my father's holdings in the contrada east of Cortona, and elevate his status, if not in title, then in the respect of his countrymen. In the year that followed that union, I was born. As my father continued to increase his land holdings, so too did he increase his family. In short order I was followed by Arturo, then Franco, and finally Giuseppe and Matilda.

O, how I remember my father, even after so many years. I see him as a young man, strong in mind and vigorous in body. He was tall and broad-shouldered and the muscles in his forearms betrayed the strenuous work that was his wont and his desire in life. His face was long and thin, his eyes were a mix of brown and green, what some would call hazel—piercing, able to look deep into the very soul and able to pierce any veil that one would use to cloak one's failings. His hair was black as the midnight sky, but later in life it would become white as the snows upon Monte Amiata, yet remain full and thick, even until the hour of his death. His nose was long and straight, progressing forcefully from his brow, in true Etruscan fashion. His lips were thin, the upper one being mostly obscured by a thick and unruly moustache.

He was of sturdy stock and constitution throughout his life, though in old age the firmness of youth, the straightness of the back, the strength of the knees and legs, and a broken heart all betrayed him to the whore of time. I remember well the tome of his voice, the calmness with which he spoke in any given situation. He commanded respect from all who knew him, not through force or aggression, but by mere presence. Respect for him was given freely, as natural as breathing, and his demeanor was such that all men, regardless of rank or station, extended him all the courtesies expected of a man of great dignity.

How foolish was I, in my brash and haughty youth, not to see the greatness in this kind and gentle soul, this man of vast experience and respect, this leader of men? How arrogant, and selfish, and stupid. I lament each day since his passing, the years I wasted not seeking his counsel nor his friendship or working harder to build a better relationship between father and son. I beg of thee again, dear Father, forgive me for my blindness and my cold heart. For all the riches I have managed to accumulate throughout my long and decrepit life, I am poorer for not sharing in the love that you were so willing to give to me.

Old age provides ample time to reflect upon every detail of the many errors made throughout one's own life, if one has a notion to do so. I have been cursed with an extraordinarily long life in which to accumulate so many mistakes. My biggest mistake was to turn away true love, for family and friends, and to seek only the love for power and wealth. I never allowed myself to truly love anyone except myself, and for most of my life I had subconsciously hated myself most. I suspect that I loved my mother and my father early in my youth but learned quickly to take what was needed and to cast away that which was no further use to me. Father was revered while he gave me what I needed—until such time as I grew too wise for my own good. Such misguided wisdom was fed with pride. Such willful pride had been spoon-fed to me by my mother from the time I sat upon her lap.

Though I did not have her for many years of my life, my mother was a very strong influence in my very early youth. She had been a scion of that race of men who heralded back through generations to the Teutonic tribes who invaded Italy in the darkest of days. Their castles and strongholds had dotted the hillsides south and east of Castellum Vetus, the oldest section of Siena. Unlike my father, she was large, fair of skin, and light of complexion. I remember her hair being the color of golden flax, and her eyes, the color of the sea. Her features were plump and soft, her cheeks high and naturally reddened. Her lips were soft and red like the petals of the most beautiful rose, and her broad smile was welcoming and a constant source of comfort. I remember how she smelled of lavender, sage and just-milled flour. She was generally mild of temperament, though when provoked, she could lash out with the fury of a cornered cignale, her sting as deadly as a viper. And she possessed an undeniable pride that had been bred into her like all those born into nobility.

As far back as I can remember, her countenance and demeanor toward my father, my young self, and the rest of her children was always loving and nurturing, though I could see, even then, that she had harbored resentment toward the life she was forced to live—the life of a farmer's wife. To me, she was Madonna, my strength, my champion, and my teacher. The confidence and bearing that was inherent in her nature was a byproduct of her nobility, traits that had been passed on to me, as her first offspring, in great abundance. She was doting of me during my first years of life and had created such a strong bond that overshadowed any other bonds I should have developed, especially that between a son and his father. Such a bond, no matter how tightly woven, proved no match for the vices that were inherent in my own heart, for in the end, as close to devoted love as I have ever come in my life, I broke her heart.

Ah, but let me speak briefly of those early days, even before the union of the Pecci and the Manenti, before the growth of the communes of Cortona and Siena. The Duchy of Tuscany had been ruled by the Countess Matilda and had begun to pick itself up out of the darkness of a feudal age. Long had she reigned, and she brought peace and prosperity to the land. Through her protection the first stirrings of commerce were born, and with them the hopes of free people to increase their lot. In her absence, the petty signatories, the so-called nobles, had grown in power and pride.

Even so, my father and his father before him were able to raise themselves out of the mud and free themselves and their family from the bondage of serfdom, while the final vestiges of the peace and security of Matilda remained. But, as ever and again the cycle of life repeats itself, so the glory of a golden age was consumed by the greed and ignorance of warring clans. Those murderous beasts, which through accident of birth, lay claim to all the lands of fair Tuscany, have ruled their individual fiefdoms with iron fists and hatred and contempt for any who dare to impede their gluttony. Long have they ravaged the land, taking all that they claim to be theirs by right, killing and raping at will, answering to none but God Himself, and to some of them, even He was cast aside for want of carnal pleasure.

Long was it that the freemen of Tuscany felt helpless to seek justice or redress from a disinterested emperor, for he was forever absorbed with matters political beyond the great mountains to the north.

In his absence these greedy nobles grew strong, the chief amongst them being the Aldobrandeschi, lords of Santa Fiora and many other castles. Before my father's time they had laid feudal claim to Monte Amiata and all the surrounding territory as far as the Mare Tyreaneo and encompassing Grosseto, Orbetello, Sovana, and Pitigliano. So numerous were their strongholds that it was said that they counted more than the days of the year. They were a fierce tribe, great in number, and their control within their territory was absolute. Still, to this day, they remain strong in wealth and politic, yet they are but a shadow of the might that they possessed a century ago. Their lawless followers pillaged the countryside surrounding Amiata and kept the populous in a constant state of alarm. Individual farms and livestock were not safe from their marauding hands. Even the monasteries were not safe from them. Although the counts themselves would sometimes show fear at the threat of excommunication from the Bishop of Siena and the Holy Father in Rome, many of their followers feared neither man nor Devine retribution. These men were devil-spawn, for they reveled in delight at the torments of Hell upon which they subjected the good people of these lands.

In all honesty I must confess to thee, Dear Lord, and to you who have received my last confession, that this apple has not fallen far from that orchard. Hopefully men will look back upon my wretched life and praise me for all I have accomplished. I hope that they will look forgivingly at my shortcomings, for though I have wronged many in my greed for success, I have tried in all my commerce with man not to intentionally cause bodily injury, nor pain or suffering. The blood of those ancient, lawless clans continues to run through these aged veins, hot with greed and avarice. Though not of the Aldobrandeschi, the clans of the Manenti, and the Soarzi, were just as menacing and culpable. Strong as these clans continue to be, they retain but a fraction of the power with which they once ruled the land. I speak openly of these injustices perpetrated by my ancestors and relations, with no fear of retribution in my heart, for I soon will go to a place where they will be unable to do me harm. In asking for my own salvation, I beg Thee, Lord, to grant salvation to my children and the children of my children, and to absolve them of the sins of the past generations.

In my earliest years on the farm, I was like a sponge, absorbing everything around me, following my father everywhere, asking him to show me everything. I constantly queried him on how things were made, their uses, how things grew, why we planted when we did, and why we didn't. My world, that tiny world of the farm, was fascinating to me. I could not get enough of it. My father, with so much kindness and an endless supply of patience, had spent hours with me upon his shoulder introducing me to all the wonders and the bounty of knowledge that was his to give. Never once did he tire of my questioning, nor try to stifle my curiosity. He took pride in the interest that I showed in his life, happy to impart his knowledge and his wisdom. He rejoiced in the false assumption that in time we would work side by side until such time as I would take his place and carry on the traditions.

As I look back to those earlier times, I can finally see that the driving force behind my curiosity was the love of my father and the desire to be just as he was. I wanted to know all that he knew, be all that he was. In my infancy, he was a giant among men. He was my world. He was the spring from which I satiated my thirst for knowledge of the universe around me. He showed me why the fields were laid out in square patterns, and how the soil was heavy red clay and needed to be turned up thoroughly when cross-plowed with a lightweight scratch plow, and how such a plow was easy to manage with a single yoke oxen, and how the size of the field depended on how far the yoke of oxen would pull the plow before stopping to rest.

He showed me why the perimeter of the field was planted with grasses for the oxen to graze upon as the beast would make one pass over the field before stopping to graze, then to be turned for a return pass. I learned early the science of crop rotation, keeping two-thirds of the arable land in production each year and keeping one-third fallow, planting one-third in barley sown in the fall, one-third in rye and oats sown in the spring, and one-third remaining unplanted for the year. Each of the plots acquired by my father, all the smaller farms absorbed into his estate, were planted in the same manner.

Throughout the year, whether planting or harvesting, the community that was bound to my father's estate would work together for the survival of themselves and the community. Smaller plots were kept and maintained by my father's tenant workers; profits of their labors were kept for their enrichment. The remaining lands were my father's to administer as he saw fit. As his holdings grew, so did the need for plows and tools with which to transform the red clay soil into verdant green crops, which were shared, for a fee, with the sharecroppers. In this way, my father never lacked for labor as his holdings increased throughout the years. He was always fair to his workers, thus the reason for his success.

Though the main crops by far were the grain crops, the money crops lay in the vineyards and the orchards. The grain crops were vital for the survival of people and the animals, particularly during the long winters, but it was the fruits of the vines and trees that provided the cash that allowed my father and other freemen to accumulate wealth and enrich their status in life. At a very early age I knew my father to be an exceptional man as evidenced by the vast holdings he had accumulated during his lifetime. As I grew, my haughtiness and my sense of self-importance led me to believe he was not living up to his full potential, or rather what I perceived his full potential to be. Even though he lacked the vices that I so readily acquired in my youth, his innocence and purity were mistaken by me to be ignorance and laziness. How foolish was I to question such success in this honest man, and at a time when the world was being turned upside-down?

Such dramatic changes in the political arena all around us, a miraculous awakening in the hearts and souls of the common man, would make it easier for me in later life to amass my fortunes and to cross the boundaries, which for millennia had shackled any not privileged by noble birth. Father knew of my opinions, for as young as I was, I was encouraged to speak my mind. My father, with great patience, would listen to me, and engage me in discussion, as if I were in possession of many more years. I would expound on the ways in which I felt life should be lived, talking such nonsense and making such unsubstantiated assumptions based upon opinions of those surrounding me, those of much lower moral fiber than my father. Not once can I remember him being short with me. He would listen, with interest, and answer with a calm, yet authoritative voice, encouraging me when my arrow had hit the target, and enlightening me when I had missed the mark. Of course, there were many times when we did not agree, but he would never lose patience or shun me for my own ignorance.

What I see now was that he marveled at my very being. He loved my inquisitiveness and was always eager to explain the simplest task or the most complicated process. He taught me in such a way that my thirst for knowledge was not slaked but only increased with my desire for more. And yet, as hard as he tried, he could not impress in me his humbleness, his kindness, his love of the land and the simple way of life. My mother's influence upon me was too great even for this marvelous man. Greedily I took from him all the knowledge that would serve me in later years. Selfishly I took, yet could not return, the love and respect that he so generously gave to me.

Not that I did not learn to love from my mother. She was so kind and loving, so caring of my father and of her children. How was she to know or suspect that the stories she had told to me of days gone by, of power and might, of wealth and plenty, would plant such fertile seeds so deeply within my heart? Those seeds would slowly sprout strong, thorny vines to ensnare my heart and to dig deeply into my soul. Such potent magic was in those seeds to doom an innocent child to suffer a life filled with lust and a desire for creature comforts and profit. How strange it is to think that the body of this young child would be a battlefield over which the blood of the Pecci and the blood of the Manenti should wage war, the good doing battle with evil, and the evil so easily claiming victory? Yet my father never tired of hoping to save my soul. In this way he may have given too much, in letting me follow those desires, for I would ever seek knowledge for my own gain. It is evident in everything I have done.

My father had always marveled at my industriousness and my ingenuity. Even as a very young child, as patiently as he would explain to me a process that was time proven, I would try to invent a way to improve the process, to do it easier, to be more efficient and more profitable. His were the ways of the past, repeated season after season, year after year, millennium upon millennium, tried, tested, and true. With everything I had learned, I felt a need to improve. It was not that my father's methods were wrong; it was just that I felt that I could do things much better and faster. Not once had I the insight to realize that my father, in this growing position of landholder, producer of goods, and leader of men, was in fact a master of innovation in a quickly changing world.

My father realized early in my life that I was too inquisitive, too interested in the world beyond the stone walls of the farm, and overly influenced by my mother's stories of wealth and indulgence, to hold me to the life of a simple farmer. He saw my potential to absorb knowledge and to use that knowledge to better my position. He knew in his heart he could fill me with every bit of knowledge that he had possessed, and still not be able to quench my thirst for learning everything there was to learn beyond the confines of his small world. He knew the world beyond the hills and plains of Cortona was vast. He understood that the excitement and the opportunities of the cities to the north and east, and the temptations of the outside world, would at some point become too strong for me to resist. He knew I would eventually leave. His only hope was that at some point I would return.

He never tired of teaching me all that I needed to know about the land and the fruits of the soil, of the cultivation of crops and the cultivation of relationships, the love of what he did and who he was, of the man he chose to be. And yet, the art of unconditional love, of building and nurturing close relationships, of seeing beyond myself, as much as he tried to teach me these things, I shut my mind to all this. It was not that I did not learn the need to build relationships or to hold someone close. It was never learned in the way that it was taught. I learned the advantage of these things and not the essence or sacredness of them. My father possessed a pure and simple soul and was capable of much love. For that he was loved and respected by most. I, unfortunately was, and still am, a complicated spirit. Because of that, I have failed my father, and all those who have loved me.

II

Education

I was ten years old when my father decided I should be properly educated in the art of reading and writing. He knew that if I were to prosper in life, I would need a proper education. I now realize how hard it must have been for him to make that decision, to make such a sacrifice.

Father had thought that I should be educated as he had been, under the tutelage of his people, the Taurisi. Mother would have none of that. To my mother, my father's people were merely a band of brigands living like wild animals in the wilds of the misty mountains. Stories abound about the wild folk of the forest—the ancient ones who lurked in the night, stealing naughty children and boiling them up for dinner. They were cutthroats and thieves, Godless, immoral, never to be trusted. Mother would never miss an opportunity to speak disparagingly about my father's people. My earliest memories are filled with fear of those wild, soulless creatures. Never would she stand by and let her son be sent into exile to be raised by a pack of thieves. She had insisted on having my father arrange for me to be boarded and schooled at the Abbazia Sant' Antimo to learn from the Benedictine monks. Many of her noble cousins had sent their most promising children there to be educated. Even her brother, Giancarlo, had spent several years there and received all the education he needed to become the successful merchant she was so proud of.

The abbey was ancient, even in those times, and was a center for learning as well as a stopover for pilgrims traveling to and from Rome over the Via Francigena. Temporal power had been given to the abbot directly by the emperor over two hundred years earlier, and that power had been expanded over the years to make the Abbot a most powerful man. By the time I had arrived at Sant' Antimo, the Abbot held authority over forty churches from Pisa to Grosseto, control of at least one thousand farms throughout the territory, and most importantly, possession of the castle of Montalcino. He had recently completed construction of the beautiful church that is currently the jewel of the abbey and attracts all manner of people—those of title, of wealth, of learning, and of piety. Father had allowed Mother to assure him that in the hands of these most holy brothers, I would receive the very best education, and he had hoped my exposure to the pilgrims traveling through the area would slake my need to travel too much afar. He could not have been more wrong.

The abbey was two days' journey from my home, but to my mind, at ten years of age, it could have been the end of the world. Though it was the first time I had ever traveled so far from my home, my fears were calmed by the excitement of seeing new lands and learning new things. Upon our arrival at the abbey, my father had met directly with the Prior in the chapter house. I remember my first impression of the Prior Filippo as a warm and wizen old man. His white robe had matched the snowy white wisps of hair that cascaded down upon his rounded shoulders. He seemed to me both wise beyond measure and ancient beyond counting. His voice was calming, and he spoke directly to me, questioning me about all manner of topics, and seemingly interested in each of my measured responses to his inquiries. In due course my father, who had been beaming with pride with my performance, spoke separately with the Prior and an agreement had been made. I can still see clearly the tears in his eyes—the expression on his face has remained so clear after all these many years. Some money was exchanged, and then my father slowly turned to me. He squatted down to look into my eyes. He held me tight, and then kissing my forehead ever so gently he begged me to accept everything that was offered with an open mind, to study hard, and to bring honor to our family. It amazes me, the emotions that have swelled up in my heart after all these years, as I recount that parting. Little did I know that our lives would never be the same. My schooling was to last for two years and yet it was to shape my life in so many ways forever. I watched as my father rode off up and over the hill. I would not see his face for another four years.

That afternoon I was introduced to the Dean of the Abbey, Brother Benvenuto, who took me into his custody and introduced me to the monks and other inhabitants of the abbey. I was brought around and shown the buildings, the church, and the surrounding fields and gardens. Several outer buildings were clustered to the south of the church, most joined together by the portico of the cloister that surrounded the quadrangle.

Extending from the cloister was the dorter, the dormitory where the novices and the young boys slept. Its front wall was completely open to the cloister, and along the entire length of the back wall ran a wooden platform upon which hay was piled. This was to be my bed for the following two years. The enclosure was constructed from stone and mud, as were all the outer buildings surrounding the cloister. It was designed to be easily cleaned and refreshed with hay. In the cold winter months, the animals were brought inside to keep them from freezing and to provide warmth for us young acolytes.

Below the wooden floor was the stable, which was dug out of the earth and opened from the back of the building. The animals were housed there during the hot summer months. The building contained a second floor, which housed the monks' cells. Though they were fully enclosed, each cell contained a small window to admit light for reading scriptures. The monks were kept warm by the heat radiating through the cracks in the floorboards from the animals and the bodies below during the cold winter months. Along another wall of the cloister ran the frater, the refectory where the monks would dine. I was to learn that only on very special occasions would we, the youngest of the abbey, be permitted to dine in the refectory. We would be allowed to serve the monks their meals but were not allowed to join them in the comfort of the frater. Our meals were taken wherever we could find the space and the time, the kitchen or most likely the dorter.

The hospital had run the entire length of the cloister opposite the frater. This was where the monks who were too old or too sick to take part in the daily routine would be housed. It was the only building, other than the kitchen, to be heated by fire, and upon many a cold evening we would fight for the privilege of serving the elders their supper and tending their needs. It had also served as a shelter for pilgrims traveling on the nearby Via Francigena, and it was here that I learned so much about life beyond the hills of Tuscany.

The Chapter House and the Scriptorium, where the clerics and scribes copied manuscripts and where the novices and students were educated, ran parallel to the frater and served as the entrance to the cloister and courtyard. In the center of the courtyard was the well from which I would have to draw water each day to meet the needs of the monks and their guests. A separate group of outer buildings housed the kitchen, the lavatorium, built upon a running stream, the misericord, where punishment was metered out for infraction of the rules of the order, and the cellarium, the storehouse for the monastery that would become my own personal Hell.

This was to be my home, my world, my Heaven, and my Hell, for the next two years. Like a sponge, I was to suck up everything I experienced on that initial tour—the sights, the smells, the noises, and the silences. How deafening was the silence in the nave of the mighty church. How impressive it was to me. How intimidating, and yet so comforting. I was held in awe by the magnificence of such a holy place. Never had I experienced such beauty, such enormity, and such divine welcoming. I still sense the magic of that first impression. Its power has never dimmed with the many visits I have made over so many years. It is a place of healing, for the mind, the body, and the soul, and it became my refuge and my sanctuary during the two years I had lived at the abbey.

I still see the golden light that streams forth from Heaven and spills through the large window in the apse to warm the alabaster, onyx, and travertine stone carvings within. Many days would I escape my chores to seek solitude and safety in the warmth of that Divine light, trying to silence the voices that began to plague me. Often, I would kneel before the beautifully carved crucified Christ and beg Him for His protection and for my salvation. O how I loved his beautiful face, in all its agony and gentle forgiveness; his sinewy body hanging lifelessly from the rough-hewn cross onto which he was savagely nailed. I was transfixed by the blood that had issued forth from the wound in his right side, the many piercings from the crown of thorns that had been foisted upon this head. I had felt his pain with each nail that penetrated through flesh and bone of his hands and feet. As a child, I should have been terrified by the nightmarish vision that hung before me, and yet his sweet face and gentleness in the quiet and sanctity of the church has always filled me with hope and peace, and determination.

I was introduced to each of the monks, thirty-six in all, and to the other boys, eight of whom were acolytes studying to become monks, their families wishing them to ultimately advance in the hierarchy of the church. Several of these were scions of noble families who hoped at some point in their lives to become princes of the church. All were expected to give up their life of earthly privilege and to seek divine guidance and spiritual reward in the service of the Mother Church. There were also three boys, other than me, who were not of the nobility, but whose family had advanced themselves in status and wealth through commerce and trade. We had been sent here to be educated and prepared for a life of temporal service, to advance in the world of business and commerce, to eventually become scribes or lawyers or perhaps to study medicine and science at some one of the universities that have come into fashion in recent years. Our fathers believed that success, whether socially or financially, was dependent upon a man receiving a good education. Such learning, especially in the art of reading and writing, was to open the entire world to me, and allowed me to recognize and to seize the opportunities that were presented to me throughout my life.

My initial introduction was met with a mixture of welcome, indifference, and hostility. Many of the community became my friends; others stood aloof, remaining indifferent, and still others, whether miserable in their own station in life or simply in possession of an incurable, evil temperament, were hostile toward me from the very beginning and would become the bane of my very existence.

My life at the abbey was structured around the Book of Hours, my day divided into eight parts. I lived my life for four years in tiny increments beginning with Matins service recited at two hours after midnight, followed by Lauds at the fifth hour, Prime service at the sixth hour, Sext, recited at noon, Nones, recited at three in the afternoon, Vespers, recited before dark at four or five in the afternoon, Compline, the last of the day services recited at six in the evening, and Terce, which was recited at nine in the evening. I was required to attend all services without question throughout the day and night. All work or study was immediately ceased during times of prayer service, and all were required to walk to the church regardless of weather or time of day. Such devotion would hopefully lead a monk to eternal salvation. For those of us who were not so inclined to accept the greater calling but were merely associated with the monks for personal advancement and education, we were forced to accept such strict guidelines of monastic life. I still feel the rhythm of the hours even today.

I was no stranger to hard work. My earliest years on the farm, with my endless questioning and emulating of my father, my willingness to learn and my eagerness to succeed at whatever task was given to me, allowed me to assimilate into monastic life quite easily. I established strong relationships quickly and easily, being so young and feeling the pains of separation from my family. I learned to trust a few, and to stay clear of others. Prior Filippo and Dean Benvenuto took an instant liking to me, and I, in turn, tried my best to impress them and to court their favor. My inquisitiveness and my intellect were beyond my years, and my self-assuredness allowed me to carry on meaningful conversation and discourse with most of the brothers at the abbey. Because of my advanced knowledge of farming and viticulture, I was on many occasions asked to work with the monks in the fields and the vineyards. Such attention elevated my status amongst the other boys and served to arouse the envy and jealousy of a few of the monks.

Brother Bernardo, the Cellarer, had never held a kind thought nor spoke a civil word toward me. He was cold-hearted and a menacing bully who led a small band of like-minded monks and acolytes, a constant source of dissention and unrest within the confines of the monastery. It was whispered that he was raised by the monks of the abbey from birth, having been abandoned at the far end of the orchard by a young witch from the woods to the east. Those woods were known to be haunted by spirits and servants of the Evil One. Although Bernardo had been raised in the goodness of the brotherhood, he had possessed a foul temperament and sought to dominate those weaker in stature and countenance than himself. He had never showed love or affection toward anyone, except for his one-eyed cat that he called Angel and had kept in the storehouse to control the rat population. Like his master, the cat was a vicious creature.

Bernardo was crafty though, for as he grew, he had managed to gain himself a higher position within the order. As the Cellarer, Bernardo was responsible for provisioning the entire monastery, and he ruled the cellarium with an iron fist. Through intimidation he had managed to spread his poison amongst the younger novices and had built himself a strong following, which was a constant challenge to the Dean and even to the Prior. He was not a person one could warm up to, nor would anyone willingly incur his enmity. It was my misfortune to gain his animosity from our very first meeting. I could never understand why a man in his position would hold such resentments toward a boy who had been separated from his family and had caused no threat to his position or himself. It is simply that some are brought into this world with ice in their veins and evil in their hearts. Such creatures are Devil-spawn and are put upon this earth by Satan to cause great harm and fear to the spirit of mankind. Brother Bernardo was the bane of my existence. It did not take long for me to learn the measure of his cruelty and the cost of his displeasure with me.

Within a few weeks I was asked to assist Brother Bernardo with a shipment of provisions that needed to be unloaded and stored in the cellarium. Learning that Bernardo had asked the Prior specifically for my assistance, I had mistakenly assumed I had finally gained some favor with the wicked cellarer. Little did I know of what horrors he had devised as punishment for my assuredness and my supposed disrespect of his authority. Together with several of his cronies, we unloaded three wagons full of wine and supplies. With each armful of goods that I carried, I was verbally taunted and physically abused by the Cellarer. He shared his abuse with the others who vied for his approval by kicking and tripping and slapping my head, which raised more cheers and laughter from the villainous pack of jackals. I had refused to cry out nor to show fear at the hands of those bullies but rather picked myself up from the floor and re-shouldered each load in silence.

My reaction and defiance only fueled the hatred within Bernardo, and he was determined to break my spirit and to teach me to respect his wrath. When all was unloaded, he sent his minions off to store the wagons and to tend to the donkeys. I was forced to stay and to stock the shelves with all the supplies. He continued his harassment for an additional hour. The muscles of my body were screaming with pain and my spirit was nearly broken. Never had I been treated in such a manner, nor could I comprehend such senseless cruelty. I foolishly asked my tormentor to explain to me what I had done to gain his displeasure and such treatment. God in Heaven! I can still see the fury in his eyes, hear his measured breathing, and feel his hatred toward me. In an icy and lifeless voice, he told me that I was too good, too sure of myself, and that I needed to be shown by him that there is true evil in this world, evil that is inherent in all of us. Salvation was to be achieved only through suffering and pain, and with penance and obedience. He told me that it was his duty to teach me how to suffer. He was to temper my spirit and I was to learn obedience by suffering with humility and in silence.

Oh, how I cowered as he towered over me. He had grabbed me by my hair and punched me with full force in the stomach, knocking the breath out of me and causing me to temporarily lose consciousness. I awoke in total darkness as my robe had been pulled over my head. My stomach had seared with pain and my broken body was now thrown across an oaken barrel. My screams were muffled, and the pain that I had felt was excruciating as he forced himself upon my helpless body. I had begged him to stop. I had fought him with whatever strength I had left in my body, and I prayed to God and to Jesus upon the cross to save me from that vicious beast. He simply repeated over and over to me in his vile whisper that I would learn humility, that I would learn obedience, that I would learn respect. He had assured me that I would be taught this repeatedly in my life, and just as Jesus had to suffer upon the cross to purge man's sins, so too would I have to suffer for my sins. Suffer in SILENCE! This last word, as if he were a viper, he hissed slowly and directly into my ear. I have never been able to erase that word from my brain, no matter how deeply I have tried to bury that memory. My hands still tremble as I force myself to relive that horrible moment. My stomach turns as I grieve for the death of the spirit of that young boy. What right did he have to rob me of my innocence? Dear God in Heaven, how could you allow such evil to walk upon this earth? How could you have forsaken me?

When he had finished teaching me his lesson, he donned his white robe and readied himself for the Nones call to service. His scruffy, one-eyed Angel rubbed its body against my trembling legs, uttered a low growl, and raked its claw across my bruised calf. The pain was excruciating. I was unable to raise myself from the barrel and just remained in a prone position, whimpering, my entire body wracked in pain, my life and spirit completely extinguished. He yanked me to my feet and commanded me to ready myself for services. He commanded me to speak to no one about the lesson or I would be gutted like a fish and fed to the swine. He had warned me that no one, not even the Prior, would believe a boy over a man of God, and he assured me my young soul would burn forever in Hell should I disclose the penance that he had chosen to meter out to such a sinner as myself. After he left, I mustered what strength I had, straightened my garments, and limped my way to the back of the church, and vomited.

As much as I tried to avoid contact with Bernardo and his crew, the monastery was small enough that I would cross his path daily. His menacing glare and threatening posture assured my silence and guaranteed his dominance. At each of the hours of service I prayed to Christ upon the cross to purify my soul and to save me from eternal damnation for the wickedness that I was led to believe was of my own making. Over time, my demeanor had changed drastically even as my physical body began to alter. I had become sullen, building my inner walls higher and thicker, segregating myself from those around me, those who could have helped me through the earliest transition into adolescence.

My father, my rock and my protector, was lost to me. My resentment toward him for leaving me in that Hellhole had festered in me. I dared not seek counsel from Prior Filippo for fear that I would break the code of silence forced upon me by my tormentor. I forced myself to do my chores and to master my studies. I strove to be the best student, to learn all that I could possibly learn. I was determined to get what I needed to get out of that miserable situation, and I blamed my father for bringing me to Hell. I was but a child, helpless and abandoned, left to endure the recurring assaults that were forced upon me by the beast Bernardo. The good Prior Filippo knew nothing of my misery. His goodness would not allow him to suspect the torture that I was experiencing at the hands of this brute, and thus could never be relied upon to intervene. The fault, I know, was all mine for not breaking my silence and exposing the monster. I allowed the abuse to continue. Of course, it was my fault for succumbing to his wicked need to drive the devil from my body. Of course, it was my fault! Bernardo had repeatedly told me so. And I had grown to believe him.

During my two years at the abbey, my studies progressed from basic reading and writing to the first trivium of the seven liberal arts—grammar, rhetoric, and logic—finally advancing to the quadrivium of arithmetic, geometry, astronomy, and music. Dean Benvenuto was so good to me, always trying to coax me out of my sullen mood. He continuously tried to engage me in discussion to test my knowledge, to elevate me beyond my self-imposed limitations. I knew I was his favorite and yet I knew that he too could not offer me protection. He was my guide through Purgatory and my hope for a better life. Prior Filippo was my example of goodness and the beacon toward salvation. Bernardo was my tormentor and master persecutor in Hell. He was quick to convince me that the changes in my body were proof of my wickedness and that the source of my lust and desires of earthly pleasures were the ultimate displeasure of God. I suffered my abuse in silence, and in time, learned not to resist. Struggle was a sign of defiance, and pride was given to man by the Devil himself. It was better to accept with gratitude the penance that was metered out by God's servant, and to suffer a silent repentance.

Toward the end of my second year, a young student named Ugolino di Conti had arrived at the abbey. He was the son of the Count of Segni and had been sent to Sant' Antimo from his hometown of Agagni, south of Rome, to be educated by the good Prior Filippo and the brothers at the Abazzia Sant' Antimo. Ugolino's uncle, Lotario, had visited the abbey on many occasions during his travels from Rome along the Via Francigena on church business and had convinced his brother the Count to allow his son to be educated by the Church's most pious order. Though Ugolino was young to begin his education, a mere eight years, he was quite bright and had possessed a self-assuredness of a boy many years his senior. He was good-looking, almost angelic, and was affable to most. He instantly gained the favor of many and had also attracted the attention of the Cellarer.

All too well did I know the burning in Bernardo's eyes as he looked upon the young boy. I knew what evil was boiling in that monster's veins. I could see him turn his rapacious hunger toward a new prey. Oh, how I hated that man! Though I had prayed to God to deliver such a diversion from my own misery, I had felt enormous sorrow for this child. I knew the horror that was in store for him, and I could not allow my nightmare to become the boy's reality. And yet, I did not have the courage to involve myself with his protection.

I waited for several days before I spoke to the boy, keeping my distance and avoiding any contact with him during our sleeping times in the dorter. To him I must have seemed like one of the aloof acolytes. My hope was that he would stay clear of the Cellarer, and because of his undeveloped stature, he might be spared the physical labor that was required for the replenishment of the cellarium. Yet, I knew this would eventually prove to be false hope, and at some point, Bernardo would act out against Ugolino.

Mustering my courage, I finally spoke with the boy, being as vague as I thought I could be without jeopardizing my vow of silence, and I warned him to stay clear of the Cellarer. I advised him to be as subservient and contrite as possible to him, but never offer to work alone with him or any of his pack of rats. I was rewarded for my compassion with a very aggressive lesson and warned by Bernardo not to fill the boy's head with my own sinful thoughts. I was but a child, helpless and abandoned. The voices in my head told me to protect myself, but my heart told me to protect that innocent child in any way I could. I offered myself to work extra shifts in the cellarium with the hope of deflecting Bernardo's attention from the boy to myself. Oh, how I suffered for my interference at the hands of that beast. My penance was increased from weekly to daily, the beatings becoming more severe and the sexual assaults becoming more savage.

At one point I was left close to my death, my body bruised beyond explanation. It was only then, after having taken my broken body down to the stream beyond the lavatorium, that Prior Filippo came upon me attempting to cleanse my body of the savage attack. He wept at the sight of the bruises upon my back and legs and bottom, all administered in areas that were easily concealed by my robe. The Prior then pressed me to identify my attacker and the reason for such a heinous crime. I knew I had to stop Bernardo's reign of terror, but I could not break my vow of silence. He helped me to my feet, clothed me in my robe, and brought me to the church to pray. Together we prostrated ourselves before the crucified Christ, who was wrapped in his own agony while He looked sadly into my soul from his suspended cross. We prayed for deliverance and for the strength and guidance that leads to our own salvation. Prior Filippo raised me from the floor and gently wrapped me in his arms, aware of the cuts and bruises that covered my body and prayed aloud to Almighty God for the protection of His young servant. He besieged the Blessed Virgin Mary to protect me and to give me the strength to face my earthly torments and to help me to overcome the demons who were plaguing me. My body had begun to shake violently, and I felt the demons who had occupied my body being pulled from within me and cast back into the abyss of Hell.

I can still recall with such clarity the beating of the Prior's heart, the warmth of his tears as they fell upon the back of my neck, at the sound of his sobbing in the silence of the church. My burden had seemed to lighten with his comforting words. I had longed to unburden myself of the sins and the horrors that had consumed my daily life, to purify my soul, and to be free of my hellish tormentor. But I could not bring myself to talk of such horrors and wickedness in God's holy house. He then assured me that when I was ready to make my confession, he would be with me to listen. As we left the church, I noticed that the Cellarer was standing close by, observing my every move, marking my steps and glaring deep into my soul.

I did not talk with the Prior that day. Nor did I dare approach him the next day, nor even the following week. Bernardo had made it a point to discipline me several time to make sure that I had not betrayed my vow. I had by then made another vow to make that monster pay for his crimes. It was only when I had overheard Bernardo requesting Ugolino be excused from his studies to accompany him on a forage for supplies in Montalcino that I mustered the courage to seek the help of the Prior.

The Prior had asked me to accompany him to Montalcino to seek the advice of the Abbot on several monastic matters. The Castle of Montalcino, home of the Abbot, was half a day's journey by donkey or by foot. Because of his advanced age, the Prior had to ride upon the back of the animal while I walked beside him. We left at dawn and walked, mostly in silence, until we reached the banks of the Merse, where we rested the animal and took nourishment beside the cooling waters of the river. The cook had supplied us with nourishing food for the short journey, and the morning's walk had increased my hunger. The clearing in which we rested was so peaceful, strewn with flowering bushes and wildflowers. The running water whispered the sweet song of the angels, and God's hand was everywhere evident. In this place of peace, I finally freed my soul.

Prior Filippo had sat in silence as I knelt before him and emptied my heart and soul of every sin and misdeed that I had committed and those that were committed upon me. I wept as I confessed, until my eyes ran dry, and continued my confession in stoic monotone as Fra Filippo shed his tears for me. When I thought I had no more to offer up to my confessor, I sat upon my heals, threw my head back, and looked up to Heaven, releasing a great cry that emitted from the pit of my stomach. I threw myself forward and buried my face into the grass between us. Fra Filippo gently placed his hands upon my shoulders, raised his face to God, and implored Him to wipe clean the marks that had marred my innocent soul, to heal the scars that ran deep throughout my entire being, and to shower me with His forgiveness, His peace, and His love.

He then raised my head, looked directly into my eyes, and spoke firmly but gently to me, saying to me that I had done no wrong. I had been used and abused by a very troubled individual, and through confession and absolution I would be cleansed of any sin that was forced upon me against my will. He encouraged me to go in peace, to live my life in the warmth of the Holy Spirit, and to try to find, at some time in my life, the courage and wisdom to forgive my tormentor, as the Lord had forgiven his. He then assured me that he would address the misdeeds of Brother Bernardo and make sure that the same fate was not metered out upon young Ugolino, or anyone else. My spirits had been lifted, and my injuries felt diminished. For the first time in two years I had felt clean. I had felt a sense of hope, of being saved. Someday I would be strong enough to forgive, but never would I forget.

At Montalcino, the Prior met with the Abbot and spent some time in his private quarters. Later I was asked to join the Prior for an evening meal with the Abbot himself. He was a generous and friendly man, half the age of the Prior, handsome of features and strong in stature. He was dressed not in the traditional robes of the Benedictine Order, but in the fashion of a noble lord, richly embellished in silks and jewels befitting a man of his station. In truth, he was one of the most powerful men in Tuscany, and it amazed me he had chosen to dine privately with the Prior and his lowly servant.

Throughout the meal the Abbot kept referring to the Prior as Teacher and had demonstrated a fondness and reverence toward Fra Filippo that betrayed a long history between the two. He spoke directly to me and asked me many questions, testing my knowledge of simple and complicated matters alike. He tested my command of Latin, of which I had excelled in my earlier studies, my knowledge of mathematics, the working of the stars, the Sun and the Moon, and the mechanics of commerce. He was impressed with the knowledge a boy of my age had commanded and would nod in agreement with a smile or a wink at the Prior, who for the most part sat quietly with a satisfied look upon his face. I was aware I was being tested for some purpose that was known only to the Abbot and the Prior, and instinctively I knew I had to make my best effort to impress the Abbot.

The meal was simple yet exceptional, the best I had ever eaten. Following the evening meal, the Abbot rose and clasped Fra Filippo's hand and asked him to make the necessary arrangements to facilitate the transfer by the end of the month. He lowered his head and Fra Filippo placed his hands upon the Abbot's head. Just as he had done with me in the glen by the river earlier in the day, he spoke a prayer of benediction for the safety and good health of the Abbot and for all his holdings. My stomach was full, my burden had been lifted, my body and my soul were already healing, and that night, in the castle of the Abbot, I slept the sleep of the dead.

Leaving at first light, we returned to the Abbazia and arrived shortly before Nones. Throughout the services, I had felt Bernardo's gaze burning deeply into the back of my head. My fears and my hatred for him had instantly returned and my body had been re-awakened to the pain of the beatings from the days earlier. I looked directly at Fra Filippo and instantly felt my heart strengthen and was sure of my protection. Bernardo met me later in the afternoon and quizzed me about my trip with the Prior. I then committed my first lie after being cleansed, looking him directly in his eyes and telling him I had not spoken a word of my sinful ways. He again warned me that I would never live to see my thirteenth year if I were ever to betray his trust.

Making myself scarce so I would not cross paths with the monster, I hid myself in a tall chestnut tree on the far side of the property, which I would on occasion climb to the higher boughs and disappear from my earthly cares. As I hid amongst the branches, I happened to spy the Cellarer walking to the edge of the wood. He had not noticed me in my secret refuge and seemed confident that none were present to witness his clandestine rendezvous with an old woman and her one-eyed cat.

At first, I assumed it to be Angel, but then the Cellarer's cat leapt forth from the folds of the monk's habit. The old crone was what the monks had called a gatherer. These women of the woods are known to be witches, and it was expressly forbidden for anyone in the monastery to have discourse with them. I had no idea why the Cellarer would be talking with the witch, but I knew it to be some evil purpose. The witch had handed him a sack, the sinuous movement within it betraying some creature belonging to the sorcerer. In exchange, Bernardo handed the witch a sack of food, and what appeared to be a set of prayer beads like the ones used by the Prior. The woman cackled as she took the beads, spat upon them, and cried "done."

The witch's cat leapt upon the Cellarer, and he swatted it against the trunk of a tree. The cat fell to the ground motionless, the woman shrieked, and the Cellarer cursed. I froze in fear, my heart turning to ice, as the cellarer turned and walked back toward the abbey. The witch collected up her cat and sack and disappeared into the woods. Angel was sitting at the base of my tree, had looked up and growled at me. Bernardo, carefully carrying the sack, had already disappeared into the rear of the Priory. After waiting until I felt sure that I could leave the protection of my perch, I returned to the dorter. There I found Ugolino hidden in darkness in the corner of the room, clutching his stomach and silently crying. The bruises on his neck and arms and the blood on the back of his legs had betrayed his torment. Bernardo had taken his newest conquest.

Immediately I sought out Fra Filippo, and I told him what I had just witnessed in the orchard and my suspicions of what had happened to Ugolino. I was told to return to Ugolino and instructed to comfort him without letting him know that we had spoken. Bernardo was summoned to the Priory and accused of consorting with a witch from the forest. Bernardo was furious he had been discovered and demanded to know the name of his accuser. Fra Filippo told him that he had been visited by an angel who told him that the Cellarer was plotting evil with the servants of the Dark One. Bernardo did not deny the charges but threatened the Prior should any action be taken against him. The Prior commanded Bernardo to remit himself to the misericord and to stay in that place until the Prior could receive Divine guidance for the Cellarer's fate. There he spent the night stewing in fury and hatred toward the Prior and toward the angel who had betrayed him. I spent the night comforting Ugolino and promised him that all would be made right.

Fra Filippo had spent the entire night deep in prayer. He was troubled that he could not find his prayer beads but held tightly to the wooden cross that he had kept above his bed. So focused was he with his prayers that he did not notice the viper that had been let into his chamber through an open window. With Divine clarity the Prior had concluded that he would return to the Abbot and seek the instant dismissal of Brother Bernardo from the Order. The revelations of the previous days had weighed heavily upon the shoulders of that good and aged man, and by the morning his health had failed him. None had noticed the puncture wounds on each of his ankles. When he was found, the Prior was weak and feverous and laying upon the floor of his cell. He was tended to as best as the monks could, and in the end, they could only gather around his dying body and pray for a recovery. By Sext, his legs had swelled and blackened, and he had fallen into a feverish coma.

As the bell tolled six times for the calling of Compline the Prior, Fra Filippo, my protector, had breathed his last breath. We all prayed.

We all wept, all except Brother Bernardo. The monster just stood and glared at me. I knew he was convinced I was "the angel" who had appeared to Fra Filippo. I also knew it would not be long before I joined the good Prior. Dean Benvenuto was then the highest-ranking monk at the abbey, and he quickly ordered the Prior's body to be cleansed and prepared to be laid in the cryptorium. A dispatcher was immediately sent to the Abbot to inform him of the Prior's passing.

The Abbot had arrived just after Noones and immediately made his way to the cryptorium to the lifeless body of his teacher and friend. I had been asked to attend the body, along with Brother Benvenuto and Brother Zacarias. We had cleaned the Prior's bloated body and burned incense to ward off the evil that had taken his life. The Abbot knelt before the deceased Prior and wept. He spoke several prayers for the Dead and for his eternal soul. All was silently still in the cryptorium. Most of the monks had been busy during the day in preparation of the Abbot's visit and the funeral of the Prior. They had been assigned to their individual tasks. The cellarer, however, was nowhere to be seen during that morning.

An inquisition was made into the happenings of the previous day to determine the cause of death. It was determined that he had been bitten during the night by a serpent that had made its way into the Priory. This explanation had become suspect when a thorough search of the compound had not produced the serpent. It has been told that the good Prior had been bitten by the devil himself, in retribution for all the good that he had done in his long life as a servant of God. With such deep sorrow and feelings of guilt, I knew I had caused this holy man's death with my revelations, and I prayed to Almighty God for forgiveness and I accepted whatever vengeance He would wreck upon my body and soul.

On the day following the burial of the Prior, Dean Benvenuto came to me early and instructed me to gather my belongings to join him in the Priory. When I arrived, the Abbot was sitting at the Prior's desk perusing a document. The Dean informed me I would be accompanying the Abbot back to Montalcino. I was to serve the Abbot well and in return I would receive further education. I was to learn later that my father had donated a large parcel of land, along with farms and livestock, to the abbey to secure a further education for me. I accepted this new assignment with mixed emotion as I still blamed him for abandoning me. I had no idea what my future would bring. I could only focus on leaving that nightmare behind. As we started down the road, I turned back for one last look at the Abbazia Sant' Antimo. Dean Benvenuto had raised his hand and offered me a benediction. I received his prayer with warm affection and then noticed Bernardo move behind Ugolino and place his hand upon the boy's shoulder. The boy winced and silently began to cry.

We traveled in silence back to the Castle at Montalcino. The Abbot was deep in thought and full of sorrow as he rode ahead upon his mighty steed. I followed as best as I could upon the small donkey, laden with my meager belongings. I could not help but dwell upon the fate of the young boy from Anagni. When we arrived at the castle, I was shown to the servant quarters where I would be housed for the next two years of my life. I was to serve the Abbot, his staff, and his guests, and in return I would be given the opportunity to further my education, and possibly to advance my station in life. I would not serve the Abbot directly until I had been properly trained in the art of domestic service, but being a very quick study, I was given my next opportunity in short order.

I progressed quickly. My affable personality had helped me gain favor with the senior staff and the Abbot himself, who would, at times, seek me out to perform some small task or to fetch something from here or there. I must say that as important as the Abbot was, he always found time to speak with me, to quiz me as he had done when first we met with Fra Filippo.

As luck would have it, a young personal servant of the Abbot had given up his position, having been called home upon the death of his father. Though I was still very young, the Abbot's valet, Buonaguida, had made it known to me that the Abbot had chosen me ahead of the other acolytes to serve as his boy-servant. I was to keep the fires alive in the Abbot's rooms, replenish his chamber pots, tend to the similar needs of the guests, and to fetch whatever was needed by the valet to serve the master. In between my duties I would continue my education in the library or in the scriptorium under the tutelage of Fra Anselmo.

Within a month following the Prior's death, I had already settled into my new position, while the abbey had remained in chaos. Although the Abbot had not taken steps to formally replace the Prior, he had not totally turned his attention away from the happenings at the monastery. With the death of Fra Filippo, the monks had gathered to nominate an acting Prior until one could be appointed by the abbot. Through intimidation and fear on the part of the Cellarer and his cronies, Bernardo had muscled his way into being elected. For the ultimate peace of the brotherhood and the good of the abbey, Dean Benvenuto accepted the will of the majority and capitulated authority to Bernardo.

The atmosphere at the abbey had drastically changed. Reports of infighting and deviant behavior finally had reached the Abbot by way of pilgrims passing through the area and staying at the monastery before traveling on to Montalcino. The Abbot was enraged at the reports and decided to clean out the nest of vipers that had poisoned the once holy abbazia. I had never stopped fearing for the life and safety of young Ugolino, who, I was sure, had become the object of Bernardo's twisted desire. I had never been able to bring myself to confess my sins to anyone else following the death of Fra Filippo. My heart and my soul were at constant war, and I suffered the torment of anxiety and guilt over the death of the Prior and the abandonment of Ugolino.

My opportunity for redemption presented itself with the arrival of Lotario di Conti, uncle of young Ugolino, who had come from Rome on official church business. The Abbot had been talking with di Conti in the study when I entered the room to place additional wood upon the hearth. Di Conti had been questioning the Abbot about some of the stories he had heard concerning the abbey as he traveled closer to its vicinity. He was concerned for the sake of his nephew and wanted to visit with him before returning home to the Count. I hurried out of the room but was determined to approach the Abbot and to tell him everything I knew.

Before dinner, while the Abbot was being dressed and I was attending the fire in his rooms, I begged to have a word with him. This, of course, was highly irregular, and Fra Buonaguida was furious at my impertinence. Amused, the Abbot bid me to enter the room and asked me what it was that I wished to discuss. I immediately began to quake, and with my eyes brimming over, I begged him to hear my confession. Fra Buonaguida barked at me to take my confession to the Chaplain, but the Abbot rested his hand upon the valet's shoulder and in a gentle voice told him to leave the room. When we were alone, he placed his hands upon my shoulders, looked into my eyes, and comforted me. That one gesture brought forth such emotion and loving thoughts of the Prior that it caused me to sink to my knees and weep uncontrollably. The Abbot raised me up and while sitting upon a footstool he patiently asked me several questions until I was in command of my emotions and able to speak.

I told him all that I had confided to the Prior. I then told him of the events that had taken place at the abbey on the day before and after the Prior's death. I told him of the clandestine meeting of the Cellarer and the witch, the items that were exchanged, and my suspicions that Bernardo and the witch were somehow responsible for the death of Fra Filippo. I ended with my concern for the safety of young Ugolino and a plea for his safety. He was extremely attentive to everything I told him but sat silently until I had finished. I begged his forgiveness for my silence in the matter and awaited his vengeance and punishment. Quietly he spoke to me, telling me that before he would absolve me of my sins, I would have to retell part of my story to another person. He cautioned me to say nothing about the death of the Prior but to relay my fears and my horrid experiences at the hands of the Cellarer. He then asked Fra Buonaguida to ask Lotario di Conti to join him in the study. I was admonished for my brashness by the valet as we waited outside the massive doors of the study. The Abbot and di Conti had spoken privately for some time, and then I was asked to enter the room to recount the abbreviated account of my confession.

As I recounted the brutality with which I, and later young Ugolino, had suffered at the hands of the monster Bernardo, di Conti could hardly contain his fury and he leapt to his feet and headed toward the door. The Abbot cautioned him to temper his steal and to ponder calmly what the next move would be. The Abbot turned to me and commended me for my courage to speak the truth and to seek spiritual guidance for myself and for the salvation of Ugolino. He then made the sign of the cross over my head and absolved me of my sins. Before the cock had crowed at first light, di Conti had mounted his steed and left the courtyard through the gate and down the road that led to Sant' Antimo.

I was to learn later that the Abbot had cleansed the monastery of all the monks who had sided with the Cellarer in his quest for power. Each of his cronies was assigned remote posts throughout the lands controlled by the Abbot. The most vehement followers were stripped of their vestments and removed from the order. They were expelled and made to live or die in the forest as outcasts or thieves. Bernardo, having sensed the wrath of the Abbot, or as most believe being warned by some demon in advance of the coming of Lotario, had managed to slip out of the abbey during the early hours of the morning and had disappeared. For many years following that fateful night, I lay in fear that Bernardo would return and seek vengeance upon me. Fra Benvenuto was instated as Prior and the handful of followers who were loyal to him were left to manage the abbey. In time, brothers of good quality were transferred to the monastery, attempting to bring it back to its original greatness. But a mighty damage was made by the Devil to this holy place of worship and learning, and it has never, in my lifetime, recovered fully from its darkest hour.

Young Ugolino di Conti was rescued from the tortures of the monster Bernardo and was taken back to his home in Anagni. Visions of this innocent youth have plagued me for many years, and yet more troublesome are the visions of the man this Ugolino would become. I am still visited in my dreams by the demons who had plagued me in those early years. Those demons continue to whisper in my ears and rob me of my peace of mind. I have seen such horrid visions of an older Ugolino di Conti, that poor, tormented soul, whose destiny it is to achieve greatness, and bring to the world such good and such evil that men will tell of his deeds for a thousand years. Of that, I will speak later. Only now, I must confess that I have always been inexplicably bound to this man, for God, in his infinite wisdom, has joined our singular paths together for what one can only hope and pray to be a greater heavenly purpose. From our very first meeting until this very day, we have been slaves to the same master.

Before the coming of spring, my service to the Abbot was to change dramatically. That winter had been unusually cold, and a thick layer of snow had blanketed the land in the weeks prior to Candelaria. The castle was cold and the need for warmth from the hearth was great, which kept me quite busy. Luckily the harsh conditions had limited the number of guests, thus limiting the number of hearths I needed to attend. Most of the winter's supply of wood had already been used, and the woodsmen were busy felling more trees, which were not seasoned enough to eliminate excessive smoke and spitting embers. The smell of smoke permeated the entire castle for a good portion of that winter, but it was the fear of fire from the embers that caused consternation amongst the staff. Fires were to be kept to a minimum, and if possible, not left unattended. Buckets of water were kept at the ready next to each hearth should the need arise.

In order to properly maintain the Abbot's hearth in his bed chamber I slept on the floor before the fire, as I had done with the Prior so many months before. On this one night, the Abbot, having consumed a large quantity of wine during the evening, had retired to his chambers and was helped into his bedclothes by Fra Buonaguida. Following his recital of evening prayers, and being assisted into his bed, as was his custom, he dismissed Fra Buonaguida with a prayer and a blessing. I lay on the floor in the corner near the hearth. Sometime during the night, the Abbot had called to me to fetch him some water to quench a burning thirst that was upon him. When I had returned with the water, he stared at me and began to berate me for my clothes were dirtied with soot and I had reeked of the fires of Hell. I felt ashamed and backed away from his presence. Seeing my reaction, his mood softened, and he looked upon me warmly. He bid me to remove my clothing and wash it in the bucket and lay it beside the fire to dry. He then commanded me to wash the soot from my body and to warm myself in the covers of his bed.

I lay beneath the covers shivering, not from the cold, but with anticipation and fear of what I suspected would follow. All the memories of the brutal attacks that I had suffered at the hands of Bernardo had flooded into my brain. My heart was icy cold, and I forced the gates of my soul to shut tight. I do not know how long I lay there, cold and rigid as a statue made of marble. In time I felt the Abbot's body press up against my own, his fetid breath hot against my neck. He placed his arm around my waist, and I felt the stiffness of his desire come alive. I made no move, but simply accepted my fate. I had hoped and prayed to be spared this new torment. In order to survive I forced myself to abandon my body to its own fate and to retreat to the inner sanctuary of my walled fortress.

When the Abbot had finished, I lay motionless in his bed, not daring to make a noise, waiting for whatever punishment lay ahead. He removed himself from the bed and walked over to a chest of drawers and obtained a small leather whip from a satchel. Panic returned as I steadied myself for the beating that I anticipated I would have to endure. The Abbot knelt naked before the gold cross that sat upon his prayer stand. The cross glowed in the light of the dying fire. His eyes glowed as well, the flames reflecting upon the tears that streamed from those agonizing orbs. He prayed for forgiveness, and with each prayer he flogged his back with the lash, gritting his teeth with pain at every self-administered penance. He prostrated himself upon the floor and begged for the strength to vanquish the evil that had taken hold of him. He prayed for forgiveness for his weaknesses that allowed him to succumb so easily to the temptation of the Devil. I continued to lay motionless, silently observing the macabre spectacle unfolding in the dimly lighted room.

In time, the Abbot rose from the floor, his back bloodied from the flogging, and made his way to the bed. I felt sure that his intent was to flog me as well for my wickedness, but instead, he lifted me from the bed and brought me close to his bosom. I could hear the pounding of his heart and felt his sobbing as he held me tight and kissed the top of my head. The Abbot, the most powerful man in the land, stood naked with his arms wrapped tightly around my naked body, and begged me for forgiveness. This was all too much for me to comprehend and I swooned into blackness.

I awoke to the Abbot washing my body with a warmed cloth, his hands trembling, and his cheeks wet with tears. Again, he begged forgiveness of me, telling me that Satan's evil was too strong to battle when channeled through the innocence of a young boy. He assured me that he would never harm me but would do whatever was in his power to protect me from what evils may happen upon my soul. Despite what had happened that night, I had still felt a trust for this good man and his conflicting soul and did not come to hate him for his weakness. In fact, I learned to use that weakness to my benefit. We knelt in the darkness as the flame turned to ember, and together we prayed for our eternal souls. Though he did not have to ask, I spoke to no one about the happenings of that night, nor of the many nights that would follow over the course of the following year.

The following days I received a new robe and was awarded the privilege of joining the monks in the scriptorium after my studies had been completed, to assist in proofing the manuscripts that they were assiduously copying. My status had been elevated once the monks became aware that I was given favor by the Abbot. My hard work and my silence were bought with a piece of my soul—a small cost, I thought at the time, for a well-rounded education of the true workings of the world. It was my primary education in the world of trade.

I served the Abbot well for two years, and in return, I was able to secure enough of an education that would qualify me, if I so chose, to pursue a degree in medicine or law at one of the universities that had become fashionable in several of the larger cities. My primary ambition, though, lay in commerce and trade. I had a great aptitude for mathematics, and my ability to improve upon efficiencies and processes, my hunger to explore new places, and my lust to obtain the wealth and power of my mother's ancestors ignited within me a strong desire to live the life of a Merchant-Captain. I dreamt of empire, not political, but financial, built upon industry, cunning, and daring.

I learned all I could from the brothers, but I learned far more from the pilgrims and visiting merchants and dignitaries who traveled through Montalcino on their missions to seek salvation or their quest to seek fortune and fame. The Via Francigena was the main travel road between Rome and the fairs at Chanpagne. Many merchants would seek hospice at Montalcino during the two years I served the Abbot. I never tired of their stories, nor closed my mind to any scrap of knowledge that I could acquire from them. I whetted my appetite for travel with the tales of the empires in the East, of the glory of Venice and Rome, the magnificence of the Imperial Court in Constantinople, the richness of the French court, and the power of the German Emperor. By fifteen years of age, I was ready to strike out on my own, to seek my fortune and to fulfill my destiny. That would happen in time, but not at that time when I was to leave Montalcino.

On the day I was to end my service to the Abbot, my father arrived at the castle, accompanied by his young cousins Salvatore and Sebastiano. I had never met these two, but I had heard stories about them from my father, as well as from my mother. My father had come to know them in his early youth, and despite what was said by many of the villagers about the wild ones or the ancient folk of the forest, he had a great fondness and trust for them. My mother, on the other hand, had held them in great contempt, calling them outlaws, ruffians, and vermin. She would admonish my father whenever he would make an excursion through the forest, repeating the gossip and wives' tales that she had heard about those creatures of the wood. I had been preconditioned to dislike and fear these men by my mother's stories. She would always use the threat of the wild ones or the ancient folk coming to take me away and making me into a stew whenever she needed to discipline me. I could never understand my father's tolerance of these people or his claim of relationship to any of the ancient ones. Though they may have been heirs to greatness in ages long ago, they had, at some point in the distant past, chosen to turn their backs on civilization and accept a life of barbarism and godlessness, and who knows what evil.

My father was so happy to see me that he wept tears of joy as he embraced me. He held me forth and studied my entire being, commenting on how I had changed and how I had grown into a young man. He held me in his arms and in his gaze. And I, in return, stood emotionless, not shedding a tear or returning his congeniality, for I still harbored resentment for his abandonment of me. I selfishly held him responsible for all my misfortunes, never considering the sacrifices that he had made to assure me of an education. He had given me everything, and in return, where there should have been abundant gratitude, there was only an empty vessel. It would be many years and many miles traveled, many experiences lived, before I would realize just how much he had sacrificed for me, and how much love he had given so that I could live the life that I was always trying to find.

For long he studied my countenance and sullen demeanor, and he was hurt deeply with the change in his young son. His conversations with me were met with respectful but emotionless responses, and my lack of enthusiasm was not missed by his two companions. Though they did not know me, their observation skills were keen, and they had sensed that something was wrong within me. I had intentionally kept my distance from those two, fearing that they would surely do me harm, given the chance.

III

Finding My True Identity

Our journey back to Cortona gave me an opportunity to understand my cousins better. Both men appeared younger than my father and were obviously well educated, though it seemed their upbringing and education were far different from my own. They were very respectful of my father, almost reverential. It did not take long for my preconceived loathing and fear of them to dissipate. Though I judged them to be complex characters, capable of extreme violence if needed, I discovered a genuine warmth in their attitude toward my father that extended to me. That they had come from the ancient forest I had found fascinating. To many, that was a mystical and deadly region. Some believed it to be a portal into ancient times, while some believed it to be haunted by the ghosts of the long-gone Etrusci people. Most believed that any who lived in those haunted hills were mad or wild or both. And yet these two seemed to be every bit as normal as my father or myself.

Sebastiano was a handsome man. His red hair and pale green eyes added to his mystique. His protruding beak and his wrinkled brow gave him the appearance of a mighty bird of prey. He was tall and broad of shoulder, his limbs and muscles hardened by years of conditioning with the sword. Through all the years I knew this man, he remained a loyal and compassionate friend of extreme complexity, intelligent, but quick to anger and even quicker to respond. It was rumored he had killed many men in his short lifetime, and his skills with the sword were legendary in the hill country. Both rumors, I was to learn over the years, were true.

His brother, Salvatore, was no less complex but much more cunning. His loyalty was unquestioned. He was the shorter of the two and fairer in complexion, with straight, golden hair that he kept short in the fashion of the ancient Romans. His eyes were a haunting blue, and yet in all their differences, the brothers bore a strong resemblance to each other. There was also a very strong similarity to my father. Even at an early age, Salvatore was known to be a master thief whose talents with a dagger had kept him well employed in the service of the local signori as well as the local merchants. There was always a very special bond between the brothers, of friendship and blood, and together they were a reckoning force. They had no problem enlisting the men of the forest to follow their lead. and they would serve me well for many years.

Upon my arrival at Father's farm in Cortona, I was reunited with my mother and my brothers and sister. My mother had aged in the years that I had been away. That softness that I had remembered in my childhood had assumed a hardened crust, though she was no less emotional then when I left her. My brothers had grown tall in their adolescence, showing the first signs of manhood that, for me, brought back a flood of sadness and anger at the memory of that which was taken from me. My sister was plump and soft and ran about chatting incessantly, like the hens in the yard. I should have rejoiced at the return to the safety of my childhood home, but my life had been changed forever. I found no comfort in those surroundings.

The first year of my return to Cortona was a period of conflict and trouble. My anger toward my father did not dissipate but only intensified each time he tried to bridge the gap that had opened between us. The horrible experiences I had faced at the abbey were buried deep, but the anger and melancholy continued to leach out and bubble to the surface. During this time the nightly visitations of demons in my dreams had become unbearable. My young mind could not cope with such physical and mental stress. I was in constant conflict with my siblings, as well as my father, and my fits of anger were a constant source of pain for my mother. She did all she could to comfort me, never knowing the true source of my anguish, but no one would ever know the depths to which my soul had been dragged.

At a point when I had thought I could no longer suffer such agony; we were visited by Sebastiano and Salvatore. I had always assumed their appearance to be coincidental, yet I suspect that my father had called upon them for help. Much to my mother's anguish and disapproval, the two wild men from the hills had stayed for several days. Each evening, they would have long discussions and debates with my father. During the days, they spent all their time with me. I had no history with these two, except for the journey back from Montalcino, so I had no animosity toward them. I seemed to be able to talk with them with ease, and they seemed genuinely concerned and attentive to my plight. Their unfettered lives seemed so tantalizing to me. The mystery of life outside the confines of established society called to me. I felt I was a misfit, my soul damaged, my spirit fatally wounded, voices battling in my head. I knew I did not belong on the farm. I knew, even then, my fate lay elsewhere.

My mother was furious over the influence that Sebastiano and Salvatore seemed to exert over me, and she argued with my father. She implored me not to be influenced by them or to throw my life away chasing after dreams of fame and fortune, but her pleading only strengthened my resolve to venture into the world beyond the city walls. Father made no effort to intervene but kept his distance and allowed me to come to my own conclusion. I made up my mind to leave the confines of the farm and the love of my family, and to disappear into the mists of the forests of the ancient ones.

My mother stood weeping as I gathered my belongings, mounted my pony, and rode off toward the hills. She and my siblings stood together in silence and watched me pass away. My father was nowhere in sight. For three days my cousins and I rode, slowly zigzagging up and down the mountainous terrain that spread out north of the city walls. The forest was thick with chestnut, taller than I had ever seen. Further up the mountains, the firs took hold and reigned supreme. The clouds blanketed the hilltops in mist. Craggy outcropping of white limestone and red ferrous stone made travel difficult but provided vantage points from which we could rest and view the world below.

We never traveled in a straight line, nor followed any pathway, yet the hill men were steady of foot and sure of direction. They knew this terrain as sure as I knew my way around the farm. We traveled in every direction, pausing occasionally to refresh ourselves and the horses in cascading springs. Travel was slow and hard on the horses. My childhood fears of these haunted hills slowly melted away as I experienced the beauty and majesty of this woodland kingdom. This was an ancient place, for sure, traveled only by those who belonged there. Such a maze would cause certain death for the foolhardy who attempted to pass unwanted.

Three days into our trek, we stopped at the top of a long ravine. Salvatore took a sack from his saddle and put it over my head to block my sight. He informed me that the pathway going forward was blocked to all but the Taurisi, those who lived in this great wood. We rode onward, my sight and sense of direction robbed from me, but eventually my mask was removed, and I found our company in a narrow gorge cut between moss-covered stone walls. The sun had set, and our pathway began to sink into darkness. We dismounted and walked our horses through the mouth of a small canyon and set up camp.

Salvatore made a small fire and prepared a quick meal of a couple of rabbits that he had snagged earlier in the day. As the fire faded and we had settled down to sleep, the blackness of the canyon suddenly began to glow red. Fire sprang from the left and the right, and the tops of the cliffs above us seemed to be lit ablaze. I panicked at the thought of being roasted alive and began to scream. Sebastiano and Salvatore both drew their blades and grabbed the reins of the horses to steady them. What I took for a wildfire now showed itself to be a hundred torches carried by as many wild-looking woodsmen. Many carried bows; others carried clubs or long staves. At the heart of the canyon we were surrounded with no means of escape, and pitifully outnumbered. A small band of woodsmen advanced upon us. My protectors lowered their weapons as the leader of the band drew close, his sword raised high. "Welcome home, Tarchon and Tyrsenos, sons of Tarquin," said he to my guides. "Long has the Zil-at awaited your return. We have been sent to meet you and to hasten your return to Curtun."

My mind was swimming; my senses were playing tricks on me. In the hazy light of the multitude of torches, my two companions, my father's cousins, had suddenly grown tall amongst the men. They appeared as princes among these vagabonds, and the woodsmen were obvious in their reverence and honor for the two. Sebastiano spoke in a strange tongue to the leader, who then moved toward me and raised his torch toward my face. He peered into my eyes and studied me closely, his expression changing from guarded disapproval to welcoming recognition. "Welcome, Giovanni, son of Vincenzo," he said to me. "Curtun awaits."

We followed the men through the narrow passages cut into the rock, over several small streams, and under several outcroppings of stone until we reached a thunderous waterfall that was cascading from the blackness above into a sparkling pool. The stars from the sky above and the light from the torches danced upon the water and made the waterfall seem like a flowing trough of gold and silver. The men leading the company began to disappear, one by one, behind the rushing wall of water. The torches behind the falls further illuminated the water, and large, dancing shadows were cast upon the surrounding rock, creating the most fantastic yet macabre vision of demons dancing at the gates of Hell. We passed behind the watery curtain, through a deep passageway cut into the mountain, and exited into a small valley.

A full moon had illuminated the floor of the valley, and the surrounding slopes of the hills were covered with a thousand buildings, lit by lamps and hearths. I had not expected to see such a city in the heart of that ancient forest and was dumbstruck at the sight. Not a word was spoken as we wound our way over stone pathways and stairs until we reached the tallest and grandest building at the foot of the central hill. As we approached, my heart stood still, and I froze in my tracks. The portico of the building was ablaze in lamp light, and at the top of the stair stood a man who appeared to be my father.

Sebastiano and Salvatore had climbed the stairs and knelt before the man whom I had taken to be my father. *What madness was this?* I thought. How could my father have transported himself to this distant place? What magic was under foot on this evening of the full moon? The two men rose and embraced the leader, calling him Zil-at, and he held each, calling them sons. His voice was not my father's, but was forceful and commanding, and deeper in tone, though no less compassionate. My blindness was lifted, and I saw clearly that this man was not my father, though as close to a twin could possibly be. He stood taller than my father, and his bearing was more regal.

He motioned for me to come to him and I hesitantly climbed the stairs. "Welcome, Giovanni, son of Vincenzo, who is known to the Taurisi as Uni-Tau," he said to me. "Long has it been since we have laid eyes upon my dear cousin, yet it is clear to all who have known and have loved him that his image and bearing is strong within his son. Be welcome in Curtun and counted as one among the Taurisi for as long as you shall dwell within these hallowed hills. Long have you traveled and most difficult is our fair city to find if you are not of the Taur. Come and be at peace in the hospitality of your kin."

I was brought to a subterranean chamber that had been carved from the limestone face of a cliff, the interior brightly lit by lamps of bronze. The walls were smooth and colorfully painted with ancient scenes of men and women and animals, obvious to me, even at that tender age, that these were depictions of a life lived long ago. The floor of the cave was beautifully decorated with tiny stone designs and strange markings that spoke of a distant language. Platforms were arranged about the room, covered with soft bedding and beautiful pillows. Along the back wall of the enclosure ran a steaming pool fed by a natural spring, heated by the earth below. I was brought a colorful tunic of strange design that was marvelously woven from the softest wool. I washed and dressed myself, enjoyed a light repast, and was then brought before the Zil-at.

The dining hall of the Zil-at seemed enormous to me, grander than that of the Abbot in the castle at Montalcino. It was lit with massive braziers and festooned with colorful drapery and elegantly embroidered furniture that surrounded a long, low table made of polished chestnut. The remains of a great feast spilled over the table. At the head of the table reclined the Zil-at and next to him, his wife, Tarquinia. On either side of them reclined Tarchon, whom I had known as Sebastiano, and Tyrsenos, whom I had known as Salvatore, now dressed in elaborate tunics like the one that I had been given. Tyrsenos smiled at me and commented at how handsome I now appeared, and Tarchon laughed, reminding all that the tunic I wore had once belonged to Tyrsenos when he was young.

I was brought a small footstool and was made to sit before Tarquin and Tarquinia. I spent the remainder of the evening being questioned and engaged in conversation with the guests. I did not speak directly with the Zil-at or his wife, for they had sat in silence and studied my responses. Tarquinia gazed directly into my eyes, and at times seemed to see right through to my soul. When my interrogation was done, Tarquinia looked lovingly at her husband and gave him a slight nod, never betraying any emotion. Tarquin rose to a sitting position and looked first to Tarchon and then to Tyrsenos, and then directly into my eyes. His stare was captivating, and immediately I knew that my fate was in his hands. His pronouncement was swift and short but would forever change my life.

"We have listened to all that was said and have taken counsel with she who shares my heart and spirit," he spoke to me, but also for the benefit of all within the room, and throughout the kingdom. "Giovanni, Son of Uni-Tau, our dearest cousin and confidante, be welcomed and accepted by your kin within the hallowed hills of Curtun. Be steeped in the richness of your heritage, as your father was steeped in his youth, and carry the flame of ancient glory within your heart, wherever you travel in this life, for the remainder of your days. Learn passionately of our ways and keep the memories and traditions of our ancestors deep within your heart. Dwell among us for as long as God grants you life, or travel beyond the sea as the ancient ones were wont to do. You are kin. You are blood. Know that you are one of the Taurisi, whose ancient people came first to this land, and who continue to honor those ancient traditions by living in secrecy within the mists of Crano's hidden kingdom of Curtun. We name thee Sandak as we welcome thee into our house. Live long and learn much. Pray to the gods to bring peace unto your spirit and to reconcile your heart with your soul and with those who love you most."

I lived as Sandak amongst the Taurisi for two years. Many of the ancient ways I learned from them. Most of what I have come to know about my family and myself I learned from the Zil-at, Tarquin, whom I had grown to love and respect as my own father, and from Tarquinia, wife of the Zil-at and tan-asha of the Taurisi. Through their patient teachings, I learned to love and respect my father, and understand the source of the misguided animosity I had shown toward him. I learned the true nobility of my father—Uni Tau, and his ancestors who were counted amongst the very first people to inhabit these lands. The first-born males of this noble line were seers, which the Taurisi call pec-ii. They have, from the very beginning, always served the Zil-at at the Table of the Council.

My grandfather, Tarxin, was the younger brother of Tarquin's father, both sons of Tarquinius, the thirty-first Zil-at of the Taurisi, who proceeded directly from Noah after the time of the Great Flood. Tarxin was a pec-ii, a star gazer who was blessed and cursed with the Sight—the ability to see into the future. He was a troubled soul who spent most of his young life preaching the dangers that the Taurisi were doomed to face. Though he was especially loved by his father and his brothers, and most of the inhabitants of Curtun, his ramblings were never taken seriously, and his frustration had ultimately caused him to leave Curtun to dwell with the lake people in the fertile plains below Cortona. He married the widow of a landowner who had been killed in the First Crusade, and he assumed the name of Adamo al Pecii, which he later changed to Pecci da Cortona. He raised my father and his other children as farmers in the manner of the lake people, hiding his identity to all except for my father, whom he had brought to Curtun in his adolescence, to be educated by the tan-asha of the Taurisi.

My father had spent several years living with the family of Tarquinius, becoming as a younger brother to Tarquin. He would eventually return to Cortona and assume the identity that he had been born into, bringing all the skills that he had learned in Curtun to the fertile plains of Cortona. He was able to increase his father's holdings and to enhance his own status within the fledgling commune of Cortona.

Oh, as I look back with these aged eyes, I realize my grandfather's gift of the Sight was true, for the fate of the Taurisi that he had seen so clearly has come to pass. His warnings had been disbelieved, ignored, and ridiculed by many. How frustrating it must have been for him to see the kingdom of Crano, which had survived for more than twenty-seven hundred years, come to an end. And yet, Tarquinius had known that his brother had spoken the truth for the Zil-at was aware of the many threats that the Taurisi had faced throughout millennia. And yet, they had survived. He remembered well the Confederacy of the Etrusci that was slowly whittled away over time by the treacherous Romans and the barbarians who followed them. He knew that Curtun was the last remnant of that mighty empire that ruled the land unchallenged for thousands of years. He carried the guilt of his ancestors for losing to those barbarians, the sacred seat of Crano, high upon the mountain of Cortona—the original kingdom. Only Curtun had remained, cloaked in secrecy by the forested hills of the Casentino, in the shadow of the great Monte Falco. As a defense, he forbade any intercourse with the outside world, closed the borders of his realm, and passed a sentence of death upon any non-Taurs who ventured into the forest. He amassed a great armory and continued for the remainder of his days to keep vigil for the impending doom.

My father was one of but a few who could cross the borders of Tarquinius' kingdom. While he resided with the Zil-at, he did little to change the leader's perception of the outside world, but his friendship and counsel with Tarquin had a profound effect on the future Zil-at. Tarquin became much more open to the happenings of the outside world. With the passing of Tarquinius, Tarquin became the thirty-second Zil-at of the Taurisi. He began to send out men to the surrounding territories to monitor the happenings of the outsiders, to keep his eyes and ears upon the enemy. He maintained a strict vigil at the borders of his kingdom but was more inclined to educate the youth of his domain in the ways of the outsiders. His scouts would have to leave behind the draping and manners of the ancient world, and to assume the mantle of the new world in order to survive. They would have to infiltrate into the highest courts and assimilate into the lowest ranks in order to obtain from the enemy any knowledge of impending doom.

Those who ventured forth were quite successful, posing as professional thieves and assassins who were much in demand by the courts of Europe, as well as in the court of the popes and the Holy Mother Church. My father was most instrumental in changing the vision of the great leader, though others of higher rank were also brought, as captives, so that the Zil-at's council was always informed of the political situation in the outside world. Father took a special liking to his young cousins Tarchon and Tyrsenos and taught them the ways of the plain and lake dwellers of Cortona. It was he who gave them their Christian names of Sebastiano and Salvatore, and it was that bond that was forged in the hills of Curtun—that would bind us all, my father, myself, and my son—to these two most noble and blessed men. Leaders of the Taurisi, they were also our guardian angels.

It pains my heart that none will know of the greatness of the Taurisi, for I have looked far into the future and have seen no sign of my people. The greatness that once belonged to the sons of Noah has faded into oblivion. Though that noble blood still courses through the veins of men, the spirit of Crano's people is no more. The hope of a future for the Taurisi was given to me, and I have failed my people and have broken my promises. I have ignored my responsibility and have shut my eyes and my heart to everything that was needed to nurture the seed of Rusellae and keep the spirit alive. Though I had saved hundreds from certain death, I have used them for my own financial benefit, stripping them of their heritage. Under the guise of protecting them, I have forced them to assimilate into a world that did not belong to them. I have made them into who they are today, while causing them to forsake who they were before. With such ease and over so short a span of years has a glorious past been erased from the memory of future generations. I mourn for the last true kingdom of God upon this earth, for the thousands who are no more. I mourn for their fading memory. Such tremendous guilt I must carry to my grave, and my failure will weigh heavily upon the Scales of Judgement.

Let me sing the praises of those ancient people before memory is stripped from me. The Taurisi were an industrious people who lived for millennia in obscurity within the protection of these hills and ancient forests. They were highly skilled with forging elements mined from the earth into metals of the purest form, transforming such metals into the most precious of objects. Their weapons were the finest pieces of warcraft ever conceived by man; their daily utensils exquisite works of art. They were masters of the forge and were most eager to impart their wisdom and knowledge upon me.

For many months I labored in the forest, selecting the most appropriate trees whose flesh would be roasted slowly to be made into the perfect charcoal for the furnaces of Vol-tuma. I was schooled in every aspect of the process of turning stone into iron or brass, of extracting pure silver and gold from rock. For many months I learned new skills and was taught many things until one day I was brought to the sacred caverns of Mania to behold the furnaces of Vol-tuma. The walls of that massive cave were intricately decorated, and the ceiling so high that it was lost in the darkness of the diminished lamp light. The cavern was filled with all manner of weaponry, manufactured or accumulated over the millennia. Elaborate headdresses of the original Seafarers were mixed with the swords and shields of the ancient Etrusci. Shields and banners of the Romans and those of the army of Hannable, axes and maces of the Goths, Huns, Franks, Normans, and other barbarian invaders, were piled high throughout. Large stores of armor and ancient mail, enough to outfit an entire army, lay haphazardly upon the floor. Another smaller cavern was used to store all manner of utensils, cups, plates, lamps, and tools crafted by the smiths and artisans, living or long dead. As I recollect even now, the enormity of such a store of artifacts confounds my belief. Back then, in my youth, I was stupefied.

Further into the earth, in a lower cavern, flowed the river of fire that was Voltuma, and upon its fiery shores stood the mighty furnaces from which the fruits of the Taurisi labors were born. Enormous bellows of wood and leather were affixed to channels cut into the rock surrounding the base of the furnace and would lose their breath upon the coals to increase the heat so that it rivaled the sun. To work the furnaces of Vol-tuma, even for a short while, one must be sturdy and fearless, sure afoot and careful of every move. One must honor yet be mindful of the gift that was given by the CUL-su, the demons of hell, to seduce the soul of man. Never are the fires quenched but live both night and day to help man to create weapons of destruction.

I learned much in the years that I spent with the Taurisi. Such knowledge would be of great benefit to me throughout my most productive years. I also learned a great deal about the art of weaving and the use of ancient looms, the fulling of wool, and the production of exquisite cloth. The invention and use of such ancient machines had been lost to antiquity in our world but had been kept alive by the practice of these industrious people. Their use would suit me well in years to come.

But most important to me was the wisdom I had received from Tarquinia, which helped me to learn the techniques necessary to handle my visions. She taught me to gaze deep within my own soul, to wrestle with the demons who reside therein, to strip them of their power and to redirect that power to industriousness, desire, and determined perseverance. From those ancient and wise people, I learned to survive, and to succeed in the world beyond the hills and forests of Curtun.

IV

Seduction

As I matured into manhood in the peace and security of the Hidden Realm, the world outside was in total chaos. The communes in the cities had begun to grow strong and had fought against the controlling lords and the more controlling bishops. The emperor from the north was in open hostilities with the Holy Father, the kingdoms to the south were scheming with the emperor in the east to usurp the powers of the Pope, and the fat lords were constantly trying to regain the power and the territory that was quickly slipping through their fingers. Reports from spies living amid the chaos had filtered back to the Zil-at, who behind his walls of secrecy was preparing his people for the inevitability of a future conflict.

Toward the beginning of the third year of my stay in Curtun, my father had fallen ill, and I was needed to return to the farm to assist him in managing his estate. In truth, I did not return willingly, for though I was upset by the news of my father's health, I did not want to forfeit my freedom and return to Cortona to a life of drudgery. With the blessings of Tarquin and the fair Tarquinia, I begged my leave of them and set forth to meet my fate in the world beyond the hills. I had pledged to the Zil-at my undying fealty, my promise to keep warm within my heart the memories of the kin and friends I had met, and to keep secret the existence of his ancient realm from those who would do harm to its existence. He spoke to me with all the emotion my father had shown to me when I first had left the farm.

"Sandak," he said to me. "Hold deep in your heart all that you have learned of the Taurisi and our ways. You will carry the seeds of tomorrow's crop. Tell no one of our realm, but keep us in your memory, always. May your footsteps never fail to find their way back to your people. Be strong and wise in your resolve and true to your heart, for I see much love buried deep within the caverns of your soul, yet it struggles with the demons who wish to subvert you to the darker side of humanity." Tarquinia gazed at me with mystic eyes and spoke directly to my soul.

"Sandak, Son of Uni-tau, seer from a line of seers, you have been chosen to lead the children of Noah to the safety of the Ark of Rusellae. I have seen this and much more. A doom is upon the children of God and our fate has been written in the stars. Much horror and death I have foreseen, yet hope is cradled in a young heart and must be carried through the carnage and into the light. Take the seeds of our people and nurture them in the fertile soil of a resurrected kingdom. Control those forces that wage war within you and never give in to one side or the other, for evil is cunning and will try to blind you to the truth of what is right or wrong. Listen to your heart for I see the truth that lies within. The truth of these words will be delivered unto you at God's will. Live long and heed well the lessons you have learned from the Taurisi."

Tarquinia then kissed my forehead and added, "Listen to your heart and stay true to the man you will become. Be at peace, our seer, our savior." Oh, so fair and loving and kind was she, that my eyes have filled with tears as I write this, for those words would forever reverberate in my mind.

Tarchon and Tyrsenos were my guides as we made our way out of the kingdom. There was no need for mask or shroud as we ventured beyond the curtained wall of water and worked our way through forest and mountain mist, which brought us into the modern world. As we descended from the mountains and traveled throughout the lands south toward Cortona, we witnessed the ravages and mayhem the warring lords and condottieri had foisted upon the helpless farmers and townspeople left unprotected in the remote villages. The total breakdown of civil law had allowed the hired murderers and thieves of the Aldobrandesch and the Ardengeschi and the Soarzi to rape and pillage while the Pope and the Emperor had concerned themselves only with their temporal struggles. Crops had been destroyed, and entire villages had been wiped out. Such evils that man can perpetrate upon women and children are best left unspoken.

The horrors I witnessed on my travel home seared my brain and filled me with apprehension of what I would find at my father's farm. We moved slowly and cautiously, keeping well-hidden as best we could. As we drew closer to Cortona and the valley below, the countryside had appeared to suffer less damage. Crops were still in the field, signs of animals and peasantry abounded, and homesteads were left intact. Many of the farms that were owned or controlled by my father had been left untouched and seemed to be operating in much the same manner as they had always been.

Though most of the farmers gathered their animals or hid away as we approached, some whom I had known showed great signs of relief and greeted me. I was told how my father had met with the great lords' men when they had come into the valley, securing the safety of his land and his tenants, by diplomatic skill, bribery, or as some believed, magic. He and his people had been spared from the brutality of the mountain lord's marauders, as he had held kinship with them. Indeed, the valley and the city itself were fortunate to have a friend in Vincenzo Pecci da Cortona.

Sebastiano and Salvatore listened without comment. They had been silent through most of our journey through the valley. As time passed, I grew angry at their silence. No longer able to control my tongue I lashed out at them, accusing them of knowing what had been happening in my world and keeping such atrocities from me. Salvatore spoke quietly to me with much anguish. "Calm thyself, young Sandak. It was your father's wish that you be spared such grievous knowledge in the hope that you would finish your education in the safety of our hidden realm. He has high hopes for his firstborn and dared not chance losing one so precious to the violence of these marauding hoards. Be at peace with his wisdom and his decision to delay in sending for you. He has secured your safety and the safety of his family and countrymen. Rejoice in the knowledge that your family and your home has remained safe, at least for a while, for though your father's influence be strong, it may yet prove futile in these times of war and great misdeeds."

My anger, I managed to put aside for another day, for I had

realized that I still had harbored ill feelings toward my father for again abandoning me, for not trusting in my abilities to protect myself, my family, and my home. Again, he had robbed me of my will, my chance to show him that I was strong, that I was able to stand on my own. Tarquin had spent much time trying to teach me how to honor, to love, and to respect my father, and I had left Curtun with great resolve to mend the broken ties between my father and myself. And yet, within a few days' journey my resolve had evaporated and the enmity and animosity that had built up over the many years I had been away from his loving embrace had begun to boil within my heart.

When we finally reached the farm, my brothers were the first to greet me. I marveled at how they had grown, these boys, now turned young men. Both were as tall as me and sported beards and the swagger and cockiness of young manhood. Mother was close behind, unable to conceal her excitement for my return. She did not even acknowledge Sebastiano nor Salvatore, and it was only with the hearty greeting of my father that my mother realized my companions were with me. Father's voice was loud and welcoming. His embrace was genuine, though he tried to mask the tears that had filled his eyes. He pressed me hard against his chest and I could instantly smell the farm, the animals, and the soil upon his person. Suddenly, all the scents of my childhood, those few years of total innocence and happiness when I would ride upon his broad shoulders, had flooded my entire being, and my hatred melted away. I was home, at last.

Father had not been ill, though, as it turned out, he did need me to help him with the farm—not just with the old homestead, but with several of the other smaller farms he had acquired. Most of the fields had been planted, and harvest time was coming in a few short months. The problem was that the workforce had been drastically reduced by the violence in the surrounding area. Many of the tenants had fled with their families as the condottieri had advanced upon the valley. Families I had known in childhood simply disappeared, leaving crops in the field and livestock to their own fate. My father and brothers had managed to collect some of the animals who wandered in the area, while the others were fair game for the lord's men. Thus, my father's pens were filled in the days when I first returned home.

His prosperity, it had turned out, was the result of the ill fortune of his neighbors and the cunning deals that he was able to make with the lords. He had convinced each to allow him to provide them with future supplies when the harvest was in, swearing to give them half of everything he and his family could bring in. He had also convinced them that by sparing the fields and the livestock, when harvested and properly fattened, would be much more valuable by being converted to cash at the markets in Siena and Arezzo. He had pledged to each a percentage of the profits in gold and silver to be delivered to them upon his return. To each he granted a lien upon certain property to assure them of his fealty. Great was my father's fortune, and even greater was each lord's greed, that a bargain was struck that preserved my father's holdings from imminent destruction. He would turn their greed into his benefit. The crops were of no use to them at this early stage, and so large were his combined holdings that it would be impossible, so they assumed, for my father and his small family to bring the crops to full harvest or to bring the goods to market. They would gladly accept what little cash was derived from the sweat and hard work of others, and the lands that once were theirs would come back into their hands through default of such a heavy debt.

I was grateful then that my father had called me back so that I could be of use to him in his time of need. I did not know at that time that I was a part of his plan to save his family and his fortune. Together on that first night of my return, my father revealed to us all that had transpired and his plans to bring the entire holdings to harvest. Sebastiano and Salvatore had been aware of most of what had happened and had been a part of the plan from the beginning. They had visited with my father shortly after he had made his deals and had devised a way to secret a workforce onto the farm to bring the crops in and to prepare the goods for market. Tarquin had pledged a force of laborers to assist in tending and harvesting the crops. Those laborers would be replaced with a small group of skilled artisans who would work their magic in turning the raw materials into the finest products to grace the markets of Siena and Arezzo.

The mills had been vacant for some time as the miller had disappeared with the initial wave of refugees and stood ready to process the harvested wheat into white gold. The milk from the surviving animals would be made into cheese, and the meat would be dried and cured in the ancient way, as none had seen in these modern times. Such help would be brought in under cover of darkness, appearing as if by magic at the farm before dawn, and vanishing into the forest north of Cortona at dusk. They would be disguised in the clothing of the local peasants as they worked in the fields or around the farm buildings and would pass themselves as relatives of my father should any question their presence.

For two months I worked with my father overseeing the outlying farms and the waves of workers who would mysteriously appear at morning's light. Many of the Taurisi I had known and come to love during my stay in Curtun. Many had known my father and showed him great respect. I had come to realize that this was his secret family, as they had become mine. Sebastiano and Salvatore would come and go, sometimes returning with other Taurisi, other times off on missions about which I never questioned. I had come to realize that our causes, though seemingly different as night and day, were very much the same. We sought to survive in our violent, war-plagued world, while they fought to keep secret their hidden realm, to keep alive their ancient ways, to live apart from the madness that the world had become, and to survive as they were.

When the chill winds of late Autumn began to race down from the hills, small armies of field laborers materialized, scythes in hand, to cut and bundle the shafts and ready them for transport to the mill. Cartload after cartload of fresh-cut wheat were brought to the yard, where the kernels were separated from the shaft, the latter piled high in barns and sheds to be used as feed for the livestock during the coming winter, and the former placed in sacks to be transported to the mill for processing. A skilled miller was brought in to reduce the wheat to flour. Autumn had brought with it an unusually heavy crop of chestnuts in the forests between Curtun and Cortona that had been gathered each day by the laborers and brought to the mill, also to be processed into a hearty flour. Farro that had been planted late in the summer was harvested, its grains left whole and placed in sacks to be sold.

The grapes and olives were abundant upon the vine and tree but would not be ready for harvest before the autumnal markets. Father's supply of wine and oil remaining from the previous year's bountiful harvest, which was secretly stored and hidden from the unwelcomed intruders, would be sent along to be sold, as would the fruits from the orchards that had been maintained by several of father's tenants. Everything produced during that season, except for a small supply that was needed for the family's survival throughout the long winter and spring, was made available for sale. Father also collected a larger portion of crops than was due to him from his tenant farmers who had survived to work the lands. They had given willingly for my father's protection and the help of his relatives in bringing in a better than normal yield. It was in their best interest that enough money was brought back from the markets to pay the debts to the lords and to assure future prosperity.

As the time of the fairs drew near, Father busied himself with making plans for the transport of his goods to Siena. He had met with my Uncle Giancarlo, whose connections to the powerful Manenti and the Soarzi had helped protect my father's lands from the lords of the hills in the first place. Giancarlo had become a very wealthy merchant in Siena and was more than happy to sponsor his sister's husband in a prestigious place in the Campo throughout the entire weeks of the market. He would provide his gracious hospitality to my father's company, provide all the necessary introductions in the Sienese mercantile society, handle all the exchange of coin and cash, and provide safety throughout our stay within the contrada of Siena. This, of course, was given for a small percentage of the profits, a deeply discounted family courtesy.

Closer to home, father had secured as many wagons as were needed to transport such a large shipment of goods over the steep road and hilly terrain between Cortona and Siena. The roads were treacherous, not only because of the physical challenges they posed to the heavy wagons, but because of the bandits, murderers, and thieves, who were emboldened by the lack of civil order and preyed upon the weary wanderer. With the increasing turmoil, these scourges of the land had multiplied and had laid in hiding places along the major routes in Tuscany. The transport of such a large shipment would be dangerous and would require a small security force to ensure its safety to the borders of Siena. Father had arranged for such a force through

Sebastiano and Salvatore, who petitioned the Zil-at to provide a small band of warriors to accompany the caravan to Siena and to escort the returning party back to Cortona at the end of the fair.

Giancarlo and Father had planned a month's time would be needed from when the first wagons left Cortona until the time they returned. One week was allotted to travel and set-up, while the second full week and a half was reserved for the actual trade of goods between merchants and local buyers. A week belonged to the moneychangers and the bankers, and the last several days were needed for breakdown and travel home.

As Hallowmas drew near, we all worked feverously to prepare our shipment. Father had collected as many wagons as would be needed for the delivery of goods and had arranged to modify many of them with hidden storage compartments where the most precious of goods would be hidden from view. Father's intent was to make the shipment appear much smaller to the prying eye of the lord's spies or bandits who would most likely be encountered along the way. The lord's agents would not know how successful or resourceful my father had been, or how bountiful a crop would be taken to market. He had arranged to pay his debts to those warlords to whom he had pledged a share of the fruits of his family's labor by meeting their agents along the way and dispatching his payments. He was careful not to allow them any knowledge of the size and extent of the cargo that would be shipped to market.

Father had planned to send two separate shipments to market. The first caravan consisted of thirty-two wagons that transported roughly half of everything produced, except for the wines, oil, meat, and cheese, which were intentionally left out of the agreement with the lords. This was sent out first, traveling on the main roads during the day, in plain sight of the lord's spies, and was enough to settle Father's debts. Father had arranged to meet the lord's agents at the halfway mark and had distributed half of the shipment to each of their men. The remaining half of the merchandise was taken to market, as agreed, and sold—a fixed percentage of the profit being given over to the lords in silver. Father was allowed to keep what was left—for his trouble. A separate stall was set up to handle the trade of the remaining merchandise from this shipment. Father oversaw the selling of everything from that stall, knowing that the lord's spies were watching every trade.

Meanwhile, the second shipment containing the other half of the harvest, plus the undisclosed goods, was loaded onto forty wagons and set out for Siena three days later, traveling backroads under cover of night. I headed up this caravan, and Sebastiano and Salvatore with an armed security force had accompanied me in case we ran into trouble. In Siena, Giancarlo had arranged for a separate stall to be erected on the opposite end of the Campo, and Father had allowed me, posing as a foreign merchant, to oversee all trade from that stall.

Fortune was good to us and we made it to Siena by noon of All Hallow's Eve. Father had been successful in his dealings with the lord's agents and had arrived in Siena the day before our wagons had entered through the Porta San Marco. Giancarlo's men had met us on the road as we entered the contrada of Siena and had escorted us into the city. He had arranged for us to position the wagons in the open fields to the south of the Campo and west of the Terzo di Citta. From there it would be easy to gain access to the Campo.

Giancarlo was more than gracious in offering us lodging. From the top levels of his magnificent palazzo we could keep watch over our wagons in the adjacent fields below and view the silhouette of the magnificent Duomo of Santa Maria that was being constructed to the north in the heart of the city. The Terzo di Citta, with the dozens of high towers constructed by the wealthy bankers and merchants of the city, sprawled out before us. Such a sight I had never in my life beheld, for though the grand majesty of the Castle of the Abbot of Sant' Antimo had at one time left me speechless, its awesomeness had paled in comparison to the wealth and grandeur of the many edifices of this wealthy commune.

Giancarlo's wealth was never to be hidden but displayed in the furnishings of his home, a great deal of which were imported from his trade missions to the East, in his possessions, in his clothing, and in his appearance. Throughout my life, he would always emphasize to me that a man's success lay in his appearance to others. If a man was perceived to be rich by his peers or his betters, then indeed he would be a rich man. Power would always begat power. Weakness, or the appearance of weakness, would always lead a man to his ruin.

Giancarlo had made a great fortune for himself, in small part through inheritance of lands held by the Manenti clan to the south between Siena and Monalcino, but mostly through his banking and trading enterprises throughout Italy and to the East in Constantinople. His skills as a money lender were renown in a city of bankers and thieves, his dealings with the Emperor guaranteeing safe passage through Ghibelline territories, and his connections with the Curia assuring his eternal soul protection from the fires of Hell. He swore allegiance to no authority but that of the Commune, yet he conducted business with popes and emperors alike. His financial empire spread far and wide with dealings in all the major capitols of Europe, the Eastern Empire, and the Holy Land. The capitol of his empire lay within the walls of Siena.

Giancarlo was a gregarious and affable man whose features and countenance was a mirror of my mother's. I had developed an early affinity to him. He greeted me warmly, and he lovingly introduced me to his wife, the fair Donata Soarzi, and her daughter Anna. Through his marriage to Donata Soarzi and his adoption of her daughter, Giancarlo's early fortune had nearly doubled in size with Anna's inheritance. Anna was several years my senior and well past the age when most young maidens were betrothed to young men of wealth or future prosperity. Alas, she had not inherited her mother's beauty, nor her wit or charm. She was, in fact, rather homely and dolorous in her demeanor, and seemed more boyish to me than the fair maiden of whom my dear uncle had so frequently spoken. She was shy around strangers and found it difficult to converse at length upon any topic. My first impression of Anna would, I must confess, remain with me throughout her life. She was not a bad person, nor was she kind or sweet; she simply existed. Father and Giancarlo had made the best of an awkward introduction by engaging Sebastiano and Salvatore in conversation with Donata Soarzi while leaving me to fend for myself with Anna.

It seems to me that All Hallows Eve, in those days, was more somber a festival than it has become in recent times. We celebrated and honored the dead, for two days, in a most reverent way. It has always been a time when spirits and demons alike walk the earth, when the ghosts of our long-dead whisper in our ear, and incubi and succubae torment the living in dreams and in fancy, causing the blood to boil with carnal lust, tempting the innocent soul to sin. It is a time when bonfires are lit in each of the piazze to illuminate the city and to drive away the evil demons who dare to walk the streets of the living. In Siena, for a boy of my age, it was haunting and magical, and so exciting. I remember the excitement and innocence of that boy even today. A massive bonfire was lit ablaze in the Campo when the full moon had risen high into the night sky. The streets and the piazze were filled with citizens dressed in horrible masks designed to scare off an evil demon or the ghost of an enemy.

We watched the festivities from atop Giancarlo's palazzo, spending the entire evening dining in royal splendor and catching up on all that was happening in each other's lives. Donna Donata was charming, adding such great delight to the conversation, lightening my uncle's demeanor and causing him to laugh many times. It was clear to see that though theirs was a marriage of convenience, a partial mending of bridges between the Manenti and the Soarzi, Giancarlo had truly loved his bride, and she him. Both were well respected in the wealthy society of an increasingly powerful commune of Siena.

Poor Anna, though; inheriting none of her mother's graces, she had contributed little to the evening's conversations. She merely sat and stared, making me uncomfortable enough to excuse myself from the group on several occasions. Sensing my anxiety Donna Donata coaxed Anna into entertaining the guests with song and lute. She handled the instrument with such gentleness and skill that the plucking of its strings reverberated on the strings of my heart. Her voice was sweet and melodic, and she sang such sad songs that filled the eyes of all who stood transfixed in the spell of that beautiful voice. A softness and a vulnerability, locked deep within her, shone forth with her tearful songs and for that one moment she captured the hearts of all in the room. When she finished, she excused herself and retired for the night, leaving me to ponder the sphinx that was Anna Soarzi Manenti.

All Saints Day was set aside to pray for intersession of those venerated by the Church and its adherents. Mass was celebrated locally in the Chiesa di San Quirico early in the morning, where many of the nouveau riche merchants living in the Terzo di Citta would parade themselves and their family. Each would try to outdo the other in their richly embroidered cloths imported from the East or obtained at the most recent fair in Champagne.

Following the Mass, the families would enjoy a morning passagiata through the congested Via di Stalloreggi and the Via Del Capitano to the Church of the Virgin Mary. The original church was ancient. It is said that before the coming of the Christ it was a temple of the Etruschi and then a temple of Diana for the Romans. Because of the veneration of the Virgin by this fair city, it has always been the seat of the Bishop of Siena, and as such has always had the attention of master builders, artisans, and dreamers of glory. In those days, the renovations to the older church were not complete, yet the edifice was still the center of life in the city. All the citizens from the three terzi came to the Duomo to hear the pronouncements of the Bishop and to hear Mass on the holy days.

I remember how beautiful the wealthy citizens looked to me, and how massive the crowd was, cordial to each other, and pious, at least for that special day of prayer. Ceremonies venerating individual saints were observed in each contrada of the city. An elaborate feast was enjoyed in those contrade that lasted the entire evening and well into the night. Tables stretched the entire length of the Piano di Mantellini, and foods of all manner were shared by the citizens of the contrada, paid for by the wealthiest of its residents. Those less fortunate gladly served the food and wine and enjoyed the festivities just as much as the seated guests. Such prosperity and camaraderie were hard for me to comprehend, having witnessed the devastation in the lands surrounding Cortona. The magic of that grand festival remains with me even to this day.

The following day, All Souls Day was observed with visits to the cemeteries and crypts to honor the deceased, as well as a celebratory Mass for the Dead at the Duomo. It also marked the opening of the fair in midafternoon. During the early hours of the morning, Sebastiano and Salvatore had overseen the transfer of a good portion of our produce from the staging area to the vender stalls. Burlap bags were placed upon the horse's hooves and the wheels of the carts to prevent any disturbance and eliminate any heavy fines for violation of any one of the hundreds of city ordinances. They worked feverously while the citizens slept off the celebration of the previous night. Quietly the small workforce transported the goods and stocked the stalls so that by midmorning, with our arrival, our stalls were ready for business.

Throughout the afternoon people had begun to pour in from all over the surrounding area, many coming in from as far as Liguria and Emilia Romagna to the north and Umbria and the Marche to the east. Pilgrims from Rome and south had made special plans to stop in Siena for this fair on their way north on the Via Francigena. The streets of the city became clogged as streams of humanity poured through each of the gates of the city. The Comunal police force was hard-pressed to keep order in the center of the city and throughout the outlying contrada alleyways.

Though there were some small bands of entertainers, jugglers, acrobats, musicians and dancers, and food vendors interspersed between merchant stalls, such as are normally found at the fairs in Champagne and Cologne, the main purpose of this fair was to bring to market those wares that had been imported from beyond the borders of the Commune: spices and fine silks from the Far East, supposed relics and treasures obtained in the conquest of the Holy Land, fine wools from Britain, rendered into lusciously colored fabrics in the factories along the Arno, foods, wines, and oils from the areas not ravaged by the warring armies of the Emperor or the Pope. Hundreds of stalls, large and small, filled the Campo, eventually spilling over into the Piazza del Duomo, the Piazza del Mercato, and along the main streets surrounding the Campo.

Wholesale buyers from far and wide made it a point to be at the fair on the first day, hoping to secure merchandise at a favorable price that would bring them increased profits upon resale in the towns and villages along their return route. Uncle Giancarlo counseled us not to sell too much in the first days, but to wait until the third and fourth day of the fair when higher retail prices could be got for the same merchandise. Being novices to this sort of trading, we were hard-pressed not to sell everything to the first bidders. Wise was Giancarlo's counsel for though we far exceeded our expectations on the first day alone, profits from the succeeding days were progressively greater, until by the end of that second week we had exhausted our supplies. The demand for local, top-quality produce was so great due to hardship and shortage in the surrounding areas that we were able to extract triple the price we had anticipated from the wealthy citizens of Siena. At the close of the second week our profit was such that all debts could be paid, to the lords, and to Uncle Giancarlo, and still a small fortune would be retained by my father.

We all rejoiced mightily at the conclusion of the second week's festivities. Uncle Giancarlo and I had spent much time together and he had developed a liking for me. He told me he saw great potential in me and played upon every weakness to win me as his prize. He was a magnificent bird of prey, and I, it turned out, was his prey. He had the eye of an eagle and could see opportunity throughout the world from his perch high upon the hills of Siena. His view of life, his manner of living, and his business acumen were very appealing to me, and he had offered it all to me freely and without attachment, or so I thought. Father had seen my uncle's effect upon me and cautioned me not to forsake my heritage for the glittering trappings of easily made profit. "The path to Hell," he said to me, "was paved with gold and carpeted with silk and gems." Oh! If only I had listened to him.

As the third week of the fair commenced, father had made his profit and had had enough of the fair. He had paid his debts to Giancarlo and his workers and had prepared his caravan for the trip back to Cortona. Feeling that he had made more than he had expected, he decided to forgo the opportunity to increase his profits through the unseemly business of money changing. He had always looked upon such activity with disdain, yet never criticized Giancarlo for his questionable practices. Father would just have no part of it. He was grateful for Giancarlo's help and guidance during the fair and wished him good fortune in his future endeavors. Giancarlo made no attempt to convince Father to stay but accepted his payments in friendship and feted us all on the night before we returned to Cortona.

During the evening I had convinced my father to allow me to stay for a short while and to try to increase his profits while Giancarlo tutored me in the ways of foreign exchange. Though most of Father's sales were consummated in silver pieces, other coin from distant regions had been used and needed to be converted into specie that would be more acceptable to his creditors. Giancarlo had obliged Father in this service, for a nominal fee, and I was fascinated with this entire process—the weighing of the coin, the mathematical calculations, and the less obvious swindling of the patron. He was a master of his trade and could easily distinguish real coin of the realm from the counterfeits. Fairs such as this one in Siena had attracted all sorts of swindlers and thieves, and counterfeit coin was prevalent. Giancarlo could spot a debased coin with ease and could just as easily pass bad coin on to inexperienced traders. Father had warned me there was a special place in Hell for the swindler and for one who would deceive another for his own personal gain. I cared not for his warnings. I saw no difference between Giancarlo swindling a swindler and my father deceiving the lords concerning the size of the harvest or the amount of profits made at the fair.

In the end, Father had allowed me to spend a few extra days with Giancarlo, to observe the closing of the fair and the settlement of payments. He allowed me the courtesy so long as Sebastiano and Salvatore remained in Siena and escorted me back to Cortona. This was agreeable to my uncle and my two guides, and I gratefully bid my father and company farewell in the early hours of the following morning. For the remainder of the fair, I attached myself to Uncle Giancarlo. He showed me many tricks of his trade, we discussed the workings of his business until the late hours of the night, and he tested me continuously, observing how much I was absorbing and how much I already knew. He was impressed with my business acumen and mentioned to me on several occasions that he wanted me to join him on his next business ventures.

My mind was reeling with the opportunities that were presenting themselves to me. This was my chance to break away from a life on the farm, a way to make my fame and fortune, a shortcut toward my long-dreamed destiny. I took all I had learned from Giancarlo of not selling oneself short and applied it to his own multiple offers, telling him that I would consider carefully his proposal, discuss it with my father, and give him my answer in due time.

It was also during my final few evenings spent at the palazzo of my uncle that I really got to know and appreciate the virtues and good graces of Donna Donata and the gentleness of Anna. Both Giancarlo and Donata had made every effort to bring Anna and me together by enticing Anna to entertain me with music and song. I knew they were intent on matching the two of us together. Anna was well past the general age of betrothal, owing no doubt to her comely appearance and reticent personality. I had grown to appreciate her gift of song but found her lacking in conversational skills and attractiveness and could find no solace in the thought of spending our lives together. Such an arrangement brought me little comfort, but the financial implications were great, and had to be considered seriously. I did my very best to avoid any discussions in that direction.

The following day, we bid our hosts farewell. We rode out through the Porta San Marco and headed east to the Val Di Chiana and on to the foothills of Cortona. Upon our arrival at my father's farm, we were welcomed as victorious merchant captains. Father was extremely pleased with the outcome of the fair. He had satisfied all his debts and had secured his fortune and the security of his family and his estates. He was eager to plan the following year's trip and assumed that I would settle down and work with him to maintain the family business. By that time, I had already developed other plans.

The day had slipped away. The sun had hugged the horizon for most of the short day and was preparing to sink behind the distant hills to the west. Long purple shadows were cast across the glistening snow-covered valley, and the sun's final rays glowed orange. Darkness was beginning to fill the room. Nikos lay down his quill as Giovanni began to doze. He had been dictating most of the day and he was exhausted. Nikos had taken the time to refresh himself and to quietly gather the supplies that would be needed later in the evening for his master's mystical journey. That being done, he curled himself up on a chair and fell into a deep sleep. A few hours later he awoke to Giovanni's call.

"Awake, Nikos. The time draws near. We must prepare ourselves."

Just as he had done the night before, Nikos began to prepare the proper elixir. Giovanni had instructed him on the amount of ingredients to be used, doubling the amount of marigold petals to enhance his insight and tripling the number of bay leaves, hoping to strengthen the Divine guidance. Nikos took it upon himself to increase the number of rosemary sprigs, hoping to ensure his master's safety while he confronted both angels and demons. Nikos had known all too well how dangerous it was to communicate with the heavenly hosts, and more so when confronting the demons of Hell. He had seen his loving friend waste away to a wraith as compensation for his special powers.

Giovanni had made sure that all was in order as the two prepared for the first night's visitation. Nothing could go wrong. His soul had depended on it. The logs in the hearth had been dried and stacked to ensure an even but slow burn. The proper incense was sprinkled upon the burning logs and the embers had already begun to glow red. Even though the room was hot because of the fire, Nikos blanketed his master with several sheepskin coverings and wrapped himself with a large woolen blanket. He positioned himself on a chair beside Giovanni and moved the small desk upon which he had been writing as close to his friend as possible so that he might protect Giovanni's venerable body and also be able to hear every syllable uttered by the seer. Extra ink and quills were made ready, for Nikos knew that the night would be long, and the spectral conversations could be lengthy.

A light snow had stopped falling and the full brightness of a blue moon had illuminated the plains below. The night air was still except for the screeching of a great white owl triumphantly claiming its prey. Nikos handed Giovanni the vision chalice filled with the magic elixir and Giovanni slowly drank it dry. The scribe sat with one hand wresting upon the hand of his master and held tightly to the quill, ready to continue to record every spoken word of the seer.

Giovanni began to slip into a dream state, his head bobbing and moving rhythmically in a circular pattern. The fire hissed and the logs spit as the embers glowed red and blue in pulsation that mimicked movement of Giovanni's head. In time, Nikos witnessed the transformation of his master—one that he had seen so many times before. Giovanni's head fell back against the headrest of the chair, his face turned ghostly, his eyes rolled back so that only bloody-white orbs stared toward the ceiling, and his mouth hung open. His skin was cold as death, and for a long moment there was no breath. Nikos had always worried when Giovanni was in this state, for he could not tell if his master had succeeded in the transition to the other world or if Death had finally claimed its prize.

Giovanni had begun his journey.

Darkness envelopes me. The drums are beating—or is that my heart? In the distance, I see a shining star. It is pulsating, and it grows larger and brighter. It approaches, and I fear not, for I have had many encounters with this gentle light. It knows me, and I know it. I welcome its embrace. How sweet the sound of the angels' voices? They soothe me and comfort me. Peace be with you, gentle spirits. Come to me and show me the way. I thank Thee, Holy Spirit, for coming back to me in my hour of need. You have never abandoned me. I am grateful to Thee for the opportunity you have given to me so that I may properly repent and gain the reward of Heaven. Speak to me, gentle spirit, as you have done so many times before. I am ready for you to guide me.

My head is filled with visions, too many to comprehend. I see my life—my incredibly long and miserable life, flashing before me. How am I to comprehend your teachings at such high speed? What is it that you are trying to show me? Are you not to be my guide, as promised? Who is it, then, who will guide me and show me the errors of my life?

The mist grows heavy. Your heavenly light is fading. Stay with me, Holy Spirit. Stay and protect me. Do not abandon me, I beg Thee. How will I ever begin to save my soul without your holy light? Darkness descends. I am alone.

[There is a long moment of silence. Giovanni labors to breathe, but I dare not try to wake him.]

Who is there in the darkness? Reveal yourself. How is it that you have happened upon my dream? Speak, spirit, and tell me if you be angel or demon and what your intentions might be.

[There is more silence, and then a strange voice speaks.]

Calm yourself, Giovanni. I am neither angel nor demon, not friend nor foe. I have not happened upon your dream as you accuse but have been sent to you by a higher power, to guide you through this night's vision. Look closer at this ethereal spirit, perchance to recognize the man who I once was.

Father! Do my eyes deceive me? Is it truly you?

Your eyes have nothing to do with your recognition; only your mind's eye can see in the spirit world. A pec-ii should know this. You should know this. I am here because of the deal you made with the light. I am here because you want me to be here. I am here to show you the path.

Tell me, Father, why it is that you appear so young to me—much younger to me than when first you carried me upon your shoulders and introduced me to the world? Oh, how I remember those early years. Those were the happiest years in my life. Then, you were a king to me.

Tell me, son, why is it that you appear so old to me? Many years have passed since last I set my living eyes upon your countenance. You were no more than a boy—a very young man intent on ruling the world. The years have not looked favorably upon you, my son. Oh, that you only had listened to me just a little. I had so much more to teach you. So many hard lessons I had to learn in my life I would have gladly passed on to you, which perchance may have helped you avoid the devilish traps laid upon your own path.

That road upon which you were destined to travel, my son, stretches out well before your birth and continues well beyond your final days. I have walked upon this same path in earlier days and for a time we walked that path together. Many of the obstacles and circumstances you have encountered on your life-journey were made manifest through actions I had made in my youth. God has allowed me one more time to retrace my own steps and to walk with you—to show you the steps you have taken with the hope that you will see the missteps you have made. Your salvation will only be achieved if you recognize your missteps, take ownership of them, and see the true path to forgiveness. Are you willing to accept that which I am about to show you?

I beg your forgiveness, Father, for treating you with such disrespect. I have regretted my behavior for many years now, and have longed to hear your wise counsel, in light of all that I have learned and have been forced to endure. I surrender my spirit to you and beg you to help me find the way. Take me now into your loving embrace and bear me once again upon your shoulders. Show me that which I was too prideful to see for myself.

The mist returns. I can see nothing. Are you still with me, Father? Where is this place?

We stand before the great sarcophagus of Crano, Son of Noah, deep in the sacred necropolis at Curtun. Look around and bear witness to the many great

Zil-ats who followed their great leader, and who ruled over the Taurisi since after the Great Flood. Strong and wise and noble were these Children of God. Many of them, like their fathers before them, lived incredibly long lives, and accomplished wonders. They built a mighty empire that ruled over the seas, and their influence was felt around the entire world. They were wise and just and prospered through friendship rather than through warfare. Our people were possessed of great learning and ability, inherited from a time before the Flood, when God spoke directly to his children and taught them many things. This you know because of the years spent living with the Taurisi—before they were taken from the world.

I do remember, Father, the Sacred Halls beneath Curtun, yet those mighty chambers paled in comparison to these I see before me. Do my eyes deceive me or has time dimmed the memory of such a wonderous dwelling?

Your eyes do not deceive you. These are the original chambers that were buried deep beneath the city of Curtun, the true seat of Crano's kingdom, which is now called Cortona. Long did the Throne of Crano sit atop the mountain which cradles fair Cortona. But the ravages of time and the savagery of man had caused the Zil-ats of old to move their once-mighty capital, to find safety and solitude deep in the forested hills to the north. The Taurisi had lived in peace and obscurity for many hundreds of years, until you changed all that.

Please, Father, please do not make me look upon that nightmare, for my conscience has been plagued with such evil visions for many years. Such visions bring me no comfort, but only misery. Please spare me your disapproval and disappointment by taking me away from this horrid vision. Spare us both the heartache and anguish of my failure.

We do not honor the greatest of the Taurisi in these hallowed halls to remind you of that terrible injustice. The sins that are yours to bear regarding that matter are to be left for another time and another teacher to visit. I bring you here to remind you of the greatness that once belonged to the Taurisi. You are a descendant of those noble lords, and their goodness and nobility, as much as it did in Crano, courses through your veins. You, my son, are a pec-ii of the Taurisi. You are a seer—the son of a seer, directly descended from a line of pec-ii that draws from the very loins of Noah. With such blood comes much responsibility. You have been given a gift that was to be used for the protection and betterment of the Children of God. Instead, you have used your powers throughout your life for the betterment of Giovanni. You let your pride hold captive your humbleness. You were given the sight, yet you chose to be blinded to its true purpose. Through your pride and greed, you took that which was good and corrupted it for your own purposes. The Children of God stand ready to judge you. But not at this time.

The vision fades too quickly, Father; what is it I must learn. The fate of the Taurisi was not in my hands alone. For my part, I am truly sorry. I have lamented my actions, or rather my inactions, since those dreadful days. And yet, are there not others who bare more blame than me? Surely you must hold some sympathy for your son. Father, speak to me.

Where now is this place, and who are these men who huddle so adoringly around that poor wretch who seems to be living his final moments? I see you, just as I see you now, a young man, not more than twenty. And bless my soul, is that Giancarlo with you? How young he appears to be. Who are the others?

We are at Clairveaux, in the Cictercian monastery of Bernard. The man on the bed is Malachy. Is this familiar to you?

Yes, Father, I was told of this event by the Patriarch of Grato, who I see there standing by the bedside. And see, Bernard has spread the prophet's papers upon the floor and is trying to make sense of it all. I have seen the result of his labor. I have held the sacred book of The Prophesies in my own two hands. The book has been the source of much mischief and conflict in the world, and now, how ironic, it resides in the vault of the one who helped steal it from the conniving emperors.

Was it not you too, my son, who stole the book? He who covets it now, at the least brought it back to its rightful owner, while you were more than happy to barter over it for your own financial gain. Your motives, noble as you have convinced yourself to believe, were poisoned by sin. Your pride allowed you to make demands of a desperate pope and your greed set the price high enough to feed that pride. But lo, see what befalls these two young travelers.

I see you, Father, kneeling beside the saint. Giancarlo has written upon a parchment and he is studying the words he had transcribed from the prophet. You are bent close, your ear to the mouth of the dying man. He is speaking to you in the words of the Holy Spirit and you understand all that he is saying for you have shared his visions, and you are weeping. What is it that he is saying to you, Father? Though my mind's eye sees clearly, my ears are deaf. What tragedy has he foreseen?

He speaks to me of my son, and of my son's son, and all of the hurt that will be manifest by the actions of the two. I had seen such horror in my own visions, and the dying Malachy showing me the same in his. Oh, such punishment is mine that I must relive this scene again and again whilst my soul is cleansed in the darkness of Purgatory. I bear the sin of not telling you that which I was told and had already known. I had carried you with me on my path and did not do enough to deter you from taking the wrong path. The decisions you made in life were yours to make, yet I, perhaps, should have steered you more forcefully toward righteousness. Forgive me, my son.

It is I who must beg forgiveness from you, Father. You had always shown me the true path, yet I was too stubborn and prideful to heed your advice and to bathe in your love. I see now that my destiny had been writ upon the stars before I was even brought into this world. Do I not deserve some degree of forgiveness for my many sins, for each of them had been predetermined and no one had moved to warn me that I might seek a better choice?

Your many sins are not so easily mitigated, for the choice was yours to make, and you constantly refused to listen to your heart and your true spirit. The Holy Spirit was always your guide, yet you listened to the evil ones and were so easily seduced into corruption. It was not always so. In the beginning you were so pure. Come, see the unsullied Giovanni–before...

I see us, Father, playing amid the grape vines. I cannot be but two years old, and you hold me so lovingly close to you. You are showing me the grape and telling me all about its life and purpose. I can taste that grape, even now. Oh, how I loved you back then. You were so patient with me, and I wanted nobody else. I was with you night and day, and you never tired of my inquisitiveness and my hunger to know more.

Look, I have grown, and I am no longer at your side. I sit upon my mother's lap. Ah, dear Mother! She too is teaching me things—wonderous things. I see castles and fat nobles, and great feasts; wild hunts, and gold and silver. She is telling me of lands far away and singing of a better life—a much better life than the one she had found on the farm. She is in love with you, Father, but she respects you not. You opened my eyes to the wonders of the earth, yet I had also learned much from her. It was she who opened my heart to all that I wanted beyond the stone walls of the farm, all that you could not give me.

Ah, my son. I saw all this happening and did not stop it. My sin of pride was thinking that I would win you over to me, without hurting the one I loved. In this, I gave you everything, and still I thought that you would eventually turn to my way, for I truly believed that my way was the right way. And yet, in the end, I lost you to your mother, to your uncle, to yourself, and the wickedness of the world.

Father, you did not lose me entirely. I had learned the errors of my ways, and had thought of you often, but I could not speak directly to you for you were gone. Did you not hear my confessions and my pleas?

Your confessions and your pleas were meaningless, for as your heart had screamed out to you and your soul had pleaded with you for salvation, your mind had turned your ears deaf, and your visions were shrouded in evil. The Devil is strong, and you, my son, were an easy prey. The night draws on and we have no time to linger here. Contemplate the root of your sin and learn from what you have revisited tonight. Come....

I know this place. Oh, Dear Lord, protect me from this evil sight. This is the cellar—the beast's lair. My stomach still aches, and I am sick at the sight of this Hellhole even after all these years. Why have you brought me here?

To face your own demons. You cannot go forward without confronting your past. This was a pivotal point in your life, and there is too much left undone. You need closure here in order to cleanse your soul.

And what is it that I will learn here?

[There was a long pause here, and then a stranger voice was heard.]

You will learn SILENCE, you miserable dog, and the insignificance of your miserable life. My master is anxiously awaiting you.

Father help me. I know this voice and it fills me with terror. And this mass of bone and charred flesh—it repulses me, and yet it is familiar to me. It speaks to me, and its stench assails my nostrils. How is it that this creature shares in my vision?

This is not a vision from your past, as others have been. This is a demon sent from Hell. Just as I was allowed by the Holy Spirit to temporarily leave the confines of Purgatory to visit you, this demon was given temporary reprieve from his eternal punishment in the fires of Hell to do the bidding of his master.

Did you think, dog, that the Evil One would allow the light to vanquish the dark so easily? I have come to thank your father for lending me his precious son, so I might educate him in the realities of life. Are you not thankful to your teacher, Bernardo, for showing you humility to counter that stubborn pride of yours? You were so smug, and good, and so sure of yourself. You thought that you could bend everyone to your will. You had a gift for that—didn't you? It was so easy to see. I knew that I could not change your powers of persuasion, so my task was to alter your point of view—to knock you off your noble steed, and let you wallow in the gutter a bit. I see that I have exceeded my own expectations.

Wicked creature—be gone! You terrorized me as a young child, but no more. You abused me bodily and mentally, but in the end, I survived and made myself a better man than you could ever hope to be. All those years that I held tightly to the fear that you would reappear on my doorstep, or release your poisonous vipers into my window, just as you had done to poor Fra Filippo, that fear only made me strong, and more resourceful, and more committed to never putting myself in such an abusive situation again.

Ah, so mighty and powerful you have become. And yet, why are we here? Are you finally realizing that you are no better than this poor Cellarer? Are you afraid of spending eternity with the likes of me? Oh, for the sins you have committed, you will be a tasty morsel for the master. He has been battling for your black soul for such a long time. He will take great delight in claiming his new prize.

I still have time to repent for my sins, and I will use every second of my life begging God to forgive my sins. It is true that you helped me to see good and evil, and to learn humility and obedience, but it was I who learned to use those lessons for good—and not for evil as you claim.

Good for whom? Good for mankind? I think not. Good for yourself, more likely. Every time you had the opportunity to do good for the world—ah, such a worthy cause—you turned a profit for yourself. You were most industrious in collecting all the deadly sins and stuffing them into your putrid soul. I was most proud of my accomplishment with my young, Giovanni—as much as I was proud of, my dear little Ugolino. Now that was a tasty little piece of meat! Oh, what fun we have had with his life. How tightly the two of your lives have been interwoven. You, a rich and powerful man, and Ugolino now wearing the papal tiara. How rich it all is. Two such precious trophies will make a fine addition to my master's collection.

I curse thee to Hell, you bastard son of a witch. Be gone!

My time with you is not done, dog. Do you recognize this place?

Yes, I do. It is the Abbot of Montalcino's palace. His private apartments.

And do you see the young boy asleep before the fire—such a dog!

I do, and I know what transpired on that night, and many nights to follow. You were not the only one to abuse me. And as I have told you, I survived.

Ah! Not the first. And survive you did. But you learned a good lesson from me, didn't you? You were old enough, and wise enough to let the abuse continue and to profit by it. You were able to take advantage of a man's weakness and use it for your own benefit. You learned the art of manipulation quite well. And you have used it throughout your life. You and I are not so different, dog. I am proud of what I taught you.

You are a pig and devil-spawn. My only hope is that we never meet each other again, for if perchance I am consigned to the pit of Hell, I vow to spend each torturous hour returning the hurt that you heaped upon me tenfold. Tell me, for my own satisfaction, how you met your end.

Ah, dog. Now that is a story! All those years wasted looking over your shoulder, afraid of the nasty cellarer, were for naught. I know that it was you who sold me out to the Abbot. It was that very morning when Ugolino's uncle, Lotario, forced me from my slumber and in the silence of the dawn he dragged me far from the abbey where I was reunited with my partner in murder, whom you have rightly assumed to be my mother. The Abbot's men were there, and they had brought with them the young boy, Ugolino. That ungrateful brat, after learning of my disappearance, had ransacked my cellar and pinned my poor Angel to the old oaken barrel. You remember the oaken barrel, dog?

They began to beat us savagely, and most unfortunate for the two of us, it did not take long for the witch to confess to the murder and implicate me. The blabbering wench still carried the Prior's prayer beads around her neck. She screamed like a demon as her familiar cat was snatched from her arms by one of the Abbot's men. I refused to utter a sound, whilst I was beaten with thorn-encrusted clubs, which infuriated them even more. The two of us were bound together and marched for two hours to a farm that was owned by the Abbot. The farmers had been sent away by the time we arrived. In the name of the Abbot and the Church, the witch was condemned to the fire. It was not a pretty sight to see her roasted upon a spit. She wildly cursed each of her tormentors and each of the cowards quaked in fear. Her agonizing screams were deafening, and the smell of her roasting flesh was but a reminder of what was awaiting us both. As her screams were silenced by the flames, that brat Ugolino, with fire in his eyes and ice in his veins, took up her familiar cat, wrung its neck, and tossed its lifeless body into the fire.

As for me, the wheel of justice is hard and cruel when determined by man. Lotario had ordered his men to seize me and to tie my hands and my legs to the posts of a hog pen. He then pronounced sentence upon me, savoring each word. My punishment was devised to fit my crime. I was to be slowly gutted like a fish and fed alive to the hogs. For my crimes against humanity, my soulless body would be dragged through the shit and piss of the hungry pigs, forever to dwell at the very bottom of Hell. Are you satisfied, dog?

I will not be satisfied until you tell me the details of your death.

Suffered I did—in SILENCE! Oh, such cruelty had caused most of the men to vomit, and though it was agonizing to my earthly body, it did gain me much status within the circles of Hell. Because of my extreme cruelty toward the boy, my hands were slowly severed at the wrists and given to the brat to throw into the hog's pen. The fresh meat had caused a frenzy in the pigs and an unnatural satisfaction in the boy. I was made to watch in agony as the pigs devoured both of my hands. For the injuries I had inflicted on the boy with every kick of my booted foot, my feet were cleaved at the ankles and handed to the brat. And again, with such hatred and delight, he tossed my feet to the pigs. My bloody body was tied to the railings, and Lotario handed the boy his dagger. He nodded to the boy, and slowly Ugolino slit open my stomach and let my entrails spill forth. Gleefully, he picked up my guts and tossed them to the hogs. Before I lost consciousness, my body was hoisted over the fence and tossed like garbage into the midst of the hogs. My last earthly vision was the cold stare of Ugolino diConti. It will not be long until we meet again. I look forward to my revenge upon the two of you.

I curse you, hellish fiend. Go back to your cesspool and rot.
Father, why hast thou not spoken or helped me to vanquish that demon?

It was your battle to fight, my son. It was your chapter to close.

Should I feel pity for such a monster?

The riddle you pose is yours alone to answer.

Father, one thing has troubled me, and I must ask. Why is it that you speak so clearly to me, when in the past visions you speak in so many riddles? If only then you were so clear, I may have made better choices.

The past is the past. It cannot be changed, only rewritten to suit the narrator. The future is fluid and can be changed, though you think it not, depending upon the choices made and the actions taken. The spirits speak not in riddles, but rather in uncertainties. They only speak of what may come to pass. Only God knows with certainty the future of all things. His servants can only guess his intent. Time is meaningless in the world beyond mortality, and the spirits are forced to witness a million variations of future events. A pec-ii can only tap into but a few brief glimpses of what may be—or what may not be.

Tell me, Father, what of me? What is my fate?

The seer's son continues to be blind, but before his journey is completed, he may yet be given the opportunity to truly see and redeem himself. Harken back to your education by my people. Perhaps there you will find some of the answers you seek.

I see me at the feet of fair Tarquinia, listening to the histories of the Taurisi. As I was with you, Father, I absorbed all that was taught to me by such a wise and loving woman. She was so pleased to train me in the Way, and yet she was also so melancholy when she spoke of her people.

Tarquinia was a powerful seer, and she had foreseen her people's doom. She was conflicted, for she had seen your culpability in their doom, and yet she held great hope that the future could be altered. She had held great hope in the power of the young pec-ii she was training, and felt that with such training, you would be able to see into your heart and your soul, and be guided on the right path to the salvation of her world.

I learned so much from her, and I loved her so. I have kept all the knowledge and the histories in the many books and journals I have written over the years. I have tried to keep the memories alive. But the task was too great. The lure of the outside world was too much for the Chosen Ones.

In the end, my son, you failed her. You failed Tarquin, my cousin, and you failed the Taurisi, our own people. You were given the precious gift of the Chosen Ones, and you corrupted them to your own purposes. Your pride has blinded you to your promise and your responsibility. This you must surely see.

I see that I have failed in my mission. Yet I feel that the mission was too great for any man to accomplish. I did my best. I did more than any man could possibly do. The Taurisi have been saved from extinction and live safely in the outside world. They are free to observe their customs in any way they see fit.

Your duty was to see that the culture of the Taurisi survived. In that, you have failed, my son. You were handed all that was precious to our people, and you have squandered it away. The Taurisi—the once-great Etruscans—are no more. Though the blood still flows, the spirit has died. All the books and journals and accounts will not bring back what has been lost. Our culture is dead. Together we must share in the responsibility of that and grieve.

I beg forgiveness, Father, from you and from all our people who were slaughtered at the hand of that madman, Barbarossa, for all the sins I have committed, the oaths that I have broken, and the actions that I failed to take. I accept my fault and I beg forgiveness.

I pray for your soul, my son, and pray you see the light and redeem yourself. The morning light approaches, and soon I must be gone. But first, there is one more memory that we must relive. Follow me, Giovanni, into the mist. Can you see the light of the bonfire?

I see it, Father, and I hear the voices of a thousand revelers. We are in the Campo—the old Campo. I remember. It is All Hallows Eve. The first time we went to the fair. Ah, the events of those days and nights are etched upon my brain. How clearly I see every detail of that first night in Siena. I was dazzled by everything I saw in Siena. It was then that I fell in love with Siena.

You were dazzled by the wealth and power that surrounded you in that city of sin. You fell in love with the money.

That is true, Father. I will not deny it. And so what of it? There is no sin in honest commerce. It was my fate to be brought to such a place—brought there by you, Father. Let us remember that, together. I was attracted to all I saw there—like a moth to a flame.

And so, the moth is consumed if it flies too close, or tarries too long. You were easily seduced, and my dear friend, Giancarlo, was all too ready to take you under his wing. You learned too late that all things easily given have a cost. Too easily did you sell your soul when you tried to barter with a master. Giancarlo always had his own plan, and he felt no shame in using anyone for his own benefit. With him, you learned much.

He was a great man, and a generous teacher. He took me in and treated me as a son. Forgive me, Father. I mean no disrespect, nor do I wish to hurt you with my words, but not for Giancarlo, I would not be the man I am today.

So truer words were never spoken, Giovanni. Had it been another man to which you hitched your wagon, perhaps we would not be here in your final hours. You honored and emulated the dark horse, and though you may have won the race, you are left with nothing of value with which to claim the ultimate prize. All that you have accumulated will have been for naught. The pity is that all the wealth that Giancarlo had accumulated on earth could not buy him a seat in Heaven. He is one of many wealthy merchants clawing in the nether regions, working for a merciless master.

Cruel are your words, Father. They sting me to the core. See there. See how generous Giancarlo was to us–to you. He helped you with your problems and he took good care of your family. My eyes have always been open to Giancarlo's nature, and I had learned to accept him, and his generosity. I was always given a choice, and with each offer, it was my choice to accept or reject. I was willing to accept his terms, so long as they were fair and beneficial to me. What harm is there in accepting what is given freely?

Freely? How can you say that anything Giancarlo gave was given freely? You have deceived yourself, and because of your stubborn pride, you have condemned yourself to follow your mentor into the fiery pit. Open your eyes, my son. I implore you, before it is too late. Look again more closely at how we were manipulated and used by Giancarlo, who like a spider had wrapped his prey in silken bonds, and had sucked out every ounce of life, leaving only an empty husk. Listen to your heart, Giovanni. Seek the truth.

Farewell, and may God have mercy upon your soul.

Father forgive me. Father come back. Father, do not forsake me...

Light dawns, and my master sleeps—such pitiful sleep. I too shall rest for my fingers ache and my eyes are weary. My heart is heavy, and I grieve with my friend. Sleep, if but for a short while, shall bring us strength so that Giovanni may continue his task. God is great.

We have refreshed ourselves with sleep and nourishment. The sun has risen over the hilltops to the east. Giovanni has eaten little, much against my insistence, and I fear that this race against time is costing him his mind, his spirit, and his life. He is aging before my eyes, and yet, when he speaks, he is filled with the passion of youth and his recollection is crystal clear. I have promised him that I would bring to his attention any inconsistencies with the truth in instances of which I have direct knowledge. I shall make such notes at the end of Giovanni's narratives.

We have readied ourselves, and Giovanni begins.

Chapter Two
Lust

V

Following My Own Path

I remained on the farm throughout that winter. There was much to do before the spring planting, and Tarquin had called his laborers back to Curtun. Father's good reputation had spread throughout the tiny villages in the valley, and many sought work and refuge from him. His kindness and generosity had worked to his advantage as many returned and worked harder and for a lower percentage than they had demanded only a year before.

My brothers had grown and had willingly taken up the yoke, helping to oversee the outlying farms and herds. The winter crops were in the field and the healthiest livestock were retained for breeding in the spring. There was plenty of feed reserved for the animals, enough to last an extended winter. The nobles had returned to their mountain strongholds and had settled in for the winter. There was a general peace throughout the valley that year, a peace that gave the peasantry a sense of hope. But for me, there was no peace.

I quickly grew to reject the values my father had seen in the land and the noble life of a farmer. My envy of the wealth and power that Giancarlo had accumulated had grown stronger. I had spent my days resenting my father and the life he had chosen for me. My nights were spent battling the demons in my head who had tempted me with visions of wealth and power that were mine to take. And throughout it all, the parting words of Tarquinia had continue to haunt me. I remained on the farm for several long winter months, always at odds with my family, especially with my father. Though I outwardly showed no lack of respect, the closeness we had when I was younger had disappeared. As hard as he had tried to convince me to follow him, I had made up my mind to follow another path to a greater destiny.

Father, I knew, was crushed, not so much with my decision to leave, but more because he had lost me to the darker, less noble part of humanity. I think that he hoped I would concentrate my interests on trade, for at least he had no ill feelings toward an honest merchant, rare as they were. His fear, of course, was that I would be corrupted by my uncle in the dark arts of the heathen and the Jew, the changing of money and the usurious sins of the banker. Though the pope and the bishops could turn a blind eye to such cardinal sins so long as their pockets were being lined with gold, the Gates of Heaven would forever be shut tight to those who cloaked themselves in such evil and villainous ways. Our parting was not acrimonious. There were no arguments, no violence, no tears. I simply left.

My mother, I would never see in this world again, for I had truly broken her heart, and she would be gone within two years of my departure. My father, I would see again on two separate occasions, but the bond that had been forged early in my life had been shattered by my decision and would never to be fully mended. Dearest Mother forgive me for plunging the dagger so deeply. It was never my intent to cause harm, but only to live my own life as I saw fit. Father, you who I have wronged so greatly and caused to suffer for so long and so needlessly, I beg thee to forgive this old fool. You were right in all that you taught me, and I was too proud and foolish not to heed your advice. I shall die a wretch, alone in my own tower with a golden purse and a blackened soul.

I left the farm and my family behind and rode back to Siena, happy with my decision to break free from my prison and accepting Giancarlo's offer to apprentice me. I was excited at the prospect of making my fortune on my own terms, of choosing my own destiny. I would learn all that there was to learn about commerce and trade, of money handling and the accumulation of power and wealth. I would know all that Uncle Giancarlo knew, and I would use him and his connections to learn even more. I had set my goal, on that solitary ride to Siena, to surpass my uncle in wealth and stature, and to become as powerful as the greatest lords in their mountain castles, a captain of industry and a prince of power. I would do whatever it took to attain my goal, for I knew that my soul was already lost, that my innocence had been stolen from me long ago. There was nothing to stand in my way or to cause me to waiver from my path.

Giancarlo was pleased with my decision as well. Though I was old for an apprenticeship, I had been educated properly in the arts and philosophies that would prove so useful to his business. I was fluent in Latin and could read and write in both Latin and Greek, talents that have proven most useful throughout my life, especially when dealing with the Curia, or with the courts in Rome and Constantinople. During my stay at Montalcino, I had picked up some of the languages of the traveling pilgrims, the languages and customs of the Normans, the Spaniards, the Germans, the Brits and Celts, and I had learned to use the numerical symbols used by the Arabs in their mathematical calculations.

Giancarlo was a kind man and a loving uncle. He was also a brutal and shrewd businessman, always surveying the horizon for opportunity, and always making it his goal to gain the upper hand with every transaction he made. He had a good reputation, not because of his morals or his honesty, but by projecting a hint of fairness in his trading, and foremost, by projecting an aurora of power and authority. Power, he would tell me, is never given, but assumed. A man is only as powerful as others perceive him to be. With power comes wealth. I knew never to ask him about happiness, for happiness never factors into the equation. He took me into his house, and because he had no true issue of himself, he treated me as a son. He showed me kindness and reprimanded me when it was needed, and never hesitated to share with me his wisdom and knowledge of business, and survival in the world of finance and trade. Though he was not well versed in the arts, he was a master of the trades, and all that I know about commerce, I owe to his patient teachings.

I became an appendage to him, present during all his dealings, observing his mannerisms, his strategies, and even the subtleties of his swindling. It was all part of the game; he would tell me. It was what he called his finesse. I would marvel at how well he would handle some of the toughest traders, allowing them to feel as though they had bested him in the deal, while he, himself, pocketed the better part of the prize. At times he would sacrifice the profits on a deal or two in order to lure the overconfident merchant into a greater take. He would call them pigeons, and he would show me how they would have to be fed a few times so they would be fat enough to bake in a pie. He would take delight in finally consuming those pies, and as time went on I too shared in his delight.

During my first year in Siena I spent most of my time in the company of Uncle Giancarlo. Business hours were long, and we were often on the road, collecting debts or rents from debtors throughout the Sienese territories. Giancarlo had financed many farmers and vintners in the area south of Siena and held mortgages upon the farms and vineyards. Payments were collected whether the farms produced or not. On many occasions the farmer would end up losing his farm, only to become a tenant to Giancarlo. It was not much different from my father's estates in Cortona, except Giancarlo's tenants were expected to pay regardless of circumstances. No quarter was given. If a tenant was delinquent, he and his family would be turned out without a thought for their safety or welfare. Father would accept excuse, and many times would make concessions. Such empathy would cost him a fortune, prohibiting him from realizing his truest potential. Giancarlo was a banker, and bankers did not have the luxury to forgive debt. A debt incurred must at all costs be repaid. I should have realized that when I first set out upon that road. I had indebted myself to Giancarlo, and at some point, my debt would have to be repaid.

Life at the palazzo was very satisfying. Donna Donata had accepted me as one of her own and sought to please me with many small and intimate gestures. She would have the cook prepare dishes to my liking, wash and mend my clothes, and sit with me in the late evening talking about a variety of subjects. Though not formally educated, Donna Donata was an intelligent woman with a wealth of knowledge, political, social, and philosophical. She was a gifted embroiderer and would sit by the fire in the evening while we talked, producing the most exquisite works of art. On many evenings, while we sat and conversed, Anna would play upon her lute and sing of distant lands or of love verses written by the fair Heloise. Such evenings of domestic bliss were well orchestrated by Donata and Giancarlo with the hope that love would grow between Anna and me. Though I cared for her, as one would care for a sister or perhaps a cousin, true love would never grow between us. True love would never be part of the deal, for I was not capable of true love, and she, I truly believe, was afraid of it. We had no ambitions to wed. Giancarlo had other ideas.

During my first few years in Siena, news had reached us that Frederick, Duke of Swabia, was on the march to Rome. The Germans had called him Kaiser Rotbart, but we Italians referred to him as Barbarossa. He had been proclaimed "King of the Romans" and had come into Italy at the behest of Adrian, the English Pope, to provide aid against the rebellious Commune of Rome. The brash young Duke and the Pope had made an agreement that was beneficial to both parties. The Pope had promised to crown Frederick as Holy Roman Emperor in exchange for protection for the Pope and the curia in the cesspool that had become Rome.

Barbarossa had left Germany, coming through the mountains at the first thawing of spring, and had traveled through the Italian countryside, surveying all that would rightly be his, as he made his way toward Rome. He first stopped at Milan, but its citizens refused to open their gates to him, not recognizing him as their sovereign lord. After a lengthy siege, they finally submitted to him. Barbarossa would never forget the insult he was given by the proud Milanese. With his patience worn thin, he approached the rebellious Tortona and again was forced to engage in a long siege there. After gaining control of that city, he razed it to the ground, murdering or disbursing all its inhabitants. After that, Pavia welcomed the King of the Romans with open arms and conferred upon him the Iron Crown and the title King of Italy.

Slowly he moved south, descending upon each of the major cities along the Francigena. Many quaked in fear while many others vied for the honor to host His Magnificence. Such honor came at a heavy price, for he traveled with a large party of court appointees, servants and supporters, and a personal guard of five hundred fully armed knights upon mighty steeds and an equal number of squires marching on foot or driving a train of supply wagons that seemed to stretch as far as the eye could see. This royal entourage preceded his marching army of more than ten thousand that traveled at a slower pace, yet at a short enough distance to be able to bridge any gap in short order.

Such a spectacle was incredible to behold. Barbarossa's message was more than clear to all: "I am your Lord above all. Do not cross me." His displeasure was terminal.

He made his way to Florence and set up camp for his large army along the Arno. We had received word that he would next arrive in Siena. The Sienese Council had spent much time in planning for his arrival. As he approached the gates of our fair city, all of Siena's wealthiest families were present to receive him. Such a fine show of wealth and respect was not wasted upon His Majesty. His party descended upon the walled city like a flock of ravens, her citizens opening her gates and hailing the young king as protector and sovereign lord. Such a warm reception only paid short-term dividends, for as time passed, the love exchanged between king and subjects would prove false on many occasions because of the fickleness of both parties

To my young eyes, the approaching king was like a god, a young Alexander leading his army to conquer the world. He seemed magnificent to me; incredibly handsome and he carried such an air that men would find no objection to following his every command. At the time of his first visit to Italy, he was at the prime of his manhood, an obvious fact that was not overlooked by both men and women alike. He was intelligent and fully confident in himself, quite ready to take the Imperial crown and rule the entire world as Augustus once did a thousand years ago. His hair was golden, curling above the forehead and cascading down to his shoulders, which were broad, for he was very strongly built. His eyes were sharp and piercing, his nose of pleasing proportion to his face, and his beard was red. He sat upon a mighty steed, cloaked in the finest red wool, and his exquisitely crafted armor gleamed brilliantly in the light of the sun.

All the citizens had turned out to greet their king, the wealthiest all vying for position and a chance to gain his ear and his affection. Giancarlo was no exception. He knew the importance of a friendship, or even a remembered acquaintance of this powerful man. He would say to me, "The importance of a man is amplified by the number and status of the friends he keeps." All were after the same prize—the Salimbeni, the Tolomei, the Buonsignori, the Malavolti, the Cacciaconti, and the Soarzi. I knew it in my heart, even as a naïve and unaccomplished pup, that my destiny would lead me to a greater status than any of those who crowded the Porta Camollia. How many showed actual love and respect for this man? How many feigned loyalty and allegiance? How many would throw open the gates of our beloved city and swing open the doors to their great palazzi, fighting for the honor to host His Most Magnificent? And how many would swing those gates shut and bar them so tightly against their Emperor, to sacrifice the Virgin's blessed city, when the tide of war and politics would change course, as it did so often in those times?

Ah, but on that glorious day, the heart of Siena was opened wide as the gate by which Barbarossa entered the city. Hospitality was extended to the entire royal entourage, with the richest and most influential families hosting His Royal Person, servants and guards. The King's hierarchy, with their servants and guards would be distributed according to rank and status within the rolls of the city. The rest of the entourage and the advancing army would make camp in the campos and fields just outside the city walls. With so many men, horses, and wagons, the city was literally surrounded as if under siege. The effect was not lost on our citizenry.

The Tolomei were by far the richest and most powerful family in Siena and possessed the finest palazzo in all of Siena. It was only fitting that the King would grace the Tolomei with his presence. The Salimbeni and the Buonsignori vied for the privilege of providing hospitality to the rest of the higher court. Their newer palazzi were also grand in scale, built in the new style that seemed to be more pleasing to His Highness and his court, and were built with many private rooms, much better suited to house a greater crowd.

Giancarlo was most gracious to offer hospitality to the Captain of the Royal Guard and a dozen of his officers. Included in this august group was the king's own son, Henry, who, as far as I could tell was not much older than I. He had not yet accumulated the titles that would be bestowed upon him in the future years but was traveling with his father and training to be a future king and emperor. He was tall and fair haired with a very pleasing countenance like his father, yet he portrayed a more genial temperament. His softer manner of speech and his more affable personality indicated that he would need much training in the hardships of life if he were to rule an empire. Being of a similar age and temperament, we formed an instant connection, and he was most cordial and appreciative of my services.

I had little time to spend with Henry but what few hours we did share were most agreeable to both of us. Because of the proximity of Giancarlo's palazzo to the staging fields within the city, he had offered hospitality to the king's quartermaster so that he might bring up his supply wagons into the safety of the city walls. Most importantly, though, Giancarlo had insisted that the chief financier and his secretary reside with us for the duration of the King's visit. Such hospitality was costly, but the future benefits were immeasurable.

Upon the second evening of the King's visit, a great feast to honor Barbarossa was organized by Jacobini, patriarch of the Tolomei. All the leading citizens of Siena were invited to attend, as were the most senior of the King's court. No expense was spared for the feast, the cost of which was incurred by Tolomei himself. In addition to this great feast, several minor, but no less grand, feasts were set up at various piazze of the city, to honor those imperial guests who were of enough rank to warrant such honor. Giancarlo was invited to attend the grand banquet of the Tolomei while I, through connections of my uncle, was permitted to accompany the intelligence officers who were staying with us, to the feast held in the shadow of San Giuseppe. Giancarlo was the sponsor for that special event, and what a magnificent feast it was. Food and drink for several hundred—enough to satisfy the hunger and thirst of the entire army. The piazza was filled with light, music, laughter, and song all night long.

As the sun rose, I helped our guests back to Giancarlo's palazzo, where they slept the better part of the day away. Giancarlo had already been home and had been waiting for our return so that he could question me about the night's events. He was pleased I had kept a clear head, and the keen eyes of the hawk, and was able to recount to him every detail worthy of note. It was another lesson in business he would teach me, to use such events to gain the friendship of people who could someday prove beneficial to our enterprise, and also to secure information about such people that could be used to benefit our position. He was quite pleased with the amount of information I had collected and was able to transmit to him that morning. My only disappointment was not being allowed to spend the evening with the king's son, for Henry was to share the banquet table with his father in the palazzo of the Tolomei.

Barbarossa and his company had stayed in Siena for a week, gaining the admiration and loyalty of many of the wealthy merchants and local nobility who saw the friendship of the future Emperor as a path to greater power and wealth and as a counter protection to the Vatican and its curia, whose greed and corruption seemed to grow with each succeeding pontiff. For the most part, the Emperor would enjoy the fealty of the citizens of Siena for many years, our close bonds of mutual respect and admiration having been built during that first official visit. Such bonds were not lost upon Giancarlo, or upon me in later years, for we were to reap many benefits throughout our lives because of the connections we were able to forge with His Highness and his son during their stay in Siena.

During that week, Giancarlo had arranged for me to entertain young Henry and the king's guard. Henry had felt more comfortable with the officers than being at his father's side all the time, for in truth, he only wished to be an ordinary young man. He did not look kindly at the prospects of someday becoming king, for in his mind, that was too much work and it very much displeased him.

I had been given specific instructions to provide whatever our guests required. Giancarlo was most interested in knowing all their wants and desires, knowing all their weaknesses, and capitalizing on whatever bits of information could be obtained during this brief but opportune visit. He had kept a journal of all those with whom he had ever transacted business, even making notes on those he had not. Over the years, I would aid him in obtaining such vital information, and in the end would ultimately inherit his most prized journal. In the interest of profit, he would tell me over and over that everything was fair game. "It was not how one plays the game," he would tell me, "but how one wins the game, that makes the difference between success and failure." I was determined to win the game, at whatever cost, and was eager to learn all I could from this wise and generous man.

The Captain of the Royal Guard had spent most of his time with Barbarossa, but several of his junior officers had found time during the evenings to enjoy the local establishments, many located within the city walls and a few illicit gatherings in the shadows beyond the walls. Young Henry had been advised to stay clear of the pastime pleasures of the officers and had spent most of his time with me touring our great city. He had been most interested in the defenses of the city and had commented on the lack of pure water sources within the city walls. His observations had resonated with me for many years and had become the impetus in my quest to find the great Diana. We enjoyed our time together and spoke on many subjects political, philosophical, and ecclesiastical. In that brief time, we had developed a lasting friendship for each other.

Entertaining the other officers was more difficult for me, for being so young and ignorant, I had not learned much of the underground offerings of my adopted city. I therefore had to rely upon the expertise of the household servants and certain street vendors, in order to provide our guests with what they had desired. The services I was to provide varied from praying in solitude, which was the habit of an amiable young intelligence officer named Sigmund whom I had come to know well, to eating and drinking, gambling till dawn, and spending the evening with prostitutes, both women and boys. In each case, apart from praying, there were laws against such behavior, which, if the offender was caught, would produce heavy fines, penalties, or even imprisonment.

It was my task to secure whatever the need and keep our guests out of trouble with the law. In several cases, it had taken the political clout of Giancarlo and the opening of his purse to secure a speedy and silent solution to the problems. Giancarlo was all too happy to open his purse, provided he obtained a detailed account of the transgression. The few days of that imperial visit had provided me with a multitude of life lessons and experiences to which a man of my tender years should never have been exposed. Yet each lesson served me well over the years as I built my own empire.

The greatest lesson was taught to me by the young Sigmund, whose allegiance to his king, and his devotion to his God, had created such a battle within his soul. I remember the hours we spent together in the Church of San Giuseppe as he prayed to God for forgiveness for the many damning deeds that he had done in the service of his overlord. He had prayed in solitude, never acknowledging my presence as I kept myself far enough to ensure his privacy but close enough to hear and record his confessions and his most personal thoughts. He was a spy and an assassin for the king, unquestioningly loyal to his lord, and driven with the strongest desire to please his master. He was also driven with such guilt and remorse for every evil deed he had committed in the service of his king. I could not understand why he had such remorse for doing so well that which he was meant to do. I felt a deep sorrow for him, and I am surprised I remember him after all these years, but then again, how could I possibly forget him? Our paths would cross again at a future time. I will say no more of that here, but only beg his forgiveness for things that were done in the interests of the masters whom we both served.

During the week that Barbarossa had spent in Siena, Giancarlo was able to secured several lucrative contracts and I was able to accumulate enough information on our guests to fill a small journal. The King had planned to leave Siena and next stop at Montalcino, and learning of my personal acquaintance with the abbot, Henry had requested that I accompany him on the journey and provide him with a tour of that town. Little did I know that his motives were to view each city on their way south to Rome to learn of the strengths and weaknesses of their defenses. Giancarlo gave permission to travel to the abbey but insisted that he accompany us. He knew of my acquaintance with the Abbot and assumed he could use me to enhance his image before Barbarossa and the Abbot. He did not know of the special relationship that I had endured during my service to the Abbot, for I had never betrayed that trust. He was only interested in advancing his standing. It was all just a matter of business.

Seeing the ramparts of the castle of the Abbot at Montalcino caused my heart to quicken. I had not anticipated the reaction I would encounter upon my return to the Abbot. Though I had had many good experiences in the service of this holy man, the demons that I had kept locked away in the dungeon of my soul had multiplied in their captivity and had sprung forth to plague me like a swarm of gnats. The Abbot rode forth from the castle with his personal guard to meet the king and his royal guard as they approached the city walls. How serene and spiritual the Abbot looked in his gleaming white tunic, his full-length white cloak trimmed in ermine and embroidered with gold thread, sitting upon his white steed. I remember to this day his long, golden hair lit ablaze in the afternoon sun, his gold and bejeweled crucifix catching the rays of the sun and throwing them into the eyes of the onlookers who lined the road leading up to the gate. My eyes had, at first, tricked me into thinking him to be crowned with a saintly halo, but as time coaxes logic in the brain and aids the eye to see beyond the supernatural, I saw him to be the man I had known, the man whom I had served for several years, the kind and generous man—the man so tormented by his own demons.

As I gazed at that kind and gentle man, I saw beyond his deep blue eyes, into the heart of the cruel and abusive man who, when stripped of his moral armor by drunkenness or lust, would call me to his chamber to satisfy his carnal desire. Yes, he would always be remorseful and repentant after he had satisfied his demon. Yes, he would flog himself, and at times he would have me use the lash upon his scarred back to inflict the pain to chase the demon away. And yes, we would always kneel and pray for God's forgiveness and strength after each episode. Yet we both had come to realize that instead of driving the demon away, he was only driving it deeper into his soul and feeding it with his pain and self-loathing.

I looked at that angelic vision in white, and I knew what ugliness had resided within the body of that holy man. His character and holiness were unquestionable throughout the abbey and throughout the land. Many a diplomat or titled traveler was compelled to stop at the abbey to seek his good counsel and blessing as they traveled the Via Francigena between Rome and their destinations to the north. Indeed, it was no mere matter of geographic convenience that Barbarossa had made plans to accept the Abbot's hospitality for several days. Though he was eager to reach Rome and receive his imperial crown from Adrian, he needed friends and allies throughout the length of Italy, and the Abbot was exceedingly rich in both. Not only had the Abbot the respect and friendship of His Holiness the Pope and many in the Curia, he had been a guiding influence for peace in most of central Italy, brokering treaties between warring states and acting as a fair and competent arbiter between the local nobility and the rising bourgeois of the independent city states. If Barbarossa was ever to rule the vast lands of Italy from his gilded throne in Germany, he would have to acquire the loyalty and support of powerful men like the Abbot.

The official greeting was dressed in ceremony as befitting two great leaders. Barbarossa, dressed in the fashion of the ancient German kings, mortier trimmed in fur and peacock feathers, a short tunic of embroidered blue silk and his jewel-encrusted surcoat lined in silver fox, dismounted his mighty steed and approached the Abbot, who had already dismounted and knelt before the approaching King. The Abbot bowed before the King and kissed his ring. Barbarossa then knelt before the Abbot while the Abbot placed his hands upon the King's head and called upon God to bless the life and reign of the future Holy Roman Emperor. Both rose and embraced, kissing each other on the cheek in a sign of fidelity and respect. The crowd cheered wildly. Both the Abbot and Barbarossa had gotten what they wanted.

It was good to see old friends again, and we spent the better part of the afternoon in conversation and introducing Giancarlo to the most important people on the Abbot's staff. As was his habit, Giancarlo used every opportunity to befriend those who would be of benefit to him, either during this brief stay or in the future. "Time was never wasted in cultivating relationships," he would always say. But of course, Giancarlo had not come to Montalcino to make acquaintances with the Abbot's staff. He was determined to talk directly with the Abbot and most importantly to Barbarossa himself. I then realized that Giancarlo had planned all along to use my connection with the Abbot to his gain. As much as I had known what my meeting with the Abbot could possibly lead to, I felt compelled to do whatever was necessary to advance my uncle's interests (as well as my own).

Through the Abbot's valet I had secured a private audience with the Abbot in his personal chambers. Our meeting was formal but cordial. I knelt before him as he placed his hands upon my head and blessed me. Many times, in the past, this man would perform the very same ritual while absolving me of our sins. How often had those sacred yet profane words been uttered to Thee, God? Did you not hear my pleas? Oh! How I remember his words; the smell of his breath, the feel of his trembling hands upon my head, clasping my face as he raised me to my feet and whispered in my ear how much he had missed his most favored servant. We spoke of small matters.

He was not vengeful, nor evil as I had anticipated, but seemed genuinely pleased to see me and to have me, once again, subjugated before him. He spoke softly, and his words were kind and tender. I told him of my decision to leave home, my apprenticeship with Giancarlo, the skills I had been taught, the places I had seen, and the people I had met. I swore an oath to the Abbot that I had never betrayed his confidence to Giancarlo, nor anyone else alive or dead. Of course, he was amused with my naiveté, and yet was extremely curious about my relationship with my uncle. Having been allowed a moment to extol the virtues of dear Giancarlo, His Excellency had agreed to meet with him the following morning. This brief audience had not been secured without paying a heavy price from Giancarlo's purse and my own body and soul.

I spent the remainder of the evening and the following morning showing young Henry around the castle and its environs. As was his custom, Henry focused most of his attention on the fortifications of the castle and the surrounding walls. The Abbot had summoned Giancarlo and had requested he bring me along to the meeting. His Excellency had already been fully informed of Giancarlo's complete history along with a detailed summary of his holdings, his extended businesses, his trading partners, his lineage, and his affiliates. Always in need of funding sources, he had concluded that a man such as Giancarlo could be very useful at some future date. He was intrigued by the Sienese merchant who had lured his former servant to the dark arts of commerce, and yet held no grudge against this man for he knew that in the bargain that I had struck with Giancarlo, I had little soul left to pledge. His Holiness had taken whatever I had left to give.

We met in the Abbot's library, where we took full advantage of the hour allotted to us. Gauging the full extent of the closeness between the Abbott and myself, Giancarlo included me in much of the conversation even though I was still just his apprentice. The Abbot was impressed with my acquired business knowledge and skills, and Giancarlo took advantage to highlight the training he had afforded me over the past years. Before the hour was finished, Giancarlo had secured several contracts with the Abbey of Sant' Antimo, and with the Abbot, himself. The two men would profit from each other for several years, but Giancarlo would never know the cost of that brief audience. I had advanced a small down payment for a greater future reward and had convinced myself that an hour's worth of pain was little compensation to the man who had given me so much. After all, I had reasoned, his success would eventually be my success.

Before we were to take our leave and return to Siena, the Abbot summoned me to the palace. As I was admitted to the Abbot's study, I was startled to see His Eminence standing in conversation with Lotario di Conti, the uncle of Ugolino, who had been my rescuer from the evil Bernardo. He had been sent by Pope Adrian to deliver dire news to the Emperor that conditions in Rome were deteriorating, and he had respectfully requested Barbarossa to make his way, with his army, post haste, to the Eternal City. I knelt before my liberator and kissed his ring. Both di Conti and the Abbot bid me to rise and stand before them. The Abbot told me that Lotario, though on an urgent mission, felt it strangely necessary to inquire as to my well-being. As a friend to the Pope, the Abbot felt it necessary to assure him that I was doing well, and in his own words, spoke to him, saying, "Keep an eye on this young man, for he possesses many talents and such a powerful drive that one day we may all be in debt to him."

Lotario looked me up and down and chuckled. Having asked about the health of the young Ugolino, I was assured that he was well and was devoting his life to the church and to God's holy work. Then being dismissed, I begged my leave of my former master and thanked him for all he had given to his humble servant, assuring him that I would always be in his debt. I knelt and kissed his ring and he lay his hand upon my head and blessed me with his holiness.

As I began to rise the door swung open and Fra Buonaguida entered and announced, "His Most Excellent Majesty, Frederick I, King of Germany, King of Italy!" Frederick stormed into the room surrounded by a dozen guards. Ignoring me altogether the Abbot and the papal emissary bowed and approached the Emperor. Words were exchanged, and a letter was produced by di Conti, which the Emperor perused, scoffed at, and threw to the ground, cursing in such a fashion that caused the Abbot to blush.

VI

Learning the Trade

For the next six months I learned all I could from Giancarlo and proved my worth to him. It was then that he decided to bring me with him on his "Grand Northern Cycle" as he called it, that would take us far to the north. I had never been beyond the borders of Tuscany, and I could not contain my excitement. We were to sail cross the sea from Pisa to Marseilles, and then use the rivers to get to the very heart of France. The trip would take us to Lyon, and to the fairs of Champagne and Royal Court in Paris. After that we would sail to the ports of LeHavre and Calais, where we would cross the channel to London.

Today, the great mapmakers of Venice and Genoa call this northern route the Hanseatic trade route. Of course, in those earlier times there was no league formed for the protection of trade, and major expeditions such as those undertaken by Giancarlo were still made with considerable risk, both on the water and on the land. A merchant risked all to the vengeful sea gods and the bloodthirsty pirates who plagued the coasts from Genoa to beyond the pillars of Hercules, even beyond to the open waters of the Great Western Sea. The mighty Mare Atlantico was filled with danger all along the coast of England and around the island of the Celts. Of course, there was no less risk in following the mighty Rhone northward from Marseilles to Lyons and transferring the shipment over land until the waters of the River Seine were reached. Bandits and thieves in great multitudes had also plied these waterways. Worse still were the wealthy noblemen and bishops who extracted heavy taxes and tolls along the way. They were no better than the thieves upon the sea. The greater part of a merchant's profit was spent on security and transport for any one trading mission, and yet in the end, I was to learn, sizable profits could still be made, and great fortunes could still be built, with cunning, courage, and determination.

The return journey would take us from London over to Bruges and then to open waters of the Atlantico. Notwithstanding devilish wind or mighty gale, a good-charted course would bring an experienced sailor close to the northern shores and would guide him to the safety of the Mare Mediterraneo. Our most-often traveled course would take us to Cadiz, and then we would hug the coast to Valencia, Marseilles, Genoa, and then back to Pisa. This western route home is now known as the Venetian trade route, for those master seamen now control most of the open seas of this world.

Preparations for this grand tour of the fairs in Lyons and Champagne had been underway for more than six months. The connections that Giancarlo had made during Barbarossa's visit had proven most rewarding in the organization of that trip. I soon learned that Giancarlo's talents as an importer/ exporter had far exceeded what I or any could have imagined.

Since my initial visit with him during the Siena fair, he had been busy managing his growing empire, bringing in goods from the Eastern Empire, Egypt and the Levant, and even from the distant lands of the Orient. He had dealt with his agents in the north throughout the German Kingdoms, and had agents associated with the courts of France, England, and Hispania. He had lent money to princes of the realm and princes of the Church and had collected debts from those who were in his debt. He had produced nothing himself save for wealth that he had accumulated by means of buying and selling other people's goods. His business revolved around the great fairs, for which he would exercise his superior trading skills, and the ever-present animosity between the popes and the emperors to the north and east. The constant political struggles had been both good for business and bad for business, depending upon which side one found oneself, and at what time. Over these many years since first I set my foot upon the path of commerce, I have found myself ever balancing upon the edge of a sharpened sword. A miscalculation or a slip could prove fatal. My entire fortune—nay, even my very life—has always been held precipitously in the hands of Fortune and the good graces of a pope or an emperor.

During the chaotic reign of Adrian IV, the English pope, we set out on my first grand northern cycle. Frederick had finally made his way to Rome intent on being crowned by the Pope, but the Pope had already run afoul of the Commune of Rome and had been driven from the city. Adrian was furious that Frederick had dallied on his way to Rome and had refused to meet him upon his arrival, refusing to recognize his legitimate election as Emperor of Germany and Italy. Frederick was furious at the insult and threatened to leave without helping the pope. Adrian then reneged on his promise to crown Barbarossa emperor in the Basilica of Rome. It was all such a mess. Yet in the end, as tempers cooled, negotiations were made, and the Pope finally placed the crown upon Frederick's head, where upon Frederick immediately gathered his army and marched north, leaving Adrian on his own to deal with the Roman mob. While this was all happening, Giancarlo and I had already begun the cycle and were making our way to Pisa.

The port at Pisa was bustling with activity when we arrived, as it does throughout the year, both day and night, never sleeping, never resting. Its citizens, even back in those early days, were increased and enriched with a growing merchant class. Its navy was a match even to that of Venice, though the latter has become so much more powerful over this past half century. Pisa was the pride of Tuscany in those days and had established trade routes and settlements in all the major ports throughout the known world. Her sailors were fearless upon the waters of the Great Mediterraneo and were no strangers to faraway lands in the east and to the west. Many a song has been sung about the valiant deeds of the Tuscans who set sail from Pisa and their adventures battling pirates in the Orient or the fantastic sea monsters of the Great Western Ocean. In my youth, I had heard many of the stories and songs from pilgrims passing through the Abby at Montalcino, yet I had never actually seen a galleon nor any large naval vessel for that matter. Such a sight, upon my first arrival, had left me speechless and gaping in wonder at the grandness and beauty of man's daring and ingenuity.

Oh Pisa! How grand and mighty were you in those early years. The pride of Tuscany! How impressive, your mighty walls, and how ordered your city streets. How many tower houses, one could only guess, tenfold more than the many churches with their own campanilli. A quarter of the world's wealth was in your purse, and yet through stubborn pride and jealousy of your neighbor's good fortune, never willing to share a piece of the pie, nor work together with your neighbor, but only to wage war after war, you have become a shadow of the greatness that was yours in those early days. How far you have fallen in such a short lifetime. How foolish it seems to me now that such power was squandered away so blindly. Your hubris has been your undoing!

In those early days, I was in awe of the richness of the port city. The port itself, like so many commercial ports, was a conglomerate of buildings, mainly low-rising, long warehouses, most with ample storage space on the ground level, and open space on the first level to accommodate business, while capable of housing a merchant and his crew. These storage facilities seemed to fan out from the docks in every direction and appeared countless in their number. Giancarlo had brought his train of wagons to several buildings that he had owned, and that were managed by his man, Genaro. Unlike most merchants, Giancarlo was not to stay in the warehouse accommodations, but rather had decided to lodge with one of his wealthier agents within the city walls further upriver. Our stay was to be brief, for the open sea awaited us and Giancarlo was always mindful of his schedule.

We were greeted at the central quay by Giancarlo's agent, Gaeta, who, through his own industriousness and cunning, had made a very comfortable living in the service of my uncle, and who had owned a sizable estate within the city walls. Gaeta was well-trusted by Giancarlo, as much as any could be, and yet my uncle would spend the better part of a day pouring over the ledgers of transactions and accounts, just to assure himself of Gaeta's trustworthiness. Giancarlo could be generous with loyal associates, but he was merciless should one show the slightest sign of disloyalty or deceit.

One only had to look around to see the wealth in the many towering palazzi that continued to be built upon any piece of vacant land. There were many richly embellished churches, including the beautiful church of San Sepolcro. It was for the greater glory of San Sepolcro and the Bishop of Pisa that I would, many years later, secure at a heavenly price an earthen jar purported to be one of the jars from Cana. At great expense did I obtain this most-prized relic from the captain of the Knights Hospitaliers who had battled Saladin at Krak and had secured temporary peace for Jerusalem. But that would come much later in time.

I was most fascinated to see the progress being made on the Duomo, which had already been under construction for a century. Its massive walls reached high into the heavens, promising to be the greatest edifice built by man. Proud Siena shall not be outdone by her rival, but alas, the completion of our Duomo will not be seen in my lifetime. For now, we look to Pisa with envy, and for inspiration. At that time, the Baptistry had just been laid out and that cursed bell tower was only beginning to be planned. Such a tragedy, and such waste, owing no doubt to stubbornness and greed, for the fools would not complete three levels of that tower before it began to sink into the soft earth. It has remained incomplete, slowly listing to one side, as if it were an ill-fitted barque upon an angry sea, a ghostly reminder of the perils of inattention to details. But, again, I get ahead of myself.

We were not there to view the sights, but rather to make money, and Giancarlo had filled his time transacting a great deal of business, arranging for shipments to and from the Pisan Quarter in Constantinople, directing shipments from his warehouses in Pisa to the docks at Civitavecchia in Rome, and securing passage for the huge inventory that would proceed and follow us as we made our way along the Grand Northern Cycle. So fortunate was I to be able to assist my uncle with his planning and to witness, firsthand, the master at his best. Such lessons would be of great benefit to me throughout my life.

Within a few days we were traveling once again upon the sea to Genoa, the waters being calm for most of that short journey, fortunate for me, for I was like a virgin to her wedding bed when I first set foot upon that vessel. I was not so fortunate as we sailed from Genoa to Marseilles as the weather had turned foul and I was to experience the full fury of Poseidon's wrath. With Heaven's protection and Fortuna's guiding hands, we were delivered intact to the welcoming arms of the harbor of Marseilles.

My heart leaps with excitement even now after so many years, when I think of the port city of Marseilles. How wonderful it was to me then. I recall the rows of warehouses fanning out along avenues that led from the docks up the hill as far as I could see. The city was heavily fortified with a wall that encircled it, with many watchtowers along the perimeter. There was no fortress, nor any large cathedral, such as one would find in Pisa or Florence, but mostly warehouses and houses of modest means, built for merchants and workers and sailors' wives. However, the magnificence of this port was in its simple and orderly construction. Its warehouses were neatly arranged, and conveniently situated for an orderly transfer of goods from the docks. Its streets were wide enough to handle several wagons across, which was so necessary to keep order amongst the chaos of this thriving colony.

From the deck of the ship I could see and smell and hear the bustle of commerce. Such a mass of humanity, the collection of smells and sounds, of languages from every corner of the world, assailed my senses. I thanked God for delivering me from a watery grave, and for bringing me safely to this fascinating place. Some of the goods we had brought from Pisa, together with those that had been previously shipped and stored in warehouses close to the dock, were loaded onto several barges and secured for passage along the great River Rhone. Duty and taxes were collected in advance by agents of princes and bishops who held fiefdoms along the waterway from Marseille to Lyons. Letters of safe passage were obtained at abysmal fees and would be used at various tariff stations along the waterways and roads. Though there was never any guarantee that a shipment would make it to its destination, it was convenient and much less burdensome to pay the tariffs in advance. For a seasoned merchant such as Giancarlo the fees were less, due to the frequency of shipments made over the course of the years, and security was understood, particularly owing to the reputation of Giancarlo's personal security force that had always accompanied him on those expeditions.

A number of barges were loaded with goods that were to be sold at the mid-Lent fair in Bar sur Aube. A large stock of inventory, some from Tuscany and others imported from exotic regions of the world, had been stored in warehouses close to the docks and would be shipped in stages and at various times for the fairs in Champagne. Giancarlo had decided to attend Bar sur Aube, then proceed to Provins' May Fair, then move on to the Fair of St. John in June. He had decided to skip the Fair of St. Ayoul back in Provins scheduled during the Feast of the Exaltation of the Cross in mid-September. He wanted to complete all his business and be back in Tuscany before All Souls Day.

Barges full of merchandise were sent upriver over the course of four months and were supervised by Giancarlo's French agent, Philippe. It was impossible for Giancarlo to oversee such a large and multi-staged operation by himself, and it was essential that he had loyal and trusted agents to oversee the operation. Philippe would join us with the final shipment in June at Troyes and accompany us to Paris. He, in turn, enlisted a small army of trusted men, some shippers and some strong arms, to protect the merchandise. With each shipment he also sent along one of his sons, each a strong and capable man with looks to mirror their father.

Accompanying us on our journey, Philippe had entrusted his most prize possession, his daughter Genevieve. She was past the age of eighteen and unmarried and seemed very like her brothers in looks and in ability. She dressed as her brothers did, and her mannerisms were as rough and masculine as any of the men. I was to learn on that journey that appearances do not necessarily speak of the person hidden within.

I remember well that first trip upon the waters of the Rhone, I divided my time between my uncle, who constantly schooled me in the thousands of minute details regarding that trade mission, and the crew, many of whom were not much older than myself. My initial interaction with Genevieve was one of annoyance; our brief exchanges were caustic and antagonistic. Giancarlo suggested that I give her a wide berth, for the trip was long and the barges were not long enough. Though I had heeded to Giancarlo's advice and gave the girl a wide birth, as the days dragged on, I had found myself crossing her path more and more frequently. I had some suspicion that the increasing chance encounters were more as a calculated way for her to torment me, and I found myself growing less annoyed with each bump and insult. In fact, I had begun to look forward to her feigned mockery and plotted in my own way to arrange to interact with her several times throughout the day.

Four days of our journeying upriver, I remember stopping at an isolated pool that had been formed at a bend in the river. It was there that our paths had crossed in a way that would affect my life forever. Nearby, a shaded glen surrounded by juvenile chestnuts and ash extending down to the bank of the river, made for a safe and refreshing landing for us to rest and replenish our body and our spirit. As the party enjoyed a leisurely meal, I wandered into the wood to relieve myself and to bathe my weary body in the cold water of a river pool. Having finished my toilet, I spied Genevieve, hidden behind a tree, casting her eyes, without shame, upon my nakedness.

Instantly, the Devil entered my body and took control of my loins, causing me to shed all sense of decency and decorum. I stood by the pool as naked as the day upon which I entered this world, with lust in my heart and the power and fury of hell pulsing between my legs. Instead of turning in shame or disgrace, I faced myself toward my fearless spectator and stared directly into her eyes, enticing her from her hiding spot. She met my stare with a haughty sneer, showing no fear or weakness or shame, and moved slowly toward me without saying a word. In silence she enveloped me like a cat, never taking her eyes from my eyes, never betraying an emotion, never uttering a sound, but grasping me firmly with her calloused hands, taking me to a place that I had never been before.

Her touch was not tender, nor was it rough, it simply was… enchanting. I know not what spell she cast upon me that day, but my mind and body had become hers from that moment on. Though she had rid me of that hell demon in a few short moments, she had substituted her own powerful will within my heart and mind and body. She released her grip and her will, and as I recovered my senses, she had disappeared. I clothed myself and returned to the group.

Genevieve was already on the barge busily making ready to continue the journey, never betraying an emotion nor a hint of shame or acknowledgement of what had just happened. We did not mention that moment to anyone, or even hinted about it with each other throughout the remainder of that trip. Had it not been for the hunger in my heart, and the aching in my soul, the longing for her touch, and the agony that I had felt with a just a word or a casual glance cast in my direction, I would have convinced myself that the encounter had only been a dream. Perhaps, a succubus, taking on the form of the lovely Genevieve, had entered upon my sleep to cause much mischief and diversion, and delighted in torturing my mind and my body. In truth, such dreams and visitations have plagued me for many nights and for many years, always in their intensity, leaving me spent and exhausted at daybreak. I still feel her presence within me, even to this day, though not as powerful as it once was, for she was another whose life I had casually picked up, used, and discarded when I saw the need to move ahead.

We arrived at the fair at Bar sur Aube by mid-Lent, sometime around the first of March. The Entrée lasted eight days, which gave the merchants arriving from all over Europe time to arrive, unload, and set up their stalls. Giancarlo had instructed the crew how to construct the stalls needed to display and sell his imports, and I had made myself available for any task needed to ensure all would be ready on the official opening of the fair. Though all the merchandise brought upriver would eventually be sold out of these temporary stalls, only a small quantity of the items was needed to be displayed. The greater portion was stored in a warehouse located close to the quay. Merchants purchasing large quantities would make the deal directly with Giancarlo, and the merchandise would be delivered directly from the warehouse. It was important to Giancarlo not only to sell all the merchandise that was transported to the fair, but also to establish important trade contracts that he would fill throughout the year.

The official opening of the fair was on the ninth day. Ten days were devoted to the sale of cloth. Wool from England and Ireland, processed in the factories of Bruges and dyed by the master dyers in Florence, as well as exotic silks from the Far East brought in from Constantinople and Alexandria, were the first items to be sold. The following eleven days were devoted to the sale of leather brought directly from the tanners and craftsmen of Tuscany. Rabbit, marten, and other skins were brought in from the north, while other rare pelts from the East and Africa, including lion, zebra, giraffe, wild elk, and water buffalo, originally obtained and imported from the markets in Alexandria, were the grand centerpieces. Giancarlo had even managed to secure several hides of dragons rousted from their fiery dens along the River Nile, though those were reserved for his most exclusive clients. Still, an opportunity was never wasted to display such magnificent finds for potential future orders.

The final nineteen days were devoted to the selling of household goods, wine, oil, cheeses, and dried meats, all brought in from Tuscany and central Italy, as well as fine salts from the salt flats in the Veneto and the salt mines on the east coast of Dalmatia, common spices from the Levant and Egypt, and more rare and exotic spices from the empires of the Mongols far to the east. Rubies and sapphires from India and pearls from the Orient, though not displayed to the general public, were gladly presented to the privileged during a prearranged private showing. Coin and specie from all over the known world were traded or exchanged for gold or silver florins most commonly used in trading in this part of the world. Giancarlo had traveled with several heavily locked armored chests in which he stored the most precious items. The risk of such a transport was very great, though mitigated by the attendance of his well-trained security force.

I had been allowed to work the stalls, under Giancarlo's guidance, as were two of his trusted agents, but the most important business, handled only by Giancarlo himself, was conducted on the banche, a cloth-covered table set up in a specially designated area of the fairground. At this table, Giancarlo would work his magic, weighing precious metals, examining precious gems, exchanging foreign coin, effecting payment for goods, and establishing terms and conditions for future payment of credits. His green tablecloth and scales informed all that this was where the true commerce was conducted. Even the representatives of lords and princes of church and state would visit the banche to negotiate for their masters the settlement of a prior debt or to arrange for additional funding for a future debt.

Guards of the Fair, most generously provided by the Count of Champagne, were posted, not to ensure Giancarlo's safety—for that, he brought his own police force—but to protect the merchants from the "dishonest Italian bankers and moneychangers." Giancarlo was used to having a hundred eyes watching over his shoulder. In fact, he relished the challenge of swindling an overbearing jackass right under the very noses of those French pigs. Forgive me, Dear Lord, it is unkind to disparage an innocent fool who performs a necessary task for a corrupt master, though most of the fools who I have encountered over these many years have been as corrupt as the masters whom they serve and have been easily enticed to look the other way when a good coin was exchanged for a bad. Little did they suspect that the coins dropped into their greedy, dirty hands, were as false as the oaths that they had sworn to their masters.

At the close of each of the three sessions, Giancarlo would set up his banche for a day and settle all accounts to that stage of the fair. The largest accounts were settled during the final closing days of the fair that came about by the middle of April. During this entire time, I had thrown myself into every aspect of this venture, assisting whenever I could, memorizing everything I had witnessed, absorbing all that was taught to me. I committed myself to Giancarlo and the business in every way…but one.

As the days drew on, my mind and my body were haunted in dreams by the specter of Genevieve of the woods. I had managed to busy myself and keep my distance for a short while, but the urges were too strong, and in time, I would find excuses to be alone with her. At no time did we ever display openly any hint of affection or attraction for each other, yet as time passed, we would deviate from our assigned task and steal a few private moments in a secluded stand of trees, a barn or stable or unoccupied shed. Though I knew it was wrong and we were courting disaster, the spell that she had cast upon me on that very first afternoon was so strong it would blind my eyes and set my loins on fire. Such intense desire is ignited only in youth, yet, though tempered with the aging of the body and the passage of time, its stirrings are still felt even at the end of my days. The lust that was born in the secluded pool of the river had grown strong and was hard to control.

We were careful to mask that uncontrollable lust for each other during the entire Bar sur Aube fair. What little sleep had been granted to me was troubled by erotic dreams, and the voices, and yet it did not hinder me from proving my worth to my uncle. I was at his beck and call and performed every task he assigned to me with ease and enthusiasm, endearing me to him and encouraging him to bestow upon me even more authority. By fair's end, he was including me in all major exchanges, and introducing me as his assistant and future agent.

Giancarlo's fortune had continued to increase with each passing day, most of his merchandise had sold out in record time, and his purchases and future contracts assured him of continued future success. The majority of his trades were "above board," as he would often say of the legitimate deals he would make, but it would be hardly worth the trip without the illicit transactions, the smooth and professional manner in which perfectly good coins were switched for counterfeit currency, or a loan made to a desperate nobleman at rates that would be considered usurious even by the Jews. By all accounts, the first fair of the Grand Cycle of 1156 was a resounding success.

The Entrée for the May Fair in Provins began on the Feast of the Ascension at the end of April and lasted another forty-five days. It was handled in much the same manner as the Bar-sur-Aube. In fact, all the fairs in Champagne were handled in a similar fashion, their rules and regulations dictated by the Count himself. The sense of order and security provided by the Count's guards was the reason for the success of these fairs and a major contributor to Giancarlo's, and in later years to my own great fortune. Giancarlo would often tell me his greatest profits were made in Champagne, above even the markets in Rome, Constantinople, or Alexandria. We had met up with the second armada of barges brought up from Marseilles by Henri, Philippe's eldest son, on the day before the Entrée was to begin.

Not only had those days grown hotter, but my lust for Genevieve had likewise become hotter. Often, we slipped off together during the busiest part of the fair. We would satisfy our secret desire and bodily cravings in a hayloft or in one of the subterranean warehouses, foolishly thinking we were being discrete and unobserved. As time passed, several of the crewmembers began to make jokes about our closeness, and Henri, Genevieve's brother, had taken me aside to castigate the seemingly inappropriate closeness that had developed between the nephew of his master, meaning me, and an insignificant barge-hand who happened to be his sister. He was careful in the way he chastised me, for he was fearful of his own station and the damage to his entire family's position should any scandal present itself because of the passions of a couple of overly amorous juveniles. Both he and the crew were very cautious to avoid any hint of impropriety being brought to the attention of Giancarlo, for they had all considered him to be a man of impeccable values who would not stand for such a thing. They also considered, quite wisely, their own position and feared any retribution that might befall the utterer of a minor insult or joke about the master's favorite, no matter how much truth was behind it.

Henri's warning to me, and his verbal as well as physical punishment of his sister, was enough to squelch, at least superficially, the attraction we were feeling toward each other during the remainder of the fair at Provins. In order to ensure that nothing unseemly would happen, Henri convinced Giancarlo to transfer Genevieve to the crew that was to return downriver with the newly acquired merchandise, substituting his youngest brother Jean-Pierre to act in her stead. He used this switch as a way for Giancarlo to observe his brother's worth so that he might advance his position within the company. The real intent was to remove his sister from the company and from my life entirely.

Giancarlo saw the merit in Henri's suggestion, though he did not know the hidden reason behind the recommendation and approved the transfer. Genevieve remained for a few days longer and then accompanied a small group of barges south. Even though I was heartbroken, I did not show my feelings, nor did I harbor any malice toward Henri or my uncle, for I had known my fate had already been determined and would not be altered by the uncontrollable longing of the heart. I had convinced myself I was strong enough to exorcize those possessive demons, who just days before had controlled my entire being, both day and night. Though those desires continued to plague me on occasion, I was able to replace them with a new lust, a lust learned from Giancarlo, the lust for the swindle.

Though I worked hard to prove my work ethic and usefulness, my sudden mood changes had caused a rift between my uncle and me. Giancarlo was far from a fool and had begun to sense a problem immediately after Genevieve had been sent away. He feigned ignorance of any problem, though I should have realized that nothing, no matter how insignificant, had escaped his notice. He chose to let time pass in the hope that the memory would fade, and the ashes grow cold.

Two days prior to the end of the May Fair, during the evening following an unusually busy day in which all the accounts had to be settled, my fate was to be forever sealed. Giancarlo was especially happy with his performance that afternoon behind the banche, much to the detriment of the inept traders, and felt very pleased with the overall success of the venture to that point. I had shared in his excitement for there was much below-the-board trading done that day. I remember sharing a light supper together, and afterwards he asked me to accompany him on a long stroll along the banks of the river. He took that time to question me about the cause of my melancholy, showing great concern and tenderness, not as a master to an apprentice but as a worried guardian to a beloved ward. The emotions that I had thought were safely locked away immediately spewed forth and I found myself confiding to him my wants and desires to be with Genevieve for all eternity. How foolish was I to think that he would see my anguish and torment and arrange for her to be brought back to me? For a brief and careless moment, I had allowed my heart to rule over my brain.

He sat in icy silence as I opened my chest and placed my broken heart into his hands, and then he unleashed all his fury and tore my heart to shreds. He grabbed me by the hair and pulled my face to his. In the frigid and controlled voice of Lucifer himself, he began to berate me for my ungratefulness, and my stupidity for allowing carnal desires to cloud my vision and ruin any chance for me to rise out of the burrowed fields and the slop of the hog pen of my useless father's insignificant farm. His voice still echoes in my head as he called me a useless piece of shit, not fit to grace the bottom of a foot soldier's boot. He had plans for me. Great plans. He had plans for a man with courage and integrity. Oh, how I should laugh today at the notion of Giancarlo preaching to me about integrity.

He said that he had plans for a man with a good head upon his shoulders and a large set of balls between his legs to stand up against the noblemen, the princes, and the curia. He had hopes to groom a champion who would take on the old-world order and challenge their hatred and envious desire to squash the rising businessmen into the dirt. He had dreams that all the gold and silver accumulated through commerce would one day be used to ensnare them all, and the captains of industry would become the masters. He then stopped and pondered aloud. How could the great Giancarlo Manenti have been taken in by such a foolish, selfish, ungrateful, son of a nobody—an ass, incapable of controlling his own prick! His words were heavier than any blow to my body. He threw me to the ground and left me whimpering, then stamped off in disgust.

For the next few days he did not acknowledge me, nor summon me to assist him, or even send word for me to fetch him anything, but continued his work for the final days of the fair, as if nothing had changed, except for the complete disregard for my ungrateful self. Foolish as I was, I was smart enough to know to give him a wide berth, to continue whatever work I needed to do and not crawl up into a ball like some wounded mire cat. Even then I was too proud for that. I was terrified I had ruined my chances of gaining the trust and respect, and the generosity of this great man, but as his words echoed again and again in my brain, my pride forbade me to crumble up and die. My lust for wealth had become strong. I was certain of my destiny, though less certain of my relationship with my dear uncle.

We packed the barges and made our way downriver, heading back east to Troyes. Philippe had met us at the dock having arrived with the fresh shipment of merchandise from Marseilles two days earlier. He and his crew had already removed the merchandise to a storehouse he had secured. His men had already begun the construction of the stalls we would use to display our goods. Giancarlo was invited to lodge in the sumptuous residence of the Canon of the cathedral. I was left to reside on the mosquito-infested barge. Giancarlo had made his displeasure with me quite clear and had chosen to teach me the true cost of a very unwise decision. His lesson did not fall on deaf ears, though my pride and vanity caused me to endure a month's worth of abuse.

My mind, again master over my heart, had told me that I would have to humble myself however possible to win back the trust and affection of my uncle. Long did it take me to muster the courage to approach him, the time well spent in formulating the right things to say to him. I knew that were I to throw myself at his feet and beg for forgiveness, my show of emotion and weakness would be met with disapproval, hatred, or worse—total disregard. Giancarlo, above all else, was a businessman, and I needed to bargain myself back into his good graces if I hoped to regain my apprentice status.

I worked extra hard during the Entrée of the fair, making myself available to the entire crew, working from early morning until well beyond moonrise. I worked in quiet solitude, asking for no favor nor reprieve, taking what little nourishment was needed to keep the body strong, and retiring in silence to the heat and the insects at the river's edge. By the end of the last day of the Entrée, I had mustered enough courage to approach Giancarlo. He had been expecting me. I presented to him a well-thought-out analysis of my actions and the implications and potential harm to his grand plan, of my misdirected energies. I apologized to him for the grief that I had caused him and for my stupidity in letting my heart rule over my mind. I was, after all, but a boy, a novice when it came to matters of the heart, bound to stumble when taking my first steps, but learning with each step the valuable lessons of life. I asked him for his forgiveness and promised him my unconditional loyalty, pledging my service to him, without question. He stared at me for a long moment, saying nothing but studying me intently.

Softly and deliberately he spoke to me, in the tone and manner of which I had, on so many occasions, observed him using with his prize pigeons with whom he was about to take. For Giancarlo, business was business, no matter how he felt about the person he was about to take. In such cases he would never be satisfied with getting even. Getting even was never an option. For those fat birds he would only be satisfied with complete domination, whether by outwitting an unsuspecting mark in the trade or by outright treachery and thievery. He would never allow himself to settle for second best but would expend all his resources to obtain unconditional surrender.

Though I was young and a novice in so many ways, I had developed an acute ability to make observations of the manner and purpose of a man's true spirit. I had much time to observe the true spirit of Giancarlo Manenti, enough to realize that should I be allowed to trade with the Master, it would cost me dearly. I had realized at that point, should I ever hope to accomplish any of my dreams, I would have to sell my soul to this man, and be in his debt for the rest of my life. I had already decided his price, whatever it was to be, would gladly be paid. I would surrender myself to him and become his vassal.

"Forgiveness and trust are not easily granted," he said to me, "but must be earned, its cost most dear when the cause for such disappointment and distrust is so great. I must think upon this act of contrition and consider the cost of my forgiveness, for I assure you that it will not come cheaply. I will allow you to prove your worth to me during this fair, giving you no promise or hope that the damage you have caused can be so easily cured by hard work or feigned affection. I will weigh the pros and cons of our future relationship, placing your character and your worth upon the scales to determine if you be genuine or forgery. Should you prove false or of no use to me, on the last day of this fair, I shall cast you aside like a forged penny and leave you upon the banks of the Seine for you to make your own way in the wild and brutal world. Should you prove true and of some worth to me, I will deliver my proposal and contract for your future." He said no more but returned to the journal.

Giancarlo kept himself busy during the remainder of the Entrée, meeting with noblemen, prelates, and wealthier merchants, all vying to make pre-market deals. Though it was technically not allowable, by act of law, to trade during the Entrée, many felt that such laws were foolish and made to be broken if one would ever hope to obtain the choice merchandise at special, privileged pricing. These individuals, of course, were counted among Giancarlo's fattest pigeons and were allowed glimpses of his most precious merchandise, held specifically for sale on the final day of the fair. In this way, he would begin the bidding process early, allowing such interests to simmer for several weeks, or as he would say, allowing the pigeon to stew in his own sauce before being served upon a tarnished platter. In several instances, promissory notes were exchanged, dating such transactions to the official opening of the fair. And, of course, the customary bribes were paid to official notaries to guarantee that such transactions were legal and uncontestable. As a result of this pre-market trading, a sizable amount of the merchandise had been claimed prior to the market opening.

Philippe had organized most of the logistics for this fair, allowing my uncle to concentrate on the deals for which he has become legend. I had worked closely with Philippe during those first few days even though it was uncomfortable for both of us, for I had suspected he had learned of my inappropriate behavior with his daughter. Though he had never mentioned any of it to me, he spent many long hours lecturing me in his own way, on duty and obligation, of status and accountability, of the foolishness of youth, especially in the privileged. He reminded me that a pup, no matter how cute or affectionate toward its master, could cause the boatman to lose footing, which could cause the merchandise to shift, which could cause the boat to tip, which could result in the drowning of the crew and their master. Nothing would be allowed to jeopardize the mission, and that should be a lesson that I would be wise to learn right quick. No more was ever said by Philippe while he was in the employ of Giancarlo, nor in later years when he continued his employment with me.

The fair progressed throughout the end of June and into the middle of the dog days of July. Giancarlo had done remarkably well selling all his merchandise and acquiring such items and promissory notes of future shipments that would benefit him in market trades later in the year. Accounts had to be settled, not only for the activity of this fair, but trades that would be conducted in port cities around the Mediterranean. My uncle was a master of the game of chess, and he constantly maneuvered his game pieces whenever and wherever he had the opportunity. He spent the latter part of the fair exchanging coin, collecting debts, and securing contracts for the following year's fair. He had sent Philippe on to Paris with the bulk of merchandise that had been earmarked for the court of Louis.

Giancarlo had summoned me to join him for a last meal before we headed to Paris. I knew his offer had already been formulated and the deal would have to be made. My fate was about to be determined. Giancarlo looked at me sternly, studying my face and my demeanor. He studied me long and hard

"Giovanni," he said. "Long have I weighed your worth to me, since the time that you drove a wedge so deeply into the plans that

I had so carefully worked out for our future together. Much have I pondered upon your qualities, both good and bad, to divide such qualities into two separate piles and to place them upon the scale of judgment. I sought after the virtues that you possess and made note of those you lack, hoping that those could be developed as you mature. I have credited you with maturity in areas of business and accountability but debited your account for your immaturity in your moral composition. You have a great damage that you keep locked deep in your soul. If left to fester and spread, it will destroy your nature, and consume all which you have worked for and all those who surround you. You are a capable and talented apprentice, and with continued training you could possibly be worthy at some future date to be considered master of the trade. You have the ability—you surely have the confidence and the ego. Yet you have shaken my confidence with your willingness to cast your fate to the wind by letting your emotion overpower your logic."

"Emotion can never be allowed to triumph over logic, in commerce or in life, for that will surely lead to death and destruction in any circumstance. I have given you credit for the stupidity of youth, though that is a minor pass, never to be credited again. With all that I have pondered I have decided that your pluses do outweigh your minuses and that there is enough material in you with which I might mold a worthy protégée, one to whom I could someday entrust my business empire. I am, therefore, advancing you from apprentice to ward and, though not my son but my nephew, I will consider you a son, worthy to assume, at the appropriate time and under the appropriate conditions, all the duties necessary to run the business that I have spent my entire life creating. My plans are about to expand and soon I will need your assistance. I need to feel that I can trust you—always. I will, if you prove true, entrust my life's work into your hands. And as part of this arrangement, I will announce the betrothal of you and Anna upon our return to Siena."

I was taken aback by his proposal and pondered in silence all the ramifications of it. I was being handed the keys to the kingdom, shown the path that could easily lead me to my destiny. And at what price? I already loved and respected this man and was loyal to him. I had no doubt that I could accept any responsibility and succeed in running the enterprise as capably as he. I would only have to marry someone I did not love, a small cost. But I would also have to be true. Could I learn to love Anna and stay true to my promise, or would I be doomed to a loveless marriage of convenience for the rest of my life? Marriages of convenience were made all the time.

I accepted my uncle's offer, without question, with much gratitude and humility. Willingly I placed my first step upon the path that had been laid before me and had pledged my unquestioned loyalty to him. I am amazed as I tell you this how easy it was for me to sell my soul to the devil. The deal had been made, and Giancarlo, as usual, had won.

VII

France and England

After a day's journey upon the Seine, we arrived in Paris. Philippe and the Provost of Paris had met us at the quay. For Giancarlo to trade within the confines of Paris it was required that he be sponsored and guaranteed by a wealthy bourgeois Parisi merchant. Giancarlo had been fortunate enough to be introduced to just such a man several years earlier, a one Francois Boileau, who served as provost of the city, and who just happened to be a cousin to Philippe. Through Francois' connections with the court and his affiliation with the various guilds, and for a retainer fee of one quarter of the profits made on any deal negotiated in Paris, Giancarlo was assured access to the highest social circles in France. It was a costly arrangement, but one that brought great gains to both my uncle and the provost of Paris.

Through Giancarlo's connections and recommendations, Francois had indeed become a wealthy man who exercised a great deal of influence in the Parisian markets and in the royal court. Like most of the nouveaux riche at that time, Francois had built himself a grand palazzo on the Ile de France within walking distance from the royal palace and the newly constructed Cathedral of Notre Dame. He was most generous as our host during our stay in Paris.

Giancarlo's merchandise had been unloaded and stored in the Hanse warehouses and awaiting sale in the markets that were held on a regular basis in the square to the rear of the cathedral. Most of the lower-end merchandise had already been traded in the other fairs in Champagne, but there were enough goods to bring to this market to have a dominant place amongst the other foreign merchants. Most of the higher-end trading, the real purpose for Giancarlo's appearance in Paris, was made in the grand salons within the palaces of the very wealthy and the royal court itself.

I was assigned to oversee the stalls in the marketplace and the replenishment of goods from the storehouses. Within a week's time, the entire shipment of goods had been sold for a very good profit. All the items brought up from Tuscany were quickly bought by the hungry Parisians. Though they had tried to drive hard bargains, particularly with the merchandise that had been acquired in the Champagne Fairs, their pockets were quite deep when it came to the Tuscan merchandise. Wines and charcuterie were of special desire of the citizens of Paris. Such delicacies, though more moderately priced than the items imported from the East, when sold in large quantity had yielded a greater net profit. This was still an essential part of the business, but for Giancarlo, it was merely a cover for the other side of his enterprise, namely the large contract deals for money, arms, and supplies needed by the king for his campaigns against his enemies, his rivals, and his supposed friends.

Louis had had a longstanding feud with Henry II of England, not only losing his first wife, Eleanor, to the younger and more virile monarch, but land and territories on the mainland, which had once been his under the marriage of France and Aquitaine. Borders had always been blurred between the two countries, and relations between both courts had been strained since Henry had won the throne of England, and the heart of the French Queen.

At the time of my first visit to the royal court of France, Louis had recently married his new young queen, Constance of Castile of the House of Burgundy. She was charming and Louis, though never fully recovering from his dismal relationship with Eleanor, had been smitten with the saintly Constance. He was eager to please his young bride, proving extremely profitable for a resourceful merchant such as Giancarlo. Louis was more than happy to purchase some of Giancarlo's most precious and exotic objects imported from the Far East. Bolts of the finest silk, dyed in the most exquisite colors of blue, green, and gold and silver, were purchased to be transformed into such beautiful dresses as to set the fashion for all the royal courtesans in Europe. To adorn her royal highness, Giancarlo had imported the finest pearls from the Orient, opals, emeralds, and rubies from India, and ermine and silver fox pelts from the northlands of Scandinavia. Louis had spared no expense to ensure that his queen would be the most beautiful woman on earth, and that her beauty would outshine all others, particularly the she-devil he had lost to the king of England.

Trading in the general market was very successful and was completed in a few days, which afforded me the opportunity to explore the areas around the Ile de France and to meet and converse with some of the other merchants. That is when I first met Pietro Bernardone, a cloth merchant from Assisi. My first impression of Pietro was that he was arrogant, loud, abrasive, and lacking in the social graces that could help him win the heart of a fair young maiden. He was of average appearance, but he had possessed the deepest azure eyes that were piercing when he looked directly at you. His specialty was finished cloth, most of which he imported from the weavers in Bruges and along the Arno, though the more exotic silks and brocades he secured from his suppliers in Venice. His main trade route was overland through the passes of the Alps to the larger cities and fairs of the north, taking him as far north as Paris and to the Low Countries and as far east as Dalmatia and the Veneto. His operation was insignificant in size compared to that of Giancarlo, but he still managed throughout his life to keep himself in a social status that befitted a successful independent merchant. He was ten years my senior and yet possessed a lifetime of experience, accumulated through the trials and tribulations of creating a successful business out of nothing but determination and a desire for a better station in life.

I found myself watching him one morning just outside the grounds of the royal palace, conversing with a couple of young courtiers and several ladies of the court. He was telling a fantastic tale of high court intrigue from the faraway lands of the Egyptian caliphates. His language was as colorful as the bolts of cloth that he held in his hands and that had been stacked high in the arms of his young attendant. Long did he spin his spell, captivating his listeners with each word. He was quite good at what he was doing. I was amused with his performance, knowing it was well rehearsed. I had learned enough about the faraway lands to know that his story, as colorfully delivered as it was, was just a ruse. For all his many faults that I would come to know and accept, Pietro Bernardone was a natural-born salesman. Though he was prohibited from transacting business in the markets of Paris, he had circumvented the laws and secured the interests and the purses of his listeners. The fabrics that his apprentice had struggled to balance would soon be decorating the bodies of the handsome young maidens and courtiers. They had followed him to his wagon that was a safe distance from the marketplace and in no time were each walking away with several bolts of colorful cloth.

Curious to see the outcome, I had followed close behind the group, and when the trading had been completed, I approached Pietro and made my introduction. He seemed to know me as a fellow merchant, perhaps only an apprentice or assistant to the great Giancarlo Manenti, and in fact, he had been watching me during the earlier days of our arrival. Instinctively his guard was raised, and the charm and command with which he had previously held his audience had disappeared. I was, as he told me later, his competition, even though a mere boy, and of no interest to him. His magic had suddenly faded, and the conversation that I thought to have with him was no longer of interest to me.

Giancarlo had met on several other occasions with wealthy patrons and officials, such meetings arranged through the guarantee of Francois. The deals he had made with his repeat clients, Giancarlo had insisted, should be of no concern to Francois, for those deals had been transacted through correspondence outside of the Paris boundaries. They were, he reasoned, not subject to his commission and should be, with the agreement of the two parties involved in the transaction, left beneath the table. The new business and introductions were, of course, part of his deal with Francois, and therefore subject to commission. Giancarlo was beginning to tire of his deal with the Provost. He had reckoned that the Provost had already taken enough of his profits over the previous seven years. Future commissions were simply a liability to Giancarlo and would somehow have to be eliminated.

On our last night in the city, Giancarlo was summoned to the palace for a special meeting with the King to discuss a matter that needed the special talents and money of a man such as Giancarlo Manenti. I accompanied my uncle to the palace, along with two of his security guards, for the streets of Paris were both dark and dangerous. Giancarlo was aware of the political situation brewing between Louis, Henry of England, and the Holy Father. He has spoken previously with Louis about the services he could render to the troubled monarch, assuring him that he was at his service should ever the need arise. Giancarlo knew he would not have to wait long before he was again invited to the royal presence. He was more than happy to help the king of France, as he had done so with many of the nobles on the Italian peninsula. He had already formulated his plan, and his price.

Giancarlo instructed us to wait while he met with the King, and then disappeared with a young courtier. We were led to the kitchen by a young maid who showed us much kindness and provided us with a hot meal and a flagon of wine. She was a pretty little thing and was quite precocious in her attitude, talking gaily with the three of us and asking us all sorts of questions about our travels. Of course, being young and French, her questioning focused upon the many pretty girls she had assumed we had courted during our journeys. Truth be told, this nervous pup had no such experience, except of course with the lovely Genevieve, whose memory came stabbing back into my heart. The friendly banter continued between us, obviously meant to exclude my other two companions. It had become clear where this was all headed, and I did not mind the diversion. So, with bellies full and their thirsts quenched, the crew begged leave of me, which I stupidly obliged, and they left me in the welcoming arms of the jovial young maiden.

Whether it was the wine or the longing thoughts of Genevieve, the fires of hell within me were stoked high, and in no time, we found ourselves together, in naked embrace, in the rear of a moonlit horse stable. Lust ignited, I had lost all sense of decency, and her advances were met with such strength and aggression that it caused her to utter the most base and guttural moans. Though I stared squarely into her face, I could only see the face of my dear Genevieve. She held me captive with her eyes, my passion blinding me to all else but the fury raging between my legs. I was in such a state as to ignore the reality and the danger in which we had put ourselves. I was deaf and blind to the approach of her boyfriend and a small group of his friends who proceeded to beat me most ferociously upon the head and body, so much so that I lost all consciousness. My broken body must have voluntarily feigned death for my tormentors ceased their attack and carried my lifeless body to be deposited in the river.

Through divine intervention, or perhaps mere coincidence, the sound of a group of strolling witnesses caused the ruffians to abort their mission. They simply dumped my body upon the bank, leaving me for dead. It was my good fortune to be discovered by Pietro and a small group of his acquaintances. Pietro recognized me instantly and wrapped his cloak around me and helped carry me back to the market stalls. As I regained consciousness, he attempted to tend to my wounds as best he could and remained with me until Giancarlo returned. From that evening forward, I was to be in Pietro's debt, and because of what had happened, his demeanor toward me was much changed. We would remain friends for many years and would share our lives, our business, our friendship, and our adventures together. Our lives would be intricately intertwined in ways that we would never have imagined.

Giancarlo was never to learn of my inappropriate behavior at the palace of the King of France. My tormentors had thought me dead and would never tell of the incident for fear of corporal punishment, and my crew members, wrapped in their guilt for leaving me and not ever knowing the whole story of the night, were summarily discharged by Giancarlo. The only ones to know the entire story were me and eventually Pietro.

News travels quickly, especially within the higher circles in which Giancarlo was transacting business. My infirmity, though quite severe, would not be enough to impede Giancarlo's planned exit from Paris. Rumor spread that the Italian Giancarlo's nephew had been attacked outside the palace, owing no doubt to some shady deal that had gone wrong, probably orchestrated by the Sienese youth. It took little effort to stretch the French imagination when it came to scandal, particularly when it involved the foreign traders, who to them seemed to be taking over the city.

Giancarlo had already planned to leave Paris within a day and to continue his journey to England. With the agreements he had made directly with the King, he did not want to overstay his welcome with the Provost. He had concluded that the current arrangement with the Provost was costing him needlessly, and so he sought a better deal with the crown. His new deal would cut the Hanse out completely, eliminating the need for "letters" and terminating Francois' contract immediately. It was never disclosed to me or to anyone else what the terms of those negotiations were, but the price must have been high and dear to both parties, for no other foreign merchant had been granted such privilege then—or even to this day.

When Francois had learned of Giancarlo's duplicity, he was furious and voraciously contested the special treatment. Giancarlo had instructed Philippe to collect any merchandise held in the Provost's warehouses and prepare to set sail before midday. We sailed to LeHavre and then hugged the coastline, sailing north, where we met up with Giancarlo three days later. Giancarlo had taken a small security force and a few pack horses and had raced to Calais, a journey that took him little more than a day with only brief stops to rest the horses. He was determined to reach the port city with the utmost speed and secrecy. He had urgent business to attend to before we met up with him to sail to England.

Though we arrived at the port several days before we were expected, Philippe was still able to secure the services of the captain of large hulc to transport the increased shipment and men to Calais and then on to London. The vessel could hold several tons of cargo, and its high and sturdy side walls made it much more preferable for voyages in the rough waters of the northern ocean. Its flat bottom allowed it to be brought into shallow water and made it much easier to transfer the merchandise from the knarrs. Within a day of our arrival at LeHavre, we set sail upon the mighty waters of the Northern Sea, picking up Giancarlo in Calais and setting sail for London the following day.

London was, and continues to be, a pale reflection of Paris. We arrived upon the River Thames and were greeted by Giancarlo's agent, Mirthwyn, who, not unlike the Provost in Paris, stood as Giancarlo's guarantee with the London merchant guilds and the court of the young King Henry. Eleanor, Henry's new queen, had brought with her some of the customs that she had observed while part of the French court, but more importantly her extravagant lifestyle and taste for the finest imported objects of beauty from the East. She was one of Giancarlo's most beloved patrons for she never quibbled about price when she was presented with a piece of merchandise of such rarity or of exquisite beauty. She knew Giancarlo to be a supplier of the most unusual objects d'art, and he knew her to be a person of refined taste with an insatiable appetite for such unique items. And she had still held a special affection for her Italian merchant.

Mirthwyn had arranged for our lodging during our stay in London, and we were immediately shown to our accommodations. I was laid upon a mat of clean hay, and Mirthwyn then arranged for a friend of his who was trained as a barber at the college of St. Cosme in Paris to look after my wounds. There, I would stay for the better part of a week, unable to see much of the city. Giancarlo had already set up an impromptu meeting with another one of his agents who represented him in his banking operations in England. He was gone before the barber arrived, leaving me in the care of Mirthwyn. With God's mercy, my wounds had remained clean, my bones had not been broken, and the cuts and abrasions had begun to heal. I was left to rest as I waited for Giancarlo's return.

When Giancarlo had returned, he told me that he had arranged a private audience with Her Royal Highness, Eleanor, in two days' time, and that he would be presenting for her consideration a selection of his finest and most valued possessions. The king would still be away hunting with his Lord Chancellor, Thomas Beckett, but he had been assured of a separate audience upon the King's return. He would be accompanied by Mirthwyn and Philippe, and because of my condition, I was to be confined to bed. I was disappointed to be left out, but in no position to plead otherwise. In silence, I accepted his decision. The men then left me with the barber to review the merchandise at the warehouse.

Philippe returned to our rooms on the following day with the merchandise brought up from Paris. Giancarlo had brought with him his personal chest, which contained his most valued gems, gold and silver, and of course his scale and weight measures. Each item that he intended to present to the Queen was most exquisite and of such rare beauty. The finest of silks, embroidered in gold thread and encrusted with jewels and pearls, the hide of the gigantic African ostrich finished to make it softer than the skin of a newborn babe, and even the hide of the Nile dragon, which, being as tough as metal and imbued with magical powers, could be fashioned into a cuirass that would render its master invincible in battle. Spices from the Orient, jasmine from the Holy Land, chamomile from Egypt, and salt from the flats of the Veneto were the Queen's favorites, always stirring mixed emotions and memories of her crusading years in the east. This initial selection was by no means all his best merchandise, for he wanted to keep an equally impressive inventory to present at his second audience with the king.

Henry had never really enjoyed being in England but preferred his own lands in Anjou. During the brief times he was forced to return to England, he would spend most of his days hunting in the countryside and avoiding the crowded and filthy conditions of London. Giancarlo had been most fortunate that Henry was holding court in England when we arrived.

Giancarlo dressed as himself lavishly on the day of his audience with the Queen, and he had reviewed each item that had been selected to present to her royal highness, paying special attention to every minute detail. I did not know then that my dear uncle, that pillar of virtue, had been, in earlier times, a lover of the young princess who had become the Queen of France. The two had filled their days and nights in passionate embrace at the Queen's Court of Love in the gardens at the Chateau de l'Ombriere, and even quite dangerously in the royal palace in Paris. It is no wonder to me now what drove Giancarlo to risk so much and to travel so far and so often from home. For Giancarlo, it was money, and love. But that was all in the past. On this trip, he would carefully fan the smoldering embers of ancient passion in order to satisfy his bulging purse.

The Queen of England had remained young and beautiful, and she had not lost her love of the finer things in life. Giancarlo was aware of the danger of stoking old flames, for stories had abound of the Queen's infidelities as well as King Henry's uncontrollable anger and jealousy. He knew that if he were to reveal even the slightest hint of a prior familiarity with the Queen, the English treasury would be shut to him, and his life could be forfeited. And yet, Eleanor was the greatest prize of all, and Giancarlo was well prepared for the challenge. Meticulously he reviewed each of the items, which were delicately wrapped in beautiful cloth and tied with spun silver ribbon. Every item was invaluable, so the presentation would have to be spectacular in order to capture the Queen's desire. Giancarlo would simply wet the Queen's appetite with his first presentation. The real money was to be made when the King returned.

Though his audience was supposed to last an hour, Giancarlo was gone for most of the day. Upon his return he quickly set about to gather his belongings, making ready to depart under cover of darkness. Upon questioning him further he told me that he was to leave immediately to fulfill a mission of utmost urgency and secrecy that was commissioned by Louis of France, and that involved the deposed king in Ireland. He was to leave for the western island on the moon tide and travel to Ireland, fulfill his mission, and return to London in less than a fortnight. Absolutely no one was to know of his whereabouts, nor was I to speak, upon my sacred oath, to anyone about his mission. I was to remain out of sight until he had sent word or returned himself from his journey. No further questions were needed. I simply obeyed my master.

It was months later that I was to learn about the secret mission that the king of France had entrusted to my uncle. Whether such a plan was actually the brainchild of the King, which I sincerely doubt after having dealings with the monarch for so many years since, or a scheme concocted by Giancarlo, which to me is more plausible, knowing the capabilities of my dear uncle, only God will truly know, for Giancarlo, throughout his life, had never revealed the true source of the plan. Of what he did confide to me when we were back in Siena was this…

He and two of his best men had sailed directly to Dun Bhun to meet with the old High King Tairrdelbach, who had been deposed by a group of lesser kings and noblemen from the southern lands. Tairrdelbach had reigned for close to fifty years over his island kingdom and was no friend to the kingdoms of England and Wales.

He had sought help from Louis, who had always been reluctant in the past to openly challenge the English crown. Funds and backing were desperately needed to subdue the rebels and reclaim the High Throne. Through connections with Giancarlo, the French king had secretly transferred a sizable sum of money to aid the High King in his domestic struggle, with the promise that when all was settled in Ireland, Tairrdelbach would turn his attention toward England.

Louis was convinced that if Henry's attention were turned toward Ireland, a swift French invasion of Britain would be possible. Giancarlo had secured the necessary funds through his banking agents in London and Bruges, and had negotiated the deal himself, with the High King on behalf of the King of France. And yet, Giancarlo, always the chess master, had seen a greater opportunity for himself in the civil unrest in Ireland.

Diarmait MacMurchada, King of Leinster, had supported the new High King Ua Locklainn, who had driven Tairrdelbach from his high throne. Grateful for his services and loyalty, Locklainn had compensated Diarmait with the finest sheep remaining in the lands that had once been taken from him. Giancarlo had seen great potential profit in the wool of those sheep. Shortly after begging leave of Tairrdelbach, Giancarlo, secretly made his way to Ferns to meet with Diarmait, who had managed to breed the largest and healthiest flock of sheep in any of the kingdoms in Ireland. The wool produced was of the best quality and had been unmatched by any throughout the textile markets of Europe. Though the best wools obtainable in large quantities still came from the countryside in England, Wales, and to some extent the wilds of Scotland, the prized Leinster wool was still beyond reach of the greedy British wool merchant guild.

Giancarlo knew that he would still have to trade through those controlling guilds if he wanted to continue trading in England, and he also knew that for him to get his hands on a sizable amount of Leinster wool, a secret, side deal would have to be made with Diarmait, now the enemy of Louis. Giancarlo's duplicity was dangerous, even fatal if found out, and would have caused an international incident. After a day of hard negotiation, never divulging his ties with Louis nor his deal with Tairrdelbach, Giancarlo had secured a contract for the shipment of one thousand sacks of Leinster's best wool, cleaned and dried, to be delivered each spring for a period of five years, with an optional right to renew the contract for an additional five years.

Such wool was to be shipped directly to Giancarlo's warehouses in Bruges—the first installment to be shipped within the month. In return, Giancarlo would pay in coin directly to Diarmait or his agent the total amount agreed upon. Giancarlo had brought with him a strongbox containing enough silver coin to cover, as he had previously calculated, the first shipment of wool. As premium paid on the deal, Giancarlo would immediately ship to Leinster from his factory in the north of Spain armaments needed by the rebels to continue their defense against the forces of Tairrdelbach and his supporters. Giancarlo was not at all certain that he could trust that the rebel king and his supporters would succeed in eliminating the threat of the old high king, but he hedged his bet on the ruthless determination of Diarmait as a changing force in Ireland and a future trading partner and ally. With negotiations completed, Giancarlo slipped out of Ireland and sailed back to London,

Giancarlo had returned in high spirits and immediately began his preparations for his audience with the king and queen. He was genuinely pleased to see me doing so well, at least I thought so, and he was obviously pleased with the successful dealings that he had made in Ireland. I was more than pleased and grateful when he announced that I would accompany him and assist him with his dealings at court. I was to dress in the finest costume available and together, with Mirthwyn and Philippe, we would dazzle the high court of Henry Plantagenet and his queen, Eleanor.

Our audience was scheduled for the middle of the afternoon, and God was kind to us, giving us mild weather and brilliant sunshine, which, as Giancarlo was quick to point out, would shine upon the most precious merchandise, giving it a halo of ethereal light and illuminating the jewels to their greatest potential and worth. Mirthwyn, Philippe, and I had waited with a good portion of the merchandise in the antechamber, while Giancarlo was allowed entrance to the royal audience. Giancarlo presented to the royal couple the entire supply of his most precious gems, highlighting those gems that Eleanor had previously favored, along with small but exquisitely crafted religious objects in gold and silver. He had brought with him several reliquaries of preternatural power recovered, at a high cost, from Muslim-held territories in the Holy Land. These sacred objects were of most interest to His Majesty and were bought at considerable cost. In order to satisfy his queen, Henry also selected several gems of varying size, shape, and color. One by one, we were brought into the audience hall with our arms full of delicately wrapped objects. It was the first but not the last time I was to lay eyes upon their royal persons.

Henry was of pleasing looks, red-haired, with a large head and a boyish face full of freckles. He was short and stocky of frame and appeared bow-legged from riding. He could be menacing with his piercing stare, which he leveled at me at my approach, and yet disarming with a warm smile when he fancied something. His bullying and his bad temperament were legendary, and yet he was extremely intelligent, being capable of speaking many languages. French was preferable to his queen, and he accommodated her in everything.

Eleanor was a handsome woman, eleven years senior to the young king. She had been one of the wealthiest women in Europe when she married Louis, to whom she remained unhappily married for fifteen years. Through all her trials and tribulations, Eleanor had become a hardened matron, yet continually sought to retain her youthful beauty. She was still alluring enough to capture the affections of Henry, while he was still Count of Anjou, and the two had secretly professed their love for each other while she was still the wife of Louis. Such scandalous behavior has been at the root of all the hatred and warfare between French and English monarchs ever since those far-off times. Eleanor's countenance and appearance were in stark contrast to Henry's. She was of regal bearing, a queen in every sense, and her taste for beauty and elegance was unmatched. Her deep green eyes shone brightly with every package unwrapped, and her ruby lips puckered with astonished surprise. She lusted after all that she saw and was quick to convince her uninterested husband of her need to possess every item.

The audience would have extended into the second hour had not the king put a stop to it by purchasing the rest of the wrapped items sight unseen. He had wisely calculated that his queen's happiness was worth more than the gold in his treasury—though it can be rightly said that the Queen had possessed a far greater wealth than the King himself. He had no more patience for shopping that afternoon, and his impatience became a boon for Giancarlo's business.

Though I did not see much of London on that first trip, I had learned a life's worth of lessons from my mentor. I was privileged enough to experience the art of the swindle at the highest levels. Giancarlo was a master of using people to his advantage, and I was so willingly his apprentice.

VIII

Our Return Home

With successful trade in the northern isles completed, we finally set out upon the channel once again and sailed directly for the Golden Inlet of Bruges. The city itself is ancient in heritage and once sat upon the shore of the sea, like Pisa, but many centuries of shifting silt and sand has cut the main city from its port upon the great channel. The Flemish, though, are as industrious as they are wealthy, and as they began to grow in power and wealth, the Brugesi caused the great canal to be built, and the mighty fortress walls that encircle the city, to be erected.

How impressive the city appeared to me in those days, and how powerful it has grown, even today. The banks within the walls are fat with the fortunes of Europe's richest families as all trade conducted in the north is somehow filtered through Bruges. They are leaders in finance, almost a match to the Sienese bankers, and renowned for their skills on the loom. They are, by far, the finest weavers in the world, being most industrious and ingenious in their techniques and their ability to produce great quantities of finely woven cloth upon the most advanced looms in Christendom. Their wealth has grown from their industriousness, for they have set up great factories all the way to Damme, dedicated to the weaving of cloth. Giancarlo's shipments of raw wool would be transformed into the finest cloth ten time faster than it would be if fashioned upon the free-standing looms in England or Ireland.

I was fascinated with the strange towers that were built in the open fields near the factories. Such towers are called windmills, and house great machines that are driven by the wind and do the work of many men. Their gigantic arms, covered in cloth like the sails of a mighty cog, catch the wind and move in a circular motion, driving the machine that is housed within the bowels of the tower. I was amazed by the number of these towers as we sailed down the canal and was captivated by their strange beauty. Before we were to leave Bruges, I had learned all that there was to learn about these incredible contraptions.

In the city we were met by Giancarlo's agent, Maarten, who had already secured our lodgings and was awaiting our arrival. Much business had been conducted in Giancarlo's name since he was last in Bruges more than a year earlier, and as was Giancarlo's way, he would spend several days poring over the books and accounts of his banking operation in this fair city. I remained by his side, assisting whenever needed and learning the intricacies of international trade. I marveled at the extent of my uncle's financial empire, for I was to learn that he was not just the successful merchant of rare and exotic goods but was the head of a financial empire whose arms reached into the pockets of popes and kings and emperors all over the world. All accounts were settled either in Bruges, Siena, or later in Constantinople. Giancarlo was a friend to many important people, and many more vied for his affection and his financial backing. I have come to learn how great this man was, and how fortunate I was to have my path follow so closely to his footsteps.

Within three days of our arrival, the first shipment of Cotswold wool had arrived from London. The wool, when it was in its raw state, had to be processed before it was brought to market for sale. It was soaked for several days by the washers in England, in a bath of hot urine, ridding it of all oils and debris, and then it was dried on racks in a heated warehouse, sacked, and brought to the wool merchant's guild for inspection and sale. The sacks that were piled in the warehouse had been handled by many hands before making their way to Bruges. Many more hands would be needed, and many miles would be traveled, before this raw material would be transformed into a thing of beauty to grace the body of a king or pope.

Next to the storage facility was another low building, long and wide enough to fit many women and young girls who sat upon benches built along the perimeter walls. Their sole function was to comb the wool and to spin it using a drop spindle into long lengths of twisted yarn. Giancarlo's wool was always kept separate from the other wools stacked in the warehouse. Only the better, more experienced spinners were employed to work on his material, as was the case with the weavers. It would take the small army of spinners one week to process Giancarlo's London shipment. The Leinster wool would arrive within a few weeks. By that time, the master weavers would be finished converting the London wool to cloth.

The weaving factory was a huge building, as big as the great hall in the palace of King Louis. Within its walls were housed many horizontal looms, designed and constructed by master Italian craftsmen. Each loom was manned by a master weaver who worked busily transforming finely spun woolen threads into cloth that measured two Flemish ells in width and finished in lengths of twenty ells. The cloth could be, if desired by a client, woven in greater lengths than any produced upon the old warp-weighted looms used in England and elsewhere. These new and improved Italian looms allowed the craftsman to sit and weave in a horizontal motion, being less strenuous and fatiguing and allowing a full day's work with minimal resting periods. It was widely known that the world's finest fabrics came from the factories of Bruges. It was my intention, even then, to someday replicate their industriousness in my own factories.

When the cloth had been woven and dressed, it was brought to the fulling mills, soaked again in urine and fuller's earth and beaten upon the fulling stocks. This process strengthens the bond of the weave and thickens the fabric. This has always been done by walkers, and it is a slow and arduous task. But again, the ingenuity of the Brugesi has made it more cost effective and less labor intensive by harnessing the power of the wind. The finished product, after several washings in pure water, and stretch drying, is a remarkably soft, yet durable, tightly woven fabric, pure as the whitest snow, and fully ready to accept the rich dyes of the Florentine master dyers. Within a month of our arrival in Bruges, Giancarlo's entire contract, consisting of five thousand bolts of fabric, was ready for shipment to the Florentine cloth dyers.

I was totally fascinated with the entire process, the methods of manufacture, the machinery employed, and the technical skills of the craftsmen. Each evening I would make notes and drawings of everything I saw, knowing at some point in time, such knowledge would be of great use to our business. There were no such facilities in all of Italy, and I had already begun to formulate a plan to someday duplicate, closer to home, all I had seen in Bruges. While my interests were focused on the factories, Giancarlo had been conducting business and making trades. He needed to fill the hull of our ship with merchandise that would be sold when we got back to Italy, in order to maximize the profits of the voyage and add to this already successful trip. He had secured a large quantity of fur pelts of ermine, mink, otter, and silver fox from Scandinavia, and a good quantity of salt from the flats of Brittany. The cog in which we arrived was not large enough to handle the increased cargo, nor stable enough to make the return journey in the open waters of the Mare Atlantico, so Giancarlo secured the ship and services of a Genoese merchant to transport us back home.

We traveled upon the frigid waters of the North Sea, making our way through the great channel that divides the north of France and the shores of England, and headed out to open water. I had never been prepared for such a sea voyage. As we headed into the Mare Atlantico, the wind was biting, and the seas were high and angry. Giancarlo had made this voyage many times, and his courage was steadfast. I, on the other hand, quaked with fear. My imagination ran wild, and I peered into the darkness scouring the waves, searching for sea monsters and those demons from the sea that, I was sure, where riding upon each breaking wave and fixing their sights upon my body and my soul. Giancarlo tried his best to calm my nerves, but he grew weary of my trepidation.

We sailed for more than a week before rounding the coast of Hispania and entering through the Pillars of Hercules. It was early morning when I first saw those mighty cliffs, and I marveled at their height and their greatness. The face of the cliffs was bathed in an angry red as the sun rose above the horizon, and the sea was dark and angry. The confluence of the two oceans caused massive waves that dashed upon the shore, creating enormous sprays of white foam.

Our ship was tossed, and I feared for my life. As we progressed into the calmer waters of the Mediterraneo, we hugged the coastline and were welcomed by the warmer winds that crossed the water from Africa. The sea was quiet, and our spirits were much comforted. We had survived that deadly passage intact; our cargo and our lives were ours to keep.

We stopped at Cardiz for replenishment. Such a wild and exotic port it was, teeming with Christians and Saracens, Africans and Jews, traders from the East and every other part of the world. Giancarlo spent the day obtaining supplies, including a strange object that was wrapped in sailcloth and that took six hardy men to bring below deck. There was much discussion between Giancarlo, the captain, and crew members about the positioning of this awkwardly heavy object. The mystery that surrounded this new acquisition quickly dissipated as we prepared to set sail on the last leg of our voyage.

As we sailed from Cadiz, we encountered our first pirate attack. We were approached by an ancient vessel with tattered sails, its swarthy crew clothed in rags, appearing as ghostly demons hellbent on taking our ship, our cargo, and our lives. My fear, which manifested itself in my gut, was quickly mastered by my hatred for such vermin who would try to take from us that which we had worked so hard to gain. We, Giancarlo and I, and Giancarlo's small security force were prepared to fight to the death to protect what was ours. We had no choice. The master of our vessel had much experience with pirates such as these, and with little trouble he steered his ship to gain the wind and was able to put some distance between the two vessels. Unfortunately, our vessel was heavy with cargo, and the pirates with their smaller and lighter ship were able to gain advantage of us. During the chase our captain was able to lure the pirates out into deep water, and as they gained speed and brought their ship close to ours, we readied ourselves to engage them in combat. I stood upon the deck with a dozen hardy men, weapons drawn, ready to battle, when I saw Giancarlo disappear below deck. I froze with fear, thinking that he was running to hide and leaving me to fight these demons. Giancarlo, however, a master of surprise and ingenuity himself, had been prepared for such an occasion.

As the pirate ship drew alongside our vessel, a mighty roar, like thunder, and a great billowing of sulfurous smoke had issued from the bowels of our ship, knocking us to our knees. An enormous gap was ripped wide open in the lower side of the pirate ship, tossing it aside violently. Bodies were thrown into the air and into the sea, its mast ripped at the foundation and brought down heavily upon those who were still standing. I heard the screams and I saw the fear in their faces, and I reveled in their misery. I thanked the Almighty God for his intervention, and I watched with delight as the demolished vessel sank below the waves, dragging most of its occupants to their watery grave. Those who survived were quickly dispatched with crossbow and pike.

We offered up prayers for our salvation as we checked to see how many of us had survived the ordeal. Giancarlo had not come back on deck and I ran below to find him unconscious, barely alive, bleeding from his ears, his face blackened with soot. We brought him up on deck and were able to revive him and tend to his wounds. He had suffered minor damage to his head that caused him to lose his hearing for several days. Fortunately, by the time we had arrived at Marseilles, he had begun to regain most of his hearing. Giancarlo's mysterious acquisition had saved us all, and more importantly, he had saved his precious cargo.

We arrived in Marseilles around the same time as the shipments of goods from the north country, and the Champagne fairs had arrived by barge. As there were at that time ongoing hostilities between Genoa and Pisa, we were forced to secure two Pisan vessels for the final leg of our journey. Finally, by the Grace of God, we made it back to Pisa. After storing the shipment, Giancarlo and I brought the finished cloth woven in Bruge up the River Arno to the master dyers in Florence. Giancarlo had arranged for the cloth to be dyed in the purest and most expensive colors available, for the finished product was expected to fetch the highest prices from the greatest treasuries throughout the empires. We did not wait for the craftsmen to perform their skills but proceeded directly to Siena, arranging for the finished products to be delivered when complete. The months had passed quickly, and the autumn weather was fast upon us.

We arrived back in Siena nine months after we had set out from there. Giancarlo's fortune had increased dramatically, and my experience in the commercial world had magnified tenfold. Donna Donata and Anna were at the main gate of Siena to greet us as we entered the welcoming city. I had not realized how comforting to me were the sturdy walls and the rows of houses so tightly packed, one upon another, lining the streets and zigzagging up and down the hills of sweet Siena. Though I had lived in Siena for only a short time, I had, at that point, considered it to be my home.

Giovanni had grown weary, his voice hoarse, and his physical strength was waning. He needed sleep and yet he was driven to complete his task. Nikos had also grown weary; his fingers, blackened with ink, were cramping from holding the quill so tightly in his effort to capture every word of his master. Though they had stopped several times throughout the day to briefly refresh themselves, Giovanni could not afford the luxury of time. The two had worked together until they could not go on, and only then did they pause from their work in utter exhaustion.

The master was roused from a deep sleep by the smell of a stew cooking in the fire. Nikos had managed to sleep for a few hours and then rose himself to prepare for an evening meal and a very long night ahead. His master was not too resistant to the meal prepared for him, and he ate it greedily, and in silence. Nikos had prepared him a pot of licorice tea to soothe his throat and stomach, and to remedy his speech. When they had satisfied themselves, the two sat in silence for a long moment.

Giovanni was the first to speak.

"Prepare thyself, Nikos. It is high time we begin preparations for my next journey."

Nikos knew what needed to be done and quickly set about the room to ensure that all was made ready. Once again, the magic elixir was concocted, and the incenses tossed upon the flames. Eventually, sleep overtook Giovanni, and he set out again on his spiritual journey.

A long time passes.

Where art thou, Holy Spirit?

No word.

I feel the icy cold waters rushing around me. This cannot be so. My mind knows that I am in a sleep. I should not feel, only observe. Yet the frigid water stabs at my body. I am cramping. I am drowning.

My ears detect the sound of oars upon the water. Help! Help me! A skiff approaches. Thy grip is strong. I thank thee for my rescue. Who are you, kind spirit, or rather who were you? Shrouded thus in weeds and rags I cannot make out whether you be friend or foe, man or spirit.

I am neither friend nor foe, though at one time I did love you—and hated you fiercely. I am no man but spirit I am. Look beyond my rags and the weeds that embrace my naked body. Such a body you once lusted after and had promised the moon and stars in order to possess it. Look closely, Giovanni, and see what you have wrought.

Ah, God in Heaven! Could this apparition be my sweet Genevieve? Cast aside your veil and let me, once again gaze upon your beautiful face. Let me set my eyes upon the face that has haunted me in all my dreams and has fixed itself upon every woman with whom I have ever dared to be intimate. Oh, how I have longed to see you again, to beg for forgiveness for the way in which I left you. Speak to me, my love.

Look upon me then. Let me cast aside these wrappings and let you gaze upon the prize that you have coveted for so long and yet so foolishly, let slip through your fingers.

Cursed demons, what have they done to my beloved. Thy face is contorted as if in a rage, and the skin has petrified around your bones. Your once-beautiful body is now worm-infested, and the dart that had robbed you of your youthful life still pierces deeply into your bosom. Oh, such a horror! How is it that you have ended in such a sorry state?

Curse the demons anon, for they had no hand in my fate. They are merely my hosts, my tormentors, my punishment. Better to curse me, and to curse yourself, for our sins have caused me to don this wretched mantle. It is your lust for that which you could never have, and my hatred for you, that has molded my spirit. Had it been only our lust, I might have fared better, but your selfish treatment of me only fueled anger and my own lust for vengeance, which was manure for the maggots who feast upon my flesh.

Your rebuke cuts me to the quick, spirit, and hampers my eyes from gazing upon you, though whether from disgrace or disgust, I know not. I confess that I used you, knowing all the while that I could never truly have you. For both of us, that opportunity was taken away when we were given to another. I too admit that our lust for each was great, perhaps stronger in me for I led you to sin against your husband. But know that I have always loved you.

We both sinned. Yours is no less than mine, but you may yet have the chance to redeem yourself. I had no such opportunity. I did love you, and you only used me. You lusted after me. You acted as though you had no control over your actions, though you have always been a master of your own destiny. You were more content in bending people to your will than to doing what was right. You used me for your own satisfaction and tossed me away when you were through with me. And I swore vengeance upon you. It was I who left the safety of my home and convinced my brother to make that final run to Champagne. I had every intent on hurting you, just as you had hurt me. So, with evil in my heart I set out upon the river. Look, Seer, see what your lust and my hate hast spawned.

I see me there standing on the dock at Marseilles. Yes, I had convinced Philippe to send your husband upriver with the first shipment. I did plan to somehow take advantage of you when all had been sent away. I remember how fortunate I was when my shipment of cloth had been delayed in Florence. It had caused me to stay as the others headed north. I confess that I strongly desired you, for my marriage to Anna had been miserable. I cared not that you belonged to another. I had sent him far away. I followed you that afternoon to the marketplace, hoping to stoke that flame within you. Our innocent flirtation was anything but innocent. You needed me as much as I needed you. I see in my mind's eye that beautiful, naked body lying there in your husband's bed. Ah, how hot the passion was between us. I can see all that we did during that day and night. Look not upon me so, spirit, for I am still mortal, and though my mortal body be decrepit, my mind still feels the flame of youthful passion. At that time, I wanted you and would have given up all I had to have you.

At that time, your logic and reason were held captive in your prick. You had no thought or regard for anything but your immediate needs. Your sweet talk had proven to be as false as your character. By dawn you had regained your reason and you left me asleep in my bed. You discarded me like an old worn sock. Like a thief, you stole my heart, my honor, and my life, and fled away.

Forgive me, spirit. I honestly see that I treated you poorly and I am ashamed for it. I beg thee to forgive this sinner for the hurt that I have caused you. Forgive me that I may go forward with my life as a true repentant.

You cannot even speak my name, nor call me love or my dear. Has your disgust finally tempered your lust? Do you truly see the error of your ways? Your sin of lust needs more than my forgiveness before it is purged from your soul. Look closer to see the results of your actions.

When I awoke, I had learned of your deceit and your wicked abandonment of me. At first, I was ashamed of my compliance, and then I was angry with you and with myself for being so easily used. I vowed to hurt you as you had hurt me. I waited for Pietro to arrive with your precious cloth and had convinced my brother to allow me to make that run. I had great evil in my heart. And it was as if Hecate had born our bark upon her winged back, for with such speed we were but two or three days from catching up to you. I had filled my soul with a lust to see you destroyed, to see you suffer, and never to be able to lord over another victim. My veins had been filled with ice, and my hatred had never cooled. It was then that we were attacked upon the water as our barge had rounded a turn and entered the shallows. A band of thieves had lay in hiding on both sides of the river behind tree and rock, waiting to pounce upon us unexpectedly and to take from us our lives and our goods. I was the first to fall victim to their cursed arrows, never having the opportunity to cast my eyes upon the perpetrator of so heinous a crime, nor shed the anger with which I had painted my soul or even to utter a prayer for salvation. I was sent to my watery grave with a shattered heart and a doomed soul. All because of you.

Sweet Genevieve, your story pains me more than had I been shot with the darts that assured your hellish fate. I am truly sorry for the evil that I caused you. I beg your forgiveness—for I truly did not know. Oh, how I grieved for you! I lamented your untimely death, and yet I never allowed myself to search for the truth to see that I was the cause of your demise. It was so easy for me to go on with my life, even though you were gone. The troubles I would have had to deal with had you lived were lifted from me with your removal, and yet my lust for you endured and served as a raft upon a raging sea onto which I have clung to for all these years. The vision of your sweet face has always cast itself before me.

Then let it be so, at least for the remainder of your days—for they be short. Gaze at what you could have had, what you chose to destroy. Look at me as I was, and not as I have become, and repent! Repent! Repent!

Genevieve, come back! Do not leave me thus. Saints in Heaven! Help me turn the wheel of time so that I might journey back to mend that which I have destroyed. If only I could give back everything and live a simple life upon the river with Genevieve. Forgive me, my love.

Ω

Nikos waited a long time in silence and then gently placed his hand upon Giovanni's withered arm. The old man bolted upright in his chair, opened his eyes wide, and gasped in a long draught of air as if he had been submerged beneath the waves for a long time, and was struggling to break free of the surface. He sat for some time, breathing heavily while Nikos prepared a cup of heated mulled-water and gently held the cup to his lips. He was back in the corporeal world, safe in a stone tower, in the care of his friend. He stared into the darkness and cried.

Chapter Three
Envy

IX

Politics, the Church, and Business

Our return welcome to the palazzo in Siena was warm and loving. There is truth in what the philosophers of antiquity have said, that in absence, the heart craves love, and grows stronger. I have seen this with my own eyes to be true with Giancarlo and Donna Donata. I have always marveled at Giancarlo's iron-hard coldness that he possessed in his business life, and, as I look back through a lifetime of experiences and disappointments, I have envied his ability to experience true love, not just for power and fortune, but for another being, one with whom he could open his heart, share his dreams, and touch his soul. I have never had that closeness in my life, for I was robbed of such a gift so early in my youth. Those who were closest to me were taken from me, or truth be told, I left them behind, before such bonds could ever be forged. My wretched soul has been doomed from birth. My only love has been for business, first and always. All else was secondary. My relationships have all been a matter of convenience or opportunity. Love has never been a part of it.

Giancarlo had already set to work planning for the following year's cycle, organizing his affairs on the continent, as well as in lands far to the East and the West. Outside of Siena, much was happening in the world of business and politics. It had been three years since the morning I had seen the emperor Barbarossa in the library of the Abbot of Montalcino. He had eventually marched his army south into Rome at the request of Adrian, and from that moment on, the two rulers had been enemies.

After again being offended by the Pope, an ungrateful Frederick marched his army back north, all the while stoking his rage with the fires of humiliation. He brought his mighty forces directly to the walls of Milan to exact his revenge, for he found the Milanese to be as proud and disrespectful as when he last laid siege to the city a year earlier. His siege was brutal and lasted for several months. He ravaged the countryside in order to supply his forces, and he subjected the citizens to constant bombardment from his war machines that he had caused to be constructed for this special occasion. The city was sealed, and its citizens left to starve.

Barbarossa was determined to exact the greatest punitive damage. The city's stores were completely decimated, and all the great palazzos and public buildings were razed to the ground. When its population was sufficiently starved and humbled, the fear and respect of their lord was duly reinstated. Frederick occupied what was left of the city and caused to be built the great San Colombano Castle, utilizing all the material and labor from within the city walls. The sweat and blood and tears of the Milanese men and women still stain the walls and serve as a focus for the hatred of the Emperor and his descendants.

Into this castle, Frederick installed his wife, the Empress, his German commanders and courtiers, and his royal guard, where they would remain while the emperor and his army traveled across the land to enforce his imperial authority. From city to town the emperor traveled throughout the Italian countryside, rewarding his loyal subjects and punitively exacting his vengeance upon those who swore allegiance to Adrian. Long did these two tyrants do battle amongst my countrymen, causing great misery and death in their struggle for total domination.

Not all was quiet in Siena whilst Barbarossa wreaked havoc in the north and Adrian schemed in the south. The commune had been growing strong and needed to feed its appetite for more territory. There were constant struggles between the bishop, the nobles, and the state.

A short time after our return to the fair city, Giancarlo announced my betrothal to Anna. Donna Donata was ecstatic. Anna betrayed no outward sign of emotion, though I would learn that she had harbored some good feelings toward me, while I accepted my fate. I had willingly paid the price of my freedom for the promise of a future and my own fortune. Our marriage was set for the middle of March, giving plenty of time for Giancarlo and Donna Donata to plan a memorable event, and so as not to interfere with the following year's grand cycle. No expense was spared, and the wedding was the major social event of the spring season. All of Siena's elite had been invited as were a host of foreign dignitaries and business associates from near and far.

Giancarlo and I threw ourselves into the operation of the business. With Pisa's increasing superiority in the region, shipping costs were constantly being raised so it became more profitable to have the eastern goods transported directly from Venice to Marseilles by the Venetian merchant fleet. Of course, there was no love lost between the Venetians and the Pisani, and hostilities were constantly breaking out between the two, particularly within the close quarters of Constantinople, from which much of our exotic goods originated. I had learned daily how much effort Giancarlo had put into each year's operation, and I was relieved that he was still closely involved to guide me through the process. Yet, I was increasingly annoyed at the costly distractions of our wedding that took him away from very important business. I had looked at the impending matrimony as a waste of valuable time and money.

My thoughts, on those lonely nights, were not of Anna, though, but more for sweet Genevieve, seeing her face in my sordid dreams and longing for her naked body to lay beneath mine. My mind had told me that I was a fool to jeopardize everything for the temptation of happiness and a few years' worth of carnal pleasure, and yet my heart ached at the thought of a loveless marriage, and a life of deceit and commitment to a woman I could never love.

At this time, Giancarlo was negotiating with Ranieri, the Bishop of Siena, for the transfer of the deed to Stigliano, which had been held in trust by the Holy See since the death of Anna's father. As rightful heir, Anna should have inherited the castle and all buildings and fields, the villages of Torri and Brenna and the village of Sufflcille and its communal pastures and farmlands down to the River Merse. The terms stipulated that upon maturity, in the case of a male heir, or if a female, upon her marriage into a reputable family, the Bishop of Siena, or his successor, would honor the claim and transfer such holdings to the rightful beneficiary. Giancarlo was confident in the documents that Donata had brought with her to their marriage and had been waiting patiently for many years. He had planned Anna's future and had formulated his plan to claim the Soarzi stronghold in his stepdaughter's name and controlling it himself.

Negotiations with the Bishop did not go very well. Though he had never bothered to visit Stigliano since accepting it onto the church's records, the Bishop had left the castle and buildings to fall into great disrepair. And yet, he was not wont to give up anything that he had felt belonged to his diocese. Ranieri had proven to be a very mean-spirited cleric, and though he was always susceptible to an attractive bribe, he was also vindictive and harbored much resentment toward the rising merchant class. He had applauded the popes' wise decision in launching their holy crusades and welcomed all the wealth and property that was brought into the protective embrace of Mother Church. Yet, as far as he was concerned, those agreements were made between crusaders and popes who no longer walked the earth nor had a need for such worldly goods. No amount of money nor legal argument would persuade him to make good on the bequest.

Meanwhile, Adrian had continued to counter Barbarossa's aggression by scheming with several loyal northern cities to form a league to oppose imperial reign. The foundation of the alliance was foolishly built upon payments of large sums of coin, a good portion of which was borrowed from Giancarlo and other Sienese bankers. Adrian had needed a quick solution to the political situation in which he had found himself, and not being a man of high intelligence or integrity, he thought to buy his victory over the scheming emperor. Popes and kings and despotic rulers throughout history have erred in this exact logic, and time has always shown this to be an unsuccessful course of action. Though the alliance had caused the emperor some grief, Adrian was not convinced it was enough to stop him entirely, so he dispatched an ultimatum to Barbarossa, threatening him with excommunication. Barbarossa had immediately sent an emissary, which included his trusted servant, Sigmund, to Rome with a proposal of reconciliation for the pontiff.

At the same time Giancarlo had traveled to Rome and had taken his claim directly to Adrian, reminding him of the large debt that he and his Curia still owed to the bankers, warning the beleaguered Pope that future financial aid would only be assured through mutually beneficial relationships. Giancarlo was able to move the Pontiff to make a solemn promise of a swift and favorable resolution to his claim, and thus he returned to Siena satisfied with the Pope's promise. But no such orders were to come from Rome, for the Emperor's emissary had arrived in Rome just hours after Giancarlo had returned to Siena. The content of the Emperor's proposal and the meeting with the emissary has always been cloaked in mystery and secrecy, but what is known is the Pope had met with only one of the imperial contingent, and in a matter of minutes had sent him back to the Emperor with a terse and angry reply. Sigmund had accepted the Pope's answer that was to be delivered to the Emperor. Adrian was moving forward with the excommunication. This, of course, never came to be, for within two days, Adrian was dead— whether by Fate or by the hand of mortal man, none will know for sure. Alas, for Giancarlo and Anna, their prize would never come to them, though, in time, it would be won by a greater pope's most humble servant.

Much was then happening to alter the course of history, and to set the path upon which I would travel toward my own destiny. Following the death of Adrian, Orlando of Siena was elected pope and assumed the name Alexander III. The citizens of Siena were now in a very precarious position. They were most pleased that one of their own had been elected by the cardinals, but the city had pledged fealty to the Emperor and were forced to support his choice for pope, Victor IV. Barbarossa had hated Orlando ever since he, as Adrian's chancellor, had convinced the Pope to make alliance with the Norman King, William of Sicily, instead of making amends with the Holy Roman Emperor.

Several Sienese emissaries were sent to Rome with loving congratulations and apologies that the city could not pledge their total fidelity to him without breaking their oath to the Emperor. Riots and fighting continued in Rome between the two opposing forces, and Alexander was forced to take refuge in the castle of Ninfa. He quickly gathered the support of Louis of France and Henry of

England, who summoned a council of western bishops at Toulouse, declaring Alexander to be the true pope. Unfortunately for our dear Holy Father, he was to be plagued by deceit and political misdeeds of the Emperor for the rest of his glorious time upon the earth.

Tensions between the two factions spread quickly throughout Italy, which was bad for business, yet it was also very good for business. War and skirmishes throughout the land had caused many crops to be burned or looted and the cost to human life was high. Men were preached to beat their plowshares into swords and their pruning hooks into spears. There was widespread hardship from famine and pestilence, and necessities were scarce in many of the affected areas. The shortage of supplies had created higher prices, and though a master merchant such as Giancarlo would reap the reward of escalated prices, the cost to obtain supplies was also greater. The security costs needed to bring goods to market were also high, thus reducing drastically the margins that could be made. Giancarlo's attention was turned away from durable goods and redirected to items that, because of the unrest, were much more profitable in the short term. Supplying arms to every side of the conflict had proven more lucrative than the sale of perishable goods. Wool, of course, was still a premium commodity, and the finest wool from Leinster was still being brought to Bruges for fulling, to Florence for dyeing, and sold to the rich nobles and the princes of the church. The agreement with Diarmait was still in effect, and its final product was bringing great profit to Giancarlo's bank in Bruges.

Frederick was angered by Siena's apparent neutrality, viewing it as a disregard for the oath of fealty that she had pledged to him as the King of Italy before he had been elevated to Emperor. She would learn then, and later again, the cost of such disloyalty. To gain support and fealty from the Tuscan cities, Frederick then granted to loyal Pisa jurisdiction over all the Pisan countryside and granted them freedom of trade throughout his entire empire. This was still beneficial to Giancarlo and his western business as he had maintained long-lasting ties with the Pisani and looked toward them for protection with his trading missions to the north.

X

My Marriage to Anna Soarzi Manenti

Donna Donata had worked feverishly to ensure all was ready for the wedding. The palazzo was completely transformed into an exotic palace fit for a sultan. Giancarlo, instead of limiting Donata in her extravagances, as I had hoped he would, provided for her every wish. Logic had told me that he was using this event as a showcase for his possessions, all of which were for sale, for he had intended to sell most of his furnishings before he relocated to Constantinople. Our wedding was designed to be a display of Giancarlo's power and wealth.

He had invited the Abbot of Montalcino to officiate the nuptial ceremony that was to take place in the partially completed Cathedral of Santa Maria Assunta. It would be decades after our wedding before the flower of our city would come to full bloom, but in those days, the central nave and apse with its partially completed grand altar were magnificent in every detail, showing the glorious power and wealth of Siena. Giancarlo had intended to have the same promise of power and wealth showered upon the young couple whose wedding ceremony was to be the first major event held in this grand edifice.

The ceremony took place on the fifteenth day of March, the feast day of Saint Nicolo, patron saint of merchants. The massive nave was filled, not only with invited guests, but with all the citizenry of Siena. The guests had traveled from far and wide and were of every rank and order. Noblemen and women of the Manenti and Soarzi, and even the Aldobrandeschi, were in attendance, as were every member of the highest order of Siena's most illustrious families. Members of the Curia and the clergy were quick to accept an invitation when word had spread that the Abbot was to perform the ceremony. Bishop Ranieri had refused to attend, feeling slighted that Giancarlo had asked the Abbot to officiate. The Pope, himself, had sent along his blessing and a unique gift of a parchment inscribed with a mysterious prose, its obscure meaning a puzzle to me at that time. It was later that I would come to realize the importance of his gift and the meaning behind its mystery.

The cathedral was not as splendid as it is today, but Giancarlo had gifted several rare and exquisite pieces that were brought in from Constantinople—obtained, no doubt, from some of the oldest churches in the Eastern Empire, supposedly obtained legitimately from his sources in that capital city. Such wondrous treasures, accompanied by the colorful costumes of the clergy and the elite of Siena, created a grand spectacle to dazzle all who had gathered at the massive entrance to the church, waiting to catch a glimpse of the wealthy and the most holy.

I had awaited Anna and her party in the small chapel to the right of the high altar, where I knelt in prayer and asked God to forgive me for what I was about to do. I had implored Him for guidance, and I had pleaded with Him to send me a sign that I would find happiness and satisfaction with Anna, that I would be a good and faithful husband to her, and that I would be a true and loving father to my children. No such sign was to come. The Holy Spirit was silent in my hour of need.

As the time of the nuptials drew nigh, the silence of the crowd within the massive cathedral was broken by a swelling of excited whispers as Anna, veiled in the most beautiful wedding gown of silk and white lace, was escorted down the center aisle by Giancarlo and Donna Donata. A small army of ladies in attendance and beautifully dressed young children trailed behind. Instead of the usual chanting of the choir of friars and monks, Donata had insisted that traditional love songs be performed upon a triad of lutes. It was Anna's wish to be joined with her new husband wrapped in the comfort of the music that had brought us together. The church elders were against such a scandalous deviation from protocol, but Donata was not one to argue with, and with much negotiation and an open purse, an ordinary traditional matrimony was made memorable. The ceremony itself would be wrapped in the sacred hymns and chanted prayers that were expected at so solemn an occasion, and the Abbot, as officiate, would guarantee that the union would be recognized in all its sacredness.

As I peered at the massive crowd before me, I caught a glimpse of my father and my siblings seated further back toward the midsection of the nave, behind the rows of dignitaries and honored guests. Invitations had been sent to the family, of course, but until that moment, I had not expected my family to attend. I knew my father was still hurt by my life choice, and by my total disregard of his pleadings, yet I could not fully believe that he or any of my siblings would not attend my wedding. Amid the crowd and the smoke of a thousand candles, I stared directly into my father's eyes and he locked onto mine. We probed each other's mind and soul, connecting as I had never done before, and after a long and agonizing moment, he broke his stare and lowered his eyes and silently wept. I too was filled with emotion and shame, and a tear fell across my cheek. My heart felt an aching and my stomach began to churn.

I regained my composure and fixed my stare upon Anna, whose steadiness and regal beauty radiated from beneath her veil. She approached with poise and grace and was a calming influence upon my trembling and weakened body. She was a vision of beauty, for which any man in Siena would have considered himself fortunate to marry, yet there I was, trembling in fear, nauseous with doubt, and full of thoughts of another. My father had read all of that in my eyes. I wanted to scream and run away, yet I knew my fate, I knew what had to be done, and I kept telling myself that all would be well in the end. The plan was a good one. Giancarlo would keep his part of the bargain, recognizing me as his rightful heir, and I would have to keep my part by marrying Anna, extending his family and his estate. I would care for Anna, but I knew within my heart that I would never love her.

My discomfort was apparent to the Abbot, for he too had fixed his eyes upon my eyes and stilled my heart with that devilish smile that I had known so well in my youth. He too could see directly into my heart and soul and had guessed the source of my agony.

He had known the stakes for which I was gambling, and I knew in my heart that he had found great pleasure in witnessing my mental anguish.

Anna was oblivious to my plight, whether finally finding love in her heart or just finding peace in the acceptance of her fate. She would stand by my side and perform her matrimonial duties to the best of her abilities, never wavering, nor failing to be anything but the model of a loving and dutiful wife. She had to have known, even on that very first day, that her love and devotion would be a solitary enterprise, that I would not be capable of keeping my end of the bargain. Perhaps she felt, in time, a long and lasting love would grow between us like the ones she often sang about.

Our nuptials were solemnized in the company of the Abbot and all those who had stood behind us, before Jesus on the Cross, in God's Holy Church. As the Abbot placed his hands upon my head, I could only feel revulsion and a strong sense of damnation as he spoke the words for all to hear. The pounding of my heart had deafened my ears, and the weight of my guilt was suffocating. He called upon God to guide this wayward son through the perils of this evil world and to send to him the strength that would be needed to maintain his righteousness in the years to come. The ceremony completed, he bent forward and whispered into my ear, "Blessed is he who works in the name of the Lord. Be comforted, my son, for it is God's will that you will, at the time of the calling, rise to the aid of His most Holy Church. So, it has been foretold."

The wedding celebration and banquet was held within the palazzo, throughout the decorated courtyard, and within enormous, elaborately festooned tents that Giancarlo had had constructed for the event. Well over three hundred guests were in attendance, and the food and wine flowed throughout the day and the entire night. Such extravagance I had never seen before, even during the previous years' visit of the great Barbarossa. No expense was spared, and I marveled at how much money could be wasted on one event. Donata was a most gracious host, accompanying Anna and introducing her to all the guests. Giancarlo did likewise with me, introducing me to those who would be of most benefit to our enterprise, and allowing me a small amount of time to converse with my brothers and my sister, before whisking me away for further introductions. My father had become ill during the ceremony and had begged leave of his hosts to rest within the confines of my apartment. I did not know the effect my wedding had had upon my dear father until much after his death, but I took his disappearance on that day as another sign of his disapproval of my choices in life.

I did not see much of Anna throughout the celebration, for it had seemed as if we were always at opposite ends of the compound talking with different people. We did dine together, and what a sumptuous feast it was, but we were much employed with conversation, as a steady stream of guests descended upon the bridal table to congratulate us. Following the dinner, and to the delight of all the guests, Anna played upon her lute those beautiful songs that had brought tears to all the maidens' eyes. Such dolorous notes of guilt played heavily upon the strings of my own heart.

The celebration was all that Giancarlo had anticipated and more, for he had accomplished many facets of his plans within that one event. Most of the items that he had brought in for the occasion were sold; the profits from the sales would help to defray the costs of the wedding. He had established much closer bonds with many of the leaders of the city as they were forced to recognize the power and wealth that he had wielded. He had finally married his stepdaughter off to someone who would eventually control a sizable estate to the south of the city. He was able to officially introduce me as his heir, enabling me to forge ties with many of the merchants and bankers, and helping me to strengthen my position as a capable representative of my uncle. Never wasting an opportunity, Giancarlo had also used the celebration to secure several contracts for sizable future trades. Our wedding was a complete success.

The winter of 1162 was extremely mild, allowing me to commence the business cycle much earlier in the year. Four years had passed since that fateful day when I had become the husband of Anna Soarzi and the son-in-law of Giancarlo Manenti. I had worked hard and had learned much about the western operation under Giancarlo's direction, and had taken on more and more responsibility. Giancarlo had finalized his plans to move eastward and had begun shipping many of his precious belongings to his new palazzo in the Venetian Quarter of Constantinople.

Anna had delivered our first child, by the good graces of the Holy Virgin Mother, a healthy boy whom we named Vannozzo. Giancarlo and Donata were pleased that their first grandson was delivered before their departure, in ample time for them to see that Anna and the child were in good health. It was hard for Donata to leave her daughter and her precious grandson, even though she had been preparing for this move for almost two years. She had known that Giancarlo's plan was to move his operation if not permanently, at least for an extended period. She had hoped that Anna and I would begin a family and had become more than anxious when after the first year of our marriage we had not shown any sign of extending the line.

Giancarlo had spoken to me on several occasions, conveying his displeasure that I had not worked hard enough to secure an heir. He was aware of my lack of feelings for Anna, but of course, to Giancarlo, feelings were of little consequence. I had a duty to enhance the operation by producing a new lineage that would become leaders and eventually replace the royal lines of inept, inbred imbeciles who had ruled the world for far too long. I had agreed with him at every instance, assuring him that we were doing everything possible to comply with his wishes. My extended travels for long periods of time did not help the situation, but at least it was something that Giancarlo could understand. I had never, ever argued the fact that he, himself, had not produced his own issue for I had known that was the one thing that had really bothered him. In time, he was overjoyed when Anna had first confided in her mother that she was with child. Fortune and the gods had blessed our family, and the Holy Family had smiled down upon Giancarlo's household.

I should have been pleased. The pressure had been taken off my shoulders to produce an heir. The Pecci line would continue and I would raise my children in the fashion of the Taurisi to be industrious, noble, and shrewd. My issue would inherit the fortunes of the Pecci, the Soarzi, and the Manenti, and in time would become kings of commerce. Though I had begun to lay the first stone blocks in the foundation of my own dynasty, I could not rid myself of the feeling that such foundations were being built upon quicksand. I was plagued with much anxiety and troubling feelings about the future of my offspring. No longer did I need to answer Giancarlo's questions, nor soothe his concerns, for I had done that which he had commanded me to do. And yet, I still could not feel comfort. But I was satisfied there would no longer be a need for Giancarlo to probe into my personal life. I was able to do what I wanted with my life, particularly since he would be a thousand miles away, or so I had thought.

Once the child was born, I was off to Pisa and then to Florence to finalize some business for Giancarlo, and then over to Arezzo and Perugia to meet with agents whom we had hoped to enlist to handle the increased activity from the East. Giancarlo was busy as well, traveling to Rome and then across the mountains to the east coast to Ancona, Ravenna, and Venice. Most of his imports would come through Venice, but shipments to the Curia and His Holiness in Rome would generally be channeled through the other two major ports on the Adriatic. All was made ready to receive a steady stream of imports from the Eastern Empires once Giancarlo was fully established in Constantinople.

Giancarlo never pressured me to be a stay-at-home family man, for, to him, business was everything. Success demanded hard work and much travel. "A man could never hope to be successful by staying at his wife's bedside," he would say to me. For me to be as successful as Giancarlo, nay to be better than he, I needed to be where the greatest opportunity lay, whether near or far, at any time of the year. I rarely found myself resting for any length of time in any of the places I called home. For me, home was where the deals were made. My deals were my children, my enterprise was my wife, and good fortune was my mistress.

Anna had other ideas of marriage and home life, but I cared little for her thoughts. Though she was mistress of a very large household throughout her life, her melancholy grew with each passing year and each extended trip I was to make. She was dutiful to me as a wife, ever faithful to me during those long periods of absence. I often felt that she was happy with her station in life. Ours was not a loving relationship, though she would still be able to muster the passion required to produce a brood of children and fulfill her matrimonial responsibilities. I could never reconcile with her melancholia, and thus found it more beneficial to be anyplace but home.

Giancarlo's move to Constantinople commenced the first of April. Hostilities between Alexander and Barbarossa had reached new heights. The emperor refused to recognize the legitimacy of Alexander and continued to support Victor IV. Riots and fighting between the two rivals had been ongoing for two years but had escalated to the point where Alexander excommunicated Victor and declared Barbarossa anathema. Henry of England and Louis of France supported Alexander, but fighting had become so horrific in Italy that Alexander and the curia decided to move to Sens in France. The Pope and the Emperor both needed funds to continue their campaigns, and Giancarlo and I continued to make a fortune satisfying the needs of such powerful men.

It was always risky business, lending to the most powerful, for their fortune could change quickly, leaving all debts unpaid or at the least, most difficult to collect. For many years, I had to delicately work both sides of this power struggle, always seeking opportunity to increase my fortune while keeping one step ahead of the executioner. Giancarlo had realized this power struggle would eventually bring death and destruction to most of Europe. That weighed heavily on his decision to move the heart of his operation to the safety of the Eastern Empire, under the most favored status of the Venetian banner and under the protection of the Byzantine emperor, Manuel I Comnenus. Alexander had already been formulating a deal with Comnenus to reunite the Eastern and the Western Churches under Alexander as pope over all of Christendom, in exchange for the Byzantine emperor being crowned Holy Roman emperor over both the West and the East.

Giancarlo had held much hope for this political deal and wanted to advance his opportunities with the Byzantine court. I was left to handle the Western operation and to advance our dealings with His Holiness and the Curia in France. We continued to foster good relations with Barbarossa and the Hanseatic League through our trading enterprises throughout the Grand Cycle. It had become easier for me to deal with the Curia since their move to France, making it unnecessary to travel to Rome except for certain business ventures that would develop with the Jewish merchants in the ghetto of that troubled city.

This had become a very dangerous time to travel over land, especially with large shipments of merchandise. Giancarlo was wise to broaden his relationship with the Venetians, whose massive merchant fleet had allowed them to rule the waves and afforded those merchants within their good graces a safer means of transportation and delivery of goods. Transportation costs had increased dramatically because of the wars, but even still, Giancarlo had managed to increase his profits with each passing year as he opened new trade routes and developed opportunities in the Levant, Egypt, Sicily, and the kingdom of Naples. He even managed to make some very profitable deals by signing a commercial treaty with the Muslim Almohad rulers of Northern Africa and Spain that ensured safe passage throughout all the lands surrounding the Mediterranean. This was a major coup and a tremendous benefit for our business as William, the mad King of Sicily, had lost his final foothold in Africa to the Almohad and had been driven from those Muslim lands.

XI

Giancarlo's Move East—My Golden Opportunity

It was early spring when the last dozen wagons were filled with the most prized and familiar pieces that Giancarlo had kept specifically for the comfort of Donata, hoping to ease the pain of being transplanted a thousand miles away from her home and her family. I had decided to accompany them to Venice and to see them off on their journey from Italy. Anna, with the child, was forced to tearfully bid farewell to her parents within the safety of the fortressed walls of Siena, for such a trip was deemed too dangerous while the hostilities continued between the Pope and Barbarossa.

We moved east through the Val d'Chiana and stopped briefly at my father's estates in Cortona, to pay my respects and to see my family. Giancarlo had insisted on bidding my father a final farewell. My father was pleased to see me and was grateful for the news of the arrival of his first grandson. He had attended our wedding four years earlier but was much pained at the loss of my loving mother, as well as the apparent loss of his firstborn son. He had appeared a broken man to me, and as the heartless son I had become, I showed little compassion for the man who had given me everything. I had refused to acknowledge then, how much I had truly hurt my father, and it would be too many years before I could finally accept my blame and beg his posthumous forgiveness. I can still see the love he had in his heart and the tears he held in his eyes on that passing day. That vision was seared onto my brain. I bid my father farewell and good fortune. It was such an inadequate parting, for I would never see this man again upon the earth.

Giancarlo and I were to spend several weeks in Venice, strengthening his contacts and working with his agents there. Accounts had been settled and the bulk of Giancarlo's fortune had been forwarded to his banks in Venice and to the imperial Byzantine city. The remainder had been kept in Siena or redistributed to money centers in Europe. Such distribution of wealth, deposited in various branches of his personal bank, enabled us to trade throughout Europe without the need to carry a large supply of coin. We Italian bankers had developed a system through which certain letters of credit would be exchanged between agents and banks in important trade centers throughout the empires.

I marveled then, as I continue to do so over these many years, at the ingenuity of these titans of trade. Such a system has enabled the good merchant to expand his sphere of trade with less fear of loss to thieves and scoundrels who always prey upon a careless traveler. Though I was young, not quite reaching my twenty-eighth year, Giancarlo had shared with me all the wisdom that he had accumulated throughout his life. He had also graced me with his love and his trust as a true son and had introduced me as such to all his associates. This had made for an easy transition as Giancarlo had planned his exit from the European theater. By the time he was set to make his move eastward, I had, with his guiding presence, been brought into close proximity of kings and queens, noble men and ladies, princes of the Church, and the Holy Father and his Curia, as well as the common merchant and the most disreputable Jewish moneylenders, many of whom were to become my closest acquaintances and mentors in the darker arts.

We arrived in Venice before St. Mark's Day toward mid-April, having enough time to finalize plans before sailing east upon one of the Doge's swiftest and most luxurious sailing vessels. Giancarlo had planned to arrive in Constantinople by the end of May, sometime after Pentecost. His entry into the Imperial City was meant to make a grand statement. He wanted to make certain that the upper levels of merchant society in that great city were aware of his change of venue and to claim his rightful position within the Venetian Quarter of the Golden Horn.

Venice

One can never forget one's first lover nor forget one's first kill. Nor can any who have traveled to the Republic upon the sea ever forget the brilliance, the majesty, the combined wonder and awe upon the first sighting of Venice in all her golden glory. Lit ablaze by the setting sun, she floats miraculously upon a green lagoon of a million sparkling jewels. She is a city like no other, although the Venice of my youth was much more rural than today's grand magnificence. Such an incredible transformation, which has been accomplished in little more than half a century, has made her the most magnificent city upon God's earth. In her newness she outshines the majestic Imperial City of Constantinople, and the eternal city of Rome, for those cities of antiquity have reached their zenith and are fading into licentiousness and decadence.

Though I have traveled to this mighty city many times throughout my life and have watched her mature into the magnificence she is today, I still can recall the thrill and the wonder in which I first held her simple beauty. As our vessel approached the lagoon, we sailed past hundreds of tiny islands, none of which were, or have been hence, habitable by man or beast. The islands, mudflats, farms, and pastures, separated by canal and river, form together, as a million pieces of stone and gem come together to make a glorious mosaic.

As our ship entered the mouth of the Grand Canal—the Rivoalto, as the Venetians call it—each side of the canal was crowded with merchant ships of all sizes. The banks were fitted with docks for berthing, loading, and unloading. Densely packed ancient shacks and modern low-rising buildings and warehouses were crammed into every available space, incredibly built upon island and wooden pier. My first impression was that all of this rested upon some ancient forest whose grand tree trunks rose magically out of the waves, each building haphazardly dropped upon the branches over the course of half a millennium. There was no bridge spanning the Canal as there is today, yet the tremendous amount of activity was not confined to one side or the other. Barges and ferries continuously crossed the waters, moving goods from ship to dock, as men moved the goods from dock to warehouse. I can recall clearly the sound of the merchants and dealers arguing their price of goods. I was fascinated at the sight of every such marvel.

Giancarlo had been to Venice many times in the past. He loved the city and was proud to share the experience with his wife and his adopted son. It was a gift he gave to each of us, a gift to Donata to help ease the pain of leaving her home, and a gift to me for staying true to his plan. It helped to convince me that his was the true path to achieve my destiny. By asking me to join him on this leg of the journey he was showing me there was more in the world to strive for than just the local markets in central Europe. The world was so much bigger than that. The prize was so much greater. If I worked hard enough, the reward would be greater than any I could ever imagine.

As we approached the quay, the warehouses became grander and much better organized. It had become clear to me that Giancarlo had built strong relationships with some very wealthy and powerful people in Venice, which allowed our ship the most prestigious docking privileges in the most favored section of the canal. The Ducal Palace and the Duomo of San Marco are situated on a separate islet; the enormity of these two buildings covers all the available land mass and extends a short distance from the Quay.

Our ship glided effortlessly to the pier and was secured by a handful of dockworkers. A man of senior years but of solid stock and appearance was waiting in the loggia of the Ducal Palace as we disembarked from the ship. As we approached, he threw his arms wide and embraced Giancarlo, raising him from the ground and spinning him around as effortlessly as one would twirl a child. His mannerism was overly cordial, and his greeting was more than genuine. His name was Enrico Dandolo. He was a very successful merchant in Venice, with far-reaching ties and enterprises. His influence was felt in Britain, throughout Europe, in Asia, and even to the far kingdoms in the Orient. His father, Vitale Dandolo, was a trusted advisor and jurist in the court of Doge Vitale II Michiel, and he was a prominent citizen of the Republic. His uncle, also named Enrico, was Patriarch of Grado and Primate of Dalmatia, making him, next to the Doge, the most powerful man in Venice. Though the family could never boast of an ancient or noble lineage, the successes and defeats of the clan over a span of several generations had propelled this family from relative obscurity to preeminent dominance in the Republic. Such it was that empires were built in a very short time in this land of opportunity.

I can easily recall my first meeting with the younger Enrico, who was many years my senior and considered by most to be an older gentleman in his sixties. Few could tell with certainty his exact age, for he was strong in stature and keen of wit. His father and his uncle were both ancient in years, yet still quite virile and active, not showing any degradation from time, and like his kin, there was no hint of feebleness, which oft' times steals into a person's countenance as he approaches the elder years. The only betrayal of his age was his long, flowing, white hair, a full, thick mane that framed his ageless face and highlighted his icy blue eyes. He had already become renowned in Venice and in the East owing to his service to the state, along with his father and uncle in the earlier crusades, where he earned the praise and confidence of the Doge and the courts of the Greek Emperor. He was of admirable quality and had been a model upon which Giancarlo had obviously fashioned his own countenance and career. His charm and stoic demeanor had enabled him to work behind the scenes, in the shadow world, allowing him to become extremely useful to the ducal court. There was no wonder why Giancarlo had endeared himself to such a preeminent citizen, whose trust and abilities would prove most beneficial to both parties. It was this charm and demeanor that instantly won my admiration and friendship—a friendship that was to last for many years.

Enrico had greeted both Donna Donata and me warmly, yet retained a sense of formality and propriety, which in an instant, had caused us to feel like we had always known him. He casually instructed his servants to gather up our belongings while he escorted us to his father's grand palazzo, which had been built directly upon the Rialto. The palazzo and the surrounding commercial buildings sat within the northern half of an immense compound, which encompassed the entire parish of San Luca and looked across the Rialto toward the magnificent palace of his uncle, the Patriarch of Grado. The southern half of the compound, beyond the church of San Luca, was owned by his other uncle, Pietro, who was at that time rebuilding his own palazzo.

Vitale Dandolo's palazzo was a magnificent edifice that spoke of power and might, yet its interior apartments maintained a sense of warmth and comfort and prudence expected from a man of business. The Patriarch's Palace, on the other hand, was far more sumptuous, being embellished with the most exquisite adornments, the finest marbles, windows of colored glass, and furnished with the most expensive examples of earthly luxury. It stood in stark contrast to the Patriarch's lifelong mission of reformation of the Church from its decadence and sins and was built to emphasize the power and might of the Church to stand against the state and the empire with unquestionable authority over the souls of all mankind. This palace was the envy of most kings throughout the land, and just as the authority over the Venetian Republic emanated from the Ducal Palace, so was the Patriarch's Palace the center of Church authority in the north.

We were hosted by the Dandolo for a period of two weeks, in which time I met Enrico's father, Vitale, and the doge himself, Vitale II Michiel. I was also to meet on several occasions Enrico's uncle, the Patriarch of Grado. Upon our first introduction, the elder Enrico had taken an instant interest in me and had spent much time questioning me about my family, my life, and my visions of the future. At that time, I found this strange and did not comprehend the Patriarch's interest, but I was very comfortable talking with the elder gentleman, and over the course of the two weeks, I was asked to visit him several times. Giancarlo had encouraged this apparent friendship, for such ties to the Patriarch would surely be a benefit when conducting business in the Eastern Empire.

I was, at first, suspicious of the Patriarch's attention for I was aware of the cost of such interest and friendship. Praise be to God that the Patriarch's motives were not of a physical nature, but rather were more devious and of a mental and spiritual nature, one of which I was not aware, nor fully able to comprehend. In time I would come to know the full intent and the mission of this holy man, and the role that Destiny had laid out for me. The drama of which I was to be a part would involve the most powerful men on earth and inevitably alter the entire course of my life.

During my stay with Enrico, I was introduced to all the wealthiest merchants in Venice and many of their associates. Several days before

Giancarlo was to leave for Constantinople, our host had arranged a dinner and had invited many of these merchants as well as other agents with whom Enrico was doing business in Europe and in the East. He had wanted to make sure that Giancarlo and Donata had been given a proper send-off, and it was at this dinner that Giancarlo worked most diligently in securing ties and contracts with the merchants of Venice, which would increase his standing in his relocated operation in the Venetian Quarter of the Imperial City.

During this event, Enrico introduced me to a young associate from Assisi who had represented him in many of the markets in Italy and France. To my surprise, it was none other than Pietro Bernardone, the same Pietro whom I had met in Paris, and who had rescued me from certain death at the hands of King Louis' stablemen. Though I was less than pleased to see him, for I was fearful the real purpose of my beating in Paris would be brought to light, I was glad for the opportunity to thank him for his assistance on that dreadful night. I had pretended not to know the young merchant, and to my surprise, he had played along with the ruse. During the evening we were able to talk at length together, and in a short span of time developed a kinship for one another. I was able to meet with Pietro on several occasions on the days prior to our departure and, as he was returning to Assisi about the same time I was leaving for Siena, we decided to travel back to Tuscany in each other's company.

The day of Giancarlo's departure was both a joyous and a solemn occasion. I was saddened to see both Donna Donata and Giancarlo leaving for the East, knowing full well that this parting could possibly have been the last time I would see either of them. My respect and affection for Donna Donata had grown strong since our first meeting, and I knew that this move, particularly leaving her home and her daughter and grandson, was harder than anything she had had to endure in her life. Even the death of her first husband, Provanzano Soarzi, was not as traumatic, for at that time she was but a child married to an old, abusive nobleman, whose death was seen more as salvation than tragedy. She had become like a mother to me, and I would sorely miss her comforting and affectionate company.

Giancarlo's counsel and guidance, I would miss, though it would not be absent, even as we were to be separated by land and sea. In truth, I was not going to miss his prying eyes, constantly looking over my shoulder into my private life. I was joyful to have fully gained his trust and respect, so much so that he was entrusting me to handle his entire western operation, yet he would never quite relinquish ultimate authority, for I would be in constant contact with my master through correspondence on a regular basis. Letters of credit and tallies would be exchanged weekly, sent on the swiftest Venetian ships, and my letters containing details of transactions or contracts would, in time be answered with instructions or advice from Giancarlo. Of course, the total response time could take weeks or months, but in time, Giancarlo came to rely more heavily on my judgment and maturing business acumen.

We had spent the entire day before this final sailing going over all the business needed to be attended to during the remainder of the year. The responsibility of a large financial empire was being placed in my hands. I still marvel at the courage and trust of Giancarlo, not unlike that of the great emperor Constantine who brought the entire Roman Empire to Constantinople and placed the western part of the empire, for safekeeping and administration, in the hands of Saint Sylvester. I was brash enough in my youth to think that if such a plan could work for the great Constantine, it could work for the great Giancarlo Manenti as well. I had no idea when or if I would ever see this great man and wonderful woman again, and our farewell was, I must admit, quite emotional. I had come to honor and respect this man, even more than my dear father, and our closeness bespoke of the mutual admiration that we had for each other.

As Giancarlo's galleon disappeared over the horizon, I prepared to set sail toward my own destiny. Both Enrico the younger and the Patriarch had come to the piazzetta to see Giancarlo off, the latter bestowing God's blessing upon Giancarlo and his growing enterprise. Surprised and honored was I that the Patriarch had taken the time to speak with me personally, and to bestow upon me his blessing and wish for much success. He had spoken to me with great kindness and with much encouragement, and most strangely he spoke to me of a prophesy, which has been forever etched upon my brain.

A seer's son from hidden realm
Will break the yoke and turn the tide,
Save church and state and heal divide
And in the end, assume the helm.
The soulless man will find no peace
But gain for all a hidden prize,
A gift to counter evil lies
The tyrant's war is forced to cease.
Tormented soul, a son cast out,
To bring the sons of Noah down,
Delivers those who left unfound,
A son to make the clerics doubt.

Though, at that time, I had no indication of the meaning of the verse, I could sense the importance of its content to the Patriarch. I was puzzled as to why he would recite them to me, yet there was a kindness and gentleness to this man, and his words were not threatening, for they had seemed familiar to me. They had touched a chord in my heart in the same way in which the Holy Spirit was able to lift my soul and comfort me in my blackest of dreams and visions. He then bid me farewell and a safe journey and assured me we would soon meet again. He then cautioned me to, "Heed well the calling, for a time will come soon enough, when your destiny will steer you back to Venice and to the world beyond, to perform a great service for God and His Holy Church."

Young Enrico too had indicated to me that we would be meeting again soon, though, in his case, I was more inclined to accept that as a matter of fact, for he was to be the middleman between me in the West and Giancarlo in the East. I would come to rely upon the good graces of the Dandolo for many years and would make every effort to see Enrico whenever Fate had blessed me with opportunity.

Pietro, as an associate of Dandolo and Company, had managed to secure cargo space on the same vessel provided to me by Enrico. We set sail for Ancona early on the morning tide following Giancarlo's departure and arrived at that port city within three days' time. My caravan and security force were awaiting us at the dock. Pietro, not being as well prepared, had to hire a few wagons and a small security force, in the port city, at ridiculously high wages, which cut into his profits from the trip. I was to learn as time went on that such unpreparedness was more habit than chance for him. His lack of planning would forever be a hindrance to his realizing his full potential in the business world. Fortune was in the habit of handing good Pietro much in this life, and he was always wont to slap her hand in return. I have often reflected in disbelief how well Pietro had done for himself. He always had the knack of sniffing out the prize truffle from beneath a pile of horse dung, as well as always hitching his own wagon to a more prosperous man's steed. This I learned quite early in our relationship, but I will always say that the man was loyal, despite his faults, and I was very fond of him in our early days.

Our convoy was brought safely back to Assisi without incident and I had decided to stop again at Cortona. My emotional farewell with Giancarlo had made me shameful for the treatment and disrespect I had displayed toward my father over the years, and I was determined to see him again to make matters right between the two of us. I had much time on my journey back from Venice to reflect upon my selfish behavior and the hurt which I had inflicted upon this good and honest man. I knew in my heart that if ever I was to grow as a decent and honorable man, I would have to face my inner demons and their true source and vanquish them. I needed to address the damage that the devils had caused and seek redemption through forgiveness and understanding. The wounds that had festered between my father and myself would have to be healed if I was to hope for salvation in this world or in the next.

XII

The Passing and The Awakening of a Pec-ii

On the outskirts of Cortona, we were met by Sebastiano and Salvatore. The two had been in Siena looking for me a few days earlier and had decided to come to Ancona to meet me. I was happy to see them and asked them of news from Curtun, for I had sorely missed my people since leaving there. They were more somber than usual, even though I had chattered on without catching a breath. I had thought it fortunate that we should meet so close to my father's farm and had confessed to them my shame and my desire to make amends with my father. The two quietly listened to my confession and my wish for salvation, and when I had finished, Sebastiano looked at Salvatore with tears in his eyes, and proceeded to tell me of the death of my father. The news cut me like a dagger.

They told me that whilst visiting him some days before, my father, seemingly in good spirits and health, had as if by cursed spell, fallen victim to such an evil malady that no remedy seemed to cure. Neither the priests with their babbling prayers nor the medicine woman whom the priests had eyed superstitiously as a witch could bring him peace or cure. Salvatore had traveled swiftly to Curtun to fetch the most skilled healer, but so swift and potent was my father's malady that he had passed before they could return. Sebastiano set out for Siena to retrieve me only to learn of my scheduled return from Anna. He then returned to Cortona in time to see my father's body laid out in the chapel, which stands beside the burial grounds. The body was wrapped for internment in the Christian cemetery, but my cousins reminded my brothers of his final wishes and convinced them that my father would be most welcomed with his ancestors under the hallowed hills of Curtun. In that fair kingdom, Uni-Tau, son of Tarxin the pec-ii, seer of the hidden realm, would be laid to rest with great ceremony and the respect afforded to the scion of the great Zil-at, Tarquinius.

My heart was broken asunder. The opportunity to make amends had been robbed from me. Never would I have the chance to tell my father how wrong and how sorry I was for not seeing the true worth of the man. I had been given that chance on my last visit with him but had squandered it away with my stubbornness and pride.

Sebastiano, Salvatore, and I traveled north into the hills, and after several days' journey we arrived at the waterfalls that concealed the entrance to the hidden realm. We were met by Tarquin and Tarquinia, and I sobbed bitterly in that regal lady's arms. Never again would I cry such anguished tears, for never will a greater prize be lost. I was brought to my father's crypt and again I wept. My tears gushed forth in endless streams, diluted with self-pity and loathing, so that no gentle hand nor comforting word could bring me peace. My father had been honored and respected by all who knew him. He was a giant among men, and rich beyond my wildest imagination. Yet I was too stupid and too blind to see. Ah, how ironic that the seer's son was so blind.

I was taken immediately to the sacred necropolis, within whose chambers were buried the most noble of the Taurisi. There was the resting place of my father, Uni-Tau, and his father, Tarxin, both pec-ii from a long line of seers. I was led down the great dromos, whose elaborate portal faced southwest toward the underworld, deep within the bowels of the earth. We moved in slow procession until we came upon the grand chamber, at the center of which rose a high dais upon which the sarcophagus of Crano had been placed. The chamber was circular and enormous in size. It had a domed ceiling with an oculus at its center, much like the dome that graces the mighty Pantheon in Rome. A single solitary shaft of light spilled through the oculus and bathed the ancient tomb in light. The walls contained hundreds of small antechambers that held the remains of so many great men and women. The dromos spread out in several directions, descending deeper into the earth. In one elaborately decorated chamber, I was brought to the final resting place of Uni-Tau. I stood before his body, flanked by Salvatore and Sebastiano, and together we wept. At my father's feet was a leather satchel, upon which, in his own hand, was written my name. Sebastiano whispered to me.

"Your father lay sick with fever for several days, at times speaking in riddles and oft times in a strange tongue. He would scream out dire warnings, and at times he would claw at his eyes as if to wrench them from their sockets and to rid his head of such horrific visions. He spoke of many places, some known to us and some not. He spoke of kings and beggars, and many times he reached out and called your name. His feverish ramblings made no sense to our mortal ears; his visions of Hell and his lamenting over tortured and rotting corpses brought anguish and dread. His grieving children had prayed to God to send His angels to mercifully end their father's agony. His fits consumed him day and night. After the second day of such torture, Salvatore lost patience with the useless mumblings of the parish priest and he rode with great haste to Curtun to fetch our greatest healer, Zarander, hoping that his healing skills would be strong enough to cure the evil that had been visited upon your father. Alas, his great skills were for not, for the two arrived back at the farm after your father had passed."

I sobbed as I heard this.

"But prior to his passing, your father had become serenely calm as if Death had finally taken him. Moments later, he suddenly opened his eyes and sat up upon his bed. He had asked me to fetch a quill and parchment so that he might leave for you a warning that was born out of his visions. He had seen his own death and had known that too late would you be standing before his dead body. He knew that he would not be able to touch you or to speak directly to you of his vision, and thus, he endeavored to transcribe the horrors that he had witnessed while captive in the spirit world. When finished, he handed me the parchment and asked me to secure it in the leather satchel, upon which he had written your name.

"He then held me in his arms and kissed my forehead, beseeching me to look after you, for he had seen your peril. He told me you were on a long and dangerous path and would need protection and guidance, for Satan had laid many traps along your road so as to rob you of your mortal soul. I pledged to him, whom I have loved as a brother, that Salvatore and I would look after you. He then blessed me with the peace of a man who had seen his end and knew full well of his next destination.

"He had called upon his children to gather close to him, and he implored each of them to trust in you, Giovanni, for he had foreseen your rise to greatness, and that you would become a benefactor to each of them. All his possessions he has left in your trusting hands to administer fairly and wisely for your siblings and their issue. His wish was to return to Curtun and to sleep beneath the forested hills of the Taurisi. He begged us not to weep for him, for he had seen a better life for himself, welcomed by his ancestors and embraced by the God's heavenly light. At the cock's first crow on the following day, he gasped his last breath and crossed over into the spirit world of our ancestors and his God. He now lays in eternal slumber amongst the people whom he has always loved."

When he had finished his tale, we stood in silence. I took the satchel, felt it with my hands and smelled it deeply, hoping as if some magic would bring my father back to life. I was envious of my cousins and my siblings for having the opportunity to see my father for one last time. I cried for not enjoying his final embrace and his parting kiss upon my brow. My heart ached for what I had missed. Through tears and with the light of the torches, I read the parchment.

Take care, my son, for the path you have fixed your foot upon is paved with promise and deceit.
Satan, in his cunning, has laid traps in which he hopes to snare your soul, and make it his prize.
That which you seek shall forever be beyond your reach.
Beware the light that guides you, for it does not always shine upon the true path.
The seer's son is blind to his own heart, and the malady of his soul shall be his undoing.
Though he shall rise to greatness and stand amongst kings and popes alike, and deliver them from evil, he shall imprison himself within his own guilted cage.

Savior of kingdoms, and the destroyer of worlds, father of demons and angels, of sinners and saints – this he shall be.

The Taur shall be betrayed by one of its own and cast into the flames of oblivion.

Plowshares shall be beat into sword and pike, and the world will run red with the blood of the innocents.

The Blessed Children of Noah shall make their final stand but are doomed to fall.

Take care! For the hands that hold the sacred seeds shall be covered in the sacred blood.

The hills shall be lit ablaze, and her sons and daughters will roast upon a spit.

Evil shall triumph, and our world will cease to be, for Cross and Scepter shall beat them into the ground.

Swift shall be the eagle for the shepherd shall prove false.

The demon unleashed by the father shall be devoured by the eagle, but the ancient line shall be broken, never to be mended.

None shall weep for the loss of innocence; the fate of our people shall be forgotten.

Though the ark shall survive, the fruit of Noah shall wither upon the vine.

The hundred shall be delivered safely but shall be swallowed by the earth.

Roots remain strong beneath the earth and shall stretch far, yet the vines shall cease to bear fruit.

The fires of Vol-tuma shall once again be rekindled by the calming waters of the Merse, but no good shall come from it.

The earth shall be opened anew amid the ancients who slumber in deep and hallowed halls, and a mighty fortress shall be built upon broken walls, yet children shall not remember the fathers.

The seer's son must regain his sight in order to lead his people to salvation. A promise shall be broken.

All is not lost, but salvation is never gained, if temptation leads the way.

Thy course is not fixed and may be altered with each step taken upon a treacherous path.
Beware, my son, for buried deep within your soul is the charted course to your salvation.
Seek for it and bring it into the light so that you may be guided on the true path.
Know always that I loved you.

I said my final farewell, hoping that his soul still lingered within his body to see my anguish. I took the leather satchel and the parchment and have kept both with me, even until this day. Alas that I did not heed his warning, for too late was I to understand its meaning. Too much damage has been caused by my unwillingness to follow his advice. Father, forgive me, for the seer has regained his sight too late, and his punishment will be to spend an eternity in Purgatory reliving the destruction that was of his own making.

I returned to Siena to my wife and child, having first stopped in Cortona to comfort my siblings and to see that the operation of Father's farm would continue smoothly, and thus I began my life as master of trade. My elevated status as Giancarlo's western partner brought with it much respect for a man of my tender age. With such a position came responsibility and expectations of proficiency and clear-sightedness. I was constantly being measured up against my master, and to many I was not shrewd enough, nor clever enough, nor aggressive enough, nor dangerous enough to play in Giancarlo's arena. It did not take long for many of them to realize just how wrong they were. Giancarlo had taught me well, and my youthful appearance was never a hindrance to me, but rather a disguise with which I was able to lure many an unsuspecting, overstuffed pigeon into my trap.

For two years I worked hard to keep up the pace of Giancarlo's hectic Grand Cycle and discovered what a monumental task it had been for Giancarlo to pull everything together for so many years. I allowed Pietro to accompany me on many trips, and charged him a fair price for protection, transport, and duty fees, which helped defray some of the costs of the trip. Sebastiano and Salvatore arranged for a small company of mountain men, fully trained and trustworthy, to complement my own security force, and on each of the trips, and when not in the service of Curtun, either one or both of my protective cousins would accompany me on various stages of my journey.

It was during this time that I met a young street urchin by the name of Galgano Guidotti from the village of Chiusdino near Siena. His tall, muscular physique had masked his young age; his ability as a streetfighter had misled me to think him much older than his sixteen years. I had happened upon him on the road leading from Siena toward Montepulciano, a section of road that had been plagued, at that time, with villains and thieves. This young Galgano had been set upon by a small band of ruffians and, though greatly outnumbered, had managed to hold his ground. Skillfully and quite lethally he was able to dispatch several of his assailants with his dagger and a short sword. His combat skills were crude but effective, a sight to behold as we approached the melee. I was wont to sit back upon my horse and watch the young assassin perform his deadly dance, but for the fact that another group of thieves had joined into the attack from a nearby thicket. Not only did they outnumber the lad but threatened our own security. I quickly released two of my security guards to assist him, and the remaining swarm was quickly eliminated.

Grateful for my intervention, the youth joined us along the road and eventually came back to Siena with us, remaining a loyal and effective member of my security team for several years, and many journeys. His temper ran hot, yet his devotion to me never quivered. Many times, did I find myself having to pull his sorry hide from the fire, for in his tenacity he would always find himself at the wrong end of an outmatched fight. Yet his fierceness and his courage and his fighting skill proved to be of great value to me and to my business. Next to Sebastiano and Salvatore, Galgano had become my best and most loyal friend, one I had grown to love as a young and stubborn brother.

For the first several years of my stewardship of the western operation, we were able to make a steady profit, admittedly not as great as when Giancarlo was running the business, but still a very impressive result from the transition period. Giancarlo was kept informed of every event and was fully supportive of my decisions to increase security and the associated costs, for he had been kept well informed of the political unrest and the violence that was overtaking the land. With each correspondence, he would end by counseling me to be vigilant of traps and opportunities, and cautious in all undertakings, for the world was an evil place, and those who harbor evil thoughts and desires to take whatever they may from an honest man were multiplying with every passing day. So true were his words, for I have seen with my own eyes over these past many years how the good souls are being dispatched off to Heaven in great numbers while the scoundrel and thief remains to ravage God's good earth.

As time passed, and I managed to navigate quite successfully the waters of commerce, a new obstacle was placed upon my charted course, one of which I had been unprepared to handle. Oh, Satan is devious in his trapping and oft times uses that which is most desirous, like the Sirenes, to lure a weakened soul to his certain death. So, it had happened to me during the third year of my stewardship of Giancarlo's business. The memory is fresh upon my mind since being visited by my sweet Genevieve, and lest I forget entirely, I wish to record the details of my most grievous sin.

Alexander and his curia were still residing in Sens under the protection of Louis, and having grown homesick for his native Siena, had commissioned a special consignment of wine and foodstuff from home. He had written me specifically at the end of the previous year to place his order for delivery in the early spring as soon as the wines had been barreled and aged and the meats and cheeses had been properly prepared in the traditional Sienese way. I had planned to take the local goods directly to Marseilles and had arranged for Pietro to accept a large shipment of cloth that was being finished in Florence, and to meet me in Marseilles. Satan had begun to set his trap by delaying the wool from being processed.

The delay kept Pietro in Florence for over a week, and I, being impatient to satisfy my most important client, decided to send my shipment up the Rhone with Philippe and his crew and most of my security guard. Galgano remained with me and would join Pietro and me and the remainder of my guard once the second shipment arrived in Marseilles. Of course, I had to pay extra duty fees along the way for an additional shipment, but because the merchandise was being brought on special order from the Pope, I was able to negotiate the fees in half. I hoped, with a smaller and lighter convoy, I could bridge the gap and meet up with the original convoy within a few days of their arrival in Lyons. It was a bad decision. Giancarlo never would have made such a decision. But the devil's snare had already been set. All he had needed was the bait.

As I waited impatiently for Pietro to arrive, I happened upon my sweet Genevieve in the marketplace. Unfortunately, the old embers began to heat, and it was not long before our smoldering passions ignited. We found ourselves captive to our denied lust, powerless to the commands of our carnal desires. We spent the night in sin, O Glorious sin! We enjoyed each other's bodies until we were spent, our minds shrouded to everything but the pleasure we were experiencing at that moment. All else meant nothing. Satan is so devious in the construction of his traps. Just as we use honey to attract the fly, so does Satan use the sweetness of the flesh to gain possession of our souls.

In the darkness of early morning, before the pale sun lightened the night sky, I had roused myself from a satisfied slumber, and with recovered logic and a strong sense of guilt, I stole myself away and slipped into the darkness. With all speed, I gathered my belongings, and after leaving instructions for Pietro to join us in Lyon with Philippe's son, I, along with Galgano, secured two horses and rode swiftly north. No one dared question the orders of the Master. They just assumed my plans had changed for good reason.

Pietro and the remainder of the ill-fated crew eventually caught up with us in Lyon. They had been set upon by a band of thieves with intent to rob and murder the entire crew, but the gang's plan was thwarted. Several of the crew members were killed but a good amount of my cloth was saved. It was then that I learned of Genevieve's death. Surprisingly to all, she had been enlisted to make that fateful run with Pietro. I was devastated to hear of her death but was cautious not to show such emotions to Henri, who grieved for his lost sister most heartedly. Galgano could only stare at me, icily, for he knew the hurt that was upon my heart, and he held his disappointment of me deep within his own heart. Pietro was bruised quite badly from his injuries, and his shoulder, which had been broken by a tossed boulder, was tied with bandages and not operable. He would eventually recover from his injuries, but his shoulder would never regain full strength or use, even until his death.

I sank into a depression and was wracked with guilt. My countenance became dark and stormy. The crew had assumed my foul mood was caused by my ill fortune and the increased costs of the trip and began to feel uneasy and even mutinous. The men were saying that their bad luck was a result of Giancarlo leaving them at the mercy of an inexperienced boy. I was too withdrawn into myself to react to such insolence and let matters get too far out of hand. Henri pushed the crew harder and harder, making very good time, and hoped that their industriousness would quench the fires of discontent. Its outcome was just the opposite.

Halfway up the Soane at Chalon-sur-Soane, violence finally erupted. Two of the crew members became drunk and belligerent, but their pathetic attempt to mutiny was quickly put down by my security guards. Their villainous actions caused me to regain my wits and authority. Though the guards were wont to slice the mutineers' throats, Henri's pleading for their lives caused me to show them mercy, so I ordered them to be beaten soundly and left upon the banks of the river in the hands of the Fates.

We pushed on further and harder until we caught up with Philippe and the first crew on the River Aube. It was not a joyous reunion, for when Philippe had learned of Genevieve's murder, he was inconsolable. Although he was quite aware of the dangers of navigating the French waterways, he was furious that his daughter should die in such a treacherous way and was angered still that such ill fortune had plagued this trip. Though he was a man of honor and duty, never one to question his superior's decisions or motives, he was also a loving father and wise enough in life and in the behavior of those whom he loved to suspect there to be some other motive behind this tragedy. Though he would remain loyal to me through the many years that he was in my employ, there was always an unmentioned suspicion between us that prevented me from truly and totally trusting him.

We made it to Bar-sur-Aube with days to spare for the Entrée. The fair was marginally profitable, but it allowed me the opportunity to hone my skills in the money-changing arena. I used the skill and tricks that my uncle had taught me and was able, by the end of the fair, to parlay my meager profits from the sale of goods into a much better return. I was also able to collect some of the debts that had been incurred in the previous year, and of course to send a full accounting of the first leg of the cycle to Giancarlo. I knew that he would not be happy with the losses that we had suffered, but I was sure that he would be pleased I was able to turn adversity into profit.

We moved on to the May Fair in Provins, but after the first week of selling, I left Pietro to handle the rest of the business of the fair. Loading three wagons with the Pope's merchandise, Galgano and I and three of my most trusted men left for Sens. When we arrived, we were invited to stay in the palace of the archbishop of Sens, William of Blois, known by many as William the White Hands. He was the brother-in-law of King Louis, and the favored uncle of the future king of France, Philip.

We were met by the archdeacon, Walter of Chatillon. He was most gracious to offer us lodging for the night before our return to Provins. I remember him to be young for such a prestigious position, and quite good-looking, and he seemed extremely congenial and most inquisitive toward me. He was disarmingly intimate in our conversations, and with not much effort he learned of my rising social status through my relationship with Giancarlo and our association with the Dandolo of Venice.

After our discussion and being provided refreshment, Archdeacon Walter came back to me and informed me that His Holiness Alexander had wished to enter conversation with me and would allow me an audience. I was most honored to be summoned by His Holiness, and though he had personally placed his orders with me, I had never expected such an audience. I thus assumed that he must have want of news from Siena. Galgano insisted on accompanying me to the audience and posted himself before the doors of the great hall. Instead of being presented to His Holiness in the massive audience hall of the palace, I was secreted into a solitary chamber, in which the Pontiff, in simple white vestments, was kneeling in prayer before a small golden crucifix in his private chapel. I stood motionless and in silence until the Pontiff finished his prayers and rose from his kneeler.

Such an intimate scene was most familiar to me and most disquieting on a personal level. My mind was clouded with fear and apprehension as I knelt before the Pontiff and kissed his holy hand.

He bid me to rise and sitting himself in a large chair near the fire, commanded me to stand before him so that he might inquire of me the political and social events happening within the walls of Siena and throughout her growing territories. He asked me of my business and my travels, of Giancarlo's move to the East, of my visit to Venice and my dealings with the Dandolo. He was most curious about my conversations with the Patriarch and pondered long upon the warnings that were given to me by so many people. Curious too was he about my family and my early life, and though I felt it wise to hide from him my life in the hills and the very existence of Curtun and its people, I found myself talking cryptically about my long lineage and my people's ability to see a clear path into the future. To this day, I do not know what possessed me to boast of such abilities to this man of God. I can only guess that his calming yet probing manner had steered me down that path to reveal that which he had already known. Ignorant of the game of which I was already a part, I opened myself to His Holiness and his inquisition.

Though I did not know it at the time, Alexander had been in contact with Patriarch Dandolo over the years since I had visited Venice, and had, himself, been visited with a series of troubling visions and dreams that he had shared with a few of his closest advisors, the Patriarch being one, and in which I was to have some small role in this most important enterprise for the very survival of the Church. Never did he share with me his visions nor his fears and apprehensions, but merely drained me of whatever information he thought useful. Well into the night did his inquisition last until, satisfied with all he had received, he wished me good fortune and bestowed upon me a holy benediction. I bowed low before him, kissing his slipper and his hand, pledging to him my love and support and my fealty. He granted me leave, then to my surprise repeated to me the charge that was recited to me by the Patriarch in Venice: "Heed well the calling, for a time will come soon enough when your destiny will steer you to the East to perform a great service for God and His Most Holy Church. Stay true to your visions, young Seer, and listen to the goodness that is trapped within your soul."

As I left the chamber, Galgano was propped against the outer wall. He had stood guard awaiting my return, but as my audience with His Holiness had drawn on, he had fallen asleep. He rose to his feet as the Pope was rising from his chair, and was struck silent as the Pontiff commanded, "Come forth, young Galgano, that I may speak with you." I took his weapons that he carried upon his person and pushed him through the doorway, closing the door behind him. Long, it seemed to me, that his audience lasted. He did not speak to me of what was said in the Pope's chamber that evening until several years later when he was fated to serve another master. Though there is more to this story to be told, I will inject here that which Galgano had told to me later.

Upon entering and kneeling before His Most Holy, Galgano had mustered the courage to ask the Pope, "How is it that I may serve Your Holiness?" Alexander placed his hand upon the young man's head and blessed him, saying, "Calm thy heart and silence thy temper, young Galgano, for great will be thy service to Our Holy Church. Your service will be needed for a short while to protect the life of the Seer of Curtun. Guard and serve him well, for his value to Us has been vouchsafed by God, and the traps that have been set upon his path by Satan and his hoard of demons are great. Keep him safe that he may fulfill his service that has been foretold to Us."

He then bid Galgano to rise and said to him, "Thy life upon this earth has been written in the Book of Saint Peter to be short, yet your service to God's Church will earn you a place at His heavenly table for all eternity. Thy name and thy deeds will be known to men for a thousand years, and strong will be thy shoulders upon which you will support His Blessed Church. He will send to thee a messenger who will show you the path to your salvation that lies within the goodness of humanity. Heed well the invitation, for though it will come twice to you, it will be Divinely sent, and cannot be ignored. Go now in peace and prepare yourself to receive the blessings of the Holy Spirit."

The bright full moon had already begun to make her descent toward the horizon. Giovanni and Nikos had had their evening meal, and while Giovanni dozed in his chair, Nikos had replenished the woodpile next to the fireplace, as well as his supply of parchment and ink. Supplies of both were running thin and Giovanni had already warned him that there was much more to tell. The Greek had thought that he knew the man whom he had always loved, yet the confessions that had been spilling out of Giovanni for the past few days and nights had given him a whole new view of the man–and he loved him more for it. He was exhausted from a full day of writing, and every muscle in his neck, back and arm, down to his fingers, burned with an aching pain. He needed sleep, a full week's worth, and yet he knew that the dawn was drawing near and Giovanni had not yet made his journey to the spirit world. He wondered how much more the aged body of his friend could take, and yet he knew that Giovanni was driven to complete his task, no matter the cost. And what was the ultimate cost? He knew that Death was waiting in the next room, anxious to collect that which was promised to him by the Holy Spirit. But Giovanni had been given seven days to complete his task. "Tonight, is not the night," he said aloud. "Seek another victim, Dark Spirit, and leave this poor repentant to his confession."

Nikos' comments roused Giovanni from his slumber, and in a dazed state he called out for his cup. Nikos comforted his friend and prepared the warming elixir. "Drink slowly," he said as he held the chalice up to his master's lips. The warm liquid felt wonderful as it flowed down Giovanni's parched throat. He could feel its magic properties radiate throughout his entire body, and it gave him a feeling of comfort and strength. "Come to me," he whispered, as he closed his eyes and gently rocked back and forth." Come to me, Holy Spirit."

The light approaches. It seems not as brilliant as I am used to seeing it, yet it comes to me, nonetheless, in the same manner. I see an angel, nay, a man, or rather the spirit of a man. I know you, spirit. Speak to me and comfort me for I am weary and have traveled much over these past few days. Are you who you appear to be, or are you some fiendish illusion? Mine eyes inform me that your countenance is that of my beloved, Galgano. Tell me that they do not deceive me.

I am or was he whom you name. You remember me as I remember you. Dear Giovanni. Thy soul is weighed heavily and perchance it will carry you down to that place where at the light cannot penetrate. I grieve for you and I pray for your soul. God is good. God is merciful, and He has sent me to help guide you on this particular part of your journey. Will you allow me to help you?

Of course, dear spirit. I place my fate into your care, dear brother, for you were as a brother to me, and I trusted you most. You were my protector and my confessor until you left me to serve a higher master. O! How I have missed you. You who were always ready to defend me against bodily harm and to speak to me most honestly of right and wrong. If only I had listened to thy counsel, my life, perchance would have been lived differently and my soul would have been less sullied. In my rush to greatness, I have failed you, brother. I have failed everyone who had trust in me. I have failed myself.

It is I who have failed you, Giovanni. I failed to keep you upon the true path as I had been instructed to do by the Holy Father. I failed to help you to see the good that was buried within you. You were always in possession of the truth that was needed to keep you on the righteous path. I should have aided you in revealing that truth during those few short years that we had together. I failed you, Giovanni, and I am truly sorry for my failings.

Nay, friend. The fault is mine, and mine alone. It is I who chose not to see. It is I who have constantly sinned. It is I who have abused the gifts that were given to me, and it is I who chose to corrupt their intended benefits to my own. You sought to give me counsel, and I took what I wanted and cast the rest aside. I never allowed myself to consider that in your wisdom lay the true path. Even after your miraculous conversion, I did not allow myself to see. I was driven most harshly by my own demons who possessed my soul and who constantly tempted me to sin. Against all of your teachings, I would argue, with great certainty, a better course that was cloaked in my own reason yet always tainted by sin. I was never frugal when it came to using any of the deadly sins to gain my desires. And through it all, t'was envy that was my task master. Envy was the driving force in my life. I have seen it so in my recent visions, and it is plainly evident in the confessions I am sharing with the world.

You make my task all the easier, my friend, for I had hoped to show you that which you have just shown yourself. Envy has always been strong in you and you let it poison every decision you made and every action you took in your life. It was the blindfold that kept you from seeing the light in your heart. It prevented you from ever becoming one with the Holy Spirit. Alas, it is too late for you to undo the hurt you have caused in your life by accepting the seduction of Envy, yet there is still time to repent your sins and to ask Almighty God for His mercy and His forgiveness.

If only I could turn Fortuna's Wheel back so I might rectify the wrongs I have done, I would gladly give back my fortune, for all the good it has done for me. I have wasted my life in pursuing a false god. I was envious of the lords and the princes of the Church. I was envious of anyone who possessed power and wealth. I was aware that such power never brought to the possessor true happiness, and it was only by giving it all away, as you did, my wise friend, that I could achieve true happiness and peace with God, yet I feigned blindness to this and allowed Envy to be my engine. Will there be time for me to shed these golden chains—to collapse an empire—or at least to set in motion the renouncement of my ill-begotten wealth? Will God accept such payment for the forgiveness of my sins?

Poor Giovanni. There is still much for you to learn. Almighty God commands not, nor accepts any material price. It is an affront to Him for you to think so. Forgiveness cannot be bought, even though it is being sold at a high price by the corruption that claims to lead His Holy Church. Forgiveness must be sought through the heart, not through the purse. Tear off that blindfold as you continue to relive your past and see your errors for what they truly are. You have much to tell, and much to forgive, but God is generous, and His love is boundless. Trust in the goodness that is hidden in your soul, for there is still a chance for you. Show the Almighty that there is still something worth saving in you. Farewell, my friend, and I continue to pray that God has mercy upon you.

Please do not leave me, Galgano! I need your help. I cannot do this alone.

Giovanni was screaming as Nikos threw down his quill and reached over to comfort his friend.

"Keep your filthy hands to yourself," hissed a demonic voice. "This soul belongs to me. I have waited too long for it, and I am growing impatient with all of these games. Goodness will never win over this one. He is too far gone even for a legion of saints and angels to save him. He has been an easy target and his sins are too great for a mere confession and plea for forgiveness to save. I shall have my prize!"

Be gone, cursed demon! Whilst I still live and breathe, I still have hope and I will do all that I can to cheat you of your prize. You have held me captive way too long, and though my mortal body is weak, there is still enough warmth in my blood, and determination in my heart to battle against your will. I have been comforted and strengthened by my protectors, and I will fight against you as long as I am allowed. I have been deceived by you for the last time. I return your gift of envy to you, and in its place, I give to you my pity, for you will, for all eternity, be consigned to the darkness and misery of your own hell.

Ω

Giovanni woke with a renewed strength and resolution. He was determined to continue his confession, and he had already begun to formulate a plan to rid himself of his worldly possessions.

Chapter Four
Avarice

XIII

The Summons to Venice

Nine months had passed when I received the summons from Giancarlo to travel immediately to Constantinople. Much had been happening during that short period of time. War had broken out between Pisa and Genoa over trading rights in northern Italy and France. The Via Francigena and the shipping lanes to Marseilles were in jeopardy. In a clash between the two naval powers, I had found my entire shipment of goods sent to the bottom of the sea. But for the Grace of God, I had managed to escape with my life though most of my men had been lost. It was only by chance that Galgano and I was plucked from the water by the Genoese sailors. We would have been imprisoned or worse had I not been able to convince the Genoese captain that I was a banker from Siena able to pay ransom, and not a Pisani sailor.

The effects of that dastardly attack were felt throughout the commercial world, for the hatred and jealousies of both states spread like fire to every port city around the Mediterranean. Even the Latin Quarter in faraway Constantinople was engulfed in those flames. That year was a financial disaster for our western operation, and our misfortunes had only multiplied as Giancarlo had found himself sitting on a tinderbox a thousand miles away in the Imperial City. The hatreds that had been festering back home were bubbling to the surface everywhere, not the least in the East. Violence had broken out between each of the Latin quarters in Constantinople, causing the Greeks and the Emperor himself to crack down on the Latins. The Venetians still held good standing with the Emperor, although that at times was upon shaky ground, but most of the other Latins felt the wrath of the Greeks. Many were thrown into prison, many were banished, and mob violence was becoming more common. More and more, the safety of the Byzantine Empire was becoming as unstable as that of the Western Empire.

As hostilities grew, I began to rethink the idea of my personal involvement in the Grand Cycle. My party had been accosted on several occasions with the high cost of loss of men and goods. Galgano had proven invaluable to me and bravely saved my life on three separate occasions, and I in turn had to pay a small fortune for his release from the Genoese. In total over those many months, I lost dozens of good men to the scourge that had spread throughout the trading routes to France. In earlier times it was necessary for Giancarlo to personally organize each cycle, accompany his merchandise to the fairs, make the sales, and settle the debts himself. But times had changed, and I needed to figure out a better, more efficient way of handling our trading business.

I knew personal reputation, especially one as great as Giancarlo's, was essential to the mastery of the art of deal making, and face-to-face dealings with our clients was most important. Giancarlo had spent many years establishing his reputation and his clients were solid, as long as we continued to meet their needs. In many cases, we were able to meet those needs through correspondence, ship the orders direct, settle accounts with bills of trade, thus eliminating the need to travel long distances with each trade. As times changed, so did our business model. I still, on occasion visited with our wealthiest clients, but I began to be more selective with my travel and with my time. I was convinced that it would be much more profitable to become less of a retail operation and began to concentrate more on the wholesale import of goods. It was more profitable and less risky. Of course, that required the employment of men of high quality and talent, worthy of our trust, not unlike the arrangement Giancarlo had sought in the past with me and other agents of his. Galgano seemed to me to be one with such qualities, and I had plans to advance him within my operation. Alas, not everything goes according to plan, for I was to suffer a great loss when my dear Galgano—my protector, my soul brother, and friend—was filled with the Holy Spirit and left me.

Let me speak of him now, for his visitation has brought back such strong memories and feelings of loss and guilt. I swear to you what I am about to tell is true.

We were returning from Volterra, having collected debts and rents in that region, when we were attacked by a small band of undisciplined bandits. Their attack was a pathetic waste of life, and the two of us were hurt. Galgano was quick to eradicate the vermin, and we hurried on our way toward Siena. As we approached the forest that surrounds the hill of Monte Siepi, we made camp for the night, in time to tend our wounds, get some rest, and make it back to the safety of the city before the sun had reached its peak.

During that night, as the embers of the fire died, and sleep had taken us, Galgano was visited by the Archangel Michael. The angel told him that he had been sent by the Holy Spirit to rescue the soul of the young sinner and to enlist him in the service of God. No longer would he have need for his sword, for though his days upon this earth would be few, they would be filled with the love and peace of Our Lord and His servant Michael, who commands a host of angels in Heaven. Galgano at once woke me and told me of his visitation. My friend had been transformed at once and spoke to me for hours of the kingdom of Heaven. As sleep fell upon me again, Galgano was revisited by the archangel and greeted by Our Lord and his mother Mary, and the eleven apostles. So rapturous was Galgano at dawn's first light that he mounted his steed and galloped full speed, his horse refusing to heed any command, to the very top of Monte Siepi. I followed behind, fearing that he, in his trance, would be thrown to his death. Upon reaching the top of the outcrop, I beheld such a sight that has forever been emblazoned upon my brain.

Galgano had leaped from his horse and was kneeling upon the barren earth in solemn prayer, speaking to a host who remained unseen to me. He was begging Almighty God to wash away his wickedness and to forgive his murderous deeds so that he might pledge his sullied sword and his undying loyalty to the service of the Lord. He vowed to forsake his violent ways and all his worldly possessions and live the life of a penitent servant should he, but for a brief period upon this green earth, enjoy the peace and the love of the Heavenly Father. He then pledged his life upon his sword and was about to plunge his steel into his body, when an invisible hand reached down and cast his blade aside. A voice then echoed down from the Heavens, saying, "Erect for Me a Holy Cross to guide My flock to their Salvation." Looking around and seeing no wood, Galgano picked up his sword and thrust it with all his might into the rock upon which he had knelt. The sword refused to break, and the stone yielded as if it were butter. At that moment, the earth shook and a bolt from the Heavens cracked the morning sky and struck the embedded sword, causing it to fuse into the rock for all time.

As time passed and I regained my wits, I pleaded with Galgano to leave that place and to journey with me back to Siena. In no way could I convince him to move from the mountaintop, nor would his horse, with any command, budge an inch from his master. With one final effort I tried to carry him from that spot, but the earth had begun again to shake violently. Seeing that it was God's will for him to remain, I threw my arms around my friend and left him, vowing to return with food and supplies for his sustenance. I will speak more of Galgano as my confession progresses.

I was in constant correspondence with Giancarlo regarding the situation developing in France and the battles over the Francigena in Italy, even into the territory controlled by Siena, and, on several occasions, used the instability of the area to further my ideas of restructuring the European business. Giancarlo was hesitant toward change but saw merit in many of my proposals. I was, therefore, not surprised with his need to discuss the future of the operation in more depth. I was surprised that he had summoned for me to travel to Constantinople, along with Anna and our child. I was not concerned about the time it would take to make the journey, nor the distance, for I had traveled many more miles over land and sea each year in order to move the merchandise to markets.

I was concerned with the urgency of his command and the mysteriousness with which he had wrapped the entire summons. He had communicated specific details for our trip, which brought me to Venice and a meeting with Enrico before sailing to the Imperial City. I was to arrive in Constantinople by the middle of May, with a very specific inventory. Anna was thrilled with the idea of seeing her parents again and with the entire trip to the exotic Eastern Empire.

Her moods were much more cheerful and her feelings toward me had become brighter. I must confess that the iciness I had felt toward her since the death of Genevieve had begun to thaw with the snows of winter, and our relationship had begun to present a promise of spring's awakening. With her lightened moods, she began to take up her lute and sing to me her sweet songs. Such a time of marital bliss, as short as it was, enabled us to plant the seed of joy, which ultimately would grow into our dearest son, my most beloved Paolo.

By the Ides of March, our caravan was ready to leave Siena. Anna was beginning to have problems as she was with child, but she refused to let anything stand in the way of her seeing her parents again. She had convinced me that she and Vannozzo would not be trouble on the trip, and as it was Giancarlo's command to bring them, I had accepted the inconvenience.

Pietro had contacted me and had told me he was being called to Venice to perform a service for Dandolo's company and had learned that we would be there at the same time. Naturally, he was delighted to accompany me to Venice, for he knew that I would be passing by Assisi on my way to the coast. How convenient it always seemed for Pietro to enjoy my company, and the company of my security force, upon those long and perilous journeys. Truth be told, I did enjoy his company in those days, and had welcomed him along for a very nominal fee. On the day before we were scheduled to set out, I was very pleased with the arrival of Sebastiano and Salvatore, who had told me they were being sent by the Zil-at to meet with the Patriarch of Grado in Venice. I was overjoyed to learn of their plans and thrilled with the prospect of traveling to Venice with my dear cousins. They would be a welcomed addition to my security force, providing me with peace of mind and good counsel along the way. Fortune seemed to be smiling upon this journey even before it was to be undertaken.

We traveled with no problem to Ancona, picking up Pietro along the way. Surprisingly, Anna and the child had taken the land journey very well. We boarded a Venetian transport and sailed directly to the Lido, taking only three days' time. The sea was calm, the weather quite mild. All was going incredibly well. Venice, in all her glory, rose magnificently from the emerald sea in the noon sun. Anna was amazed at the sight of everything. She ran from one side of the ship to the other, not wanting to miss the tiniest detail. She leapt with joy at being in Venice, and the thought that soon she would be seeing her parents. Her melancholia had disappeared, and it pleased me to see her so happy. The piazzetta was as busy and as loud as ever, more so because Venice had become master of all of the Eastern trade and the ruler of the Adriatic. The center of the financial and mercantile world was right here in the Republic on the Sea.

Unlike my first visit to Venice, there appeared to be no welcoming party to greet us. I felt it strange that Dandolo had not met us upon our arrival, but knowing how important he was in his city, I did not think too much upon it. I sent a runner to notify him of our arrival and waited with anticipation for him to recognize us. In the later part of the afternoon a messenger was sent to notify us that Master Dandolo had been unavoidably detained and that he would meet us at the Red Sail tavern located within a ten-minute walk from the Piazzetta. I walked with Salvatore, Sebastiano, and Pietro to the Red Sail and awaited our host. Anna and the child remained on the ship and awaited instructions. It was not long before Enrico appeared, encircled by a large mob of friends and associates. He dismissed them all before he joined us at our table.

He seemed to have aged since I had last seen him, but still had retained his vigor, and his piercing blue eyes still sparkled with youth. He was as amiable as I had remembered him to be and he spoke to us in an openhearted manner, greeting each of us by name. I had found it strange that he had known my cousins by name, for I had assumed that they had never met. I put aside my suspicions and greeted our host with much affection and formality. I had not forgotten that I was in Venice under specific instruction from Giancarlo to discuss some sort of business arrangement and needed to secure safe passage to Constantinople on one of Enrico's galleons. Enrico offered us refreshment and sent a servant to retrieve our personal belongings and escort Anna and the child to our lodgings. Again, I was surprised he had not offered us lodging with him at his father's magnificent palazzo as he had done before, but then I figured that this was a routine business trip and such lavish lodgings should not oft' times be expected.

I graciously accepted his offers and his hospitality, and following an enjoyable evening of drink and conversation, he accompanied us back down to the piazzetta. I remember so clearly the moon being full as it shone its brilliant light upon the face of the ducal palace and the golden domes of the Duomo, her many statues casting long shadows across the piazza below. The landscape beyond was hidden in darkness, the closer buildings but mere silhouettes. As we passed the rows of buildings that bordered the piazzatta, it was only then that I realized all the land spreading out to the north and east—the area of San Luca and San Salvatore and the entire area of the Dandolo compound—was an empty void. The silver beams of moonlight were absorbed into a vast wasteland. The smell of charred wood and rotted destruction weighed heavy in the air and cloaked the land in the stench of Hell.

We all stood in silence and disbelief. Enrico, his white hair and beard glowing in the moonlight, had tears running down his cheeks. He said nothing at first, but finally broke the silence of the group. "It has been but a mere dozen years since the Dandolo were returned from exile, only to see our homes, our possessions, all that we held so dear to us in this city, destroyed by mob and fire. They were not satisfied to have brought a mighty house to its knees. They reveled in the destruction of every building, palazzo, and warehouse, even the smallest shed, and caused the very stones upon which those buildings sat to be crushed to dust, so that all could see the end of the troublesome Dandolo. Gone are they now, every one of them who would have had our skin stripped from our bodies and our bones crushed to dust. Dust are they now, the ones we trusted most, and the mob who blindly followed them. Strong and fearless we have proven to be, and as Fortuna saw fit to reverse her mighty wheel, we re-entered the city and steadily vanquished our foes. We rebuilt our property and broadened our power, like the Phoenix of old, arising from the ashes to be stronger and more beautiful than the original. My father and my uncle are amongst the most powerful in the land, and their palaces were the envy of many throughout the republic. You know this from your last visit. Yet Vulcan has again laid claim to our most sacred sestiere, and has taken from us our home, our business, our churches, and our monasteries. Gone are San Luca and San Salvatore, gone is the light and our salvation."

He then told me of a fire that had broken out in the small church of San Luca on Christmas Eve that had spread with the wind to destroy all in its path. On Christmas Day, the day on which all good men celebrate the birth of the God of Light, the city was still smoldering, and thousands of Venetians had been left with no home and no hope. His home, his father's mighty palazzo, and the entire Dandolo compound was gone, again. But hope, he said, would never die for the Dandolo, for that, as well as courage and perseverance, were the greatest treasure held by his family. That which was is no more, but would be rebuilt, only bigger, and better.

He beckoned us to follow him and we wound our way through the rubble and along the tiny canals that led to the Rialto. Just across the Grand Canal stood the Patriarch's grand palace, miraculously saved from the flames. A boat had been awaiting us, and we were ferried to the palace. It was there that Enrico, his father, and his family took refuge and would reside until they had rebuilt their palazzi. It was at the Patriarch's palazzo where we would stay while in Venice.

The palace was as grand as I had remembered it to be. We were not offered private accommodations because the Patriarch had been hosting a major conference at the time of our arrival and the palace had been filled with important guests. Enrico showed us to a separate wing, an area set aside to house his family, and showed us to a large salon where makeshift couches had been prepared for our use. The accommodations, though confining for four men and one pregnant woman with a young child, were no less elegant than the finest establishment one could imagine.

Sleep came mercifully quickly for some, but I was less fortunate, plagued by visions of death and destruction. Horror upon horror washed upon my blinded eyes and my head ached with an evil pounding and the agonizing screams. I saw myself and Salvatore bearing Enrico's dead body through the streets of a foreign city. I witnessed the destruction of Curtun and the death of all whom I had loved. I held the body of Giancarlo in my hands and cried over the rotting corpse of Donna Donata. I watched as the Holy Father danced upon the imperial neck of the mighty Barbarossa, as a steady stream of wars fought upon the land and sea flowed through me.

My restlessness was too great and, leaving my companions to their peace, I found my way down to a terrace that overlooked the water. Inky black and tumultuous were the waves, and the lapping rhythm helped to ease the dread of my nightmares. I remained deep in thought until Enrico rested his hand upon my shoulder to comfort me. He too had been plagued with dreams and demons and had always sought the comfort of the water's whispering voice. I did not tell him the details of my visions, nor asked him of his. But in the darkness on that morning, as we contemplated our fates, and the fates of those around us, we shared a closeness of friendship that bound us together for the rest of our lives.

Later we shared a breakfast while Enrico arranged for our needs. A grand banquet had been planned at the palace for that evening, and we were invited to attend as Enrico's guests. He made sure that we were all suitably attired for the evening and then excused himself for the remainder of the day. The purpose for my summons to Venice would have to wait until after the banquet. The palace was busy the entire day preparing for the banquet and we were left on our own. Pietro busied himself with the Jews of Cannaregio. Sebastiano and Salvatore also begged leave, their whole business seemed so mysterious and intriguing to me, but I had known enough not to press them for details. Anna spent the day resting and caring for Vannozzo.

I was left to my own devices, and instead of spending the day at the market, I decided to seek solitude in the library of the Patriarch. I was surprised to see two guards posted at the massive doors to the antechamber of the library and more surprised when the guards stepped aside and opened the door for me to pass. Within the brilliantly lit room, beyond the massive bookshelves crammed with bound books, scrolls, and ancient texts, in a far corner, sat the Patriarch and another man whose silhouette I could not discern. They were conversing in whispered tones, but when I entered the room, they ceased their talking.

The Patriarch rose and walked toward me with a welcoming demeanor and said, "Welcome, Giovanni of Cortona. We are so pleased that you have seen the need to visit our fair city once again. We were just speaking of you." If I was surprised to hear that the

Patriarch of Grado was speaking of me, I was doubly surprised to see that the Patriarch's guest was our Most Holy Father, Alexander, himself. "Greetings, once again, Giovanni Pecci da Cortona, or should I call you Sandak of the Taurisi, pec-ii of Curtun. How fortuitous to meet again, at the answering of the calling."

Never had I nor anyone uttered my given name beyond the borders of Curtun, and I was struck with silence as my identity, and the existence of my ancient people, echoed throughout the chamber. How could anyone know of my secret? It was mine to keep and mine to give, and yet I shared it with no one. Sensing my discomfort, His Holiness assured me that the existence of the Taurisi had been known to many beyond the hidden walls, since the time before the Romans. Many of the true and most holy pontiffs had enjoyed certain agreements with the Zil-ats through the ages, and their requests for anonymity had been sanctioned with sacred oath and legal contract in return for specific pledges and favors.

None of my kin had spoken of such arrangements or interaction with the outside world in all the time I had spent with them, so I was skeptical about what had been unfolding. My fears were somewhat dispelled when His Holiness told me he would meet with Tarquin's emissaries, Tarchon and Tyrsenos, later in the morning. The Pope was pleased I had come to Venice with my cousins and wanted to assure me that our meeting was not simply one of chance but rather part of a plan that had been revealed to him through God's messengers. I was to trust in God's plan and His instruments, and in return for such faith and upon the success of a holy quest that I was about to undertake, I would be rewarded in this life and in the next. I spoke directly to the Holy Father and inquired of him the details of his plan. Alas, my audience was abruptly ended when he rose from his chair and placed his hand upon my head, whispering in my ear, "All in due time, young pec-ii. All in due time." The Patriarch bowed low and Alexander exited the library.

The Patriarch seated himself and beckoned me to sit beside him. He then asked me if I had come to the library seeking knowledge, and when I said that my life had been a long quest for knowledge, he laughed and promised to share with me a knowledge that he was sure would answer many of the questions he had seen in my eyes and in my heart since the first day we had met. He told me he had been waiting for me to arrive in Venice, not just on the previous day's tide—but for many years. He then told me that all he was about to unfold had been told to him by his dear friend and mentor, Bernard of Clairvaux, who had also been mentor to the great seer Malachy Ua Morgair of Armagh.

Malachy had been a great reformer of the Church in Ireland and had accomplished many miracles in his life. He was a powerful pec-ii, and like me, had been blessed with extraordinary visions and communications with the Holy Spirit. Many of his prophesies had already come to pass since his death, yet many more had been left to unfold in the near or distant future. The Patriarch went on to tell me that he had met Malachy during a synod in Rome in 1139 where Bernard of Clairvaux had eloquently presented Malachy's miraculous accomplishments in Ireland to Innocent II. The Patriarch was much impressed with the Bishop of Armagh's prophetic gifts and his zeal for reformation of the church. The two had spent time together in Rome and had kept up a close relationship through friendly correspondence for the remainder of the seer's life.

The Patriarch had likewise remained faithful to Bernard and had helped the abbot organize the hundreds of pages of Malachy's visions into a book titled *The Prophesies*. Copies of the letters exchanged between the Patriarch and Malachy, as well as copies of many of the letters written between Malachy and Bernard, were contained in the library in which I sat. The Patriarch had made it his mission to accumulate copies of as many of the individual visions as possible and had codified them into his own volume of work by the prophet. He showed me the volumes of parchment dedicated to Malachy's writings and gave me permission to peruse the work at my leisure.

The Patriarch told me that Bernard's exquisitely crafted book of *The Prophesies* was presented to Eugene III as a gift on the eve of that pope's launching of the Second Crusade, with the hope that the Pope could clearly decipher the true path to victory using Malachy's visions. His prophesies accurately named the participants of the holy war and the battles that were theirs to be won. Unfortunately, the Pope had chosen not to share the visions with the leaders of the expedition and the campaign was a dismal failure, for though

Malachy had predicted the defeat of the Latin armies, Eugene had intentionally kept the information to himself for fear of losing the support of crusaders.

Word spread of the power of *The Prophesies*, and when Adrian, the English pope, tried to use it to force Barbarossa to come to Rome, the would-be emperor arranged to have the book stolen from the Papal Archives and brought to Germany. Because *The Prophesies* are not complimentary to the Emperor, Barbarossa vowed to destroy the book, but yielded to his bishops, who insisted that the book was divinely inspired and could not be destroyed. He then had the book transported to the library of the Knights Hospitaller in Rhodes, where, he hoped, it would be buried beneath the thousands of ancient holy texts. Not long was the book in Rhodes when agents of the emperor, Manual I Comnenus, stole it and brought it to His Magnificence in Constantinople. The book had then been in the hands of the Eastern Emperor, who refused to acknowledge its existence in the imperial capital or even to discuss potential ransom for its return.

The book, he told me, was of immense importance to the Church and to the future of the West. Its return to its rightful owner was to be the ultimate quest. At that point in time, I still did not fully understand what the Patriarch was attempting to convey. He spoke to me of his own compilation and of the many prophesies that were specific to the Dandolo. He had, in fact, dedicated a separate book of such prophesies, along with correspondence between himself and Malachy and Bernard, discussing possible interpretations of key lines in *The Prophesies.* Though he did not tell me any of the predictions during my conversations with him, I was able to view this book later, and to make a copy of certain passages of which he had referred.

Malachy had written to Bernard of the anguish he had lived with as a result of his communion with the Holy Spirit and had begged the scholar for help in organizing the Prophesies and getting them into the proper hands. Shortly after, Malachy made the trip to Clairvaux where he was received most lovingly by the Abbot Bernard, who was a very honest and holy man. At the time of Malachy's return to Clairvaux, the Patriarch had been sent into exile, along with his entire family, by the Doge Polani, and he had sought refuge and guidance in Clairvaux, bearing witness to all that I feel compelled to present to you, so that you may know of its truth and its influence upon the direction in which my life would take.

Malachy had arrived, an aged and dying man, carrying with him a large portfolio of sheets and mere scraps of paper, inscribed in ink or charcoal, on front and back, legible and at times totally blurred—a satchel of order and chaos, comprising the essence of his communion with the Holy Spirit. He was weak yet determined to finish his holy assignment and to deliver his life's work into the hands of his venerable mentor. God did not see fit to instruct Malachy as to the purpose or ultimate use of his visions, but merely used the Bishop as a chalice to receive His sacred font of knowledge. As Bernard and Dandolo had learned, there appeared to be no logical order to Malachy's visions, though the prophet had insisted he had been divinely inspired to make an order out of the chaos. The visions were at times quite clear and succinct, and at time completely deranged and had made no sense. Some were quite lengthy, rambling on for pages, while others were mere words and phrases scribbled upon a shred of paper. Some were eloquently written in perfect iambic, while others were in clear prose, and still others appeared to be gibberish. None could tell if the compilation was the rambling of a madman or the whispers of the angels.

Determined to see the good bishop's life work completed before his passing, the arduous task of making sense of it all was completed over several months' time. In the end, the hundreds of pages were compiled into an orderly fashion to the satisfaction of the prophet. During that time, Malachy continued to have visions, and had continued to transcribe them. Some of those visions, because of his close association with the Patriarch, were more directed toward the Dandolo of Venice. Those visions were given directly to the Patriarch, who, at a later date, had them bound into the beautifully illustrated book that had held an honored place in the Patriarch's library. I have, on several occasions, been allowed to view the contents of this sacred book and have lived to see many of those prophesies come to fruition.

It was also during this time that a young merchant from Siena, having finished his yearly trading mission to Bar-sur-Aube, had visited the abbey with news from friends in Venice for the Patriarch. His name was Giancarlo Manenti. He was accompanied by a young friend named Vincenzo Pecci da Cortona. The two had delivered the news from the Patriarch's young nephew, Enrico, and were only meant to stay the night before journeying on to Provins, but fate had caused them to remain for more than a week. Upon their first evening's stay, the prophet, having grown considerably weaker, had been seized with a horrible stream of visions that had almost taken his spirit from this earth. His visions were mainly focused upon the fates of the two travelers and yet were intricately woven into many of the visons that he had foreseen for the Dandolo and others. So intense and disturbing were these visions, their meanings almost impossible to decipher, that Bernard insisted the two remain for a few days.

The prophet continued to be visited with visions of great intensity, crashing upon his weakened body like mighty waves crashing upon the shore. So weak was he that he could not record the visions himself but entrusted the sacred task to Bernard. Malachy died in the arms of his beloved mentor, Bernard, just as he had predicted, happy in the knowledge that he had completed his usefulness to the Holy Spirit and had commended the fruits of his life to the one whom he trusted most to fulfill God's plan. Such a violent end to such a frail and courageous man brought tears to my eyes with the Patriarch's tale. So too did the tears that filled the Patriarch's ancient eyes reveal the love that he had for this holy man.

For months Bernard worked tirelessly to reorganize and to have crafted an exquisitely illustrated copy of the manuscript, hand copied by the most skilled monks in the abbey upon the finest Egyptian papyrus given as a gift by the merchant Manenti. The book was bound in the softest kid leather, engraved with gold, and encrusted in jewels. He had the book sealed with a golden lock, having only two keys fashioned in gold. Bernard included a preface section and a dedication letter to the Holy Father, Eugene III, and when the sacred work of art was finally completed, he carried it himself to Rome and presented it to His Holiness. *The Prophesies* has remained in the hands and under the watchful eyes of the pope ever since, except for a brief period, about which I will soon tell. The Patriarch secured his copies, as well as copies of the prophesies concerning the Manenti/Pecci merchants and brought them back to Venice when he was welcomed back from exile upon the removal of the disgraced Polani faction.

The Patriarch had grown tired and was about to leave when I asked him to tell me of the Manenti and Pecci prophesies. He stared into my eyes and spoke this verse.

All hail the mighty Dandolo,
Head of State, Healer of Church, Admiral of Christ's Fleet,
Blessed and cursed by pope and king,
Who blindly leads his flock to victory upon the wall,
And dispenses His justice without fear for himself.
Leader of men, both seen and unseen, servant and master,
Fortune's son and Envy's bastard child.
Listen well to the word of God, and seek the help
Of the seer from the hidden realm,
To reclaim what was stolen from His house.
The viper's sting shall be denied,
And the Word shall be returned to Rome.
The seer's deeds shall remain unseen, yet his reward shall save the chosen ones.
All for naught. His boon shall be his bane. He shall have everything, and end with nothing.
All hail Enrico Dandolo,
Maker of Peace, Wager of War, Builder of Ships,
Savior of Souls, Destroyer of Empires.
Men will sing of thy mighty deeds
For a thousand years to come,
And men will shed a tear for what was lost and won.

As he began to leave, he told me of the visions Malachy had foreseen about the seer from the hidden realm who would come to the aid of the Church in its darkest hour and help the Vicar of Christ regain that which was taken from him. He was not certain I was the seer who had been mentioned in the prophesy, nor had he assumed the prophesy had referred to himself. He was only certain of the legitimacy of the current Holy Father and of the righteousness of the mission that was to come.

XIV

The Company and The Quest

It was late in the afternoon when I was reunited with my party. Anna was feeling better and joined the group. She had been provided with a most beautiful blue gown in the style preferred by the ladies in Venetian high society. She looked radiant, well-rested, and in the full blossom of motherhood. Pietro had returned from his dealings in the Cannaregio and chattered incessantly about the Venetian markets. Salvatore and Sebastiano had reappeared after meeting with the Patriarch and said not a word between the two of them. I was anxious to talk about my time spent in the library but then felt it wiser to keep the day's experience to myself. I had also thought it wise not to discuss any of these meetings with Anna or Pietro, unless they were directly involved. We had all dressed in the clothes Enrico had provided for us and as the guests began to arrive, we were escorted to the great hall. It had seemed to me that all of Venice was stuffed into the room. Lords and ladies were showing off their finest fashions, and Anna had commented that all the silk and fur and jewels in all the world must have been brought to this special event. Princes of the Church, bishops and archbishops were in the majority, no doubt having been summoned by the Patriarch to honor and support his special guest. Throughout the evening we saw no sign of the Patriarch nor his nephew, Enrico, but did upon chance come into the presence of Enrico's father, the senior Vitale, who was most gracious to me and had even introduced me to the Doge. Lord Dandolo had taken a liking to me, and his powerful position as head council to the Doge was enough to gain me admittance to any conversation within the room.

Throughout the evening I had noticed several groups of high-ranking clerics being ushered into a separate wing of the palace. Each group would remain for a brief period, and then be replaced by another group. Some of these groups were comprised of men within the ducal court, including Lord Dandolo, and a separate emissary was sent to escort the Doge to a private meeting. As the evening progressed, many of the guests, having been sufficiently feted, disappeared into the night. Anna had already retired to our bed. At close to the midnight hour, I was summoned, together with Salvatore and Sebastiano, to the library. I had expected to see the Patriarch, but I was happy to see Enrico as well. Both were gathered at the far end of the library where I had first seen His Holiness. I had assumed I was brought in to discuss the matter that had brought me to Venice at the behest of Ginacarlo, and my suspicion was partly confirmed when the Patriarch greeted us as his bankers from Siena.

I was pleased to see Enrico. The mysterious summons and the meetings earlier in the day had been most disquieting and had piqued my curiosity and apprehension. I had hoped that Enrico would be able to finally answer all my questions. The Patriarch immediately began to speak. He told a more condensed version of the story he had shared with me but spoke most insistently of the importance of the holy book to God's Church that was under siege by the emperors of the East and the West. Though we wanted to question the Patriarch more, we each held our tongues until the Patriarch was finished.

"The book had been in the hands of the Pope Eugene for several years and had provided him with divine guidance through those years of political unrest throughout the world. The Pope's ability to outmaneuver his opponents brought him success and strength during his early pontificate and had also raised the suspicion of his archenemy, Barbarossa. When the emperor had learned of *The Prophesies*, he sent down to Rome several agents to infiltrate the Lateran Palace and to steal the book from the Pope. The book was brought to the Emperor while he was laying siege to Milan."

"The holy text was deciphered by the Emperor, who was encouraged with the eminent death of Eugene but had become furious with the predicted election of Orlando of Siena as Alexander III. The Emperor had considered Orlando an attack dog for Eugene and had come up against the Archbishop's steely tongue on several occasions. Barbarossa could not allow Orlando to become pope and he sent his assassins to make certain the prophesies would not be fulfilled. He was wont to have the book destroyed, but being convinced by his bishops that God's wrath would be visited upon his imperial head for destroying the word of God, the Emperor sent the book to Alexandria to be buried amongst the thousands of ancient holy manuscripts accumulated in that city. The assassination plot failed, and Orlando was made pope by the cardinals assembled in Rome.

"Barbarossa was furious and called a conclave of northern cardinals together to elect his own man as Pope Victor IV. As we now know, this was not the only attempt to eliminate the true pontiff. Barbarossa had failed in eliminating Alexander III, but he could not bury the Word of God for long, for the duplicitous Greek emperor, Comnenus in Constantinople, had also learned of *The Prophesies* and had sent his agents to Alexandria to retrieve the holy book. The Holy Father has been advised of this imperial treachery and has vowed to emancipate the holy book from the thieving hands of the Greeks."

The Patriarch fell silent and let Enrico finish the narrative.

Enrico told us that His Holiness had commissioned him to form a company of seven valiant warriors to set upon the open sea and sail with utmost haste to Rome's great rival in the East, to liberate from the pit of Satan's guardian serpents, who reside in the sacred halls of the apostles, that which had been stolen from the True Shepherd of Christ's flock—the holy book containing the sacred words of the Holy Spirit. He looked at each of us in our eyes and studied our faces. In shock and disbelief of what I had heard, I met his serious glare with innocent inquisition and asked him where he was planning to get these seven valiant warriors. Without changing his expression, he said to me, "Three I have, and three have been sent to me."

I looked around the room, seeing none but our small company, and then I laughed aloud. In all seriousness he looked at me and affirmed that the plan had been formulated and the company, as God had foretold, would be brought together in the heart of the Imperial City. I listened in disbelief, as if it may have been some marvelous joke, but the serious look upon Salvatore and Sebastiano's face had told me that there was much more to this story than I had been told. I then asked them both if they had known about this madness as it had been described by Enrico, and both nodded in solemn agreement.

Sebastiano then told me that in addition to the letter given to him by my father upon his deathbed, he had delivered a final prophesy to Tarquin, begging him to act quickly and wisely for the fate of the Taurisi would soon be at hand. He told him that a great contest would be waged between the Church and the State and would last for a hundred years. In the infancy of such enmity, Curtun's assistance would be sought by the church, and by giving of her sons, she would be spared annihilation. The fate of its people was in the hands of the seer's son. The outcome of his quest would spell doom or guarantee a reprieve for the sons of Noah. The hyena had stolen from the jackal and the Prophet's words were resting amongst the ancient bones of the apostles. Lo, should those sacred words not be rescued from the serpent's hold, the two beasts shall form an unholy alliance and lead an army of darkness over all the world. Survival of the Blood of Noah rests within the seer's son, and he shall be called upon to rectify the Imperial wrongs.

Tarquin had been implored to heed the calling, "for when the king of eagles resides upon the golden hall of the Zil-at, the time is nigh to send forth his two mightiest warriors to aid The Master and vouchsafe the return of the Word of God." The eagle had come and the two brothers, Tarquin's two sons and mightiest warriors, were sent to seek out the seer's son. All looked upon me, and Sebastiano said quietly, "You, Giovanni, are the seer's son."

I had found it difficult to comprehend all that was being said, even though such fantastic tales had been told by so illustrious a gathering—a prince of the church, a prince of commerce, and two princes of the hidden realm. And yet, who was I—the seer's son? My question to Enrico was quick and to the point. "Here you have two mighty warriors, their skills in warfare and subterfuge I can attest to most hardily, but I ask again, with utmost respect, where are the other warriors of which the prophesy speaks?"

Enrico smiled at me and assured me that the company was coming together. Already he had two mighty warriors and the seer's son. He too would be counted amongst the company, as would Giancarlo and his young associate, Nikos, in the Imperial City. I was stunned to hear Giancarlo's name, yet not surprised about his involvement. In fact, it started to become clear to me that Giancarlo had been involved with a lot more than he had ever claimed to me. Nikos, I had met earlier in France and was not impressed with his abilities at that time. Neither he nor Giancarlo appeared to me to wear the mantle of valiant warrior. Enrico laughed and stated that the company then numbered six, and the seventh member had been given by the Holy Father, Himself. With that, the Patriarch stood and walked to a small door at the far end of the library. He motioned to a young cleric standing in the antechamber and ushered him into the room. At that distance and in the fading light of the candelabra I did not instantly recognize him, but as he approached, and with the vail of distant memory lifted from my eyes, I beheld a mature Ugolino di Conti.

Though it had been twenty years since I had last seen him, the helpless frailty that was his in his adolescence had matured into a stone- cold hardness, his body and features chiseled into the same sharpness as that of the statues that grace the portico of San Marco. Twenty years had not dimmed the icy stare of his charcoal eyes, nor tempered his stoic countenance. In fact, the years had made him colder and more guarded.

He approached the group and observed each one of us, never betraying a hint of emotion. The Patriarch turned to his nephew and announced, "The company is now complete." No more would be discussed until the company was brought together in Constantinople. Ugolino knelt and kissed the hand of the Patriarch, and without uttering a word exited the room.

I did not have a chance to talk with him, nor to find out what had befallen him since those horrible days in Sant' Antimo. I would not know, at that time, for when I had attempted to find him in the morning, I had been informed by the Patriarch that he had left Venice under cover of darkness. No one in the palace nor in the city had known that di Conti had been there. We were to remain in Venice for the remainder of the week, telling no one of our meeting or our charge, but transacting such business as was requested by Giancarlo and Enrico. Pietro was intentionally kept in the dark concerning the real reason for our mission and was eager to visit the Imperial City as a trade negotiator for Enrico.

I had no time to question Enrico further, for some time during the following day, having given Pietro final instructions regarding the shipment of goods that he was to deliver to agents in Constantinople, Enrico secretly slipped out of Venice, leaving word for us to meet him in Constantinople on or before Pentecost. He had matters to attend to that would bring him to the Kingdom of Sicily, but he would send word to Giancarlo of his progress and the intended date of his arrival. He had secured for us and our merchandise safe passage on one of his largest galleons, which, though having to make several stops in port cities along the way, would still get us to the Imperial City with time to spare.

On the evening before we were to leave, the Patriarch summoned me to the library and implored me to have faith in God's plan, to have courage in this holy task, to have hope in the successful outcome of our mission, and to have trust in my fellow valiant warriors to accomplish that which need be done. Victory was to be ours, and great reward was the price for our successful service. It was at that moment, in the presence of the Patriarch of Grado, the one who had the ear and the personal welfare of the Holy Father, I decided to make my deal and state my price. Relying upon all the training in negotiations that I had received from Giancarlo, I named my reward.

Upon the successful retrieval and return of "The Prophesies of Malachy" to its rightful owner, His Holiness, Alexander III, I, Giovanni Bartolomeo Pecci da Cortona would receive transfer of title of the Castle Stigliano and all the land and surrounding properties as currently held in trust by the Bishop of Siena for the benefit of Anna Soarzi Manenti. I would be granted, in perpetuity, Most Favored trading status within His holy kingdom, being able to trade duty and tariff free on all manner of merchandise.

Another prelate would have been shocked at the bartering being proposed for so holy a quest, but the Patriarch was first and foremost a Venetian, and he smiled at my boldness. "Giancarlo has trained you well," he said to me, knowing full well that Stigliano was also the reward that Giancarlo had sought. "Very well," he said. "It shall be recorded, as has the demand of your uncle. The Holy Father, with the guidance of the Holy Spirit, will make the final determination as to what reward shall be made, and to whom."

We made ready to set sail the following day on the noon tide. Anna was sad to leave the enchanted city, and nervous that the next few weeks would be spent upon the sea, yet she showed a brave face toward the final voyage that would bring her to her parents' arms. Vannozzo, already used to a large seaworthy craft, had made himself busy running throughout the main deck, and making mischief with the merchants and crew. All the merchandise had been loaded upon the ship that Enrico had arranged for the journey to Constantinople, a galleon of some size, though not as large as the war vessels anchored in the lagoon. It was heavily laden with goods destined for the Eastern markets. It was not long before we saw San Marco slip away, and we headed into open water.

We traveled east across the Adriatic to the Dalmatian Coast. The weather was mild upon the water and the winds were strong, pushing us along at such a pace that within several days we had made port in Zara and within a week we had made the port city of Ragusa. Several of the merchants had disembarked, along with their cargo, and others were replaced. We circumnavigated the Principality of Achaea without problem, and our charted course was to take us along the coast of Athens, across the Aegean to Chios, to Byzantium before sailing through the Straits of Saint George and on to Constantinople.

However, as we rounded the coastline of Sparta and sailed the turbulent waters of the Aegean, a mighty storm had blown down from the north and forced us off course, landing us on the western coast of the island of Crete. We were thankful that we had reached the safety of the island but became frustrated with the delays caused by the bad weather. Anna and the child had been sick throughout the storm and were both very weak when we made land. I could not blame them for their discomfort, but I had begun to regret my decision to bring them along on the trip.

As days passed waiting for better weather, tempers began to flare. Upon the fourth day in our delay I watched as two of the merchants we had picked up along the route were begrudgingly unloaded along with their cargo. They were angry at being displaced so inhospitably and complained to the Captain that they had paid good money to secure passage to the Imperial City. The Captain could do nothing but return a portion of their purses and help secure passage for them on an alternate ship. While the crew idled away the rest of the time on the island, we found it best to stay aboard the ship.

As the weather changed and we readied to set sail, a stranger boarded our ship and was escorted directly to the Captain's quarters. The man was tall, dark of complexion, like a Nubian, with hair and beard as black as a moonless sky and braided in the style of the Saracen. He was dressed in a loosely woven robe, like sack cloth but black as coal, hooded to conceal most of his face, and making him look more like a phantom from the Underworld than a mortal man. He was accompanied by a youth garbed in the same sack cloth, only of lesser quantity, enough to cover his loins and not much else. The boy had a small rug, or some sort of thick fabric rolled in a tight bundle, strapped to his back, which served as a short cloak as well as his sleeping mat. He followed the dark stranger carrying a trunk, which held the elder's belongings.

Though it was not unusual for a merchant ship to pick up an additional passenger on an unscheduled stop, I found it strange that this mysterious traveler had displaced a couple of good-paying merchants and their wares. Stranger still was the very large and apparently heavy crate and a simple wooden coffin the stranger had caused to be loaded into the cargo hold. The contents of the crate could not be determined as it was sealed tightly and bore no markings. The crew felt uneasy about bringing the stranger and his coffin aboard and made their feelings known to the Captain. I shared the same feelings with them.

The stranger and his servant were most mysterious in deed, the elder having kept himself locked within the Captain's quarters for the remainder of the voyage, never showing himself, not even to relieve himself or to take in fresh air when the day was calm. The boy was as mysterious as his master. His manner of speech (when he spoke at all) and his appearance was that of the natives from the Kingdoms of the Nile. He had no interaction with any of the passengers on the voyage and slept on deck at the entrance of the Captain's cabin. He ate by himself and sat in deep meditation during most of the day, stopping at intervals throughout the day to kneel upon his mat to offer prayers to his heathen god. Even though he was taunted by crew and passenger alike, he kept his guard, and his strangeness of manner kept most away.

He did show some affinity to Vannozzo, who toyed with the youth, causing him to occasionally smile. During another stormy evening, as most had sought shelter from the falling rain, I felt sympathy for the boy and brought him a cloak to cover himself. Truth be told, I cared not for the youth, but thought that a small kindness thrown in his direction would yield some information about his master and the mysterious cargo that had been brought onto the ship. I sat with him for a brief period and tried to engage him, hoping to pry his tongue loose enough to answer some of my inquiries.

With much perseverance I learned that the elder was a scholar in search of truths and answers to many of the greatest riddles of the world. He had traveled throughout the ancient world and had most recently been to ancient Alexandria and to the great libraries in Rhodes. They had been on their way to Constantinople to seek additional knowledge at the massive Royal Archives when a storm had diverted their ship to the island just a day before we arrived. The boy never spoke the scholar's name, only referring to him as The Master. The more I questioned the boy, the more reticent he became, until he fell completely silent. Silent he remained for the rest of the voyage.

Our vessel followed the established Venetian trade routes, and with skilled navigators and exceptional weather we were able to cross the Aegean, pass through the Dardanelles, and reach the Sea of Marmara, gaining a few days that had been lost to the tempest. As we approached the southern outskirts of Constantinople, under cover of darkness, the captain set anchor close to the abbey of St. Stephen. There, the scholar and his boy quietly disembarked and were met by a group of black robed and hooded monks, all carrying torches and moving in total silence. A fortified wagon, like the ones used to carry large blocks of marble from the quarries of Carrara, was awaiting The Master's arrival, and it groaned when it received his mysterious cargo. As surreptitiously as their arrival had been, so too was their sudden departure. All on board were muttering, some were cursing and making the sign of the evil eye. None dared ask the captain any questions, but all felt a sigh of relief when the strangers were finally away.

The walled city of Constantinople is more impressive than any can imagine, especially as the sun breaches the horizon and casts its golden light upon ancient stone. Its massive walls can hold all the cities in Tuscany together and still have room for a hundred vineyards. In all my travels to that point, I had never beheld so many grand palaces, nor seen so many and such varied domes and towers of the Orthodox churches. Our ship sailed passed the mighty walls of this ancient city, and then right under the great Palace of Bucoleon and the magnificent Hagia Sophia. We circumnavigated the city in all its glory and entered the famous Golden Horn.

As we approached the great chain that spans the Horn and is connected to the Tower of Galata, our ship was forced to weigh anchor until inspections were made and all the necessary tariffs were paid. Though we were sailing a Venetian vessel and most of the merchants still enjoyed the privileged status granted to all Venetian merchants by the previous emperors, there were, still amongst us, a few Tuscan traders whose purses were made lighter by heavy tariff. Pietro and I were trading under the protection of the Dandolo, who held a very special place in the hearts of the imperial court, and thus did not have to pay any tariffs to the customs agents.

This privilege would only last for a few more years as the fickleness and duplicity of the Greeks would cause imperial promises and contracts to crumble into dust and cause major upheaval throughout the world. But at that time, after all duties were paid, the chain was lowered to allow further passage of our ship into the Horn. We watched from the deck of the ship as we sailed past the Genoese, Pisan, and Amalfi Quarters, all greatly diminished with the exile of most of the Latin merchants, whose petty bickering and jealousies were brought to the East with every ship and caravan.

Violence between each quarter had been simmering and eventually had spilled into the streets of the Capitol itself. Many innocent Greeks were injured, which caused such political unrest that the Emperor, in a furious state, caused all Latins, except for the

Venetians, to be cast into prison, exiled, or worse. News reached us back in Siena of the demise of many of our countrymen who had met their untimely destruction at the hands of the angry Greek mob. Many of the magnificent villas of the wealthiest Pisani and Genovese were burnt to the ground. Many had lost everything, and many who had still retained holdings in the West were ransomed off for exceedingly high prices, only to be banished from the imperium forever. Those were the fortunate ones.

I gave up a prayer of thanks to Almighty God that Giancarlo was given the wisdom and foresight to ally himself with the Venetians, for he had written to me from the safety of his palazzo in the very heart of the Venetian Quarter of the horrors that had beset our brothers all around him. Those horrors of which he had written had unfolded before our eyes, the stark contrast evidenced as we sailed into the Venetian Quarter. It was as if we had sailed from the Inferno into Paradiso. Though it was then two weeks past Pentecost, all in the company thought it was most auspicious to have arrived in the capital city by mid-June, on the feast day of San Marco. There were great celebrations being observed throughout the Quarter, and thus very little activity in the large piazza that spread out from the docks.

We had expected to see Giancarlo at the dock and were quite disappointed when our expectations were not met. Instead, we saw several very large wagons, being led by a young man who was familiar to me. Giancarlo had been detained and had sent his servant, Nikos, to greet us and to escort us to his villa. Nikos had offered himself to oversee the unloading of the merchandise and its transport to Giancarlo's warehouses located within a few blocks from the pier, but my pride and youthful insecurity would have none of that. I insisted I would oversee my own shipment.

Nikos sent the servant back to Giancarlo to tell him that all would be along once the merchandise was securely stored, and he was most agreeable as we completed our task. Although I had held a jealous suspicion of him even from our first encounter in France several years earlier, there was an endearing quality about him that caused me to warm to him as the days went on. Though I had found him rather stoic and reserved in France, he seemed a different man in his homeland. He talked incessantly, and by the time we reached my uncle's villa, we had been informed of every major event that had happened in the Imperial City for the previous hundred years.

Forgive me, dear Nikos, for any slight. I marvel at the clarity of my memory of that day.

The villa of Giancarlo Manenti, situated in the very heart of the Venetian Quarter of the Golden Horn, was a magnificent edifice. Unlike most of the other residences in the area, the villa stood apart from the other buildings. In his planning, Giancarlo had purchased several contiguous properties and had the aged buildings torn down. He then erected his grand villa in the center of the combined properties. The villa was built upon a raised foundation, and Giancarlo had wisely instructed the builders to slope the land away from the foundation in all directions. The perimeter of the entire property was enclosed with a sturdy wall as tall as two men. The grounds within the walls were planted with fruit trees and vegetable gardens.

As we approached, Giancarlo arrived at the doorway, and Donna Donata pushed past him, sprinting across the courtyard at the front of the villa and throwing her arms about Anna's shoulders. With tears in her eyes, she embraced young Vannozzo and smothered him with kisses. Finally, she enveloped me in a loving embrace and kissed me upon both cheeks, holding my face within the palms of her hands. She was so pleased to see us, and longing for news from back home, she completely ignored etiquette and would not let any of us go. I must confess, in our absence I had longed to see both, and at that moment, did not feel compelled to follow Sienese protocol. The lady did not even acknowledge my companions but brought us directly to Giancarlo. Sebastiano, Salvatore, and Nikos followed behind.

Giancarlo remained in the doorway but showed his happiness with a huge grin that covered half of his face. He threw his arms around me, kissed me on both cheeks, and welcomed me into his household. He accepted a formal curtsey from Anna, who then threw her arms around his neck and held him tightly, crying tears of joy. Giancarlo picked up his grandson, twirled him around, and threw him into the air. He was amazed at how much the child had grown in the few short years we had been separated.

Fighting my emotions, I bowed to him and respectfully began to make introductions when he interrupted me and said to Nikos, "Well met, my friend. You have brought us our dear friends, Sebastiano and Salvatore. Welcome, friends, to my humble home." He hugged each of them and gave them a quick, impish wink. I was surprised that Giancarlo had remembered my cousins, but then again, I was constantly being surprised by this man. I knew that there was so much more to him than he would ever let one know, and I anticipated there would be many more surprises left for me to learn.

We were shown to our quarters and allowed to refresh ourselves, after which we met our hosts in the central courtyard, in the cooling shade of the palm garden. There we talked about Siena, Anna, and the baby, and business in general, though Giancarlo and I would talk more seriously about the details of our business in the privacy of his study. Donna Donata hung upon every word and asked Anna a million questions. The conversation was more for Donna Donata's sake, for I had kept up very detailed correspondence with Giancarlo since he had left Siena, keeping him abreast of all the political and social happenings, including the gossip within the city and abroad. However, he did show interest in most of the idle conversation for I rarely, if ever, included such news in my letters to him, and such idle chatter made him feel at home.

The ladies inquisition produced more facts than all my letters over the previous few years. My companions said little but politely listened and added some color when we talked about the happenings outside of Siena. Giancarlo reiterated to me his condolences for my father's passing and extended his condolences to both of my cousins in such a way and with such emotion that I found it quite strange, for I had thought that Giancarlo had thought little of my father. I was shocked when he told me in a very sincere voice that my father was a great man. Both Salvatore and Sebastiano nodded solemnly in agreement. Again, I felt that there was much more that had passed between these three than I had ever known.

We talked until early evening and then we were all called into the dining salon for the evening meal. Donna Donata had taken great delight in having all my favorite Tuscan dishes prepared and served with the finest wines from my father's estates so that we would feel at home, though in truth, she had been tremendously homesick, and it helped to ease her melancholia.

Following dinner and before we retired for the night, I privately met with Giancarlo in the courtyard to talk business. We spoke of what had happened in the past, yet, most discreetly, he made no reference to Genevieve. He also made no mention of the real reason for his summons nor of anything that was to take place in the future. When I did question him, he stopped me and told me that all would be revealed when the entire company was assembled at a dinner that he was hosting in three days' time. Though I was tired, and the cool night air gave promise to a good night's sleep, my emotions ran high and my head was swimming with questions. Why had I been brought there? What plans had been made? What peril lay in store for me? Sleep did not come to me until just before the sky was to lighten, and then, only a fleeting moment filled with all sorts of horrible visions.

I spent the next two days being introduced to Giancarlo's acquaintances in the Quarter and throughout the capitol city. During this time Nikos had done his best to entertain me and it was then that our friendship began to take hold. Pietro seemed a bit weary, or maybe more jealous of the relationship that had been developing, but truth be known, I had, in the very brief time I had spent with Nikos, developed a greater affinity to him than I had with Pietro. Nikos and I had become, and have always been, kindred spirits, and have trusted completely in each other. It wasn't so with Pietro, for so many reasons.

At a mid-morning gathering in the shaded courtyard of Giancarlo's palazzo, Nikos had introduced me to his uncle and guardian Nikelas Choniates, who was the Imperial Librarian and Keeper of Antiquities in the Church of the Holy Apostles, a very important position. He was a historian and trusted advisor to the Emperor, and his duties included acquisition and oversight of the Emperor's private collection of artifacts. Giancarlo had long done business with the Librarian and was working on a very special deal about which he had been extremely secretive.

I was surprised to notice how similar in appearance were the younger Nikos and the elder Nikelas. Though the elder had longer hair and sported a lengthy beard, both of which were the color of silver, his facial features were as youthful as his nephew's and his eyes, like the younger, were a light hazel. They were of similar height, though the elder's stature was slightly bent with age, and he walked with the slowness of many years. He was dressed in a long, white, hooded robe, and he leaned upon an intricately carved wooden staff. I was also amazed to witness the sudden appearance of the Master, that mysterious scoundrel whom we had encountered on our journey. The two stood against each other in total contrast.

Apparently, everyone seemed to know each other, and after being invited to sit at the table, Nikos and I were excused to attend to our own business. The Master appeared to be the shadow of the Librarian, his hair and beard black as coal, his features ancient, except for his piercing blue eyes, with his long, black, hooded cape and robe. My interest had surely piqued and I wanted to stay and listen in on the business that was to be conducted, but a quick glance from Giancarlo informed me that I was not invited.

As we left the compound, I questioned Nikos about the Master and shared with him my distrust of the scoundrel. Nikos assured me that Giancarlo was aware of the character of the Master, for they had been doing business for many years. Nikos had shown no fear of the Master, but rather feared that his poor uncle Nikelas would, once again, end up with the short end of whatever bargain they were discussing. He then tried to assure me that all would be well, and that I would change my opinion of the Master when I got to know him.

We spent the rest of the morning and afternoon transacting business with several prominent Greek merchants. As afternoon faded into evening, we found ourselves back at Giancarlo's villa for the evening meal and that most important summit meeting. Our dinner party consisted of Giancarlo, Nikos, Salvatore, Sebastiano, and me. Donna Donata had a separate dinner prepared for the ladies and served in the far end of the villa. Such talk of business was of no concern to the women. I questioned Giancarlo as to the whereabouts of Enrico, and he told me that he had arrived in the city and would be joining us toward the end of the meal. He also indicated that the seventh member of our party, the young diConte, would also be joining us at the meeting. I had forgotten about Ugolino and was anxious to talk with him again.

As darkness fell, a servant announced the arrival of one of our missing guests. I turned in anticipation of seeing Enrico again, and was surprised to see the Master being admitted into the courtyard. In the blackness of the night, he appeared to be a shadow from the depths of Hell. Giancarlo raised himself and embraced him, welcoming the Master to the table. In a most formal gesture, Giancarlo introduced each of us to the Master, who, in turn, bowed most respectfully with each introduction. Despite Niko's assurances, I had become most watchful about the stranger and quietly leaned toward Giancarlo to whisper my caution into his ear. The Master turned toward me and admonished me for being most impolite as to whisper before, and about, an invited guest. His voice, though seemingly familiar to me, assaulted me, as if I had been slapped across the face, and it caused me to sit upright, in silence.

Giancarlo grinned as the Master seated himself at the table and began to help himself to the food that had been laid before him. He stared at each of us, never removing his black hood from his head, and motioning to Giancarlo with a half-devoured lamb shank, he said, "Thought I would miss the meeting. Where is the other?" I caught a glint of his icy blue eyes in the moonlight and continued to stare at the demonic apparition in silence.

Finally, I broke my stare and turned to Giancarlo, saying, "Where is Enrico and Ugolino, and what does he," pointing to the Master, "have to do with this?" The Master turned to me and in a mocking voice said, "The seer's son is truly blind, just as it has been foretold. Look closely, young pec-ii, and see what your heart should tell you and what your mind refuses to acknowledge. See now what Giancarlo and young Nikos know, and even what young Tarchon and Tyrsenos have realized."

As if a veil had been lifted from my eyes, I saw before me, in the darkness of that imposing menace, the twinkle of Enrico's vivid blue eyes and the warmth of his broad smile. The saints in Heaven must have been rolling with laughter as the charade was ended and my dear friend and mentor was revealed to me. What manner of devilish tricks, I had asked myself, would cause such a powerful and respected man to transform his person into such a menacing character? What, I asked, was this subterfuge, all about?

Before I could gain an answer or explanation, the servant announced the arrival of the Scholar. Another puzzle, I thought. We had been awaiting Ugolino's appearance, and we were instead being joined by another mystery guest. The announced guest entered the courtyard, dressed in a white robe with a hood pulled forward upon his head so that his facial features were completely obscured. He approached the table but unlike the Master, the Scholar did not seat himself. He stood a few feet away in total silence. Giancarlo raised from the table and gestured to us all, "All hail, the Scholar of Athos. Welcome to our little party." With that, the Scholar pulled his hood from his head and revealed himself to be none other than a totally unamused Ugolino di Conti.

Giancarlo summoned the servants, the table was cleared, and more wine was brought. We waited until all was settled, and the company was guaranteed total privacy before Giancarlo began the meeting.

"The world," he began, "is in total chaos. The very soul of man is in danger of being cast into the darkness. A mighty game is being played out upon the world stage, and the forces of darkness are battling to win superiority over the forces of light. The Muslim is taking over every port from Egypt to Cardiz; the Mongol is spreading his dominion from the Far East to our very doorstep. The emperor from the North has risen time and time again to reclaim the realm that he thinks was left to him by the great Roman emperors, and the emperor in the East conspires to reclaim that which was taken from him by the West.

The Church stands alone to bring peace and order to the lands, and by doing so, is being attacked on every front. The one true shepherd of Christ's Holy Church has been openly challenged by Barbarossa and his surrogate popes, and His Most Glorious Emperor Comnenus schemes with anyone to use subterfuge to gain that which he feels is rightfully his. The world is falling apart, my dear compatriots, and that is not very good for business." At last, I thought to myself, the true Giancarlo reveals himself.

"Our dear cousin, His Holiness, Alexander, and the church he heads, is in dire need of our help. Some may believe in prophesy, and some may say that the outcome of the coming battle has already been cast in stone, but I care little for prophesy. I believe in action. I do not believe that we sit and do nothing while we watch our predetermined destiny play itself out. We must be the architects of our own destiny.

We must rise up and lend our support to the one true constant in this world, the one true entity whose purpose it is to shepherd all of the inhabitants of the world and to nurture peace and good commerce between men, the Roman Catholic Church.

"It is up to us to help the fates to set things right in this chaotic world. We must come to the aid of the Church in her hour of need and secure the Chair of Saint Peter, lest it fall into the hands of Barbarossa. Its rightful heir, His Most Holy, Alexander, who was chosen by the Holy Spirit, has had to endlessly battle with that powerful emperor to the north—he, whose sole ambition it is to eliminate any who stand in the way of his quest for world dominance. It is true that many of us have benefited from his supposed protection and grace. I, for sure, am counted first amongst the many. Yet I truly believe that such beneficial arrangements, however lucrative at the time of their consummation, are mere devices in which to snare an unsuspecting populous in advance of complete military subjugation and tyrannical over-lordship. We have seen how the great Barbarossa has used his favors to turn our countrymen against each other and to spread dissention throughout the land. We can look beyond these very walls to see the destruction that has been wrought by that villainous emperor of the West and which has been allowed to fester within this mighty city by the unwitting emperor of the East. We have seen the wrath of the Holy Roman Emperor inflicted upon his own subjects who voice opposition to the injustices to which he subjects his own people.

"The way I see it, is though the Church has not always been a fair and beneficial partner to commerce, it has always been our most steadfast consumer, and the one true force to motivate the people's hearts and souls to stand against the imperial tyrants. With its sacredly chosen leader at the helm of that Most Holy Ship, he alone will be able to navigate these dangerous waters and keep afloat that binding force of Commerce, which is the lifeblood of our society. Alexander must be proven to be the rightful captain of that holy ship, to all the clergy, to all the kings and rulers throughout the lands, and to the masses of humanity upon whose faith he draws his earthly strength.

"That proof has been given to us directly by the Holy Spirit, through his humble servant Malachy, the Seer of Armaugh. It was transcribed and verified with my own eyes, and with those of Giovanni's father, by the Most Reverend Bernard of Clairvaux into the Holy Book of Prophesies. That most sacred text, through treachery and deceit, was stolen by the servants of Barbarossa from the very bosom of the Holy Church, and has been stolen again, by the thieving Greek agents of the Emperor Comnenus. It is here in this very city as we speak. Great is the greed of these two tyrants that they would covet the very word of God and keep such wisdom locked away from the eyes of Christ's own flock.

"I, through fortune or through what others would claim to be destiny, had, upon arriving in the Imperial City, learned of the theft and subsequent safekeeping of this most sacred text from my young apprentice, Nikos, who, most fortunately claims to be the beloved nephew of Niketas Choniates, Director of Antiquities. Under his careful watch the holy book has been entrusted. No one here knows of the origin and the importance of this sacred text. I dare say not even the Emperor himself knows of the power that rests in the written word of God. I, alone, together with Giovanni's late father, and Enrico's aged uncle, The Patriarch, have looked into the eyes of the godly Malachy and have listened through his own voice to the spoken word of the Holy Spirit.

"Alexander, in his constant war against Barbarossa, has learned of this precious gift from Heaven too late to prevent its theft and its subsequent journey to the East. No kindly words for the Roman Emperor are written in that text, but glory and honor and ultimate victory of the Vicar of Christ and Christ's Holy Church have been foreseen. The great battle has been revealed to us, and I, as always, intend to mitigate my potential losses by staking my wager upon the winning horse.

"Over the course of several months, I have labored over a plan to steal the sacred text from beneath the very nose of the Greek tyrant and return it to Rome, and its rightful steward. I have had the counsel of the Patriarch of Grado, whose wisdom and guidance have comforted me, and whose intimate knowledge of the entire manuscript has proven most valuable to the formulation of my plan. His Holiness, Alexander, has been well appraised of my plan and has, both financially and spiritually, pledged his support for this endeavor.

"Each of you have been chosen because of your abilities, though the Patriarch and His Holiness both believe that the choice has not been mine alone but has been made before the beginning of time by a power far greater than mortal man. We are the company of seven valiant knights, chosen by the Holy Spirit, to carry out this most important quest. I ask you, each unto himself, to speak freely your intent and to swear upon your life, and the lives of your children, to fulfill the task that has been laid before you."

He looked at each of us and in turn spoke our true names. "Some of you have answered the call of His Holiness, while some of you have answered the call for your own reason. Still others may perhaps believe in prophesy and feel it is your destiny to join this company on this sacred task, for grace, for glory, or for gold. My good friend Enrico Dandolo of the Republic of Venice, and I, Giancarlo Manenti of Siena and of late from the Golden City, both master merchants of land and sea, accept the call for love of gold. We make no shame of that, for that is who we are and what we do."

The Master spoke, saying, "Long have I been preparing for this very role that I play, though in the beginning, I was totally ignorant of the reason for my choice for such disguise, nor of the valiant use for which the Spirit would have for me. I have, for years, on occasion, made special acquisitions for the Most Glorious Emperor and his wealthy associates, cloaked in the disguise of the Master. Niketas Choniates has long been eager to welcome me back to Constantinople with open purse to purchase for the pleasure of his master any treasure that I could relinquish from the Holy Lands to the East. My partnership with the great Giancarlo Manenti has been most satisfying and rewarding, and he commands my utmost trust and respect. We have counseled together over the details of his plan and I find it to be both sound and logical. I pledge myself to this quest, for the safety of my family and all their enterprises upon the land and upon the sea, and to the honor of the Great Republic of Venice, who has, despite the personal desires of many of the previous pontiffs, always come to the aid of the Mother Church in her time of need.

"Young Nikos Choniates of the Golden City, apprentice to the great Giancarlo Manenti. You have been chosen for your obvious closeness to the situation here in the city and your astute perception of the value of the treasure that is hidden away within its walls, and for bringing such a valuable weapon to my attention. Your closeness, and I must say, the uncanny resemblance to your uncle, will be most helpful to our quest. You have served me well, and in this you will ultimately be providing a service to a much greater master. Are you willing to give your life for what some would say to be a Western cause, though intelligent men would say that the outcome of this quest will affect the entire world? I seek from you the true reasons that have brought you to this table?"

Nikos spoke. "You have been as a father to me since your arrival in the Holy City. You have guided me and elevated my status amongst its leading citizens. You have placed great trust in me and my abilities to handle your business affairs, and you have treated me with much respect that should not ordinarily be due to a person of so low a station in life. I am willing to pledge my life to you and to your cause, for if you have accepted such risk unto yourself, and have so craftily formulated a grand plan, I will swear to you my trust and my service. I come for glory, Master, and out of loyalty, to serve my master and his son. I seek no gold nor care for chasing destiny. Where thou shalt go, so I shall follow?"

Giancarlo was obviously pleased with his apprentice's response. I must admit that Nikos' words, spoken in truth and from the heart, had awakened my youthful jealousies, and yet, his sincerity and his unquestioning loyalty to Giancarlo had caused me to feel shame at my pettiness, and in some way had ultimately strengthened my fondness for the young Greek. It was, from that moment onward, that I considered Nikos more of a brother and less of a rival.

Giancarlo turned to my two cousins and asked, "What say you, noble Tarchon and Tyrsenos of the ancient house of Noah? Your people have, since the time of the flood, kept themselves apart from the quarrels of western men. Why have you come to pledge yourselves to the cause of Mother Church?"

Both men looked at each other and then at each man seated around the table. Sebastiano spoke first. "We come out of loyalty to our cousin, and to honor a promise that was made to his father that we would protect the pec-ii of our people and to follow him to his destiny, for our destiny is woven into him, and our salvation will be met through him." And Salvatore added, "We seek no gold, nor glory, but bear witness and follow the Prophesy, as is our duty by the command of our father, the great Zil-at of Curtun. We hold the Most Holy Alexander to his pledge to lend aid to our people in our time of need and to keep hidden that which has remained unseen for a thousand years."

Turning his inquisition to the Scholar, Giancarlo demanded, "And you, Ugolino di Conti, son of Anagni and Scholar of Athos, what cause is it you seek upon this holy mission?"

The cleric spoke in a soft and measured tone, "I serve my master, the True and Holy Father who rules the world with the Blessing of Christ as proven in the sacred whispering of the Holy Spirit. I come to retrieve that most holy text that was dictated by God Himself, transcribed by his reverent servant, Malachy, and given unto the safekeeping of the Successor of Peter. Such holy book was stolen by the bastard German King Barbarossa, and was, in turn, stolen by the thieving Greek King Comnenus. I seek the safe return of that which belongs to the Holy Father, and I seek divine retribution against those who have wrought great harm to our Mother Church."

As each of my companions stood to present the reason for their calling, I gave much thought to the true reason why I had joined this quest. I knew it not to be the actual calling of Giancarlo to discuss our business, for such details had, over the many months, been chronicled in our monthly letters. I thought it might have been for glory and adventure, for youth does cradle such wild and stupid ideas. Most plausible to me was the promise of reward—Giancarlo's longtime, sought-after prize of Stigliano. Was it the castle itself, or was it the thought of besting my mentor in this incredible deal? Only now do I see that it was gluttony that drove my desire to speak. I would never be satisfied merely inheriting whatever was left of Giancarlo's empire; I wanted it all. I was prideful enough, envious enough, and audacious enough to see that moment as the golden opportunity to build my own, even greater empire.

As sure as I was, I found it hard to focus for my mind was a whirlwind of possibilities. Lack of sleep had hindered logical thinking. Since my first sleepless night in the Patriarch's palazzo, the night in which I had been plagued with horrid visions of the destinies of my closest friends, I had been beset with dreams so bizarre and frightful, as to cause me to dread the goddess of sleep's loving touch upon my eyes. Such visions I attributed to the anxiety I was feeling for this very meeting, the results manifesting themselves in the deterioration of my mood and physical complexion. I had thought I could convince my companions that my malady was due to the long sea voyage and the perils that we had managed to avoid, but Giancarlo was not so easily deceived, and Enrico was sure of the source of my melancholia, having discussions with me prior to our leaving Venice. Giancarlo had seen the look I was carrying before. He told me he had seen it when he and my father were companions about my age. Casting an affirmative glance at the Master he demanded, "Tell us what the seer has foreseen." I had not been prepared for his demand and stood frozen as all eyes turned toward me. Hesitantly I shared my visions.

"All is dark. The smell of death is strong. A knight lies beneath a sleeping king—awakened before the crystal box that holds the sacred word of God. The Apostles weep as the demon serpent slithers 'round the holy prize. A lesser eagle will fall and give false testimony as the shards conceal the lie. The great eagle will be defeated by the bishop's knights as the hand-less saint will sanctify the eagle's servant. All praise to a false god! The white bishop will gain his prize, but the black knight will be no more. Lo, he will come again—a blazing white knight to follow an unseen path to glory and fame. He will push the lion from his golden throne though never claim the jeweled crown for himself.

"All praise to God, for the eagle, with his keen sight, will be blinded to the bishop's deception, and will be caught in the snare of his own making—forced to accept the mercy of the shining bishop. The white rocci will build their castles, one for good, and one for naught, for one will be a sanctuary and one will be an unrealized dream. Two knights will stand strong against the eagle but will be betrayed by one of their own. They watch as their world is consumed in treachery and fire. The bishop's pawn will take the bishop's seat. For good and for evil he will reign. His war against the strega's cat will cause the rat to feast upon the carcass of men and cast the world into darkness and sin."

All were silent, and then all spoke at once. Some had offered their interpretations of my visions, some questioned me further, while others sought answers from Giancarlo and the Master. Finally, Giancarlo spoke. "And how sayeth the seer's son of this holy quest?"

Again, I thought long and hard before answering. Then, in a calm and steady voice I replied, "I, Giovanni Bartolomeo Pecci da Cortona, son of the great Vincenzo Pecci, also known as Uni-Tau, son of Tarxin, Pec-ii of the Taurisi people, accept this quest for grace, and for glory, and for gold. I open my heart most honestly before this gathering of truly noble men and admit that I seek the glory and the honor that will come to us from the Holy Father should we succeed. I seek the Lord's Grace as I enter into his service and I hope He will show me mercy, should I wrest His Holy Book from the powers of darkness, and free me from the hellish visions that have plagued me both day and night. And I pledge my life to this quest, for gold and the promises given to me by His Most Holy, Alexander III, the true heir to Saint Peter's throne. Though my vision is clouded, and the future has not been clearly revealed to me, I have great confidence in our band of thieves and feel very certain that Giancarlo's plan, whatever it is, will guide us to victory, or at least keep us upon our own paths to our destiny."

Giancarlo gave me a quizzical stare and then grinned. "Spoken as a true Corsair."

Although you would perhaps find such a derogatory appellation quite offensive, I did not then, nor do I now, for during those times the Englanders in the court of Henry had begun to call the Sienese bankers 'Corsari" and had held us in contempt as much as they did the Muslim or the Jew. Giancarlo's growing contempt of the English, even though they were a main supplier of wool for our business, had caused him to wear such insult as a badge of honor, and he would smile most wickedly whenever he used the term.

"So be it, then. Our company has been formed and our task has been laid before us. From here there is no turning back." With that, Giancarlo proceeded to disclose to us his plan. All in the party agreed it was a sound plan. Much time and effort had been put into its design and Giancarlo and Nikos had spent many months preparing for its execution. Giancarlo had bought the Director of Antiquities' trust with many choice acquisitions obtained from reliable sources in the Latin Kingdom in the East. The two had become great friends, especially since Giancarlo had used Nikos' knowledge of his uncle's habits to provide the old man with all his earthly wants and desires.

Their meeting on the previous day was to discuss a most precious acquisition that the Master had brought with him from the ancient city of Alexandria. The Master had also been busy for several months laying the groundwork to make the plan work. He had been working from Venice, through his agents in the East, to locate certain objects of special interest to the Emperor. Through a bit of luck, and a vast amount of gold dinari, the Master had obtained the burial sarcophagus of the great Macedonian king, Alexander, Ruler of the Ancient World. The Emperor had heard the legends of the power and beauty of this sarcophagus and had insisted upon having the treasure brought to Constantinople to be used for his own personal burial chamber that was being built in the Church of the Holy Apostles.

The ancient relic, in its protective casing, would have to be positioned in the church and placed under the watchful eye of the Director. To ensure the Director's unsuspecting collaboration in Giancarlo's plan, the Master had also obtained the incorrupt body of Saint Nicephorus, the ancient Patriarch of Constantinople, whose remains, minus his holy hands, had been discovered in Prokonnis. The Master, through endless inquiry, had located the hands of the venerated saint in a monastery on Mount Athos. Ugolino, in the guise of a scholarly monk from the monastery of Lavra on the Holy Mountain, had sailed directly from Venice on the evening tide following our meeting at the Patriarch's palace. At Mount Athos he assumed his role as the Scholar and, with help from Vatican agents within the monastery, was able to steal the hands of the saint and a couple of other treasures and set sail directly to the Imperial City. He had slipped into the capitol several days before our arrival, and with an introduction from Nikos, the Scholar had gained the trust of the Director and access to the sacred scrolls kept in the library on the upper levels of the Church.

To endear himself further with the Director, the Scholar had offered to convey to the imperial treasury, at a reasonable price, the severed hands of the ancient patriarch, St. Nicephorus, he had brought with him, at great risk, from the Holy Archives in his ancient monastery. He would not tell the Director how he had come into possession of such a treasure but had dangled the holy bait in front of the Director's nose until he was given free rein to review the library's sacred scrolls. Ugolino had used the opportunity to scout the interior of the church for potential entry points and exit routes.

It had seemed that Sebastiano, Salvatore, and I were the only newcomers to this game. As risky as this business would become, I possessed the confidence of youth, and the drive of greed, and convinced myself of the ultimate success of the mission. My only trepidation was that I had brought Anna and the child along with me on this journey, needlessly placing their lives in jeopardy. But how was I to know the peril that was about to unfold?

XV

Execution of the Plan

The plan was set in motion on the very next day. Nikos and I met with the Director and brought him to one of Giancarlo's warehouses just inside the Venetian Quarter. There we were joined by Giancarlo and the Master. In a remote corner stood a large wooden crate and a smaller wooden coffin. The Master recounted how he, after much searching, had located the final resting place of the Great Alexander, amid the ruins of the ancient city of Sidon. At great peril to himself, and at considerable expense to Giancarlo, he had managed to eliminate the guards and gain access to the prize. The sarcophagus was loaded onto a wagon, whose wheels had been covered in sack cloth, and silently transported to a waiting vessel that Giancarlo had provided. The theft had gone flawlessly, and the Master was anxious to get his prize to the safety of the Imperial City.

Fortune had seemed to turn against the Master as the ship was almost sunk in a gale but had managed to make safe harbor on the island of Crete. The Master's misfortune continued as a band of pirates stalked the Venetian ship in the Sea of Marmara and caused the Captain to pull into port at the island of Buyukada, where the Master and his cargo were delayed for two days. But the Master's luck had again turned, for news had reached the docks that the pirate ship that had been plying those waters had run afoul of another Venetian ship and had been destroyed.

Feeling that he had been saved by the intercession of Saint Nicholas, the Master visited the monastery of Agios Nikolaos, and there discovered the hidden resting place of Saint Nicephorus. The saint's remains had been defiled by the Stoudites, who had stolen his body from his tomb within the Church of the Apostles and had hidden it in this monastery. The zealots had chopped off the saint's hands, which had penned so many bold ecclesiastic writings and had sent them to Lavra on Mount Athos. The Master had learned all of this from the monks who had invited him in for prayer and hospitality. Seeing it his duty to restore the ancient Patriarch to his rightful resting place in the Imperial City, the Master decided to remove the remains in the early morning hours when the monks had finished Matins and were still half asleep. The body, remarkably undefiled by time and still covered with the Patriarch's original vestments, was wrapped in a sail cloth and brought to the ship, where it was placed in a simple wooden coffin; it traveled the rest of the way along with the sarcophagus of the King of the World.

The Director was captivated with the entire story, which I knew to be a complete fabrication. I did not know exactly how Giancarlo, or the Master had come into possession of the two relics, but I did know that the Master was in possession of both when he boarded our ship in Crete. His story sounded plausible to the Director who was delicately caressing each crate and its contents. The large wooden crate was opened first to reveal the intricately carved sarcophagus, and the Director let out an audible gasp at the sight. He reveled at being so close to greatness and swooned at the touch of the gleaming white marble. He was no less in awe of the simple wooden coffin that held the remains of the saint. The Emperor, he insisted, would be most pleased with his acquisition and the heroic return of the city's beloved Patriarch. A space had already been prepared to receive the large crate containing the sarcophagus, and the saint's tomb had been prepared for his return.

Giancarlo was pleased his clients were satisfied with the merchandise and agreed to have both delivered to the Church as soon as payment had been received. The Director was more than accommodating and then sent Nikos to the Imperial Treasury with instructions to transfer Giancarlo's payment to him by midafternoon. Giancarlo arranged to have the crates loaded upon a specially constructed wagon designed to hold such a heavy weight, and transported to the church, to be placed under the care of the Director.

Giancarlo then invited the Director to his villa for a midday meal and a celebratory glass of Tuscan wine.

The plan, to that point, had been going quite well. While Giancarlo was entertaining the Director and the Master, I was left to oversee the loading of the wagon and the transport to the church. Two guards had been posted at the main entrance awaiting the transfer. We were instructed to move the crate into a predetermined position in the east side of the transept that was accomplished with the help of six of Giancarlo's strongest men. The coffin containing the body of the saint was laid to rest to the right of Alexander's sarcophagus before the alter in the chapel. The men were discharged and sent back to the warehouse with the wagon.

As I stood there, I spied in the center of the transept a large glass enclosure atop a dais. Within the center of that enclosure stood a pedestal upon which rested the Book of Prophesies by Malachy. The entire floor of the glass enclosure had been filled with all manner of vile and poisonous serpents. The Director was ingenious in his methods for keeping his valuables very safe, no doubt expecting some future attempt of thievery of the holy relic. The guards remained at the door not interested in what was transpiring within the church, and enough noise was made to allow the Scholar to exit from a secret side panel at the bottom of the crate that had concealed a chamber large enough to fit the man and the equipment needed. He immediately disappeared into the shadows with a large sack he had been carrying. I quickly sealed the secret chamber and exited the church, leaving the Scholar inside to unlock the doors on the upper levels so that the rest of the company could gain access. I left the guards at the entrance and returned to Giancarlo's villa just as Nikos returned from the Imperial Treasury. The money had been transferred and the goods had been delivered.

Nikos excused himself from the group under the guise of finishing a business transaction for Giancarlo, and the four of us—the Director, the Master, Giancarlo, and I—returned to the church for the Director's final inspection. We entered the church and removed the lid of the smaller crate containing the remains of the saint. The body was still wrapped in sail cloth as the Master recounted. The saint's original vestments still enveloped the his corpse. The gold thread and embroidered jewels still gleamed in the sun's rays. The Director brushed his hand gently over the fabric and whispered a prayer. The ancient saint's hands, which had been delivered by the Scholar several days earlier, had been placed under lock and key in a reliquary behind the main altar. The Director was ecstatic over the return of the city's patron saint. Thanks to the noble efforts of the Master, and a most fortunate and timely visit from the Scholar, the body of Saint Nicephorus would be made whole again, and his eternal soul would once again reside within the hallowed halls of this mighty church. He was convinced that this miracle, of which he had played a small part, was indeed, Heaven's will.

As we made ready to depart, the Director closed and locked the large iron gate that sealed the entrance to the imperial chapel. The key to the chapel as well as the keys to all the locks in the church were hung upon the same ring that was attached to a chain that girdled the Director. Nikelas knew the Emperor would be pleased with him, as pleased as he was with himself.

A lavish dinner had been planned as a pretense while the real plan was unfolding. Giancarlo had invited the Director and several of the wealthiest and most powerful citizens in the city to celebrate my first Eastern trading mission and to bid farewell to his dear family, as we were scheduled to set sail on the next midday tide. The Director had been pleased to accept the invitation and had hurried back to his home to prepare for the event. He had donned his costliest robe and sandals and his most expensive walking staff in order to mask his financially inferior status, and Nikos had convinced him to leave his bulky key chain hidden in his secret hiding place in his rooms. He did not want to appear less important than his title and his closeness to the Emperor led others to believe. Nikos had also recommended that he stop by the baths in order to be cleaned and scented before he attended such a grand event, another reason to leave his valuables behind.

Once the Director had left, Nikos gathered his uncle's clothing, walking staff, and his key chain and hurried to Enrico's warehouse. He was met by one of Enrico's servants, who skillfully applied cosmetics, wig, and facial hair in such a precise fashion as to render Nikos into the mirror image of his uncle. Donning his uncle's clothes and leaning on his staff, Nikos had been transformed into the Director. He had perfected his uncle's manner of speech and his overall mannerisms so that, in the darkening hours of late afternoon, he could pass into the church with ease.

Salvatore and Sebastiano had been dressed in the uniforms of the imperial guards, and when all was ready, the four of us returned to the church. Nikos, as the Director, needed to send the sentries on an errand that would buy enough time for the company to complete its mission. He informed them that a silver chalice in one of the chapels needed repair and was to be taken immediately to a certain silversmith in the Pisan Quarter. He retrieved the chalice and told the guards to deliver it to the silversmith, await his inspection, and report back his assessment. Salvatore and Sebastiano had been sent to relieve them. The smith was, in fact, an agent hired by Enrico to delay the guards for a minimum of two hours. As they waited, he was to offer them a very special wine.

The sun had already started to set and the light in the church was fading quickly. As we entered the church, Salvatore and Sebastiano sprinted up the stairs to meet the Scholar on the top level. He had already unlocked the small door that led outside to the roof. The Scholar had taken from the sack a small crossbow and a coil of rope that he used to shoot a line and grappling hook to the roof of a building beyond the rear of the church. Securing the end of the rope to one of the stone fixtures, he pulled the line tight, testing it with his own weight. He then took another coil of rope from the sack, tied himself to it, and handed it to Sebastiano. He had already fastened several sacks to his legs, and after Salvatore had broken one of the eight small windows in the dome just above the imperial chapel, the Scholar eased his way through the opening.

Nikos and I had entered the chapel and had lit enough candles to illuminate the area, waiting for the Scholar to be lowered down by the others. Slowly he descended until he was hovering just above the glass encasement of the Prophesy. The serpents hissed and raised their heads, ready to strike. The rope slipped slightly, sending the Scholar to within inches of sudden death. Quickly he was raised and proceeded to work. Dangling with his head closest to the pit, he removed a small metal hammer and shattered the top piece of glass in the case. The noise seemed deafening as it echoed throughout the empty church. The hissing of the snakes was unbearable and caused a great fear in me.

Such a precarious position did not seem to frighten the Scholar as he busily performed his task. He replaced the hammer with a small golden key given to him by the Pope before he had left Venice and proceeded to open the sacred text. He deposited the key in his mouth and retrieved a short dagger with which he pried open the binding of the book and gently removed the pages from the spine. From another sack, he took a stack of aged papyrus sheets, similar in size and condition and quantity as those held within the elaborate covers of the book. Those pages were completely blank. Carefully he placed the consecrated pages into the empty sack, and gently tossed it to me.

With incredible skill and precision, even in haste, he gathered the blank pages together and reinserted them into the binding of the book. Taking the key from his mouth, he secured the lock and arranged the book so that it had appeared untouched by human hand. From a larger sack he produced a lifeless eagle that had been caught a day earlier. Its neck had been broken and the carcass was gently laid upon the top of the case, making it appear as if the poor creature had inadvertently flown into the window above and then crashed down upon the glass case.

The task was completed, the transfer made, and the Scholar was hoisted back up to the rotunda. Taking a candle from the chapel I made my way to the upper levels while Nikos secured the iron gates to the chapel. In the darkness I encountered Sigmund, Barbarossa's tormented assassin, who had been sent to retrieve the book for his master. He had been waiting for his chance to gain access to the church, and we had provided him ample opportunity while we were busy retrieving the book that he sought to take from me.

I instantly remembered the kind and gentle, yet tormented, soul whom I had to entertain in Siena so many years earlier, and yet I knew that deadly killer would not let me live to tell of his thievery. He lunged at me with drawn dagger and nearly pierced my chest but for the sack that I had held in front of me. He lunged time and time again and I deftly avoided his sting. I called for help as he lunged at me one last time and his dagger pierced my side, getting tangled in my leather belt. I screamed in pain and turned my body away from him, causing him to lose his footing.

At the same time, Nikos came up from behind and took a large crucifix and brought it crashing down upon his back. I jumped aside and gave his body a forceful kick that sent him over the railing, crashing to his death. The others heard the commotion and finally came to my side. We all peered over the railing into the darkness below. My side was aching, and I could feel my shirt becoming wet with blood. We needed to come up with a new plan and our time was running out. Quickly we moved to the lower level and made sure that Sigmund was indeed dead. Using whatever we could find, we cleaned up any traces of blood and swiftly moved his body to the chapel. Nikos open the gate and we moved the body toward the coffin.

At my command we stripped Sigmund of his clothing. Making sure there was no evidence left to identify his body, I took from his neck the golden eagle amulet that signified his servitude to the German emperor. His naked and badly bruised body lay lifeless upon the cold marble floor, yet in the candlelight, his beautiful face appeared almost angelic. Such was the dichotomy of that poor wretched soul who was Sigmund.

Carefully we unwrapped the venerated saint and dressed the preserved body in Sigmund's garb. The Scholar, with the key provided by Nikos, had removed the saint's hands from the reliquary at the main altar and stuffed them into his sack. Returning the key to Nikos, he took the sack containing the holy pages from me and had Salvatore carry the body of the saint to the roof. As the two disappeared into the darkness, the rest of us took Sigmund's naked body, sliced both of his wrists, being careful not to sever the hands from the forearms, and wrapped the body in the sail cloth covering it in the garment fragments, being careful to eliminate all traces of blood. We then placed the body back into the coffin and sealed it. With luck, I thought, the deception would go undetected until we were safely away, or perhaps a miracle would be proclaimed that the saint had been returned and had become whole again to protect his loyal worshipers. Sigmund could, at last, make peace with God through the misguided prayers of the millions of faithful in Constantinople.

On the roof, Salvatore had fitted several small pullies to the rope, and the Scholar, along with the holy relics, quickly traversed the line to the safety of the building below. The body of the saint was sent flying into the waiting arms of the Scholar, who unceremoniously dumped it in an alleyway a short distance from the Church. The Scholar of Athos was never to be seen again in the East. Salvatore had removed all evidence of our presence on the roof, re-entered, and locked the door.

Two hours had passed since our arrival when the guards finally returned from their false mission. They had seemed quite drunk on the wine that had been offered to them, owing to the drug that was added to cause delirium. Nikos took the opportunity to chastise them for their unreliability. He told them the guards he had brought with him were needed elsewhere and berated them for their poor performance, ordering them to compose themselves and to finish their post. How unfortunate it was for them that they would be found asleep at their post and blamed for the theft of the chalice. None would believe their excuses or their incredible tale. The law's swift justice would eliminate our only witnesses.

We returned to Dandolo's warehouse and were met there by the Master, who had excused himself from the festivities at Giancarlo's villa. The Scholar was nowhere to be found, nor was the holy book. The Master seemed not to be concerned, for he knew the city and he felt assured the Scholar would be found. He showed more concern for my wound, which looked worse than it really was, and had his servant clean and bind it while Nikos and my cousins shed their disguises. The Master was pleased with our success and with my resourcefulness in handling the complications presented by Sigmund. He cursed Barbarossa for his constant meddling and vowed to make the tyrant pay for his deeds.

We gathered our belongings and headed back toward Giancarlo's villa. Nikos had to return the articles and clothing borrowed from his uncle, so we made our way to the Director's rooms. As we headed down a darkened alleyway, we encountered a small group of Barbarossa's men standing over what they took to be the badly disfigured and lifeless body of Sigmund. It was, of course, the body of poor Saint Nicephorus that the Scholar had left propped up against a dung wagon. In the dim light one of the men had recognized me, for they had been working with Sigmund in the emperor's espionage, and the group fell upon us.

Salvatore and Sebastiano feverously battled four of the assailants as the fifth attacked the Master. A sixth one lunged toward me and wrestled me to the ground, where he began to pummel my face with his gloved hand. Nikos tried in vain to knock the man off me with his uncle's staff, but the brut just dug his fingers deeply into my throat. Before he could snuff the life from me, Nikos wrapped his uncle's key chain girdle around the ruffian's neck and placed his foot upon the man's back, pulling tightly upon the chain. Blackness consumed me and the carnage surrounding me faded.

When consciousness returned, I saw Nikos sitting against the wagon holding the chain that still girdled the thug's throat. Salvatore had dispatched the two men he was fighting and had moved to help his brother with the other two. The fifth one had somehow bested the Master, who was prostrated upon the ground. The attacker hit the Master upon the head several times with a shovel that he had taken from the wagon and was about to deliver one final blow when Salvatore ran him through with his dagger. Sebastiano had just finished off the other two and the melee was over.

The six Germans and the holy saint lay dead upon the ground. The Master lay bleeding, but still breathing. Nikos sat stunned with the chain in his hand, and my two cousins moved throughout the victims to make sure that they were truly dead. I, having witnessed the aftermath of the carnage, staggered over to the Master and cradled him in my arms. Immediately I knew we needed to be free from that place, so we carried the unconscious body of the Master back to Dandolo's building. I sent Nikos to his uncle's house to return the clothing, as was part of Giancarlo's plan.

I felt certain that Enrico could be saved if we acted quickly, for I had seen a longer life for this great man. Giancarlo had once told me of the miracles that had taken place in the Monastery of Transfiguration, and Enrico himself had mentioned this place to me when we had spoken in Venice. We secured a wagon and I instructed the servant to take the Master, accompanied by Salvatore and Sebastiano, immediately to the monastery. I returned to Giancarlo's villa and advised him of what had happened and hoped to rejoin my friends as soon as possible.

At the villa, Giancarlo and his guests were horrified to see me so badly beaten. Anna let out a scream and fainted, causing much confusion amongst the women. Giancarlo embraced me and was about to whisk me away, but I insisted on telling my tale.

With all the emotion I could muster I told the group that my cousins and I had been making our way back to the villa after having gone to one of Giancarlo's warehouses to inventory the goods being shipped the following morning, when we ran into the Master. He had left the festivities in order to retrieve a special gift that he had planned to present to the emperor for his generosity with the recent acquisitions. We had walked several blocks together when, in a darkened alleyway, we were set upon by a large group of men whom, at first, I thought, intended to rob us. Their dress and their manner of speech had led us to believe that they were foreigners in the service of the emperor, Barbarossa. Their intent was still hidden from us until one of them called the Master by name and referred to us as Venetian dogs. It was then that I knew their intent was to murder us. The reason for their evil actions remains a mystery to us for they spoke little, only to say that His Highness would be most pleased with their catch.

They set upon us, and though we fought valiantly and managed to vanquish some of them, several had beaten the Master into unconsciousness and had taken him, bound hand and foot, into the darkness. Salvatore and Sebastiano gave chase and I thought it wise to come back to seek help.

Giancarlo and I exchanged a long glance. The captain of the Imperial Guards, who happened to be one of the guests at the dinner, called several guards into the room and, after telling them of the approximate location of the incident, he quickly dispatched them to assist with the search for the Master. The Director was anxious to hear if his nephew was involved but I assured him that I had not seen Nikos during the evening. Giancarlo, now knowing the direction of my story, played to his audience by lamenting that Fortune had been most unkind to bring such tragedy upon the very evening in which we were celebrating his family's great fortune and success. He suggested that continuing the celebration might temp the Fates to hurl more offenses in our direction, so he bid his guests to return to their homes. The guests all agreed and were more than quick to make for an early exit.

When all had gone, I recounted in detail the night's events. Giancarlo was pleased that his plan had worked so well, but he was extremely concerned for Enrico. He was also very troubled by the disappearance of the Scholar and *The Prophesies*. He complimented me on my quick improvisation in the church and my far-sighted thinking in getting Enrico away to his only hope for survival.

We immediately made our way to the Monastery ofTransfiguration. When we arrived, we found Salvatore and Sebastiano and the servant standing around the badly beaten body that the monks had washed completely of its disguise. The black shroud had been stripped from his lifeless body. On the dais lay Enrico Dandolo, his snow-white hair and beard washed clean of the ink that had cloaked his identity and the blood that had plastered his skull. His body radiated in its whiteness, and for a moment I assumed we had lost him to the angels. The monks were attending him, their faces grave, and they refused to render up any hope for his recovery. Enrico Dandolo's fate, whether he lived or died, had always been in the hands of God. The Master's fate, however, was in the hands of man, and he would never be seen by the Greeks again. We could do nothing, so we returned to the villa.

Giancarlo had arranged for us to delay our departure until we had heard news of Enrico's recovery. My own injuries and Anna's melancholia, which had returned, were used as convincing excuses for the delay. The Imperial Guards found the bodies of Barbarossa's men, but found no trace of the Master. The Emperor Comnenus was so furious at the brazen insult committed by Barbarossa's men that he had all of the Western citizens who were suspected of any connection with the German Emperor thrown into prison. Pietro thought it wiser to join us at Giancarlo's villa and was shocked to see me in such a wretched condition.

The city was beset with turmoil over the next few days. Fortunately, the commotion had created great distraction, as the Director was most aggravated to have to clean up an entirely unexpected mess caused by a wild eagle that had gotten into his church and had caused much damage within the imperial chapel. The glass enclosure had been damaged by the creature but luckily no damage was done to the relic stored within. We would be long gone before it was discovered that the hands of the saint had disappeared from the reliquary, and a miracle would be declared. The body of Saint Nicephorus, still wrapped in its vestments and sail cloth shrouding, would be witnessed by a host of bishops to be in a state of incorruptibility, and his holy hands reattached to his saintly arms.

Three days passed before our ship was finally readied for departure. Giancarlo had let me know that di Conti had successfully left the capitol with *The Prophesies* and was on his way back to Venice. The company was expected to meet again at the palace of the Patriarch in three weeks' time. Anna and the child were extremely sad to leave, not knowing if ever they would see her parents again. I was anxious to sail back to the West, though I was still concerned for Enrico's recovery. Giancarlo tried his best to assure me that Enrico had escaped danger and that his health was returning at a miraculous speed. He assured me that I would see Enrico again soon, yet somehow, I felt that he was hiding something from me.

Our departure was marked with no fanfare. Pietro, Salvatore, and Sebastiano joined me on the deck of the ship and commented on how empty the dock area seemed, as it ordinarily would be teeming with people on a busy afternoon. Only Giancarlo and Donna Donata stood waving upon the dock. Anna and the child were grief-stricken at our departure and waved, all teary-eyed as the ship moved away. Nikos came up on deck to join us as well, for he was to travel back to Venice with us on some business given to him by Giancarlo. In truth, I was pleased that Nikos was coming with us for I had grown to love him, and he had proven his love and devotion to me by saving my life not once, but two times in the short span of one night.

We sailed the Golden Horn from the Port of Bucoleon and out across the Sea of Marmara, heading toward the open waters of the Aegean Sea. On the third day of our voyage the Captain brought me to his quarters, in which, to my joyous surprise, I saw laying upon the Captain's bed a sleeping, but very much alive, Enrico Dandolo. Though I could hardly contain my excitement, the Captain counseled me to still my composure and to keep my discovery secret from everyone else on the vessel. I gave him my oath but insisted that I be given the opportunity to visit him from time to time on the voyage.

Fortune deemed to show some kindness to us, possibly with the intercession of Saint Nicholas, for we encountered fair winds and calm seas for most of our voyage and we sailed directly to Venice with few problems. I visited with Enrico on several occasions, trying not to cause suspicion, and upon my fourth visit I was fortunate enough to find him awake. He sat up on the bed but was staring blankly at the ceiling. I spoke softly to him, and for a moment I thought he was still asleep. He lifted his hand to mine and whispered how good it was to hear my voice. I was heart struck for it was then that I realized he could not see me. The blows to his head had caused such damage that even the skilled monks of Transfiguration could not give him back his sight.

It pained me to see such a virile and energetic man reduced to a state of helplessness. He thanked me for my concern and for my affection, and he praised me for my duty to His Holiness and the Church. The plan, he said, had worked well, even though Fortuna had only sparingly bestowed her blessings at the behest of Envy. His sight, he said sadly, was a small price to pay for us to set the world aright. He held my hand and said to me, "Tell me, seer's son. What fate do you see for this old, blinded fool?" Holding back my tears, I heard the voice of the prophet Malachy echo in my brain, and I spoke,

All hail the mighty Dandolo,
Head of State, Healer of Church, Admiral of Christ's Fleet,
Blessed and cursed by pope and king,
Who blindly leads his flock to victory upon the wall,
And dispenses His justice without fear for himself.
Leader of men, both seen and unseen, servant and master,
Fortune's son and Envy's bastard child.
Listen well to the word of God, and seek the help
Of the seer from the hidden realm,

Great will be the name of Enrico Dandolo,
Maker of Peace, Wager of War, Builder of Ships,
Savior of Souls, Destroyer of Empires.
Men will sing of thy mighty deeds
For a thousand years to come,
And men will shed a tear for what was lost and won.

Enrico had placed his head upon the bed and drifted back into a peaceful sleep. I wept in silence for this most worthy man, and in time I left him to his sleep. Never did I disclose to any of my companions that Enrico was aboard the ship nor his most pitiful condition.

We arrived in Venice with much more fanfare than when we had left the Imperial City. Giancarlo had already arranged lodging for us with a state diplomatic friend of Enrico's father, through an official emissary who had left Constantinople a few days before we set sail. Anna was glad to be safe upon dry land, but her melancholia was unrelenting. She would battle such depression for the remainder of her life, which had already extinguished any fire that had been kindled between us before we left Siena. Nikos and my cousins remained with the ship and presided over the customs check and transfer of merchandise from ship to warehouse. There was no word from the Patriarch or the elder Dandolo, nor any indication from His Holiness, that di Conti had made it safely back to Venice. I also had no word of Enrico's triumphant return.

Several days passed when, in the early hours of the evening, a messenger was sent from the Patriarch's palace with a specific request for the immediate presence of my cousins, Nikos, and myself at the palace. Pietro was furious that he was not included in the request. At the palace we were warmly met by the Patriarch, who hailed the return of his valiant knights and gave each of us his blessing. We were then escorted into the Patriarch's library and sat with him for over an hour, during which time he asked each of us many questions concerning our mission.

Following our account, the Patriarch summoned a servant, who, having accepted whispered instructions, bowed and disappeared. A few moments later the door to the library opened and before us stood a magnificently attired Enrico Dandolo. My companions had been amazed to see Enrico alive and well in Venice, and I was equally amazed to see that his sight had apparently returned. He bowed to the Patriarch and then to each of us in turn, saying, "Well met, my friends." We were all overjoyed with our reunion and had much to talk about, but the Patriarch raised his hand and demanded silence. At that moment, the door to the library opened and through it walked His Holiness, Alexander III. He was followed by none other than Ugolino di Conti, dressed in the red vestments of a bishop of the Church. All bowed low and the Pope seated himself upon a simple chair. He looked at each of us and nodded a simple welcome.

He spoke to us, saying, "Blessed be our holy knights, for through your great deeds of courage and sacrifice, you have returned to the Holy Throne of Saint Peter, the Sacred Word of God, which was stolen by the heathen kings for their own selfish purposes, and whose evil deeds will be judged by God as crimes so heinous as to earn each of them an eternal sentence in the fires of Hell. The Sacred Word, as spoken to Malachy by the Holy Spirit, has been brought from the serpents' pit and delivered into the hands of Christ's true vicar. All praise and honor are to you for your righteous deeds. Your loyalty to Christ's Church will be rewarded in Heaven, and your earthly rewards, each will come to you. Men shall not hear of your deeds, for it is the Lord's will that those deeds remain in the hearts of those in this room and of this company, but His Holy Saints have written of your courage and deeds upon the pages of the Holy Book, and will rejoice in your victory when you enter into the Holy Realm of Heaven.

"We miss our dear cousin, Giancarlo Manenti, but do not forget his allegiance to the true successor of Peter. His bold plan and his faith in the valiant knights whom he had assembled to carry out his plan, has earned him a special place within our heart. His motives, like most of yours, may have been other than the preservation of Christ's Church, yet we know, as surely as some of you in this room know," and he looked directly at me, "that we are all driven by the Holy Spirit, even as it has been foretold. Even so, we hereby grant to the great Giancarlo Manenti his worldly price, which was agreed upon at the beginning of this quest. Let the ledger reveal that the task has been completed and the debt has been paid."

With that the servant handed to me a notarized document transferring ownership of the Castello di Montalto and a large tract of territory straddling the Sienese and Florentine border. Such an important and strategic holding would bring stability to our Western business by enhancing the security of the Francegena and would bring great wealth to Giancarlo and his descendants.

"Enrico Dandolo, Master of the Seas, to thee we have caused to be transferred twenty warships which we have, of late, confiscated off the coast of Zara in that unruly skirmish with the Genoese. Be master of this brigand fleet and turn its use to the good of the Church and the most loyal Republic of Venice. Blessed be the Admiral of Christ's Fleet." The servant handed Enrico a sealed document of ownership for the Genoese ships.

"Tarchon and Tyrsenos of the ancient house of Noah, thy loyalty to our cause has won your people our deepest gratitude and eternal love. We pledge our filial loyalty to the Zil-at of Curtun and swear to protect the anonymity of your hidden realm. Our armies will always be at your service should need arise and the call be sent." With that, His Holiness presented Salvatore with a small golden medallion and said, "Send this to Us and Our armies will follow. And to each of you We also bestow Our admiration and respect for the love and concern that you have shown to the pec-ii of the Taurisi, whose safety and encouragement has assured the success of this holy quest.

"Ugolino di Conti, son of Anagni, for your loyalty to the Vicar of Christ and His Church, you have earned Our love and trust. Great you will become, yet your service to Christ's Church be far from over. The Holy Spirit has other purposes for Our loyal servant as has been foretold. The Holy Church is in great need of your courage and your abilities, and it is thus that We have elevated you to the Bishopric of Anagni.

"Nikos Choniates of the Golden City, you have given your service to the Mother of All Churches in Rome, even though your allegiance and devotion be to Our brothers in the Eastern Church. Nonetheless, you have sacrificed all that you hold dear in your life for the love and fealty of these western merchants. Your example of brotherly love and fidelity is a shining beacon for men of all means to follow. Thou hast asked not for gold nor for greatness, but for the opportunity to serve and protect thy betters. Glory and honor in the Kingdom of the Father is yours by right and by the fulfilment of thy sacred vow. Twice the life of the pec-ii was in peril and twice you lacked the proper means to protect your charge, yet, the Holy Spirit was with you and inspired you to use whatever means were at your disposal. As a token of Our love and esteem, I herewith present you with this gift and reminder of He whom we all serve."

The servant handed Nikos a small bejeweled case that held a golden dagger onto which was affixed the crucified body of Christ. Nikos bowed most gratefully.

"And finally, to Giovanni Bartolomeo Pecci da Cortona, son of the great Uni-Tau, and scion of Tarxin, greatest of the pec-ii of the Taurisi, with your vision and your cunning, your loyalty to your master and your companions, and for your service to God's Holy Church, according to the terms of the agreement between you and the Patriarch of Grado, with whom We are in much debt and agreement, We herewith grant your petition for the transfer of ownership of the Castello di Stigliano and all properties identified in such deed currently held by Ranieri, Bishop of Siena. We also hereby grant most favored status in perpetuity to thee, Our most cherished cousin. You have done the world a great service, young seer. Be wise with the gift that the Holy Spirit has given to you and be at peace with your soul so you may be guided to the true path." His Holiness then rose from his chair and bringing me to my feet he handed me a sealed document and kissed me reverently upon my forehead. "May the peace of the Lord be always with you."

Night has fallen. Giovanni sleeps. The day was endless. I know not how he maintains the strength to narrate his story. Such an incredible story. Such an incredible life. He is driven to complete his task; he hopes to save his soul. Who is to tell what awaits him when he is finally done? God in his wisdom and mercy must see the effort that my master is making. Will it be enough? I pray that it is.

There is no time for me to rest; there is too much to do. Giovanni seems to gain strength each time he pulls his sins from their filthy lodgings and beats them upon the rocks to cleanse away the evil toxins. His spiritual strength is incredible, and his determination is great. No other could endure the task that has been given to him; no other could pass this test, but I believe in him. I admire his openness, and I have learned to love him more because of it. I can never complain about traveling with him on his final journey. I am honored to share his love and his pain.

Giovanni sleeps soundly and I fear that no draughts will be needed tonight. I hesitate to disturb him, even for the potion of protection, though I have prepared it–just in case. I have increased the incense and have placed his crystals about his neck and arms so that his earthly body will be anchored more firmly to this world. I sit and wait.

I know this place. I am in the library of the Patriarch of Grado in Venice. Long has it been since I have seen this room yet the memory for me is crystal clear. Books, the manuscripts, the fireplace, the armchairs—they are all here as I remember them. I hear voices, familiar voices, but I see no one in the room. Hark Spirits! It is I, Giovanni Pecci. I come seeking guidance. The spirits do not hear me but continue their conversation.

...but can we trust him?

Yes, Holy Father, I feel it strongly in my heart. His coming was foretold by Saint Malachy, himself. I heard it with my own ears, and it has been written upon the sacred pages of the Prophesies.

The Prophesies are clouded and are subject to interpretation. He has never been mentioned by name. He is young and brash, and he is troubled. An insidious poison festers in his soul and feeds his greed and gluttony.

I recognize these two voices. It is the Holy Father Alexander, and the Patriarch, Dandolo...

That is true, Holy Father, but his drive and determination give hope to the success of our plan. Our mission is a holy one, but we cannot expect the instruments we use to be as holy as our motives. Greed shall drive the engine of our quest. The Holy Spirit is strong with this one, yet he blinds himself to the power of the spirit and succumbs to the temptations of the flesh.

There must be merit in him else the Holy Spirit would not send us this hope. We have been warned of his shortcomings well in advance of his coming. It is our task to keep him focused on the path to the greater glory of God. His companions will help us to keep his feet upon the true path. His greed will push him beyond his own limits.

He will succeed, Father. The prophesies bode well for our cause, for our struggles against the Emperor, and for the glory of your reign.

The prophesies bode well for you as well, Patriarch. The Dandolo have much to gain and to lose by the actions of this boy. I know well what Saint Malachy predicted for you.

Together, Holy Father, we will be invincible in glorifying Christ and His Church. With the Prophesies back safely in your hands, you will be able to command all the armies of the world and bring peace to all God's creatures. With Barbarossa's demise and Comnenus' subjugation, the Eastern Church will be brought back into the fold and the threat from the north will be no more.

Dear Enrico, there will always be threats, always be wars, always be hatred. That is the way of man. We can never stop it. But with the Prophesies to guide us, we will be better prepared for those struggles and perhaps mitigate Satan's evil intents....

Oh spirits, if this play be true, then I have been used, even by those I most trusted. Whether this farce be revealed by Holy order or devil-spawned, it cuts me to the quick. I see my weakness, though I was blind to it then, and accept my responsibility for my actions, hoping that God will forgive me. Yet these two, the most holy of the holy, knew of my weaknesses and exploited them for their own gain. What difference is my sin to theirs? Through my own weakness, I have sinned. I admit my guilt. Yet through strength and cunning, I was allowed to sin. Was theirs not the greater sin?

Again, I was blind to their manipulation. I am ashamed for having been so easily used. Like a cheap whore, I was used, and then discarded.

You were well compensated, my son, and never discarded.

Holy Father? You are here?

Calm thyself, young pec-ii. We have all been used in life, just as we have used others. Was that not how you advanced yourself over so many years, and so many lives. Were you not the master manipulator? How many lives have you used and ruined in order to obtain all you desired? Your gluttony has been fattened with used-up lives. Do you deny it?

Nay. I own my actions and will pay for them at the time of judgement. But surely, you must share some culpability in my sin.

I am not here to share in your misery. I have already stood before Our Heavenly Father and have accepted His judgement and have received my sentence. I am here to show you that you, like all mankind, had a choice in everything you did, every decision you made, every action you took. Just as there is light and darkness, there is good and there is evil. Man must choose between good and evil, and though we have been made in God's image, we were not given his inherent goodness. Satan and his minions are always ready to tempt us to the darkness.

You, Giovanni, have been given a rare gift of seeing good and evil in its primary form. It is a gift that few men possess, and even fewer can handle. We had high hopes for you, pec-ii, as did all those who depended upon you. Yet you were blind to goodness, time and time again. You were easily seduced by the darkness, and in that, you have failed them all, and have failed yourself.

What more can you tell me, Father, that I do not already know?

Time grows short and there is much for me to do to atone for my own sins. I leave you with my love and hope that you may find your path before it is too late. Look now, Giovanni, at all of the decisions you have made in your life, and the consequences of those decisions.....

Ω

For two hours my master has remained quiet. His face is as if made of stone; a horrific grimace has captured his countenance. He has not moved and at first, I had feared that Death had finally taken him. But for the slow breath and the slight pulse, he shows no other sign of life. I hesitate to wake him, for I know that he needs to complete this part of the journey by himself. I wait, and I pray.

The sun has risen, and Giovanni is awake. He returned to this world in the early hours of dawn and sobbed bitterly for a long while. I had no way of consoling him, but merely held him in my arms and rocked him as a mother does a child who has awoken from a terrible dream. I feel so protective of him, and yet there is nothing that I can do but to be here for him, and to accept my role as witness for his confession and visions. I must be strong, mentally and physically, to perform my duties, for he cannot do this on his own, even though it is killing me to see him thus.

I have given him nourishment and he is insistent on carrying on with his narrative. God, be merciful to my love.

Chapter Five
Greed

XVI

Building Business and the Ark

My life was changed after the quest and my reward. Great fortune would come my way although not everything came to me without problems. Opportunity, wealth, advantage, and power seemed to flow to me just as the River Arno flows to the sea. Yet, at what cost? I cared not, back then. I chose not to see. I was driven by greed. With my summons to Venice, Opportunity had once again knocked upon my door, and I was more than willing to let her in.

We had returned to Siena by late July. I was riding high upon my victory, while Anna was in a state of misery with her losses. She had lost her inheritance and had left her family behind. I had lost some time with the diversion to Constantinople but had increased my fortune and position as a result of the journey. Though I would never, under solemn oath, be allowed to disclose the true nature of our trip or my involvement with the successful recovery of the Prophesies, I had gained the personal friendship of the Pope and the Patriarch of Grado and was then held in high esteem with the ruling merchants of Venice. I had become the sole master of Stigliano, much to the displeasure of my wife. I had solidified my relationship with Giancarlo and Enrico and had gained the friendship of Nikos and Pietro.

During this time, communes such as Siena and Cortona had continued to wallow in political turmoil. Siena had been pushed to its limits having to deal with a growing number of adversaries, as she annexed each parcel of land or estate. The special benefits granted to the city by Barbarossa had emboldened the leaders of the Council and had fed the envy and jealousy of its enemies. I knew, as I drove our wagons through the streets of Siena, that I would have to work hard to build my empire and equally hard to control the city that I had begun to call home. I was willing and excited to take on both challenges, for I wanted to control it all.

At the same time, Cortona had been undergoing similar growing pains as Siena, though their commune had not been able to free itself from the influence of the bishop of Arezzo, nor curry the favor of the Emperor as had Siena. It too had begun to exert greater influence and authority over its citizens living behind its massive walls. The privileges awarded to its citizens did not come without cost. Full rights and citizenship were granted to landowners only, and those owners with large enough holdings outside of the walls were required to maintain a residence for at least two consecutive months in the year within the city walls. Though my father had been considered a most important and influential Cortonese, his holdings, which were extensive but not within the city proper, would not qualify me, or my brothers, for citizenship. Thus, I needed to establish residence within the city for my brothers and myself. Being practical, I decided to forgo building a massive palazzo like Giancarlo had built in Siena, and instead built several small but comfortable row houses just inside the Porta Santa Maria. I was able to carve out a small section of land, constructing four two-story, simple residences that abutted the wall and fronted upon a paved alleyway that is now called Via Janelli. Into these dwellings I would deposit my family each year to meet the minimum occupancy requirements. Nikos had supervised the construction of the residences, which were completed and ready for occupation before the spring crops were planted the following year.

Back in Siena, Anna delivered our son whom we named Paolo Enrico Nicholo. He was born out of the love Anna and I had found in the spring before our trip to Venice. That love had abruptly been lost in the heat of summer and our return to Siena. Anna had never forgiven me for making the deal with the Patriarch and for accepting the deed of her Stigliano from the Holy Father. At that time, I had cared little for her reproach or her needs and had consumed myself with my business and the construction of the Cortona residences. She had confined herself to her rooms during the final weeks of her pregnancy, and it was only at Nikos' insistence that I traveled back to Siena to witness the birth of my son, Paolo.

Even though I had felt nothing for my wife, I was amazed by the newborn child. I remember that day as clearly as if it were this morning. I was deaf and blind to all in that room, save for that tiny baby boy. How could I not have seen my eldest son, Vannozzo, nor listened to Nikos' warning to me of a malady that had possessed the young child since our return from Constantinople? Blind was I to the hatred that festered in the elder boy toward his younger brother. Little did I suspect the evil with which the senior would eventually do to his junior. My eyes would not be opened for many years, and then, only at the insistence of others, and for that, I beg forgiveness for my blindness and my apathy. Where I failed so miserably, I thank God that my dear Nikos was able to provide the love and protection of a father, which my children so desperately needed.

My marriage had become a misery, and I found myself longing for another extended journey. I initially decided to forgo the Grand Cycle for that year in order to complete the required residence ordinance in Cortona and anticipated making a larger profit at the Siena fair. Trying to manage both Giancarlo's and my businesses had taken up a tremendous amount of my energy, and the diversion of the Cortona construction put a great deal of stress on my time. Feeling the need to get away, I then decided to attend the later fairs in Champagne, only to deal in a select number of high-end goods, but mostly to handle the money changing and lending at the close. Giancarlo had a few important trade deals that I was not totally comfortable leaving up to Philippe or Henri, so I thought to oversee them myself. I left Nikos in Siena to organize the growing August fair, and to complete the construction in Cortona.

Having most of the exports shipped ahead to Marseilles, I had Philippe transport the goods directly to Provins. I decided to take the shorter and faster route through the Alps and met up with him in time for the close of the St. Ayoul Fair. I devoted a week to money changing, lending, and other banking business, and was pleased to report to Giancarlo that profits from this short trip had been exceptional. I decided to bypass Louis' court and return home, having to make a short stop in Sens to deliver a special relic that

Giancarlo had secured for the Archbishop William de Blois. I brought it with me from Constantinople with orders to deliver it personally to the Archbishop, who purchased it as a wedding gift for Louis' son, Philip, who was a favorite nephew of the Archbishop.

The tiny relic was purported to be the petrified foreskin of the baby Jesus, verified by the Patriarch of Jerusalem, himself, which Giancarlo had obtained at a very high price. It was encased in a blood-red glass vial and housed in a jewel-encrusted carved box made from the purest of white marble. The Archbishop was mesmerized by the object and cradled it in his hands, kissing it with loving devotion during the entire time I was negotiating the deal. He ended up paying a ridiculously high price without question, his coffers no doubt having been enhanced over the years by his brother-in-law, King Louis.

I was surprised to learn that my friend, the Archdeacon, Walter of Chatillon, had been discharged by the Archbishop under very mysterious circumstances, and was living in the outskirts of Sens. I had desperately wanted to obtain a copy of Walter's *The Alexandreid*, a work based upon the life of the great Alexander of antiquity, which had become the rage of the courts throughout Europe. I had intended to send a copy to Emperor Comnenus on his dedication of that grand tomb that we had been instrumental in bringing to the Imperial City. Only later did I learn of the scandal that had whirled around the Archbishop and the Archdeacon and had caused the poem to be written. Love, hate, betrayal, revenge, remorse—ah, such powerful motivators! It was Walter's great love and contrition, which he so eloquently expressed in his poem, that brought me to the outskirts of Sens. He was living in seclusion on the outskirts of the great town, with only his niece, Dona Pica, to care for him.

I recognized him when I saw him, though his countenance was contrite, and he had seemed to lose the looks and vitality with which youth cloaks its host. He remembered me and invited me in to supper with him. It was then that I met the enchanting Dona Pica. It was as if a ghost had been conjured from the recesses of my heart. As I stared in disbelief at her innocent face, I saw only the living image of my dear Genevieve. Like my lost love, she was of poor means, yet she was pure of heart and spirit, lovingly attentive to her uncle, and she exuded such innocence and a charming vulnerability that immediately captured my heart. She served us in silence, yet our eyes seemed to be transfixed upon the other's every movement. The Archdeacon rattled on and on about the mistakes he had made in his life, and the regrets he had carried because of his jealousy and stupidity that had caused the loss of his one true love. He hoped his act of contrition would someday win him his love's forgiveness. So, it is with me, like poor Walter, that I hope and pray, with all my heart, that God may forgive me my mistakes, and grant me His mercy and His love.

I asked of him the honor of being allowed to read his *Alexandreid*, and gleefully he produced his original copy, complete with notations and deletions. Being of considerable length, and with the evening light beginning to fade, I requested I be allowed to return the following day to give more attention to his work. Graciously he bid me to stay the night with him, and my men and I were made comfortable in his barn, with wine to drink to warm our bellies during the chill night. During the late-night hours, I left my companions to relieve myself of the drink that had earlier brought comfort to me, and there, in the silver moonlight, I saw the spectral image of Genevieve, beckoning me to follow. The phantom's bidding brought me sleepily into the trembling arms of Dona Pica. For a long moment, we held each other close, fending off the chill in the air and becoming awkwardly aware of the hardening of our bodies. Our lips found their mates, and I could hardly contain myself.

Though I found some initial resistance, our hearts beat fast and loud and we feared we would wake my companions or her uncle or the sleeping angels in Heaven. Quietly we moved to the protection of a haystack a short distance from the house, and within its protective embrace we became one. Along with her simple robe she removed her veil of innocence, and our hidden lust took us on a most incredible journey. Ending our blissful pleasure, we donned our robes and our innocent masks and returned to our roles, she to her bed and I to my mates. Sleep would not return to me for I was haunted by the image of Genevieve and the guilt of betrayal of Anna.

I spent the better half of the following day engrossed in the agonizingly beautiful writings of the Archdeacon. The work touched me deeply and spoke to me of my own pain of loss and betrayal. I knew even before I had finished my review that I must have a copy of this masterwork. I convinced the archdeacon to allow me to have two copies made, one for my own private collection, and one that I planned to send as a gift to the Emperor of the Eastern Empire. I paid him handsomely for a second copy that he had kept in his library, and I promised to return the book upon my return visit to the fairs during the following year. Dona Pica made herself scarce throughout most of the day, never once looking upon my face nor betraying the pleasures that we had shared only a few hours earlier. She prepared for us a noontime meal, and I caught her gazing at me from afar, yet she maintained her dignity and dutifully played her role as devoted caretaker to the Archdeacon. When I left, I found it hard not to turn and gaze into her longing eyes, yet I was aware of the traps that had been laid at my feet. My failure to control my desires had caused me to blindly step into those wicked snares again.

Shortly after my return from the fairs of Champagne, I began to spend more time in Cortona looking at other parcels of land within the walls of the city that could be bought at a good price. On one of my excursions with Nikos to the northernmost part of the city, we climbed to the very top of the mountain, where sits the ancient ruins of the great fortress built by Crano, himself. It has been said that from this great mountain fortress Crano could survey his entire realm, from the great mountains of the north to the receding waters of the Mediterranean to the south, from his distant home upon ancient Mount Ararat in the east to the vast ocean beyond the wild Celtic Isles in the west. Mighty were the sons of Noah, and their kingdoms were prosperous and their people rich in all the abundance that God had bestowed upon them. Their greatness has diminished over the millennia; their kingdoms, with the ultimate destruction of Curtun, have been erased from the knowledge of man. Yet their great power and magic remain upon the earth, in the blood and hidden memories of its unwitting sons and daughters. Nikos and I stood in awe at the greatness that was before us, and I, better than he, could feel the power that was still warm within my veins.

Seating myself upon a pile of stones that the locals had called the Throne of Crano, I pondered long upon the fate of those ancient people. Though we had arrived in that sacred place in the brightness of the noon hour, whilst I had sat pondering, the sky had blackened as if turned to midnight, and a gale had blown down from the north, causing Nikos to take refuge amongst the ruins. I sat through rain and hail, my mind possessed of a vision so violent and so vile that it continues to haunt me, even in my aged years, and it brings tears to my eyes with each recollection. As lightning cracked above my head, I saw the valley below illuminated in an eerie green glow. Spread across that valley, an army of thousands marched, their banners and pikes stained scarlet and dripping with blood. Above the army, a two-headed eagle soared high, its screeching call piercing my ears and turning my heart to ice. I was filled with such fear and loathing that I could not bear to keep my eyes open, and the phantasmal scene was burnt upon my brain. Lightning had singed the feathers of the eagle, and yet it did not hamper its flight. Its deafening screeches morphed into the screams and agony of a thousand souls being butchered and roasted alive.

Satan was sitting upon a hill toward the north and was smiling as he played upon his wicked flute. A red dust from an army to the south gave a promise of relief, yet all hope faded away as the dust settled back upon the waters of Tresameno. As if glued to those mighty rocks, I tried in vain to wipe the visions from my eyes. Yet I found no comfort, nor relief. I saw the hills to the north lit ablaze, the sky blackened with smoke, the putrid smell of death heavy in the air. Prying my eyes from the horrid vision to the north, I searched the horizon toward the west, and in the distant vale, in the shadow of the great Monte Amiata, I spied a splendidly built castle, illuminated in pure white light, standing as a beacon of hope against a blackened sky.

Far could I see, into the bowels of that stronghold, to the billowing smoke of the furnaces of Vol-tuma. I was drawn into the darkness and led by the red glow, down secret passages into the earth, to the fires of the furnace. I felt the dampness of the stone and the heat of the blast upon my face. Joyously I heard the clanging of steel, the gurgling of water, and the pounding of hammers, and I heard the lamenting of women and the weeping of children. Yet I also heard their cries turning to laughter and song.

Though my skin was saturated by the wind and rain, in my mind's eye, I was being refreshed in the cooling waters of a winding river, feeling some relief from the visions that had assaulted me. As I watched the children play and the women weaving cloth, I was suddenly swept away downstream. Frantically I reached for the safety of something or someone upon the shore. My mother was sitting upon the banks of the river, but she did not move to save me. My father was also upon the shore and he held out his hand to save me, but the bloated body of Giancarlo had enveloped me and had dragged me farther from the shore. Tarquin and Tarquinia were standing silently while Donna Donata sat grieving further downstream. Tarchon and Tysenos were trying to hold the branch of a mighty oak tree across the water, but as I approached, they were cast into an open fire pit by the shadow of my son, Vannozzo, who laughingly began to light the surrounding forest on fire.

Long I struggled, weighed down with heavy chains of gold, until by Heaven's intervention I sought my salvation with the outstretched hand of a young beggar in a brown ragged robe. This haggard youth, so alike to my young self, was being held over the river by a richly dressed young merchant who kept yelling, "Hold tight, brother, I shall not let you go!" The merchant's grasp was strong though his efforts were hampered by the Holy Father, who appeared to be the aged Ugolino Di Conti. He seemed to be struggling, not for my salvation, but for control of the young beggar, whose hands and feet began to sprout rivers of blood that stained the earth and turned the murky water red. My chains were weighing me down below the roiling waves, and I was drowning in a sea of blood.

Feverishly I fought my way back to reality and I threw myself from the stones to the soaked earth. Nikos ran to my side and pulled me to the safety of the ruins. Though only a moment had elapsed since I first ascended those stones, I felt as if I had experienced an entire lifetime. My body was drenched and ached with pain, and my mind was in a haze. Nikos helped me back down the mountain and tended me while I recovered from that grueling ordeal. It was then that I turned my attention to Stigliano.

I only visited Stigliano one time during the year that followed my return to Siena, and then only to assess the physical condition of the tower and to survey the extent of my holdings. I was determined to return to the ruined castle and to delve deep into its foundations and the surrounding hillside upon which it had been constructed. With my brothers managing my father's estate nearby, I felt more comfortable having Anna and the children in Cortona, for Siena was beginning to have its problems with wandering bands of juvenile delinquents. I took Nikos with me to Stigliano to assess the damages and to lay out plans for the fortification of its buildings and walls.

The tower had suffered great damage over the long span of time since it had been built upon its mighty foundation. The surrounding buildings were in great disrepair, dilapidated to a point of being just a pile of rubble and debris. Most needed to be razed to the ground. In their place, I intended to build several adjoining low-rise stone buildings, encircling the main tower, each sitting solidly upon the contour of the hill into which the castle sat. Further in the valley below I would later build a series of warehouses and factories, and toward the banks of the Merse I would erect the very first windmill and waterwheel in all of Tuscany. I was driven by the vision in my head and my plans for the transformation of this castle into a major manufacturing center were innovative and aggressive. I would spend many years building and rebuilding, experimenting and improving, and gaining the most efficiency from my prize.

My plans were more than ambitious, but I still possessed the optimism of youth and the audacity of genius. I always felt that I could, with hard work and determination, show the world that improved profitability could be obtained with cunning, guile, and ingenuity. I had assured myself that with the right workforce I could reclaim the glory that lay hidden within those crumbling walls for so many centuries. I had seen that glory in my vision as I had seen so many good and horrible things, but I would need help. Just as my father had done in the past, I had decided to seek the help and guidance of Tarquin, to share with him the visions that had been torturing my soul and to warn him of impending doom of his people from the Germans to the north.

XVII

The Council of the Zil-at

The journey to Curtun took me longer than I had anticipated, for though I had lived within the hidden realm for two years, I had journeyed to the Gateway Falls only one time, and for most of that journey I had been blindfolded. I had wandered for several days, and having brought minimal provisions, almost perished, but for the grace of God. Border scouts had observed me for a day and seeing that I had taken some of the hidden paths only known to the Taurisi, did not cut me down. Word was sent to the Zil-at, who dispatched Tarchon to assess the situation. My savior admonished me for my carelessness and happily welcomed me home. My spirits were immediately lifted, and as I made my way through the cascading waters, I finally felt a deep sense of home. As we moved further into the realm, I began to sense a deep sadness and grief in the air, in the trees, and all around me. Tarchon urged me forward but I stopped and begged him to tell me the reason for the melancholy that had overtaken his land.

"The Lady Tarquinia has passed," he said. "Just as your father had been taken not so long ago, my loving and wise mother, counsel and comfort to the Zil-at, had met her destiny." With tears in his eyes he spoke. "For many days she burned with fever and was deprived of nourishment and sleep. She suffered such horrid visions of doom and destruction and wasted away such that Death finally took pity upon her and granted her eternal sleep. Her body now rests in the sacred burial chamber of the Zil-ats, awaiting the future reunion with her beloved partner."

I wept openly at the loss of so fair a lady but spoke no more of it until I was summoned to the Council of the Zil-at. Tarquin had aged since I had seen him last. In his haggardness and grief, he looked more like my father did when I spoke my last farewell to him in Cortona. And yet he still possessed his nobility and determination of life. Weariness and grief had not spared Tyrsenos either, as he sat at the right hand of his father, where his mother had always sat. It was his job then to lend comfort and support to his father.

"Sandak," the Zil-at spoke. "You travel to the hidden realm as a stranger, lost and unescorted. The darkness that consumes you prevents you from seeing the true path. Tell us why you have traveled to Curtun for counsel and what doom you bring to us."

"I grieve over the passing of the fair Lady Tarquinia." I began. "I beg forgiveness of the Zil-at for my lack of composure, for when I learned of the manner of her passing, I was reminded of my own father's pain and torture, and the heaviness of the burden that must be borne by a pec-ii. I know something of the pain she must have suffered for I have been plagued with such visions that torture my own soul."

Tarquin's countenance softened and bid me to sit before him. "Tell us the doom that has caused such heaviness upon your heart, young pec-ii," the Zil-at commanded. Without hesitation I shared the terrible visions that had been visited upon me whilst I sat upon Crano's Throne. I told him of the threat from the Emperor of the North, of the massive army marching across the Val di Chiana, of the burning of the mountains to the north and Satan's delight at the destruction of the hidden realm. I wept as I recounted the agony of those whose fate it was to be slaughtered, and I tried to give hope with the vision of the shining tower in the West whose secret chambers would become a new home to those who survived the holocaust. I told him every detail of every vision except the one that had involved my son, Vannozzo, for I had convinced myself that the young boy in my vision was some other youth or demon. When I finished, I sat silently as the Council debated over what they had heard, until the Zil-at spoke directly to me.

"Sandak, our pec-ii, the doom you bring is great, but it has not been yours alone to carry, for many have delivered such warnings over many years. Your grandfather, Tarxin, a great pec-ii, had similar visions that he shared with my father Tarquinius, and because his warnings were ignored, he chose to live in exile amongst the Latins in the valley. Your father Uni Tau, dearest cousin and friend to me, was also plagued with such visions and convinced me years ago to prepare for our ultimate doom. My beloved Tarquinia, a pec-ii of extraordinary ability, has agonized over these visions and has perished because of them. I am not a seer, yet I am not blind. I have listened well to those who came before you. I have listened well to Tarquinia, who was my heart and my soul and my eyes. I mourn her loss but find some comfort in the fact that she has escaped the doom that she knew for certain was ours to bear.

"It was through her counsel and that of your father that I began to make plans for the future of the Taurisi people. Our builders have labored for years to construct a fortress deep within the bowels of the mighty Cel-Tin, which the Latins call Montana Favolta. It is large enough to shelter our women and our daughters and whatever food is necessary for their survival for a short period of time. The best of the best of our art and our heritage has been relocated to secret burial chambers in locations spread out across the old empire. Our men and our boys are trained and equipped to defend our homeland and are ready to stand against any army that dares to cross into Taurisi territory. We know our doom is upon us and we are prepared to challenge it."

Looking directly into my eyes Tarquin continued. "It was not by chance you have come to us, nor is it a small part you are destined to play in the survival of your people. Tarquinia warned of your coming and said to me, 'The Seer's Son will bring us our doom. The Seer's Son will also deliver us our hope. The Ark must sail for ancient Rusellae, before the boy can lead the great army against us, for it is there, beneath the White Tower, the seed of the Taurisi will thrive. Time is not on our side and the end is already in motion, yet he will not strike until Rusellae is brought to life and can welcome her children home. Look to the west, for the two-headed eagle will swoop down from his mountain eerie in the north seeking to right a false wrong, and the gates of Sena Vitas will be closed to her Master. His rage will be diverted by the lure of gold beneath ancient hills, and his strength will be diminished before the She-wolf's gates. His arrogance shall increase, as he is driven by greed to condemn the innocent. The sacred pledge of assistance will be buried with the dead—the promise denied. The eagle will devour all in his path before it is cast into a watery grave. Yet for all the doom he will bring upon us, he will fail to destroy us. We are saved so long as the Seer's Son is Master of the Ark."

Tarquinia's warning hung heavy in the air. All were silent, and then all began to speak at once. The chaos was deafening. Tarquin raised his hand, and all fell silent.

"Again, I say to thee, young pec-ii, it was not by chance that you were called into the service of your Pope Alexander, for after discovering your true self and those gifts that you possess, you were foresighted and bold enough to claim the prize that is now under your control. Tarquinia saw all this from the first day you entered our presence. She was most loving and protective of you for she knew the fate of her people would someday lie in your hands. It was she who presided over your initiation into the Etruscan ways with the hope that her memory and the memory of all of her people would be imprinted upon your soul and would provide a guiding light for you to follow upon your darkest paths."

Tarquin continued. "The history of the Etrusci is long, as you know, and spans beyond the mists of time from after the great flood until this very day. In her greatness during the time of Crano, her children multiplied and prospered throughout the land. Cortona was the heart and the soul of the Tyrsenoi people, and her blood flowed throughout the Italian peninsula. Her abundance from the land and the skills of her craftsmen made her greatest in trade amongst the peoples of the world. As the centuries passed, her children spread across Tuscany and great cities were built. It is from our great wealth and the splendor of our stone cities that the Latins, who were living as animals in their mud huts, began calling us the Taurisi, which meant in their tongue "Tower builders." In the beginning, we shared our knowledge with them and helped them to establish their settlements along the coast to the south of our border. One of those cities we named Romu, though they have changed it since, and we helped to raise it from the pasture that it had been to a splendid and thriving city. We gave it our art and our culture, our heart and our soul, but its people were bred to war and lusted after all that was not theirs. Hoping to subdue the warrior race of the Latins, past Zil-ats had encouraged intermingling with the chieftains of those barbaric tribes, becoming themselves leaders and kings of the growing city. But alas, their aggressiveness could not be bred out of them and they cast aside the ways of their mentors.

"During the reign of the Zil-at Alex-Xi, Tarchun, and Tyrrhenus, two wealthy merchants from the kingdom of Lydia had convinced the Zil-at that the strength of the Etrusci lay in a powerful union of the great cities we had built. Thus, the great federation of the Etrusci was born. Ten great cities were joined together, their hearts beating as one, their council led by Zil-at of Cortona. The wise Alex-Xi believed that the council of the federation, in order not to favor one city over the other, should meet in a central location. So it was that the small but imposing citadel of Rusellae, which sat upon the banks of the river Merse, became the seat of the Council and the heart of the federation.

"But, as the centuries passed and the cities became complacent, the bastard child to the south became voracious in her appetite for conquest. Even through our friendship with the Carthaginians we were unable to stem the tide of Roman aggression. The sins of the great African General Hanibal caused the Romans to war against Catharge and obliterate that great empire. With our strong ally eliminated, one by one our sisters fell to the Romans until only Cortona and Arezzo stood.

"It was during the reign of the tenth Zil-at, the great Uni-Taur, that he and his wife Dinae first shared the vision of the Doom of the Taurisi. Mightiest of all Seers, Dinae was so overpowered by the visions that her grief for her people totally consumed her, and she was no more. Uni-Taur grieved mightily for his wife and vowed to protect his people by removing them from the clutches of the voracious conquerors. While the Romans were warring amongst themselves and expanding their empire throughout the rest of the south, Uni-Taur led the proud Etrusci of Cortona, deep into the forested hills of the ancient Umbri, establishing the hidden kingdom of Curtun. All that was Etrusci, the best of that culture that had been brought to these western shores by Crano and the Tyrsenoin, once a showcase for all the world to see, is now buried in obscurity in the mist and the hills of the Hidden Realm. Rusellae, like her sister cities was destroyed. Only its mighty foundations were left above the ground, and what the Romans could not find and destroy, time managed to do great damage. The ruins of that once beautiful city sit beneath the fortress that you call Stigliano."

In an instant, all became clear to me.

"Through the ages, powerful pec-ii have warned of the coming doom, for the world is changing, and the madness and the lust for conquest that once belonged to the Romans has been reborn and is spreading like a plague throughout the world. The time for peaceful co-existence is over. The wolves are about to slaughter the last of God's children. I have spent my life preparing for the final days of my people. Though this heavy burden has been born by me, and of late, my dear Tarquinia, we have labored long and in secret to assure the survival of our people and our heritage. Just as Uni-Taur did a millennium ago, I have built a haven for our people. One hundred men, women, and children I prepared to secret away, each possessing the skills, abilities, talents, and temperaments of our people. In them is the hope of survival of the Taurisi culture. And yet, upon the insistence of Tarquinia, I have been persuaded to alter my plan for 'The Chosen Ones' and to deliver them unto your safekeeping to sail within the bowels of the Ark of Rosellae.

"Like Noah before the Great Flood, we have trusted in the salvation and protection of The One True God, to ensure the survival of Noah's bloodline, and I have looked to the prophetic visions of the pec-ii as proof of God's willingness to protect his beloved children. Just as he instructed Noah to build the ark and to save His creatures from annihilation in the Flood, so too has He instructed us to build a new sanctuary to safely house His children. The seer's son has been chosen to lead the Taurisi flock, and to keep safe the spirit of our people. To aid thee in this task, I will send with thee my finest architects and builders and a host of strong men and boys so that you may make ready the ark for the Chosen."

Tarquin gave me his blessing and his support, praying I swiftly fulfill the commands issued to me by the Holy Spirit, which he had judged to be the only salvation for his people. With a small army of laborers, Tarchon and Tysenos accompanied me back to Stigliano. Tarquin's uncle and chief architect, Gontarz, and two of his sons, both masons of the highest ability, were sent to oversee the rebuilding of the structures and the excavation of the ancient subterranean chambers and passageways.

When first I laid eyes upon the ruins of Stigliano, I had only guessed the foundation walls were built by the Etrusci in the distant past. Yet upon my return from Curtun, I developed a greater respect for those ruins, which once were called Rosellae. Deep did I delve into the rock and the earth, with the help of the Taurisi, seeking what my visions had shown to me to be the hidden secrets of our ancestors. We had sought the subterranean passageways, which we knew to be most common in the ancient kingdoms, and it took little time for us to find them. Many had been sealed or rendered impassible due to quake or the destruction of man, but most bore the same markings that I had studied upon the sacred walls in Curtun, and the Taurisi had known so well.

Deep and far did those passageways spread out, like the tentacles of an enormous sea creature, until the air grew heavy and the heat of Hell's furnace weighed heavy upon our chests. As we cleared away the debris and opened the damaged tunnels, we gained access to the ancient burial chambers, which had been stripped of any treasure centuries before. Though, still surviving in the dead air of the sealed tombs were the defiled bones of the great leaders of that ancient race. Reverently, Tarchon and Tysenos helped to restore those ancient bones to their proper alcoves in the walls of the circular vault. Although the castle had been left to ruin above the ground, the subterranean caverns, once reopened and cleaned, were magnificent. There were many decorative chambers, and their sizes, though varied, were enormous. Under Gontarz's direction, each of the chambers' domed ceilings were opened in the center and shafts were dug through the earth to the surface, creating an oculus through which natural light poured in to illuminate the floor below. In a relatively short period of time, the underground vaults of the dead became the Ark, which was destined to be the salvation of Noah's children.

Following the same basic architectural footprint as the mother city, we continued our excavations until we ended in a sealed-up tunnel that ran a great distance from the base of the foundation walls. With ax and pick and sweat and labor, we finally broke through an avalanche of rock and debris and found that which I had sought—the fiery furnaces of Vol-tuma, a gaping hole in the earth under which flowed a river of molten magma. The surrounding chamber had been damaged as its ceiling had fallen in upon itself, but when cleared, it provided access to the furnace from within the tunnel system or, more easily, from above. I was overcome with excitement for I had seen the potential for such a natural forge and the uses that the Taurisi had made of such a gift. Gontarz had immediately set his best men to rebuild a working forge so that the skills of the Taurisi smiths would never be lost.

With all the natural resources needed for steel production so readily available to me in the surrounding area, I began to replace my vision of the salvation of my people with a new vision of turning Stigliano into an underground manufacturing center, capable of producing many of the products that I had spent so much money and travel time importing for resale. My mind was filled with calculations of how many products could be manufactured within the secret confines of this complex and how many middlemen would be eliminated to the great benefit of my profit. And yet, as much as I tried to alter my sacred visions, I was in constant dread of what those original visions revealed.

We worked for more than a year restoring the mighty tower, which glistened white in the sunlight. Encircling that tower, I erected a dozen buildings that were cut deep into the stone outcropping of the hill. The stones from the ancient buildings that were scattered haphazardly over the hilltop, along with rock and debris carried out of the subterranean tunnels by the Taurisi boys, were once again molded into functional structures, large enough to house many people as well as the best looms designed by Gontarz. I envisioned utilizing the expertise of the Taurisi in fine weaving, for they were far superior to the weavers in Bruges and creating a textile center that would be matched by none. The tunnels and caverns, now opened to sun and air, would remain hidden from the prying eyes of friend or foe and were likewise reinvigorated with life and purpose.

The massive system had been transformed from mausoleum to hostel and working factory. When the work was completed, many of the workers and all the boys returned to their families in Curtun, for their tasks had been completed. We had all developed a close bond during that year of construction, and some of those who left me would eventually return with their families to dwell in the caverns that they helped to resurrect. Before the final chapter of the Hidden Kingdom was written, the men, women and children who made up the one hundred Chosen Ones were brought to Stigliano and eventually became the heart and soul of my manufacturing empire.

No longer was Stigliano a pile of rock or a ruin of past glories; she had been transformed into a mighty stronghold. Its position upon the Merse and near the Via Francigena had made it a vital point for the security of the area. Well before I was able to bring her to her full glory, the wolves had begun to circle, each vying to claim jurisdiction over the area. The bishops of Grosetto and Volterra were the first to try to nibble at the prize, but both were quickly countered by Ranieri of Siena, who had the backing of Pope Alexander, who felt that my soul (and of course my property) and the souls of those living within the borders of the territory that he had bequeathed to me would be better shepherded under the Siena diocese. The Sienese commune, of which I was beginning to take a more leading role, felt the property had been legally transferred from the stewardship of the Church to private ownership and thus from ecclesiastic jurisdiction to civil jurisdiction. Since being situated within one of their own contradas, they claimed my entire holdings to be under their territorial authority.

The greedy nobles also conspired together and made a claim to the imperial court for the return of the property to the Soarzi clan, claiming that the Pope had no right to transfer the property left in its care by Provenzano Soarzi to anyone other than its legal beneficiary, Anna Soarzi. Though I had invested a tremendous amount of money and labor to breathe life into a dead corpse, the wolves were hungry and threatened to tear my creation apart. Much time and energy were needed to eventually bring the jurisdiction of the newly created village of Stigliano under the protection of the Commune of Siena. I have struggled until this very day to maintain that precious relationship with my beloved city, to enjoy her protection and the many benefits she owes to her leading citizens.

During this time the power and the pride of the Sienese Commune had grown strong. Barbarossa saw an opportunity to drive a wedge between the Pope and the city of his birth. Many of the leading citizens, now instrumental in the governance of the city, had come from noble families who were loyal to the Emperor. They had harbored resentment toward the greedy Bishop Ranieri, who had taken their power and their possessions, all in the name of the Church. It was but a matter of time before the troublesome Bishop Ranieri had outlived his usefulness to the people. Meanwhile, the Emperor had assured himself of the allegiance of the city by being most generous with his benefices toward our wealthier citizens.

I must confess that though I had remained loyal to the Holy Father, I decided to play both sides of the wall. How was I so easily lured by that devil from the north, having pledged my loyalty to our dear cousin and benefactor, Alexander? Truth be told, I allowed myself to be bought, like so many of my fellow Sienese, accepting his benefices, his contracts, and his money. Oh! Judas had betrayed our Lord, Jesus, for a mere thirty silver pieces. I had demanded a much higher price to sell my soul and to betray my promise to my people. We are both cut from the same cloth, only mine was the color of blood. God forgive me for what I have done.

Barbarossa knew full well that which is so easily given can just as easily be taken away. He continued to favor our city and allowed the Council to elect our own Consuls. The animosity between the imperialist government and the Church finally came to a boil when the consuls openly declared themselves loyal to the Emperor and forced the clergy to support Barbarossa's puppet-pope Paschal. Ranieri tried to anathematize the chief magistrates and their supporters, but the magistrates acted swiftly and boldly, seizing all his holdings and sent the old bishop into exile. Alexander was furious and placed the entire city under an interdict. This did not bode well for my business, for we relied heavily upon doing business in the Christian world, and I had enjoyed a very profitable relationship with His Holiness and the Curia, not to mention the Christian royals throughout the empire. On the other hand, as much as I hated Barbarossa, I was fully aware that all commerce within the borders of the empire was under the jurisdiction and the pleasure of the Emperor. The struggle of power between Alexander and Barbarossa was quickly coming to a head, and my business was in jeopardy.

While this was happening in Tuscany, troubles were brewing in Ireland, which threatened my entire fine-wool import business. Diarmait MacMurchada had been treacherously replaced by the renegade Norman, Strongbow, whom he had brought over to help him maintain his kingdom. With Diarmait out of the way, Giancarlo's contracts were nullified. After consulting with Giancarlo, I decided to travel to Ireland myself and attempt to negotiate a new contract directly with Strongbow. Giancarlo had written to his contacts in London and Wexford to help facilitate a meeting with the usurper. In the meantime, I had made my way to Marseilles and secured passage on a Venetian galleon bound for Santiago de Compostela. Once the captain had unloaded his pious cargo of well-to-do pilgrims, I was able to pay him a goodly sum to make a detour to the eastern coast of Ireland, where I had hoped to meet with Strongbow in Wexford.

I had been assured that the negotiations with the new lord looked promising, and I was hopeful an amiable business arrangement could be reached. When I arrived, I quickly learned of Strongbow's treachery from a longtime business associate of Giancarlo, a Norman of some means by the name of William Du Vall, who had fallen out of favor with Strongbow because of his loyalty to the deposed king. Through his contacts he had learned of the renegade's intent to lure me into a trap where his men had planned to eliminate this Corsari once and for all. By gaining the favor of the wealthy Sienese, DuVall thought to find a solution to his own problems in Ireland.

I was met by DuVall at the dock and warned to return to the ship with great speed for he had feared some of Strongbow's men were close at hand. I count myself lucky that I had barely escaped with my life, and even luckier that events had distracted Strongbow from his prey. Henry of England had launched an invasion to eliminate Strongbow's threat, and as we sailed through the harbor, we passed a great number of Henry's ships. Some had been there and had already unloaded their war-ready troops. Others were entering the harbor from the open sea. I thanked God for his protection, and though I should have immediately returned home to lick my wounds, my only wish was to exact revenge upon the traitorous Strongbow. I paid the captain additional money to take me north to Wicklow, for I was determined to return home with the wool that had been swindled from me.

There I met with several of the "mere Irish," Gaelicians of the O'Neill clan who owned a substantial flock of sheep. All of them were loyal to Dairmait and had been known to openly oppose the treachery and tyranny of the Norman Strongbow. Too long had they witnessed the slaughter of their kin and the raping of their lands by the English and their Norman lapdogs. I was able to convince them, with a sizable amount of coin and a promise of a better life, to sell me the remainder of their flock. I reckoned that since I could not negotiate a deal for the wool, I would buy as many sheep as I needed to produce my own wool in Siena, thus cutting out the middlemen. That grand open green space that abutted Giancarlo's palazzo in Siena would be the perfect place to begin the breeding of a new strain of Leinster sheep, much stronger and healthier, nourished by our sweet Italian grasses. I left Ireland satisfied I had turned a sour deal into a great opportunity to enhance future profits with the production of fine lana di Stigliano cloth. I only needed to build the factories and acquire the manpower to produce such a valuable commodity.

Meanwhile, Barbarossa continued to have trouble with his Italian subjects. Angered by the lack of respect and fealty from the northern Italian provinces and their refusal to pay the annual tribute to the imperium, he marched his army south in the spring of 1176. As a matter of defense, Alexander worked to enhance the Lombard League by allying Milan with the small towns of Verona, Vicenza, and Padua. He was also successful in gaining support from Venice and even the Kingdom of Sicily and Constantinople. The drive for imperial dominance had been fueled by the personal vendetta between the Emperor and the Pope. Barbarossa wanted to send Alexander to Heaven, and Alexander wanted to send the arrogant emperor to Hell. The western world was not big enough for two supreme rulers, and the ultimate contest was inevitable. The final battle happened in Legnano, at a time when the emperor did not have his entire army with him. His smaller force numbered only two thousand cavalries and a mere five hundred of his bodyguard men-at-arms. The Milanese had learned in advance of his intended plans and had mustered the town forces, any who could wield a weapon, and summoned help from surrounding towns and the League. Some say the ragtag army numbered twelve thousand cavalry and an equal number of infantrymen. I am more inclined to believe that the two armies were more evenly matched, for the Milanese are prone to exaggeration, and there did not appear to be enough time to muster too great a force.

But cunning and guile was on the side of the Milanese, for they intended to drive a wedge between Barbarossa's small forces and his main army that was camped west of Milan. Lying in wait in a forest near Legnano, the Milanese surprised the imperial forces and engaged them in battle. Fighting was vicious, but at the end of the day the Milanese had taken the victory. Barbarossa's banner, the two-headed eagle, had fallen early in the melee and his horse was killed beneath him, though he, himself, just barely escaped death. He remained missing for many days, until finally he reappeared in his army's camp at Pavia. God had granted him his life but had stripped him of his dignity, for later he was forced to sign a treaty with Alexander and the League. This treaty was authored by Ugolino di Conti, the Pope's secretary and his uncle, Lotario di Conti, the papal nuncio.

Alexander had finally won his battle with Barbarossa. The treaty forced the Emperor to recognize Alexander as pope, and it gave him many concessions that His Holiness felt were fair and just in the eyes of God. That following May, the Emperor was forced to sign the Treaty of Venice, pledging a truce with the Lombard League and the Kingdom of Sicily. Though he would never again trouble the northern cities, the eagle would swoop down one more time some years later to wreak havoc in the lands of the Tuscans and our fair city of Siena, and in his final act of contempt for the Italian people, he would savagely destroy the world of the ancient innocents.

XVIII

Venice–Treaties and Deals

When word of Barbarossa's defeat reached Siena, the consuls and the ruling citizens of our fair city gathered to discuss Siena's political and financial future. Our city was in a precarious position. Our emperor and protector had been defeated. No longer could our fair city be guaranteed the protection and the favors of the Emperor. The Pope and the northern Italian cities had been the victors. Siena had incurred the displeasure of His Holiness and was living under an interdict. Miraculously he had managed to escaped death at Legnano, though he had lost a great portion of his army. All in Italy had assumed that Barbarosso would have to forsake his ambitions of empire and turn his attentions to his homeland if he were to retain his power and his head. He had lost the respect of his German princes at home, and instead of gaining empire he would be forced to sue for peace and forsake his ambitions in the lands south of the Alps.

Siena's consuls acted quickly in assessing the need to regain the trust and affection of the Holy Father, and quickly drafted a resolution of contrition, begging forgiveness for their betrayal of his trust and pledging undying loyalty to the Pope and His Holy Church. Knowing of my deep loyalty, love, and affection for His Holiness, the Council enlisted me to act as Siena's emissary and sent me to Venice to treat with our "dear cousin" and his representatives.

I surprise myself to this day that I accepted this assignment so willingly, for its outcome was questionable and it could have had a disastrous effect upon my business and my relationship with the

Holy Father and his curia. But I was young and had seen a great opportunity to increase my personal status within the commune and within the curia itself. Such favors, I gambled, would free me from Giancarlo's mighty shadow.

I was given little time to organize my business deals and had to leave instructions with Gontarz for the needed fortifications of the castle tower and the surrounding buildings. I had anticipated completing my mission and returning to Stigliano within a month's time for I could not afford to linger. Before we departed, my gift for Emperor Comnenus had been completed, a handsomely scripted copy of *The Alexandrei*. I had planned for Nikos to deliver my gift to Constantinople in time for the official dedication of the Emperor's mausoleum. The present was meant to gain favor with the Emperor and to help open direct communications between me and the imperial court. Nikos was now acting as my agent, even though he still owed loyalty to Giancarlo, and he had to walk a very thin line in order not to betray his loyalty to either of us.

We arrived in Venice in a week's time. Enrico was gracious to host us in his newly constructed palazzo, as most of the decent lodgings had been taken by the visiting elite. Lord Dandolo had opened his very spacious villa to visiting high-ranking state dignitaries, and the Patriarch Dandolo had filled his palace with the high echelon of the church, including the Pope and his closest advisors who occupied a separate wing of the palace. Alexander had been staying in Anagni whilst the battle had been fought and was quick to receive Barbarossa's envoys who brought peace offerings from the Emperor. Lotario and Ugolino had been instrumental in crafting the truce agreements that brought the Emperor to Venice. Alexander and the allies had been welcomed to lodge within the city proper. Barbarossa and his supporters were encamped in the Lido at the mouth of the Venetian Lagoon. Because of my past service to the Pope and his church, I was recognized as emissary of the Commune of Siena, even though Siena had been a supporter of Barbarossa and still lay under the heavy weight of Interdiction. It was only through the intercession of the Patriarch that I was promised an audience with His Holiness on the day following the signing of the treaty.

Every piece of land surrounding the Basilica San Marco was

crammed with people. Clergy and dignitaries flooded the three main portals and spilled into the narthex of the Basilica. The heat of the crammed bodies, the stench of humanity, and the deafening chatter echoing off the mosaic walls was overpowering. All had been arranged by their rank and station, and I, as representative of a city that was suffering under an interdict of His Holiness, had been fortunate to be included, instead of being dumped into the canal. Determined to get a clear view of the ceremony, I was able to elbow my way to the front of the massive crowd. A great canopy had been erected under the grand arch of the central portal and a high throne was erected upon a raised dais. The throne was embellished with gold and encrusted in jewels and pearls and was draped in the richest red fabric that the Easterners call velvet. Upon this high throne sat the Holy Father, clad in vestments of the purest white silk and embroidered in gold and beset with pearls, and his slippers were made of the same red velvet, ensuring that they would be seen by any spectator in any corner of the piazzetta.

Barbarossa was escorted from the Lido to the shadow of the Basilica by the doge and the Patriarch of Aquileia, with a large contingent of northern cardinals. No longer was he that young, virile stallion who rode beside the Abbot to the Castle of Montalcino so many years earlier. In his place was an older, battle-hardened, and defeated warrior. The gashes and bruises upon his body and the hairs of gray that then dominated his golden locks and red beard betrayed a life of war and aggression. The cost of glory for this man was his youth. As Barbarossa was brought before Alexander, all were silent, and the world stood still as the two titans locked eyes. T'was the mighty emperor who broke the spell of silence by dropping to one knee, laying his sword at the feet of the Pope, speaking one word, "Holiness." The Pope extended his ringed hand and the Emperor kissed it.

Barbarossa spoke directly to the Pope, never diverting his eyes, and formally acknowledged Alexander as the one and only true pope of the Roman Catholic Church. He was then forced to renounce his own anti-pope. Placing his hand upon the Bible, he then swore an oath of peace with Alexander and his allies, the cities of the Lombard League, William II of Sicily, and Manuel I Comnenus of

Constantinople. As was demanded in the peace negotiations, he was made to humble himself before the great Alexander and, as penance for his pride and arrogance, was made to kiss the Pope's holy slipper. Before the thousands of witnesses in the piazzetta and within the walls of the Narthex of the Basilica, the Pope then placed his holy foot upon the royal neck of Barbarossa, reminding him of the ultimate power over mortal man of God's Holy Church. A deafening cheer rang out from the crowd as the Emperor was brought to his feet. His Most Magnanimous and Holiness then absolved the Emperor of his sins against the church, and officially lifted the excommunication. The eagle had his wings clipped, but his talons were still deadly sharp, and his anger was boiling beneath his clipped feathers. Peace was finally won throughout the land. Such hope and euphoria would not last for long.

Later that evening, I dined at the palace of the Patriarch, who had become the second most powerful man in northern Italy. More powerful was he than the doge, for doges came and went, and ever steadfast and cunning was the Patriarch, for he had gained back all that he had lost and had increased his wealth and power by providing counsel and security to the Holy Father. Close did he hold the heart and the ear of Alexander, and that close relationship benefitted me greatly. His interest in me was far greater than I had imagined for he had been well informed of all my business dealings and of the reconstruction activity that was happening at Stigliano. Young Enrico had joined us as well and I was glad to see that he had gained prominence through his own craft by expanding his web of business ventures and partnerships, both legitimate and illicit. He had still chosen to keep a low profile, handling most of his business through trusted agents, but continued to have problems with his sight. He had become of great use to the doge and the ducal court, because of his trustworthiness as well as his mysterious persona, and had been enlisted for many covert operations and back-deals with many foreign contacts. Enrico's hidden influence was felt throughout the world, and though he showed no open display of wealth, his purse had grown considerably large. I had already begun to forge a partnership with him in our banking and currency operations. And the church would become our biggest client.

During dinner we spent a great deal of time discussing the political and economic situation in Constantinople. He had been there several times since we last met, and he gladly shared with me news of Giancarlo and Donna Donata. It troubled me that there was so much unrest in the capital city, especially amongst the Latins, and it seemed the tinderbox had been set to ignite. I feared a great deal for my partner's life, and I feared for our business. Enrico was also troubled with the turn of events in the eastern empire. Hatred for the Latins had increased with each wave of Crusaders that crashed upon the eastern shores. War is a terrible business, but one that benefited Venice greatly, and that also was necessary to increase my own coffers. The waging of these Holy Wars had the unintended result of making Venice the most powerful naval force in the world and had also increased the personal wealth of those of us who provided weapons and supplies to the Pope's holy cause. Every heathen soul sent to the furnaces of Hell brought coin to our treasuries. Such is the duality of commerce; one man's loss is another man's gain.

Later that evening, I met with the Holy Father in his private apartments. He was kneeling in prayer as I was brought into the room and I noticed that he had aged since last I saw him. The years of strife and worry in his struggle with Barbarossa had taken their toll on him as well. His movements were slow, and it was evident that the burden of carrying Christ's Church upon his shoulders was great. He rose from his kneeler and lowered himself into a cushioned chair next to the hearth. His breathing was labored, his eyes were red as if he had been weeping, and a darkness of fatigue had circled each orb. He spoke in a hushed whisper.

"The battle between good and evil rages on, as it has been waged from the beginning of time and will continue until the Day of Judgement. Yet, today, young pec-ii, the scales have been tipped in favor of God's Goodness. Today, God's Holy Church has been victorious, through the blessed intervention of the Queen of Heaven, and the courage and steadfastness of the League. Though Our body is weary, Our heart is singing the praises of Our Lord and Our God, for the salvation of His Holy Church and His chosen people. The victorious celebrate their victories—and the defeated licks his wounds. But you and I both know the evil will never be vanquished. It merely slinks back to its mountain lair to fester and grow strong again so that it can meet us upon the next battlefield, and the next, until the end of the world. You know this, young pec-ii, for you have seen it, as have I. Today we rest easy, yet Satan's poison seeps slowly within the hearts of man and will cause great harm and calamity before much time has passed. Tell me the future that you have seen, and which drives you with such determination to rebuild the Ark of Rusellae within the bowels of that prize that was so fortuitously granted to you. Speak to me from your heart, and without trepidation, for I am aware of your inner struggle and wish to heal your soul of this tremendous hurt."

I spoke with His Holiness for a great while about the visions that were visited upon me on the mountaintop of Cortona, of the return of the two-headed eagle, and the destruction of the Taurisi. I wept openly as I told of the horrors that had clouded my mind and had torn my heart asunder. Nothing was kept secret from my confessor and my spirits had been lifted. Alexander, too, had seen the return of the Emperor, and had also seen the Church not standing against her foe. He had grieved for the Taurisi, though their fate had been predetermined, because the pledge that he had given to protect the sons of Noah would not be honored. He would not be upon the Earth to make good that pledge at the hour of need. He had seen his beloved church descend into darkness but had also seen hope that it would be lifted from the turbulent waters by a beggar of simple means.

Together we prayed for the salvation of my people and the time that would be necessary to complete the mission that was given to me by the Holy Spirit. His Holiness then made a promise to me that he would assist me in my endeavors and would post sentries along the northern borders of the Papal State to give advanced warning of any future incursion of the imperial troops into Italy. I had professed my love and fidelity to him and then had begged forgiveness for any offense that I or any of the Sienesi had shown to him. I implored him to accept the deepest and most sincere apologies of all the citizens of Siena, the city of his birth, and the city who wished, more than anything else on Earth, for the forgiveness of her dearest cousin, the Holy Father, and for the opportunity once again to bask in the blessedness of his familial love. I begged him to consider the souls of his misguided cousins, for their greed had blinded them to his love and the temptations that had been laid before them by Satan's agent, Barbarossa. The golden chains with which the Emperor had shackled their necks weighed heavily upon each of them, and the jealousies and hatreds of her neighbors were a mighty burden upon the soul of the city. I begged him, with all the honest and true emotion within my heart, to lift the interdict that he had placed upon our city, so that our people could, once again, be welcomed back into the loving arms of Christ's Church.

His Holiness thought long and hard over my plea. "Long has my heart been broken because of the disloyalty of my own people. Their support of my enemy, and the enemy of God's Church, has caused us much hurt and angst for far too long. Had you come before me in the weeks or months before the great battle of Legnano had determined the fate of your emperor, I would have gladly accepted your plea, without reservation or skepticism, and my decision would have been much easier. It grieves me to think such pleas and acts of contrition are made with political expediency and out of self-preservation, only when the victor is the one to whom our dear city has given so much offense. The fickleness of your consuls is only matched by their audacity. The hurt is too deep to ever be mended."

Without hesitation, but with utmost respect, I interrupted, asking, "and yet, did not Jesus forgive the treacherous Judas for his betrayal of He who loved him most dearly?"

"Your masters were wise in sending you to me, for though they know not the reason of our closeness, you and I share communion with the Holy Spirit who brings a brotherly love into our hearts and opens our minds and our hearts to the forgiveness of those who trespass against us. You have represented the pleas of your people well and have struck the chords of peace and harmony, and forgiveness, upon the strings of my heart. Listen now, and hear the words of Alexander, Supreme Pontiff of God's Holy Church. With love and much affection for our dear city do I accept your act of contrition and your plea for forgiveness. With your apology, I accept your oath of allegiance and your pledge of fidelity. I herewith grant to the citizens of Siena my solemn promise to lift the interdiction that was placed upon our city, after a formal apology and oath of fealty is given to Our Holy Person in the blessed shelter of the Cathedral of Santa Maria Assunta on All Saints Day.

"Return to your city and tell the consuls I accept their invitation to visit the city of my birth and to renew familial ties with my dear brothers and sisters. I also accept your invitation to consecrate the new cathedral as it is being built to the glory of the Queen of Heaven. Go in peace, Giovanni, with God's blessing for the mission that you must complete. Until I see thee again, may the peace and the strength and the love of the Lord be with you, always."

I returned to Siena with a lightened soul, for the peace of the Lord had been bestowed upon me by His Holiness, and the promises of forgiveness for my people had lifted my spirit. I was imbued with determination to complete the fortification and reconstruction of Stigliano before the return of the impending doom. Nikos had gone on to Constantinople, bringing with him my reports to Giancarlo and my gift to the Emperor Comnenus. I had brought with me the terms and conditions for the Pope's official pardon, which I had negotiated with his secretary, Ugolino di Conte, before I left Venice. The cost of forgiveness was high and included coin and penance. Twenty thousand florins would have to be paid to the papal treasury. The consuls, being astute businessmen, gladly accepted the terms of the agreement, and conferred upon me much honor and acclaim for helping to bridge the divide between the Pope and our beloved city. I was also elected to oversee the organization of the ceremony, which was to take place in less than three months' time. With so much to plan for the event, I was regrettably detained from my work at Stigliano, and spent my days in Siena.

It was during this time that my son Matteo was born. Anna and I had spent little time together in those days, but on the rare occasion I took her to my bed, Venus had smiled down upon us and blessed Anna's fertile womb. My family was growing, yet I was not present for any length of time to enjoy their growth. I beg forgiveness of Venus for ignoring her gifts, as I beg forgiveness of my children for providing them everything in this mortal world but a caring father. At that point, news of another child was merely a footnote in my business journal, a day's delay from my busy schedule in order to make sure that Anna had survived childbirth and the child was healthy. There would be time enough to give attention to the family when the work at Stigliano had been completed.

I must confess, I showed more emotion when Pietro had returned from France with news of his impending nuptial to a French woman who had captured his heart at the fair at Aube sur Bar. He had pursued her endlessly during the weeks he had worked the fair. Reluctantly he left her behind, but not before professing his love for her and asking her guardian for her hand in marriage. They would have to wait another year before business would bring the merchant back again to his love.

I was reminded of my forced separation from my beloved French maiden, Genevieve, and sought to convince him to send for his love and to take her to marriage right here in Siena, in the Cathedral of Maria Assunta, on the day following the great Consecration and Reconciliation. He accepted my advice on condition that I stand at his side during the ceremony. Caught up in my friends' happiness, I even offered to accommodate the bridal party at the palazzo and, for a small fee, host his wedding reception on the grounds. I had failed to comprehend the enormity of hosting a wedding, in addition to organizing the biggest event for Siena since the imperial visit of Barbarossa. I had never considered the amount of work required to organize either event—never mind both, and still conduct my business as usual. Oh, how wrong a fool can be! The cost nearly sent me to the poorhouse. Even though most of the cost of the Pope's visit had been reimbursed by a special assessment from the state treasury, I had been put in a tenuous position of fronting the costs while having to wait for the final reimbursement. Though I was permitted to assess a modest interest rate for my advances, the entire transaction was still a drain upon my working capital.

Work at Stigliano had slowed considerably, which caused me much angst, and the pressure of producing a memorable and flawless event was overwhelming. All the leading citizens had vied for the honor of hosting the dignitaries who were invited to travel to Siena for this most auspicious occasion. Those who paid the most were awarded the highest honors, and of course, the guest of honor, His Holiness, was won by Jacobini Tolomei, for he still possessed the fattest purse as well as the grandest palazzo in the city. This became a major problem, for when invitations and arrangements were sent to the Pope, His Holiness showed his displeasure with the wealthy banker, who had previously hosted Barbarossa in that same palazzo, and refused his invitation. Instead, the Pope opted to stay at the palace of the unseated Bishop Ranieri, who had died in exile, and whose unfair treatment at the hands of the Sienese mob had caused the Pope's wrath in the first place. This insult was to show the proud Sienese that His Holiness could be able to forgive, but he would never allow himself to forget.

The palace had been ransacked during the Bishop's removal and had been left in a dilapidated condition. Much money and manpower were needed to return the palace to its original grandeur, and a special tax was levied to raise funds for the restoration. The council and the citizens were furious at the escalating costs of this reconciliation and began to question the wisdom of their original actions. No less furious were the Tolomei, for they would have to satisfy their honor by hosting several less eminent dignitaries and would be forced to relinquish their personal seating places in the new cathedral to the curia and other such guests who accompanied the Holy Father. To add additional bitterness to an already-bitter cake that he fed to his hosts, His Holiness had insisted upon seating me, as organizer of the event, in Jacobini's personal chair throughout the entire proceedings. Though it would gain me no favor from the wealthiest of the wealthy in the days to follow, I savored the honor that was bestowed upon me.

In the short span of three months, the city had been made ready for the Pope's visit. Invited and uninvited guests began to pour into the city gates, swelling the already crowded population by thousands. Hundreds of tents had sprung up upon every green space within the city walls, and hundreds more had been erected just outside of the walls. Siena had rivaled the greatest fairs of Champagne, and her merchants happily plied their wares and set up their bance. Security had to be increased, at an additional cost to the Council, as troops were employed from neighboring towns throughout the contrada. The city had become a mass of humanity; the filth and the stench of such a large crowd had threatened to undo months of beautification.

The Pope arrived a week early with his entourage and occupied the refurbished Palace of the Bishop. Though emissaries were sent to greet the Pope's party at the Porta San Marco, His Holiness refused to grant an audience to members of the Council until the day of the consecration ceremony. Water and sanitation became a problem because of the mass of people, for Siena had always lacked a reliable source of drinking water. We had no river nor lake or aqueduct such as other large cities to handle an enormous and thirsty crowd, so water had to be brought in from the Sorra and the Merse to the south, at a great cost to the treasury. I took charge to rectify our deficiency, In the years that followed this event, I made it our chief civilian engineering project to seek Diana, the purest of underground springs, and to bring her nourishing waters to our citizens within the safety of our mighty walls. In those days, however, the wagon trains loaded with barrels of water ceaselessly traveled from river to city to satisfy the needs of a thirsty mob.

Upon the second day of Alexander's arrival I was summoned to the Bishop's Palace for an audience. His Holiness had continued to be visited by visions of the beggar sent by Christ to help mend His beloved Church. He had heard stories of the beggar of Monte Siepi, who had been visited by the Archangel Michael and Christ's Holy Apostles and given instruction to cleanse the Church of sin. He was not surprised that this beggar was the young and tormented Galgano, whom he had met in Sens and had remembered his prophesy, nor was he surprised to learn that I had been present when the beggar had witnessed the Holy Visitation. His Holiness was captivated with the story I told him and was most anxious to meet with Galgano again. He enlisted me to lead him and a small party to Monte Siepi, so that he might hear from Galgano's own lips his holy mission. Together with Ubaldo, the Bishop of Ostia; the Pope's confidant, Ugolino di Conti; and several of the Pope's curia, we set out for Monte Siepi. To my surprise, the bishops of Grosseto, and Volterra, the Archbishop of Sens, and the Abbot of Montalcino had all arrived that morning and had insisted upon accompanying His Holiness on the journey.

Upon hearing of the Pope's mission, the entire council and Siena's wealthiest citizens scurried out of their palazzos and into the streets to view the papal procession. All were aghast to see me riding at the head of the column with His Holiness and the Abbot, speaking to both with familiarity and personal affection. The negotiation of the papal pardon, the organization of the papal visit, and the arrangement of the papal consecration had done much to raise my social status within the city, but that march through the streets of Siena and our journey to Monte Siepi brought me a greater level of honor and respect than Giancarlo could ever gain from his native city.

We traveled southwest from the city, making a brief stop at Stigliano to refresh ourselves. His Holiness was most impressed with the progress that I had made with the restoration of the castle and questioned me privately about the completeness of the subterranean renovations. I assured Him all was going well, and with God's Grace, I would be able to prepare the ark to receive the sons of Noah when the time arrived. Such activity was kept well hidden from the envious eyes of the bishops of Grosseto and Volterra, for they had both coveted my holdings, not knowing the hidden purpose and need of my people, but only viewing the military advantages that my castle would bring to their bishoprics. The full potential of the compound, above and below the ground, was not lost upon Ugolino, for he seemed to know, or rightly assume, I had hidden plans for my fortress.

Fortunately for me, His Holiness had pushed the party to move on, for he was anxious to make Monte Siepi by noon. Upon our arrival at the base of the mountain, I showed His Holiness the area where my company, including Galgano, had camped for the night and where he had first been visited by the Archangel Michael. I recounted every detail of the event to the entire party as each of the holy men looked questioningly to the other, some with obvious looks of disbelief. All remained silent in their opinions, for they had seen His Holiness listening to me with great intent and nodding in agreement as if he, himself, had witnessed those spiritual events. Only Ugolino and the Holy Father knew of my special abilities, and therefore did not doubt my account.

We left our horses at the base camp and made our way on foot to the mountaintop. There, upon a large slab of stone, sat Galgano. He was clothed in a brown ragged robe of a beggar, preaching a sermon to a small group of penitents. His iron sword still protruded directly from the stone upon which he sat, casting a shadow of the Holy Cross. He was speaking with such conviction and holy authority that none noticed our approach. Long did we stand in silence, listening to and observing the evangelist, enraptured in the force of his spoken words and witnessing the aura of holiness that emanated from the young preacher. At one point, the Bishop of Volterra made a movement and coughed, and broke the spell of the gathered crown. The Pope looked disapprovingly at the Bishop as all eyes, including Galgano's, turned toward our party. Galgano rose from his stone and approached the Pope, prostrating himself before him. The Holy Father bid him to rise and to return to his sermon. To everyone's amazement, the Pope then positioned himself before the preacher, seating himself upon the ground and behind the small group of Galgano's followers. Uncomfortably, and with obvious incredulity, the rest of the papal party followed their pontiff's lead.

Galgano had been imbued with the Holy Spirit and continued his sermon. I was amazed at his transformation, for no longer was my young, hot-tempered companion speaking uncertainly before his small group of followers, but rather an ageless and sage prophet sat confidently before the world and spoke of Heaven's dictates. He totally captivated his audience with his simple and direct manner of speech, and His Holiness was wont to engage him in inquisition and dialogue. Such it was that the afternoon had slipped away. Knowing we would never make our way back to Siena before nightfall, Ugolino and I made our way down the mountainside and sent several of the Pope's guards to ride with all haste to the castle at Stigliano, there to secure food and supplies necessary for an overnight encampment of the papal party. When the guards left, Ugolino questioned me about the authenticity of Galgano. He was very skeptical about the beggar who had seemed to capture the soul of the Holy Father. Ugolino was very protective of his master, and I knew he would offer his own life in the protection of His Holiness, yet there was doubt in his mind to fully allow him to see what His Holiness and the others were witnessing on the mountaintop.

We returned to the mountaintop to find Galgano and the princes of the Church engaged in theological debate. The Pope and Ubaldo listened with the utmost interest and respect, as if they were communing directly with the Holy Spirit. The other members of the party, fearing to gain the displeasure of His Holiness, felt committed to engage in polite interrogation. Hard did they try to catch the preacher in some dogmatic trap, but Galgano's simple logic and speech seemed to untie every knot that the prelates had tried to tie around the young man's tongue. His Holiness was very impressed with the authenticity of the preacher and had become convinced the beggar's mission had been delivered from God, as had been affirmed in his own dreams and visions. Before total darkness set in, we removed the papal party to the campsite below while Galgano and his followers remained upon the rocky hilltop, satisfying themselves with the meager rations that they were used to. His Holiness was very moved by his experience with Galgano and remained in silent meditation throughout the rest of the night, conferring only with Ubaldo, his trusted advisor.

As the sun rose, we discovered His Holiness had left the group and had made his way back up the mountain trail. Alarmed at his disappearance, Ugolino and I raced to the top of the mountain and found His Holiness kneeling in silent prayer upon the slab of stone with his hand upon the hilt of Galgano's sword. Tears were streaming down his cheeks, and it appeared to Ugolino that he had been robbed of his consciousness by some malicious spirit. Only Galgano and I knew the rapture that our pope was experiencing while in communion with the Holy Spirit. The papal guard and several members of our party climbed the path to join with us in patient silence. When his consciousness finally returned, the Holy Father rose and embraced Galgano, whispering at length in the young man's ear.

Turning toward the crowd that had gathered to witness this mystical event, he spoke, "Behold the Lamb of God, He who is the heart and soul of God's loving creatures. Blessed is he who walks with the Holy Spirit and speaks in the name of the Lord. Blessed are the meek, for they shall inherit the world, and their purity shall be the honey upon Christ's feast table in Heaven. Heed the wisdom of the Holy Spirit as it flows through His humble servant, for before our Lord and Savior, we all must come as beggars with open heart and open soul. Peace of the Holy Spirit be with you, Galgano, for your time upon this earth grows short and your mission has far to go before its end. We grant thee Our love and support, and Our gratefulness for your enlightenment. Help us to heal the poison that is corrupting this earth and help us to mend God's Holy Church that has been torn asunder. Our tasks are greater than the time that has been allotted to us, but I say to thee, work diligently in God's Grace and when your service to God has been fulfilled in this earthly kingdom, I shall await your soul and prepare a place for you at the feast table of Our Lord in Heaven. The peace and the love of the Lord be always with you."

XIX

Reconciliation

Back in Siena, the commune and the Curia had finally agreed that the reconciliation ceremony would take place on the steps of the new cathedral, for the Pope would not welcome the commune into the consecrated church until the interdict had been officially lifted. The Duomo itself was still under construction, but it was sufficiently completed to support the arches that spanned the nave and supported the vaulted ceiling. The massive Campanile had been built upon the foundation of an old tower and at the time of the consecration was the tallest structure in all of Tuscany. Before the enormous portal of the Cathedral was erected a large canopy, similar to the one used in Venice for the humiliation of Barbarossa, a massive, multicolored pavilion and a lavishly festooned throne, situated high upon a dais so that all the citizens appearing before the Pontiff to beg his forgiveness and to swear their undying loyalty, would be prostrated beneath his holy foot. Rather than red velvet as had been used in Venice, bolts of the most expensive Leinster wool, dyed in vivid colors, were draped in great profusion around the papal enclosure.

His Holiness was clad in his white silk and gold embroidered robe, encrusted with pearls and precious gems. His feet were similarly clad in white and gold silk slippers, studded with pearl and gold coins. The purpose of the ceremony was meant to celebrate reconciliation but was clearly designed to show power and humiliation as the price for forgiveness. His Holiness had surrounded himself with loyal princes of the Church clad in purple or red, as befitting their station. Positioned upon the steps of the cathedral, to the right and to the left of the pavilion, were clergy, guests, and dignitaries who had come to witness the events. The grand Piazza del Duomo was filled, except for a small aisle that had been roped off and left vacant, so the penitents could file in a solemn procession before the papal throne. The air was filled with excitement and the heaviness of contrition. Men, women, and children crammed together to witness the greatness of the Holy Father and to share communal confession and forgiveness. The Virgin had blessed us with a beautiful day, although an unexpected summer's heat on that All Saints Day had made the long line of penitents most uncomfortable. Under the burning rays of the sun, each awaited his turn to supplicate himself before the papal throne.

In addition to the monetary concessions made in the agreement that I had negotiated with the curia, each penitent was expected to deliver unto the Holy Presence twenty-four candles of the finest beeswax for the illumination of the new cathedral, and thirty gold coins to ease the indignation of His Holiness. One by one the members of the Council, the heads of the leading families, the entire membership of the Merchant Guild, the leaders of each of the thirteen contradas, and even the bankers and moneychangers prostrated themselves before the Holy Father, begging his forgiveness, kissing the Holy Slipper, pledging fealty to the One True Pope and His Holy Church, and presenting their offerings. One by one, the Holy Father accepted their acts of contrition and offerings, absolving them of their sins, and welcoming them back into the loving arms of the Church. The ceremony lasted for most of the morning, ending with the Holy Father raising from the dais and giving general absolution to all present within the piazza.

The consecration ceremony, though steeped in tradition and holy sanctity, was much more uplifting, for it represented a path forward for Siena and held promise of warmer relations with the Pope and his Holy Church. The overall cost of these two ceremonies was extremely high, but the benefits to our dear city were great. Commerce could proceed, much expanded, throughout the Western world, and the Sienese banking houses could reestablish credit lines with Catholic royals and leading merchants without reprisals from the Roman curia. The stigma of the interdict, once washed away, had emboldened our businessmen to expand operations and grow in wealth and power. Such benefits were not lost on me, for with the successful negotiations for peace between the Council and the Pope, I had risen to a position of power and notoriety, greater than most of the leaders in the Council. My service to His Holiness in this matter, as well as his gratefulness for introducing Him to the holy Galgano, had earned me his eternal gratitude and the title of Banker to the Pope and the Roman Curia. Letters of introduction and recommendation, issued with the Holy Seal, allowed me to deal with any court in Christendom, and had become a great value to me and my business, allowing for such growth as to dwarf the empire that Giancarlo had built in the West.

I was exceedingly pleased with the efforts I had put forth over the preceding several months and enjoyed the celebratory banquet and feasts that were held at the Palace of the Bishop and at several palazzi around the city center. The Patriarch of Grado and his nephew Enrico had arrived in Siena in time for the official ceremonies and were guests of the Holy Father, as were the Abbot and the other bishops. I had arranged for Enrico to reside with me at Giancarlo's palazzo, as guest of honor, and to repay him for his generous hospitality that he had always shown to me. He was pleased to accept the invitation and was equally pleased to be present for Pietro's wedding celebration. Although I had been all-consumed with the reconciliation ceremonies, I had left Anna in charge of arranging for the arrival of Pietro and his guests, as well as the bridal party, welcoming them into the palazzo and seeing to their needs. I had done this against my better judgement, for Anna had grown increasingly unreliable with her fits of melancholia, but Nikos had not yet returned from the East and I was much too busy with the Pope's visit to devote the adequate attention required of a responsible host.

The papal feast and other banquets lasted well into the night, preventing me from meeting Pietro and his wedding party. The wedding ceremony was to be performed on the following day in the newly consecrated cathedral, with a small party of friends and relatives present, and my palazzo was prepared for a great feast to be held on the afternoon following the ceremony. I had anticipated there would be plenty of time in the morning to meet Pietro's bride and her family. As fate would have it, I received an early morning summons to the Bishop's Palace to meet with His Holiness and the Patriarch. The elder Dandolo had asked me to return in order that I may convey to him, directly, the story of Galgano and the Visitations of the Archangel Michael and the Apostles. Pietro was disappointed for his bride and her party had not yet presented themselves, so again I had to leave them to the hospitality of Anna and her household staff. Duty called and I begged pardon of Pietro, assuring him that I was anxious to meet his bride before the ceremony, promising him I would not be late. I assured him I would bring with me such honored guests to bring Holy Grace to his very special day. Little did I know the hurt I was causing my friend, nor the cruel revenge the gods had devised for me.

My meeting with His Holiness and the Patriarch lasted most of the morning. Ugolino and Ubaldo were both brought in, as was the Archbishop of Sens and the Abbot. There was much debate as to the holiness of the beggar on the mount; much was said, and much was not. By noon, I begged leave of the company, and both Ugolino and the Archbishop, having known Pietro, agreed to accompany me to witness the ceremony.

As we walked through the streets of Siena, a small crowd of citizens recognized me and the two dignitaries and began to follow us. As the crowd swelled, several of the metropolitan police fell in behind us for our protection. The unintended result of our arrival at the Duomo was that a small mob led by the Pope's secretary, the Archbishop of Sens, and Giovanni Pecci created a commotion amongst the guests. Pietro seemed surprised and annoyed but upon seeing my two companions, he bowed low and humbly welcomed his most honored guests. More surprised was the Archbishop to see his ex-lover, the Archdeacon, Walter of Chatillon, standing between Pietro and his veiled betrothed. In that instance, Mighty Zeus let loose his fiery thunderbolt and split me asunder. I had known in an instant that the bride was none other than Dona Pica. I could not tell from beneath that virginal veil if her stare was of loving remembrance or pure hatred, but I thanked Heaven she was so veiled, for the look of surprise was quite evident upon so many faces—all except Pietro.

The ceremony commenced and the deacon spoke loudly to all those assembled before the church. "Before all else, let those who are to be joined in the marriage bed come before the doors of God's Holy Church." The sun had risen high in the sky, yet the air had grown chill. My head was swimming in a pool of self-loathing, doubt, betrayal, and anger. My heart was mastering my mind, for I knew I could never have Dona Pica, and yet I could not acquiesce to allow Pietro to have her for his own. The Fates were indeed cruel to all of us, forcing us to play our bit parts in their drama, upon the steps of Santa Maria Assunta. The words of the ceremony were lost to me. I recall quite clearly the rage that had welled up within me as Pietro spoke the words, "I receive you as mine, so that you become my wife, and I your husband." I nearly cried out loud as Dona Pica repeated, in her sweet and gentle voice, "I receive you as mine, so that you become my husband, and I your wife." No cracking of her voice, no tears of regret and sorrow streaming down her rosy cheeks.

Dona Pica lifted the veil from her face, revealing a radiant beauty filled with love and affection for the man who stood beside her. The deacon then took both of their hands and joined them together, binding them with a richly embroidered scarf that Pietro had acquired from me on one of our trading missions in France. Oh, how cruel the gods can be!

"As two hands are bound together in love, so too shall two lives be joined together in life and happiness, in prosperity and in fruitfulness." He blessed the wedded couple with holy water and recited an invocation and a charge to go in peace.

It is incredible to me even now that I could have put myself in such an uncomfortable situation, having to don a mask of happiness for the newlyweds, having to officiate over the wedding banquet and provide lodging for the entire party for several days. Such penance I was forced to accept for all the wrongs I had committed in my life up to that point, though now, I see, t'was only a down payment for the many wrongs I would perpetrate during the remainder of my life. Pietro was the happiest I had ever seen him or have seen him since. Dona Pica, I knew to be in agony, yet she showed no outward sign of her inner misery, playing the loving wife. But I knew the true devil who resided within her. I knew she really wanted me. And I knew I would have her again, and I vowed when that day would come, I would be ready to bring her true happiness.

God in Heaven forgive this sinner for coveting the wife of my friend. Forgive me for bearing false witness upon the steps of Your Holy Church, and in the eyes of my friends. Forgive me for abusing the loyalty and trust of a friend and for ruining the sanctity of the marriage of those whom I loved. Oh, give me strength that I may complete this confession and transfer to parchment the mighty burden of all my sins that weigh so heavily upon my soul. My body grows weak and my spirit is pained with these reflections. I submit myself to Your judgement….

Rest nor sleep shall be awarded either of us for Giovanni is possessed with a maniacal urgency to completely purge his soul of every sin he has ever committed. I praise his commitment but there is not enough parchment nor ink nor strength in my blistered fingers to satisfy his need. He refuses to rest and is now searching through the stack of papers that have been produced over the past several days and nights, searching for inconsistencies or inaccurate statements. I swear to Almighty God that I have done my very best to record every word or thought of my master, whether it be truth or fantasy, which is not for me to judge. I have merely acted as the receptacle into which his stream of consciousness and unconsciousness has flowed. Through me, his spoken words have sought quill and ink, and have been grounded upon the firmness of the parchment. Long after my master has gone, his words will live, perhaps to plead for pity and understanding, or perhaps to prevent a future sinner from suffering a similar fate as he.

I marvel at the accomplishments of this man. His confessions move me to tears for I know the goodness in him, and I know the agony he has suffered all of his life. He has done so much good for the world—more so, I fear, than will ever be revealed in this journal. Yet he is obsessed with only the sins of his life. The goodness of the man has prevented him from highlighting his positive attributes despite his fear of the irreversible damage done by his pride and envy, his gluttony and his greed.

Lord, I beg you to consider the good that is in this man and all that he has done for Your Church, the state, and his fellow man. Please be merciful to him.

Night has returned. Giovanni has stared into the murky waters of his seeing chalice and has drunk deeply of the potent contents. His body rests as his spirit has begun another journey. I wait.

Welcome, kind spirit. I have anxiously awaited your visit and am most welcoming of your counsel. Help me to see what I must see in order to save my soul. Let me look upon you, spirit. Do I know you? Thine image is obscured from me, for a swarm of flies envelops your face and prevents me from seeing your countenance. Speak to me, spirit, that I may know you.

Know me, Giovanni, as the man that I was, not this tormented spirit that I have become. Listen well to my counsel, as you have done in years past, for the time to settle up upon the banca of your life is drawing near. The scales of judgement are ready to receive your soul and they are not weighted in your favor. As I had once weighed the debits and credits of your character before choosing to accept you as my son and heir, so will Almighty God be weighing the pluses and minuses of your life before making His final judgement of your worth.

Blessed Giancarlo! Father and friend. Forgive me for not greeting you more respectfully. Your appearance has unnerved me.

Look upon me, Giovanni, and fear what you see, for worse may await you unless you can somehow alter your fate. I was given no opportunity to confess my sins and beg mercy from God. My life was taken, as was my poor Donna Donata in the darkness of a filthy Greek cell. Your delay in getting our ransom money to our captors—in counterfeit coin, no less—had sealed our fate, and robbed us of any chance for confession and redemption. Your greed had doomed us. For all we had given you, you failed us. You failed us, as you failed Anna and your children; as you failed your own people; as you have failed everyone.

Giancarlo, please. Forgive me. Please. I never meant to hurt you or to fail you. I loved you and Donna Donata as I loved my own parents. Perhaps I loved you more. I only wanted you to be proud of me. I only acted as I was taught by you. I felt sure that you would have been proud of the way I attempted your ransom and rescue. I grieve that it did not turn out as planned. I truly grieved, as so many others did, at your loss. You were a great and honorable man, and I have missed you dearly.

Not so great or honorable to avoid my punishment. The flies do not feast upon a good soul. I was a great sinner. I knew my behavior was wrong and yet I reveled in feasting upon my fat little pigeons. Remember the pigeons, Giovanni? Ah, how I delighted in swindling them of everything they had. And with each pigeon I swallowed, a hungry fly was added to my sentence. See the cost of such gluttony!

You loved us not, nor have you loved anyone in your life. Such is a pity. For all that you have accomplished, you have never been able to accept true love. You cannot see it, even as it sits beside you in your final hours. How could you possibly return that which you refused to receive? You will die the poorer man for lack of it.

In place of love, you envied me. Your pride and your lust for power, your gluttony and your greed, all filled your heart and left no room for love. You did not want to honor me; you strove to best me in everything you did. You coveted all that I had, and you wanted more. Your greed has been your undoing.

Your words shame me, Giancarlo, yet you speak the truth. I did envy you and I lusted for the power that I saw you wield so masterfully. I channeled all my energy into besting you, for as great as I had thought you to be, I wanted to be greater. I wanted my empire to be ten times greater than yours. My pride would not allow me to be second best. I took what you had done and made it better. I took it all, and I wanted more. Only now—maybe too late—do I see that I was wrong. The note is finally being called and my soul is bankrupt. Even if I liquidate all that I have, I fear that I may never satisfy the debt. I have paid too high a price for my success, and Satan will prove to be the victor in this bargain.

Forgive me, Giancarlo. Forgive me for all that I have done. I am truly sorry, not for my own soul, but for yours, and for Donna Donata's, and for every soul I have tarnished. I am not worthy of your forgiveness and I shall accept my fate as it is given to me.

It pains my heart to see your life end thusly. I had hoped that you would do better than I, and somehow managed to see yourself as others were wont to see you. There is greatness in you, Giovanni, or at least there was at one time. That shall be judged by those you leave behind. There is also good in you, my son, and that will be judged by God, Himself. Be honest with yourself as you make the close and let the chips fall as they may.

God in Heaven give me the strength to carry on for I am failing you, just as I have failed everyone else.

Nikos, sweet Nikos. Hold me, Nikos. I need to feel your love.

Chapter Six
Anger

XX

End of an Era—Life Goes On

I am failing, Nikos, and there is still much to tell. I praise God and I thank Him for granting me this time and what little strength I have remaining so that I may complete my task. My story at this point is far from over; my unconfessed sins are many and are so clear to me now. No longer is the seer's son blind—only too late to right the wrongs that I had so willingly foisted upon those whom I should have loved. It is only with God's good grace and mercy that I continue my confession.

Siena had reconciled with the Pope, and had forsaken her oath to the emperor, but Ghibelline sympathies had run deep amongst the upper merchant class, and the Guelf influence was weak. Alexander was stronger in his victories and had returned to Rome. The Patriarch had returned to Venice and Enrico had sailed east on a diplomatic mission for the Doge. The Archbishop of Sens had forgiven his lover, and both had returned to France. Pietro and Dona Pica had returned, as husband and wife, to Assisi. Nikos had returned from Constantinople, and Siena had returned to the prosperity she had enjoyed before the interdiction.

I had removed myself to Stigliano, partly to avoid the petty jealousies that had been born amongst the leaders of the Council, but mostly to resume my work with the restoration of Rosellae. Gontarz had already erected a fulling mill on the banks of the Merse, using a similar mechanism as I had studied in Bruges but modifying it to be driven not by wind and sail but by a large paddled wheel, turned by the running waters of the Merse. Affixed to the wheel shaft I had designed a series of pounding mallets that were used to full the cloth that was derived from bleached raw wool. The pounding process was far more effective than the walking method used by other fullers for a thousand years, and it enabled my factory to produce a greater quantity and higher quality of cloth, at a fraction of the cost.

I intended to construct several of these mills while my flock of Leinster sheep grew, figuring to cut out the processors in Bruges and avoiding the higher cost of importing wool from Ireland. The expert weavers and the superior looms I had built by the craftsmen of Curtun had assured the best, most luxurious fabrics attainable. My plan, however, was foiled when tragedy struck in the night and a good portion of my flock was mysteriously stricken dead. Some claimed it was God's punishment for a prideful entrepreneur, while other claimed it was agents of a vengeful Strongbow. Those of the Guelf persuasion placed blame on agents of Barbarossa for my involvement with the Pope. I am more inclined to believe that the perpetrators were much closer to home.

I did not let the setback change my overall plans, though it was several years before I was able to approach the high level of production, I had first envisioned. I would eventually negotiate a better contract with King John of England after he took the throne from Richard. The deValles of Wexford had become my main suppliers of the Leinster wool, which augmented my growing supply of lana di Stigliano.

I eventually collected all debts owed to me by the commune for my service in the reconciliation affair, even though some on the Council had attempted to renegotiate the terms of our contract, complaining that the demands and wishes of the Pope had far exceeded their initial estimates of the cost of forgiveness. I did not hesitate to rely on the assistance of some of my most powerful and influential friends, including His Holiness, himself, to ensure the Council honored our agreement. My new position as Banker to the Pope and the Roman Curia allowed me to concentrate more on the financing business and less on the import/export trade. The increased violence and security risks throughout the empires had put a great deal of strain on margins and profit, while the financing of enterprises was much more profitable and safe because of my access to banking centers throughout the lands.

I began to travel at a lessened pace, the logistical problems of moving a convoy of goods safely across a continent were minimized, and much of my business was then being conducted through letters of credit with agents and banks. No more did I face the risk of thieves upon the roadway, but rather had to face the thieves who masked themselves as friends and associates. And of course, there were always the delinquent debtors, both noble and clerical, whose word and honor, in some cases, meant nothing. Occasionally a prince of state or the Church would try to wiggle off the hook of a well-executed contract by using the prohibition of usury or the threat of excommunication in satisfaction of the debt. Though many of my associates have fallen into ruin because of such traps, I always had the good fortune to have the support of friends in very high places.

As Siena was again flourishing, the Eastern Empire had been thrown into chaos. Violence between the Latins and the Greeks had escalated and forced the Emperor to increase restrictions on commerce and trade. As in the past, the mobs, and subsequently the Emperor, had driven the Genoese, the Pisani, and the Amalfani out of the Golden Horn and this time were intent on eradicating them altogether. Tensions between the Greeks and the Venetians began to boil because of Greek jealousy, and the beneficial status the Venetians had earned and had been rightfully awarded. Enrico had been sent to negotiate with the Emperor for the release of a great many Venetian hostages who were taken unlawfully during a major political upheaval. Giancarlo had been spared imprisonment because of his close association with the Emperor, but many of his associates and contacts had been killed or had suffered imprisonment. Business in the Eastern Empire had dried up, and survival had become the main cause of concern. Fortunately, Giancarlo's importance and imperial friendships, as well as his connections throughout the Mideast, had protected him from the mob violence. Along with his own increased security forces, his personal safety and the safety of his family had been vouchsafed by imperial decree.

Giancarlo was wise to see that his survival was only dependent upon the good graces and the whims of the Emperor, and his usefulness was tentative, at best, in the land of the duplicitous Greeks. He could see that the future of the Latins in the East was growing dim and his vision for success in that area of the world was clouded. He decided to return to Italy until such time as peace and security had returned to the empire and instructed me to make ready for his return. Carefully he orchestrated the transfer of most of his wealth through various Eastern banks to safe harbors in Venice. I was instructed to move those funds to various banking facilities in the West.

The Emperor was growing old, and for many years he had been battling the Seljuk Turks. During this time, he had suffered several decisive defeats and despite his vanity, had started to display vulnerability. And in his weakness, the wolves had begun to circle their prey. Not only from outside his imperial borders; they had lurked within his own empire. Many attempts had been made upon his life, which only added to the chaos and the uncontrollability of the mob within the Imperial City.

Finally, in the summer of 1180, Manuel Comnenus, Most Blessed Emperor of Constantinople, was stricken with fever, and while cradled in the loving arms of his wife and empress, passed out of the world he had sought to conquer. Empress Maria of Antioch, who had been a patron and benefactor of Giancarlo, did not want to lose her power, and so assumed the role of regent, having imperial power transferred, not to the eleven-year-old son of Manuel, Alexios II, but rather to Manuel's nephew, the protosebastos, also known as Alexios. It appeared that this nephew had been the Empress's lover and co-conspirator in the murder of the Emperor.

Emperors are known to rise and fall, and so, while attempting to satisfy the appetites of the usurper and the regent, Giancarlo secretly planned to leave for Venice. This major upheaval caused me to travel to Venice to receive Giancarlo's shipments and to oversee the conversion of the gold hyperpyrons to Venetian lira. At that time, it took almost five lire to make one gold hyperpyron. The large shipments of the gold coinage from the East had flooded the market and had caused additional debasement of the Venetian coin. When Enrico finally came to power a decade later, he eventually solved this debasement problem for Venice by minting the marvelous grosso, which is the standard used around the world today.

Giancarlo was not the only Venetian merchant of high standing to attempt a massive sell-off, and such frenzied trading, coupled with the heighten jealousies of the Greek populous, created pandemonium in the streets of the capitol. Chaos reigned for two years, until Andronikos, that murderous snake and first cousin to the murdered emperor, with eyes fixed upon the imperial crown, entered the city with his army and overthrew the government. He was proclaimed the savior of the people and granted ultimate power. He deceitfully maneuvered to have Alexios II crowned emperor, while retaining all the power behind the throne, and proceeded to eliminate anyone close to the throne. Playing to the hatred of the Greek mobs, this Satan-spawn systematically also rounded up all the Latins in Constantinople, including Giancarlo and Donna Donata, imprisoned only the wealthiest in order to ransom them off at a future date, sold the serviceable women into slavery, and massacred eighty thousand poor souls, whose only crime was not being born Greek.

Merciful God in Heaven, I do not pretend to know Thy plan nor Thy reasons for such atrocities, but only question what good was born out of such tragedy! The Venetians fared the worst. The many months of negotiations and the large sums of money that Enrico had paid to Alexios and the Empress on behalf of his Venetian brothers and sisters were wasted, and the unspeakable atrocities that took place under that devil's reign shall never be forgotten.

Having successfully handled Giancarlo's transfer of assets, I was then faced with trying to negotiate terms of his release and his deliverance from the madness. Enrico had narrowly escaped the Imperial City with his own life and had returned with a handful of refugees and the horrendous news of the massacre of the Latins. He had no news for me of Giancarlo and Donna Donata. I had prayed for help from the Vatican, but my prayers were unanswered, for Alexander III, our Holy Father, had been exiled again from Rome by the commune, had fallen ill with fever, and had died at Civita Castellana at the end of August. He was succeeded by Ubaldo, as Lucius III, and though I had known him to be an honest and honorable man, he had proven to be a weak and ineffectual leader during his short reign. The only meaningful decision he made during his three years as pope was to canonize my dear brother Galgano, who had passed from this world only a few months after Alexander. Lucius' prayers were of no use to the Venetians and his call to arms would never come.

Louis of France also joined His Holiness in Heaven in that same year, Henry of England was embroiled in wars in Ireland, Scotland, and France, and the relationship between the papacy and Barbarossa had never been mended. No help nor hope for rescue would come from the West. Nikos' Uncle Niketas, working in Constantinople with palace sympathizers, had missed an opportunity to have Giancarlo and Donata transferred to the Monastery of Agios Nikolaos on the island of Buyukada, and having raised great displeasure with the devil Andronikos, narrowly escaped death by fleeing in the last remaining Venetian vessel to the Island of Crete. From there, he was able to get a message to Enrico as to the exact whereabouts of Giancarlo's prison cell. With such information, Enrico and I quickly formulated a plan of rescue. We made our way to Crete, where Enrico had enlisted twenty of his best men and had secured for them the uniforms of the Royal Guard of the Kingdom of Sicily. At great risk and expense, we were brought onboard a Napolitano warship, which was making ready to depart for the capitol. With a small sack filled with gold coins and a forged document from King William, Enrico was able to bribe the captain to allow our party to join several envoys from William's court, whose mission it was to negotiate a peace treaty between the Norman Kingdom of Sicily and the Eastern Empire.

The emissaries were informed that the Guards had been sent by William for their protection in the Imperial City. I had never questioned how Enrico had managed to get all of this done, for such skills must remain unquestioned for a master of infinite resources. We sailed directly to Constantinople and having been kept waiting a day and a half for permission to pass beyond the Great Chain, our ship was escorted by a royal naval vessel and an armed Imperial Guard to the Bucoleon Palace. The emissaries were separated from us and escorted into the palace. We found ourselves close enough to the location reported to be the prison where Giancarlo and Donna Donata were being held but sensing we had been led through treachery into a trap, we quickly revised our plan. As we were led to a desolate alleyway, the Greek guards were silently and effortlessly dispatched, their bodies thrown down a nearby well.

Silently, we breached the wall that surrounded the prison, and after slaying the unsuspecting guards, were finally able to gain entrance to the holding cells of the last of the Latin prisoners. My heart froze instantly as I looked upon the lifeless body of my dear Donna Donata, strangled and savagely defiled by her barbarous captors. A similar fate was met by all the women who were held in that Hellhole. In a darkened corner of the room, in a locked cage, were piled the bodies of a dozen withered men, their eyes gouged from their sockets and their tongues ripped from their mouths. The horrid sight brought on such nausea as to cause me to vomit. I sank to my knees and wailed like a woman, cursing the Devil and God alike, and vowing vengeance upon those hated Greeks, should I be allowed to escape that nightmarish scene.

Violently we hacked away at the lock on the cage until it split apart. The smell of death and decay assaulted our nostrils, and again I found myself sick to my stomach. Most of the bodies lay lifelessly upon the floor, save for one, the badly broken and emaciated body of Giancarlo Manenti. Still did he have life within him, even though his tormentors had left him for dead. I gently raised his head from the cold stone, and I cradled it in my lap, wiping the blood from his face as my tears helped to wash away the dirt from his cheek and brow. I called to him and told him I had come to take him home, and in that instant of recognition and relief, Giancarlo Manenti breathed his last breath.

Enrico insisted that nothing further could be done, and we needed to quickly leave the city. I could not leave Giancarlo and Donna Donata behind, and implored Enrico's men to assist me in carrying the bodies with us. Enrico led us through a series of mazes until we made our way to the Harbor of Theodosius. We shed our disguises and donned whatever rags we could find or steal so as not to bring attention to us. The bodies were wrapped in cloth and placed into large baskets, which one of the men had managed to take from an unsuspecting shopkeeper, along with his clothes—and his worthless life. Though the Venetians had been driven from the land, Enrico still had friends who would risk their lives to hide and safely transport us out of the city. As we waited, deals were made, and safe passage was arranged upon an Alexandrian vessel setting sail for Abidos.

There we transferred to a Pisan ship bound for Corfu. In two weeks, we had managed to break free of the Byzantine threat and had gained safe passage on a Venetian ship bound for home. My rescue mission had been a total failure, a disaster of which I will never fully recover. My only consolation was I was able to retrieve the bodies of my adopted parents and bring them back for proper and honorable burial within the womb of Sena Vitas.

Upon my return, the news of her parents' deaths had caused Anna such consternation and misery that she sunk irretrievably into depression and madness, until, one stormy night, as Jove's thunderbolts illuminated the blackened sky, Anna Soarzi Manenti threw herself from the topmost window of her palazzo and dashed her brains upon the rain-drenched pavement below. With the death of Giancarlo, of Donna Donata, and of my wife, Anna, I had become the sole master of Giancarlo's entire remaining financial empire.

From then on, I continued to expand my empire by taking advantage of bankers and merchants who, through mismanagement or bad fortune, were forced to sell their businesses at distressed prices. All the while, I was dealing with the restoration of Stigliano and serving on Siena's council. Pietro was also showing promise by expanding his own business enterprises. He had seen greater profits from the silks and other fine cloths he was able to find in Venice. His major customers were wealthy nobles and merchant class citizens in the major commercial centers in France, whose demand for those exotic fabrics had only increased as the supply of such goods had dwindled.

I decided to travel to Assisi with a business proposal for Pietro. I needed trusted agents, especially in France, and I decided to employ Pietro to oversee my French operation. My timing was off, for I had missed Pietro by a week. Dona Pica met me coldly and informed me that her husband had gone to Venice. I then pleaded with her to allow me the time to explain my deceptive behavior toward her in the past. Long did she berate me for stealing her love and leaving her behind, and in silence, I listened, and I took full responsibility for my actions. She then surprised me by telling me she had known full well that Pietro was a friend of mine and had agreed to travel to Siena and accept my offer to host them in order to get even with me. She had intentionally kept herself hidden from me until the very moment it would create the greatest hurt to me. I was furious at her confession, and yet I had found myself enchanted by her deviousness.

We both knew that Pietro had loved his wife, but he loved making money more, and had spent more time away from his young bride than she had expected. She knew that a good merchant's wife must expect her husband to be away from the hearth, providing for his family and building his fortune, more so than staying at home to hold his wife's delicate hand and comfort her lonely body in the cold, dark night. Pietro had provided her a good life, better than most, with a nice home, fine clothes, security—and yet she had wanted more.

With her confession I decided to take her for myself. With Anna's death, I no longer was plagued with feelings of guilt, and had on many occasions, in the loneliness of my own bed chamber, turned my thoughts toward my friend's wife. Merciful God forgive this sinner, for you had turned a deaf ear as I pleaded with you to drive those adulterous desires from my mind and my body. Only now do I see the wisdom of your plan, for it was those thoughts and desires that drove me to travel to Assisi, hoping that Pietro would be far away. Those desires forced me to sin against my friend by coveting his wife and helped me worm my way into her home and into her heart, to rekindle those hot coals of passion that had warmed our naked bodies in the haystack at her uncle's farm.

Like a satyr I played upon every string of her heart, complimenting her upon her beauty, comforting her in her lonely state, listening to her wants and desires, and falsely confessing to her my undying love. I convinced her that all of the obstacles in my life were no longer a concern of ours. Until finally, with weakened resistance, she became mine. We spent the remainder of the day and night fanning the flames of passion, which had engulfed both of our hearts and which had burnt away all reason between the two of us. Lust and passion are powerful weapons against virtue and reason and can easily wash away the hurt and despair of a loveless life. Yet, their power is not lasting. The darkened silence of night brought calmness to our exhausted bodies and brought reason back to my mind.

With reason came guilt and self-loathing. I knew what we had done was wrong. I had taken from my friend that which he loved most, that which was so easy for me to take. I did not love Dona Pica, nor did I want to hurt her, and I certainly did not want to hurt Pietro. I had gained nothing in this action, save an evening of carnal pleasure, but had increased my liabilities by debasing my friend's wife, and risking my friend's hatred. I had realized that no good would come from this liaison, and nothing could be done or said to rectify my wicked actions. I had to get myself away from Dona Pica as quickly as possible, and refrain from ever having contact with her again. I hoped that in time she would see the logic in my decision to leave her, and never speak of our unwise indiscretions. In darkness and silence, I left her asleep upon her marriage bed and stole away, like a thief, into the night.

I traveled quickly back to Stigliano and threw myself into my work. I was imbued with a drive to make things right, to finish all I had started, and to prepare the ark to receive the Chosen Ones. I was determined to make Stigliano the greatest commercial complex in the region. My days were long, and I had to force my mind to focus on a myriad of projects. The nights, however, were still an agony to me. I tried hard to convince myself I had made the wise decision to distance myself from Dona Pica, but the guilt continued to plague me. I felt my only salvation lay in the counsel and guidance of my dear brother Galgano, but as I set my mind to traveling to Monte Siepi, news reached me from Cortona that my infant child, Giuseppe, had died.

Immediately I made my way to Cortona, where I had left my family's care in the hands of my sister, Matilda. Nikos was overseeing the household in Siena for the eight months when my family was moved there, and upon hearing of the infant's death, had made his way quickly to Cortona, arriving there before I had made it from Stigliano. Matilda was distraught when I arrived at the house. She had taken very good care of the children and had come to love them as her own. Such love, and the attention that Nikos had shown them, was all they would get during those juvenile years, for I had been too consumed with building an empire rather than building a loving family.

With all the care and nurturing one may possibly give, Fate is cruel at times, and can easily cut down a sapling before it has time to flourish and grow. Such it was with Giuseppe. A healthy and jovial child was tucked into his crib for a peaceful slumber, only to be found hideously bloated and blackened by the touch of Death's icy grip. None could have known that Satan's agent, a venomous viper, would make its way into the child's crib and wrap itself around the warmth of living flesh to claim an innocent life for its own. Terrible was the effect of this child's death upon my entire household, and I could only assume that it was God's retribution for my wickedness.

Young Paolo was most affected, for he has always been kind and gentle and loving to the helpless. Vannozzo was also affected, though for him, the child's death was more a fascination than a fright. He seemed to marvel at the lethal power that a smaller creature could have over a larger, unsuspecting victim. His reaction made my skin crawl and brought back to me the visions of the destructive force that I had seen in him. Nikos had warned me of the boy's inherent evil, and he was convinced the boy had inherited the curse of the sight, from me, just as I had from my father. As he began to mature, his fits and visitations were becoming more frequent and more violent, and he did not know how to handle them. Nikos was convinced the boy was being visited by a demon rather than by the Holy Spirit and had reported to me on several occasions that the boy had become increasingly cruel toward his younger brother.

Both Matilda and Nikos had kept a close eye upon the growing animosity and had made sure the two youngsters were kept separate whenever possible. Fearing for the safety of young Paolo, Nikos had taken measures to train the seven-year-old in the art of self-preservation. Such action, he thought, would suffice until Vannozzo could learn to control his outbursts, but he also pleaded with me to step in and bring my eldest to live with me at Stigliano for he was convinced that the boy had something to do with the death of the infant. Too late did I listen to his pleas. I could only remember the torture that I had known as I grew to adolescence trying to deal with the power of the pec-ii, and the comfort I had finally found through the training and patience of the Taurisi, I had decided to ask Tarquin to accept the boy into the community. I was convinced that, with time, Vannozzo would learn to master his curse and use his powers to help our people. I wanted desperately for the future that I had seen in my own visions to be altered so my son could be turned from the darkness and live a productive life at my side. I vowed to Nikos that

I would take the boy to Curtun upon my return from Monte Siepe. I sought the peace and wisdom of Galgano, for I had felt my life was becoming uncontrollable. Laying the infant to rest in the crypt with his mother and grandparents, I left the rest of my family in the care of Nikos.

XXI

A Sinner Becomes a Saint

I rode swiftly past Stigliano and made my way to Monte Siepi, longing to speak with my confessor, Galgano. I had looked forward to seeing my spirit-brother, for he, above all else, knew my true self, and his words and his counsel were always a relief to me. As I climbed to the top of the mountain, a large crowd had gathered. Many were kneeling with heads bowed low. Others were openly weeping. A small group were praying in a circle around the sacred stone, hands above their heads raised to Heaven. In the center of the circle, upon the sacred stone, lay the emaciated body of my brother. His breathing was labored, his eyes wide open and staring into Heaven. I broke the circle and I knelt beside him, gently cradling his head in my hands, and I could not hold my sorrow but gave out a loud cry to God, and then fell silent. I had sensed his spirit was already preparing for its journey home and I did not want to interrupt his communion with the Holy Spirit. My tears fell upon his cheek and provided moisture to his parched lips. Silently I prayed with him and wept. He died as the sun began to set, and the shadow of his broad sword touched upon his brow. His last breath was carried to Heaven upon a gentle breeze as the mountaintop was blanketed in silence. My friend, my brother, my confessor, was gone.

Just as His Holiness Alexander had prophesied to him, Galgano did not live a long life, though those few years which were afforded to him were, indeed, filled with peace and the joy of the Holy Spirit. The young street urchin turned master assassin, whom I had grown to love and to call brother, had, in a few short years, become known throughout most of Europe. All who heard the story of his visitation and conversion were drawn to visit the man, to bear witness to the miracle, and to hear his holy words. Alexander's visit to the mountaintop, and his acceptance of the authenticity of the holy beggar, had confirmed the miracle of Monti Siepi. Those who had born witness to the conversion of the Holy Father on that mystical visit had helped to spread the name of Galgano throughout Europe and around the world. Many had come to him seeking penance for their sins and forgiveness from Heaven, and many remained with him as followers.

Never again would I hear his counsel or gain comfort from his loving acceptance. But never have I forsaken my vow to provide my brother with sustenance. Though his followers continued to grow in number, their care I have accepted as my charge, for he lives in each of them. And through the years, as his reputation has spread across the land, I have found I am constantly asked to recount that first night of miracles upon the hill. Kings and queens, princes of state and princes of the Church, merchants, bankers, and laborers alike, all are fascinated with the story of the sword and the stone, and through those stories I have kept my brother alive. Many of the wealthiest, as well as the poor, have made pilgrimages to the site to witness for themselves the miracle

Galgano Guidotti had passed from this earth at the tender age of thirty-three, and was buried in a simple grave to the right of the stone from which he preached to his disciples, his only marker being the shadow of the Holy Cross cast from his sword by the rays of the setting sun. In his memory, I have since constructed a small chapel near his grave. He had lived and had died as the Lord had commanded, and in death he will, as promised, live forever.

I returned to Stigliano in utter despair. The world, it seemed, was closing in on me. I needed to throw myself back into my work in order to exorcise my soul of all the evil that had plagued me during the long and grueling year. Construction of the water-powered mill had been completed. The long stone building with waterwheels, built upon a stone foundation, miraculously laid upon the bedrock of the river, sat upon the waters as if it were a giant seagoing vessel. Its two wheels turned constantly as the river's current flowed around the foundation.

Gontarz had retrofitted the cams on the shafts of two separate tappet wheels, enabling a dozen fulling hammers to automatically do the work of two dozen walkers in a fraction of the time. The steady current of the river provided an endless and even supply of power to the hammers, which fell day and night. With this new facility, I would increase my output a dozen-fold, and by streamlining the entire process, I would manufacture great quantities of the finest wools in Europe. Through cunning and ingenuity, I would make a huge fortune.

Several weeks had passed when small groups of The Chosen Ones began to arrive from Curtun. We had made sure that each band had traveled at night once they had left the safety of the Hidden Realm, and new identities had been established for many of them. The roads and villages were full of suspicious eyes and wagging tongues, and I did my utmost to avoid waking the anger and jealousies of my neighbors and my enemies. Supplies and artifacts were also transported at night, and I established several warehouses along the way so that rest and concealment were assured during the daylight hours. Over the course of a month, the entire one hundred Chosen were brought to Stigliano, along with about fifty craftsmen who were on loan to me so I might finish the establishment of the settlement and bring the mighty furnace of Vol-tuma to life again.

With the last shipment of goods and men from Curtun, I was met by Salvatore and Sebastiano. My heart was heavy knowing that doom was quickly drawing down upon Curtun, and I prayed that my visions were false. I held hope that the future could somehow be changed by miracle from God or heroic deeds by men. We enjoyed the brief time we had together, assured of our love and friendship, and recounted the many journeys we had shared together. I could not convince them to stay at Stigliano, for their duty was to their father, the Zil-at, and I had begrudged the sun's rising, for I knew by midmorning my cousins would depart, and quite possibly I would never see them again.

That following morning, Nikos was seen galloping at full speed into the compound. Upon his horse sat Vannozzo. I had been so engrossed with the rebuilding and the many promises of Stigliano that I had forgotten about my pledge to Nikos to take Vannozzo to Curtun. Not saying a word, Nikos dismounted and dragged the boy from his steed. He then pushed the boy to the ground before my feet. Not knowing the cause for such action, Salvatore grabbed Nikos' arm, questioning him as to the manner of such disrespect. Nikos turned to me and admonished me for breaking my oath to remove the boy from the rest of the family, and through my negligence, placed my entire family in great harm. He told me that Vannozzo had become unmercifully cruel to his siblings following the death of the baby, unleashing his hatred and abuse, especially toward young Paolo. No manner of separation had seemed to work, and Nikos believed the possessed boy was determined to kill his brother, as he had done so with the infant Giuseppi. I found it hard to fathom that one so young could hold such hatred for another human. I have since learned that evil can make manifest in any susceptible vessel, young or old.

Nikos then told us that Vannozzo had lured the innocent Paolo into the hills beyond the northern borders of Cortona, telling him his father had been held captive by the hill people and was in desperate need of their help to escape his captors. High on the mountain, as forest gave way to rock and cliff, Vannozzo cast Paolo over the cliff and left him for dead. For two full days and nights, that monster feigned ignorance of his brother's whereabouts. Nikos and my brothers searched in vain for the boy, and all the prayers of the priests and the family could not bring the boy back. The angels were with young Paolo, for Death was robbed of his young and durable soul as he fell from tree branch to tree branch, cushioning his fall. Though badly bruised, he was strong enough and smart enough to find his way back down the mountain.

He made his way, in secret, to his Uncle Arturo, who together with Nikos decided that for the safety of the entire family Vannozzo had to be removed. Nikos insisted that a devil had possessed the boy. Vannozzo silently looked back at Nikos and sneered. Had the boy been Nikos' he would have been stoned to death, as is the custom in the East, and his broken body would be cast over the same cliff from which he had attempted to end the life of his brother. Still, the boy was mine, and we were not living in the East. Our laws were no less clear or just, yet I could not bring myself to proclaim a sentence of death upon my son's head. Lo, that I did not have the courage to act as logic dictated. Instead, I listened to my heart and sought an alternative solution to the problem. Dear Lord, I beseech Thee to help me understand Thy wisdom in allowing me to choose the greater evil of mercy over punishment. My compassion has cost the lives of an entire race.

I did not make my choice lightly but listened to the counsel of Nikos and my two cousins. In Salvatore and Sebastiano's counsel I heard my father's words and listened to the wisdom of an ancient people. They had known of the powerful effects of the sight upon an adolescent struggling to control the voices and the visions that threaten to overtake a young body and mind. Sympathy and understanding seemed to rule their guidance, while fear and vengeance seemed to dictate Nikos' arguments. It became clear to me the boy could not be left to reside with the family. It was also clear to me I had not the time nor the inclination to keep him with me at Stigliano, for my business would always dominate my attention and would keep me away for too long. I could not afford to have the boy's mischief endanger all I was attempting to create.

I also considered that if the boy had been truly possessed by the devil, he may have been manipulated by Satan to destroy all that the Holy Spirit had commanded me to build. Was my vision of the boy, dancing with delight at the destruction of the world, a portent of things to happen at Stigliano and not Curtun? I concluded it was better to send the boy to the Hidden Realm to be trained to control and accept his gift, as I had done, and not leave the threat anywhere near the Ark. But I needed my cousins to accept the responsibility of taking the child to Curtun and presenting him to Tarquin. Both men were fearful of the uncertainty of my visions and the fate of the boy, and yet, in the end, they saw the wisdom of removing him from the ark and preventing any knowledge of the importance of the new Rosellae to be disclosed to hostile ears.

Tarquin would have the final decision about the boy's fate. If he saw merit in him, he would be accepted into the community to be trained as a Taurisi. Should Tarquin see no possibility of redemption, the boy's life and his curse would be ended. With the decision made, and not so much as a kind word or farewell to the boy, I watched my cousins and my eldest son ride down the road and disappear.

XXII

Deliver Us from Evil

We worked throughout the winter months. The weather was milder than usual, which allowed for the transport of goods and equipment from Curtun and from other parts of the countryside. The number of relocated Taurisi had been kept to the agreed upon one hundred, though the number of craftsmen and laborers had increased substantially. Many of those not counted amongst the Chosen Ones were hesitant to return to the Hidden Realm, some having grown accustomed to the outside world, and some fearing what would befall them should they return to their secret kingdom. They knew their fate was in the hands of the Zil-at, and his need for them was to return to Curtun. Though they knew they had been on temporary loan to the Rusellae project, they had developed an affinity to the subterranean palace that they had helped to bring back to life.

In those cavernous chambers, they had felt a sense of hope and permanency, and the prospect of returning home was only clouded with sorrow and doom. Tarquin believed the instructions to repopulate the Ark at Rusellae with the One Hundred had been sent to Tarquinia directly from the Holy Spirit. In God's mercy He would protect the culture and the memories of the Taur within the seeds of the Chosen Ones. Oh, if only I could take the entire populous of the Hidden Realm under the protection of my ancient walls, I would surely have found a way to feed and clothe the multitude. Yet my fate, and the fate of the Taurisi of Curtun, was in God's hands. Each of us had known the parts we were to play in His celestial plan, and had accepted His will, trusting in His mercy, and praying that our fates were not cast in stone, but could be altered with hard work and spiritual fortitude. Sad was the day when I bid farewell to those laborers whom I had grown to know and respect. I could only hope I would see them again, to hear their cheerful songs and to listen to their ribald stories.

Alas, I have only the echoes of their voices to keep me company in the long dark hours of the night. The Chosen Ones had now become my charges and my family. Their care and protection had been entrusted to me, and it was my sacred duty to nurture this transplanted vine and to see its roots dug deeply into the ancient soil of Rusellae, and its branches spread widely and weighed heavily with young fruit. It was my charge to see that the ancient ways of the Taurisi were not forgotten, and that the names and the deeds of their heroes were kept alive in the world of today and tomorrow.

I was determined to make Stigliano into a self-sustainable and prosperous manufacturing center, utilizing the knowledge and skills of the Taurisi, employing only the most qualified workers, using only the best raw materials, and producing only the very best products. The quality of my products would become renowned, and the wealthy would vie to purchase my goods. I would build upon the core of my commercial center, erecting more buildings, constructing more mills, both wind- and water-powered, and employ more laborers. The commercial power of the ancient Etrusci would return to Tuscany, and the Sons of Noah would thrive. The possibilities seemed endless to me at the time.

By spring the sheep needed fleecing, the mills were fully operational, and the spinners and weavers had already been tutoring a large group of young children, some orphaned and living on the streets of the larger townships surrounding Siena. Most, very appreciative for the opportunity of a good meal and dry bed, would be trained in the ancient ways, spinning the raw wool into tight threads that would be used to produce our cloth. So adept were these children, and so easily and skillfully did their tiny hands make quick work of the mounds of raw wool, that they soon became the pride of their mentors. With such excellent threads, the skilled weavers began to produce such fabric as to put the master weavers of Bruge to shame.

We began to employ Gontarz's fulling mill, and with minor adjustments and very little waste, the cloth was washed and fulled with magical speed. Within a month of the shearing, my workers had produced enough cloth to fill several carts, which were immediately dispatched to the master dyers in Florence. Only the very best dyes would be used for the richest cloth in Christendom. Within a few weeks' time the entire shipment had been returned to me—one thousand bolts of the most luxurious crimson fabric ever created by the hand of man. Only the wealthiest and most powerful men could afford my lana di Stigliano. Shipments of lesser-grade cloth, made from the wool imported from England, mixed with a quantity of our locally produced wool, would keep the Florentine artisans busy throughout the year. That product would fetch a lesser but still very decent price on the open market.

Meanwhile, the furnace of Voltuma had been brought to life and the smelting furnaces had been built. The forests to the south and east of Siena are rich in natural resources, particularly in chestnut and ash, which are converted to the charcoal needed to produce high-grade steel. The ferrous hills to the east, which had been mined by the Etrusci in ancient times, were once again brought to life, producing large quantities of iron-rich ore to feed the furnaces. The Taurisi smiths were eager to utilize their talents and equally eager to share their knowledge with the younger apprentices. My metal-producing workforce had increased tenfold as the furnaces began to produce pig iron and steel, and it was no time before we began to produce armaments on a large scale.

I would continue to supply princes and popes with product produced in foreign lands, for it was cost effective to supply my customers in Ireland and England with weapons produced and shipped from Spain, or lords of France with steel from the mines of Suderland in Germania. The god of war had provided me with a steady stream of customers, and the profits from my arms business became the lion's share of my annual income. The turbulent political situation in the East had forced me to suspend most of the business that Giancarlo had worked so hard to build, but Fortuna is fickle, and the winds of opportunity have changed many times during my long lifetime. Profits from the East eventually came back, but for this extended period, I concentrated on building my own commercial center closer to home, increasing my fortune through banking and arms supply.

I continued to supply arms to Henry of England as well as to each of his sons who were in open revolt against their father while that monarch lived. Phillip, like his father Louis, had become one of my most profitable clients. He had an insatiable appetite for holy relics and weapons of war. With the continued exposure to the Holy Land through pilgrimage or crusade, every court and church in Europe had sought to acquire a relic that could bring tremendous income to the one who possessed such a treasure.

I had financed two separate armories on the continent just to handle the needs of England and France and had always been careful to keep my involvement in both a closely guarded secret. Through transfers of credit between several banking houses in the Low Country, I was able to operate covertly using Nikos as the principal partner in the entire enterprise. This required much trust on my part in Nikos' complete loyalty to me, and it also required us to travel together to negotiate trade deals with the two monarchs and their courts. We had operated successfully for a couple of years, but as rebellion continued to escalate between Henry and his sons, and the ties of both kings' offspring became stronger, it became more difficult for me to mask my loyalties.

My cloak of duplicity was ripped from my shoulders in the spring of 1181 when Louis of France died. At age fifteen, Phillip was crowned King of France. Nikos, and I had made a trip to Paris in order to negotiate a new contract with the young king's court. I had also planned to journey further north to meet with Henry, who was leading a campaign against his rebellious eldest son and the boy's supporters in Normandy. I hoped to renegotiate a new contract with Henry as Lord of Ireland to reopen our old trade agreement. My fine cloth production in the mills at Stigliano had escalated beyond my limited supply of raw material, and I had needed to reopen channels with my Irish suppliers. It was an extremely tenuous time for my business and for me, personally, as I steered my ship between rock and reef in a tempestuous sea. As a businessman, I could never appear to be political and hope to survive in a world in which most of my customers were at war with each other.

I had planned to travel the land route to Paris, after which I would sail up the Seine to meet up with Henry as he was camped outside of Rouen. Nikos had convinced me to take young Paolo along on the journey, as he was well into his eighth year and was remarkably astute and eager to learn. Nikos had a special affinity for the boy and was determined to do whatever it took to strengthen the bond between me and my son. I had felt guilty that my neglect had almost cost the boy his life and hoped the trip would possibly bring some closeness and understanding between father and son. Paolo was eager to accompany us and had proven to be a sturdy workhand and a capable companion. He reminded me of myself, in my innocent youth, on my father's fattoria. I marveled at his capacity to learn and found great pleasure in teaching him everything I had learned.

Upon our arrival at the court of Phillip, I was most surprised to find young Richard, then the Duke of Aquitaine and Normandy, and son of the King of England, residing with the King of France. Richard had accepted the hospitality of Louis and had been living in Paris when the king had died. He had developed a great fondness for Phillip, and rumor was the two were inseparable, even dining from the same plate and sleeping in the same bed. I bring this up not to perpetuate a sordid, unsubstantiated rumor, but to highlight the delicate predicament in which I had found myself.

I had met Richard at the court of Eleanor in Aquitaine, and he had known, through his mother, of my dealings with Henry of England. I had to make it clear to Phillip that though I had provided a most beneficial service to all of the crowned heads of Europe, and though I had had a most beloved relationship and true respect for the late King Louis and his dear wives as they lived and breathed, it had always been well known that my affection, admiration, and respect was equally matched with my service to young Richard's loving father and mother, the Fair Eleanor. In truth, I had pledged no fealty to any master, save our Most Holy Father, to whom, as His most-favored banker to the Curia, I owed my love and my allegiance.

I extended to Phillip, my deepest condolences on the passing of his beloved father, Louis, and offered my congratulations and services to the new king. I felt no shame in reminding him that it was I who supplied that special gift that was presented to him by his uncle, the Archbishop of Sens. The closeness of the two young royals had then proven a benefit to me, as Richard related to Phillip the many marvelous treasures that I, and Giancarlo, had obtained for his mother and Henry. Phillip, too, had recalled some of the most revered holy relics that we had brought to the West from the Holy Land and had presented to his father over the years. In my short audience with the monarchs, I had recounted the horrors that had transpired in the Eastern Empire, the demise of the great Giancarlo Manenti, and the unfortunate decline in available goods from the East, but I had assured them that certain items could still be acquired, though at greater risk and cost if the buyer was determined.

I did not leave Paris without securing several new contracts with Phillip, as well as with Richard, who was in open rebellion against his father and king over Normandy. I was commissioned to provide three shipments of arms to be delivered to his loyal troops in the Limousin and Perigord from my armories in Nuremberg so as not to raise suspicion and the ire of Richard's father. All shipments sent to Henry's troops would come from my Catalonian operation.

I met with an aging and ailing King Henry at Rouen. Our meeting was cordial, and we spoke of earlier times and a less stressful life. I was most sympathetic of his troubles, for I knew of his suffering by the betrayal of his family. I spoke warmly of those early times and the love that had been evident at the court of the Magnificent Henry and the Beautiful Eleanor. Though his heart and his spirit were broken, his eyes rekindled their light as I spoke of the promise of his beautiful children. I shared with him the losses that I had suffered over the recent years, and he was grieved to hear the vivid account of Giancarlo's death, for their friendship was greater than I had imagined. I found myself pitying the King of England. For all he had accomplished, he had become an empty shell, a man driven to fight the rest of his life in order to make his family whole again. My audience with Henry at Rouen was filled with sadness and regret, yet I was still able to secure from him the agreements that I needed to ensure continued supply of Leinster wool from Ireland through my agents, the deValles in Carlow. In addition, I negotiated contracts to deliver to him arms that were needed in his battles with his sons and his enemies.

After another successful cycle I returned to Italy by way of Champagne, intending to stop at Sens to transact some business with the Archbishop, and decided to work the closing days of the St. Ayoul fair, where I would teach young Paolo the art of money changing. At the fair, we encountered Pietro, who was finishing his own successful mission. I was pleased to see my friend again, even though my guilt still weighed heavy upon me. Nikos sensed my discomfort, for he knew me well and could read the slightest subtlety in my manner of speech or behavior. Thankfully, Pietro was oblivious to such subtleties. He was thrilled to see his old friends, as well as my son, and told us that he was anxious to return to his most beloved Dona Pica, who was heavy with child when he had left Assisi. He was most honored to accompany us back on our speedy journey home.

We made our way overland, through the Alps and down into Italy. Along the route I hired a small security force to accompany us through the more hostile stretches along the Via Francigena. We were within the borders of Tuscany in less than three weeks, and Pietro insisted we accompany him back to Assisi to bear witness to the birth of his first child. He implored me to be the child's godfather, and I knew that such a request meant everything to Pietro, not only because of our history and friendship, but because of the status he and his child would gain with the support of one of the wealthiest men in Italy. Reluctantly I accepted his request.

Foolishly I had released the security guards after unloading in Siena, and we traveled without guard to Assisi. Pietro was anxious to return home before the child was born, and as anxiety most often breeds stupidity, Pietro foolishly decided to leave the main road near Perugia and cut through the forest that surrounds Assisi and Monte Subasio. I was very skeptical, having sent away my security force, and knowing full well of the growing reports of roving bands of brigands who were roaming the hills and forests along those major traveling routes. My keen senses had been clouded with recurring guilt and apprehension at seeing Dona Pica again, and my logic had been impaired. I did not even think of the safety of my son and Nikos, for all I wanted to do was to witness the child and leave the walls of Assisi as soon as possible.

My attention had been drawn inward and thus I did not see the first boulder tossed from the thick branches overhead. Just as it had happened on the River Soane with my dear Genevieve, the attack was swift and unexpected. Pietro's luck was with him for the boulder missed his head and landed square upon the back of his pony, causing both horse and rider to plunge into an overgrown ravine. Several brigands immerged from behind the trees to spring upon their prey. Nikos was quick to jump from his horse, daggers artfully clasped in each hand. I had just enough time to draw my short sword and dagger and leap from my steed. I commanded Paolo to ride swiftly through the wood and not to stop until he reached the safety of Assisi. Nikos moved swiftly and was able to bury his steel deeply into the guts of two approaching villains. Several more immerged from the woods.

I have had enough skirmishes in my life to know how to effectively wield a sword, and two more thugs were quickly dispatched. Pietro was nowhere to be found, and my sense was he had been fatally struck by that boulder. Nikos and I stood back to back as several more brigands began to circle us, jabbing their knives and feigning attack. With sudden swiftness and surprise, Paolo reared his horse and drove directly into the circling group, crushing two of them under the hooves of his charging steed. Nikos lunged to the left and slit the throat of one of the attackers.

I had been engaged in a struggle with two of the thieves, one of whom seemed to be the leader. He managed to wrap my cloak around my sword arm and had me pinned while his cohort charged and attempted to run me through. Nikos was able to deter him with an accurate knife throw to the back of the neck, but not before the bastard buried his blade deep into my leg. Nikos was distracted by one last tormentor and could not come to my aid. My captor, smiling at my unfortunate predicament, raised his dagger over his head, making ready to sink it deep into my heart, when his grimacing face turned to a dead stare, and he toppled over on top of me. Like a wild lion cub, Paolo had jumped upon my tormentor's back and sunk his small dagger deep into the monster's back, piercing the devil's evil heart. Nikos finished off the last of the thieves and rushed to my aid. Little else did I see until I awoke in a bed, one that was very familiar to me, in Pietro's house.

I was weak, in tremendous pain. My mouth and throat were parched, and I was burning up. I could hear whispered arguments and weeping, and I could hear a baby crying uncontrollably. A priest was praying over me while Paolo and Nikos each held my hand. Cold compresses had been laid across my head and my leg throbbed with an unspeakable pain, causing me to cry out in agony. I lay naked upon the bed, my body covered in sweat that cooled my skin but sent me into convulsions. A bitter concoction was forced down my throat, and I eventually sank back into oblivion.

Long did I sleep. Hours or days, I knew not. Shame and remorse weighed heavily upon me, and my dreams were filled with horrible demons who took great delight in pushing me through a quagmire of scaly, blackened, groping claws of the wretched souls roasting in the fires of Hell. My only comfort was in the image of my dear Galgano, who beckoned me on toward a Heavenly light. I woke with renewed strength and a firm commitment to set my foot upon a new path, to adjust my moral compass away from avarice and reset it toward righteousness. Nikos and Dona Pica were applying fresh dressings to my wounds while Paolo sat cradling an infant in his lap. The child and the young boy seemed intertwined as a peace and calmness enveloped the two. Pietro was gone. Not a word was spoken for the remainder of the day. The following morning, I was able to raise myself from the bed, don my clothes, and ask questions.

I had learned that Pietro had not been injured in the attack, though his horse was mortally wounded. The thieves had all been eliminated, and Nikos had carried my lifeless body upon his steed to the safety of Assisi. Paolo had saved my life, showing great courage and skill with a dagger, and had remained behind to help Pietro transfer his belongings to my horse. Together they rode with great speed to Assisi. I had already been brought into the house and had been placed upon the bed, while Dona Pica sent a neighbor to fetch a healer who lived a short distance down the road.

When Pietro arrived at the house, he ran directly to the bed chamber to see if I was alive. He had not even noticed that she was no longer carrying a child, nor the healthy baby boy laying in a basket near the hearth. Only then did he realize that he had fathered a son. Immediately he went to the basket and lifted the infant high in the air and danced with delight. The baby began to scream, and Pietro quickly handed the howling infant to its mother. He turned his attention to the healer and watched as the priest prayed over my body. I was told that shortly after the healer had done all that she could do, she was sent away, and then a bitter argument developed between Pietro and Dona Pica.

Pietro was told that his son had come into this world earlier than expected—several weeks before Pietro's return. Fearing for the safety of the tiny infant's mortal soul, Dona Pica immediately had the baby brought to the church by the priest and baptized on the Feast of San Giovanni. The child was given the name of Giovanni di Pietro, to honor the cousin of the Christ Child, and to honor the child's father. Pietro then stormed out of the house and did not return until after I regained my strength and was able to leave. As I regained consciousness, I was met with the icy stare of Dona Pica. Her voice was hard and cold, and she cared not whether others could overhear.

"I curse the day I met you, Giovanni Pecci," she said. "You misled me. You used me. You threw me away once you were done with me, like everything else in your pathetic life. And when I finally found happiness and security after being forced to mend my own broken heart, you forced your way back into my life. With your silver tongue you wooed me, and you caused me to lower my defenses just enough for you to play upon my weaknesses. How evil you are. How foolish was I. I must live with the guilt and the shame for what I have done for the rest of my life. I will have to live with the agony of my betrayal of my husband. I will pay for my sin of weakness. And you will continue to live your life as you see fit, for you have no conscience, you have no soul, and you fear not the fires of Hell that await you. Know this. I hate you and I curse you for what you have done to me. And still, knowing that you will always profit while you live upon this earth, I charge you to care for and protect our son, Giovanni, for his life is doomed through no fault of his own. He will always be known as the bastard child, and he will need guidance and protection from all who would do him harm. Give me your word and swear an oath to whatever you hold dear to you, that you will protect our son." As weak as I was, I swore upon young Paolo's life that I would watch over and protect our son.

As soon as I was able to mount my steed, we returned to Stigliano. I was grateful for the care and attention that was so vital to my recovery, but I longed to be away from Assisi, from Pietro, from Dona Pica, and the child, and the reminder of my sinful transgressions. Paolo had grown exceedingly attached to the child in such a short period of time, and I could not help but notice, as he held and kissed the baby for one last time before our departure, the similarity between the two. I could not help but notice also that Pietro had been looking the same way.

From that day forward Pietro refused to recognize the child's true name, referring to him always as Francesco. He would later insist that he chose to honor the people who gave him his wife and true love, but I will always know in my heart that he had a greater, darker reason for not recognizing the boy's true name.

XXIII

Betrayal

Barbarossa's love and gratitude for the free citizens of Siena was short-lived, and in four short years melted away like the March snow. Short-lived, too, was Siena's innocence, for greed had fueled the deterioration of the political and economic situation throughout Tuscany. Some will argue that it was Siena, in her pride and aggression, who caused the enmity of her neighbors by reaching too far and eating more than her share of the pie. Such gluttony only causes to stir up hostilities and acts of wars amongst brother Tuscans and trading partners. In defense of the City of the Virgin, I must say that such envy and hatred and constant plotting of her rivals had been brewing for decades. Jealousy had been fed by Fortune from the moment the Emperor had bestowed most favored status upon his loyal subjects.

With poisoned deceitfulness, many of Siena's neighbors, those most loyal to the Pope, had schemed and plotted to rob her of that which had been given to her by a grateful imperial sovereign. Little by little the Florentines, the Genoese and the Pisans, the Montepuciani, and those from as far away as Arezzo and Perugia to the east, and Grosseto and the Maremma to the west and south, all tried to wrest from her those territories that were rightly hers to control. But Siena had grown strong as she basked in the good graces of His Imperial Majesty and was more than capable to meet the challenges of her envious neighbors. Raids and minor skirmishes had escalated into wars, and territories were lost and won, only to be lost and won again. Such hostilities, as is always the case, spread death and disease, and much misery and pain. Chaos reigned supreme. Man's attention was turned from industriousness and welfare to destruction and warfare. Fields were destroyed or left untended, supplies were stolen or depleted and unable to be replenished, as long-established trade roads became battlefields.

Counted among her many enemies were Siena's greatest adversaries, the fat lords and greedy noblemen, whose undying mission has always been to see the usurping communes crushed into the very earth that had been taken from their undeserving hands. Cunning are they, for though they never reveal their villainous faces from behind their smiling masks, and they feign loyalty and friendship upon the stage while spinning their webs of deceit and revenge behind the curtain. Always they have strived to regain their glorious past, even though most would agree that their past has been far from glorious. Was it not God's will to reshape Man's world and raise the common class to replace the nobles? … and the meek shall inherit the earth.

So content were they to sit back and watch while city bore arms against city, and freemen perpetrated such evil upon each other as to cause the angels in Heaven to weep. Happy were they in our misery and discontent, and lethal were they in their nefarious deceit, as they sat and they watched, and waited for their chance to strike back. With letters writ in poisonous lies and false testimony against his most loyal subjects, they sent emissaries to the imperial court beyond the Alps, to fill the ear of the ill-tempered Barbarossa, and to stoke the furnace of his flammable rage. While Siena fought to protect herself and her sovereignty within the Tuscan borders, the insidious lords had awakened the rage of the eagle and had caused it to leave its aerie in the northern mountains.

So that I am not allowed to paint an inaccurate picture, I must confess to you that during those years of misery, some had managed to thrive under Fortuna's protective cloak. War, though devastating for most, brings opportunity to the shrewd and the industrious merchant who sees benefits amid the chaos and seizes Opportunity by the balls. Stigliano continued to flourish, and the furnaces of Voltuma never slept. Never was there a lack of demand for the weapons that my skilled armorers could so efficiently produce in the underground caverns of my mighty fortress. Many of the farmers from the surrounding countryside had abandoned their fields and sought protection and employment from the Master of Rusellae. Many worked willingly, and for a meager wage, in the ferrous hills extracting ore, or in the great chestnut forest cutting wood and rendering it into charcoal to feed the voracious appetites of Gontarz's smelting furnaces. Our colony had become self-sufficient and had been transformed into the leading industrial center in Tuscany. The ark, cloaked in secrecy, had successfully navigated a whirling sea of disorder and mayhem.

Over the course of several years, Sebastiano and Salvatore would visit Stigliano and bring news from Curtun. As a gift from the Zil-at, they brought with them trained pigeons, whose natural instinct was to navigate their way back to the royal roosts in the palace in Curtun. So highly trained were they that they could successfully navigate no matter the weather or the distance. Such rare birds, I was told, had been used in ancient times by the Etrusci to communicate between each of the seven high seats of power. Tiny notes were secured to the claw, and the bird would be released to carry a message over great distance with little danger. I marveled at the ingenuity of those ancient people and accepted the gift with gratitude. So important did I see the application of these tiny messengers, that in short order, I had bred a small flock, feeding them from infancy with my own hands, and becoming very attached to each of them. Over time, I sent breeding pairs to many of my agents throughout Europe, which improved contact with my operations and allies in the major banking center. Such faithful creatures have been my extended eyes and ears throughout the remainder of my life.

Tarquin had been spending his days enhancing the fortifications of the Hidden Realm, while distributing its vast trove of riches to various secret strongholds deep in the distant mountain halls. I was told early of the Zil-ats' decision to accept my son into the clan and to have him trained in the ways of the Taurisi. Tarquin, himself, had taken the boy under his protection and had patiently helped the boy to learn to master his supernatural gift. He was taken into the tribe and given the name Vani-ri-Sandak, which in the language of the Taurisi means Gift of Sandak. It shames me to this day how I had failed in my duties as a father and had allowed myself to be convinced that the boy's salvation could be found in the loving embrace of an innocent people. Happy was I to learn of Vannozzo's rehabilitation and the progress that he had made in controlling his demons.

As time passed, I received warnings from the northern cities that Barbarossa had mobilized his mighty army and was bringing it through the passes of the Alps into the plains of Italy. The Emperor had broken the promise he had given to Alexander and had brought a mighty army back into Italy. He had insisted that he had come in peace, with his son, Henry, and a mere body guard of fifteen thousand men, and that his only desire was to meet with Lucius in Verona, and to offer his royal assistance to the beleaguered pope, who continued to have problems on the Italian peninsula. Of course, Barbarossa's real purpose for returning to Italy was to force the weak pope to crown young Henry as co-emperor to secure his own dynasty amongst the ravenous German princes. The indecisive Lucius stalled sufficiently to drain the Emperor's patience and finally refused his help altogether. In a curt note Lucius declared that two men could not be emperor at the same time.

The unintended consequences of the Pope's callous pronouncement proved most unfortunate for the cities to the south. Standing confidently with the backing of the combined armies of the Lombard League, the Pope thought to pluck the tail feathers from the eagle, as his predecessor had done in Venice. His actions had only served to insult and infuriate the hot-tempered Emperor. In a fit of rage, Barbarosso then turned southward with his army to enforce his rule over the disobedient city-states in Tuscany. His heart being filled with poison and malice, he turned his hatred and his fury toward loyal Siena.

Fortunately for Siena, my carrier pigeons had brought messages from my agents in Verona to warn us of Barbarossa's advances southward toward Siena. Quickly I rode to Siena to warn the Council that a malicious doom was upon them in the form of a revengeful and misinformed emperor and his imperial troops. I gathered up my family and most of my precious possessions, including my store of hard coin and my business ledger books, and led a small wagon trail, under heavily armed guard, back to the safety of Stigliano. I had hoped that the distance between Stigliano and Siena would be great enough to escape the reach of the Emperor's mighty hammer. We had had several days in which to hide my valuables deep within the cavernous bowels of my stronghold, and to minimalize any outward appearance of prosperity in and around the compound. Food and water were stored in the deepest vaults in the event the stronghold came under siege by a smaller force. In no way did I believe the walls of my castle would withstand an assault of Barbarossa's entire army, but I prayed for the mercy of the Virgin and the wisdom of the Holy Spirit to protect and guide us through the worst of times, until a deal could be brokered.

I stood upon the ramparts of my tower and peered into the blackness of the night sky, facing northward toward Siena. I can remember the cold of the night air, the black sky painted with a million stars, and the feeling of dread as thick as a fog. The wind was whispering through the trees, warning of the doom to come. So clear it is to me now. The screech of the owl on her midnight hunt, and the squealing of her prey as talon and beak ripped into flesh. The insects and the toads competed with their mating calls, and the wolf and the wild dog gave warning to man that night belonged to the beast. My senses became heightened and the sounds became deafening, when in an instant I was plunged into blackness and silence. I could not feel my body, nor the brush of wind against my face, but have memory only of a solitary point of light that came toward me from the east. It grew in intensity and washed over me like a wave in the mighty ocean. Suddenly, I was comforted by the peace of the Holy Spirit, and shortly after that, an anguishing terror had consumed me.

In my mind's eye I had seen fair Siena, her gates securely locked against an invading army, her impenetrable walls surrounded by Barbarossa's imperial forces, and like the coils of a mighty serpent, it was crushing the life from its prey. Behind those sturdy walls, I could hear her people, thousands of people I have known, laying bloated with disease and emaciated with hunger and thirst. A multitude of corpses had been strewn amongst fields of rosemary or hung like cured meat upon a hundred gibbets. My head was filled with the wailing of women and children pleading for mercy from the Queen of Heaven, and the shouts of angry men atop the city walls, hurling curses and insults, like weapons, to their nemesis below.

Loyal Siena would not raise lethal weapon to her overlord but would only pray for God's intervention in all the madness. Barbarossa sat smiling upon his mighty steed before the gates with his son Henry, sitting upon his right with head bent in shame, and to the left sat the black shadow of Satan, grimacing in delight as he held my son Vannozzo upon his lap. The boy was holding the eagle standard of the ancient Roman legion that had been lost to the great Hannibal's rapacious horde. He was armored in brilliant gold, and his tunic was the color of blood. The Fires of Hell burst forth from his eyes, and his gaping laugh revealed the forked tongue of the serpent.

The hills to the east had been lit ablaze, and the night sky was filled with the screaming shades of those being roasted alive in their mountain fortresses. So intense and horrid was my vision that I lost consciousness, and it was not until morning that Nikos found me. Instantly, I set to warn Tarquin of my visions. I prayed that my pigeons would fly swiftly and directly to the Zil-at's palace, for the Doom of the Taurisi was at hand and Tarquin would need time to prepare his people for their final stand.

Within hours after sending my message out, Sebastiano arrived at Stigliano. He had traveled directly from Curtun to deliver terrible news and to warn me that my life, and all of Rusellae, was in danger. The horrendous tale he told to me caused my blood to freeze and tore my heart asunder. He told me that my son had gained the love and respect of the Zil-at and the Taurisi people. He had worked hard to learn control of his special gift, and even harder to become a valued asset to the Taurisi. Proud were they of their dear little cousin, and all were convinced of the merit of the Zil-at's wise decision to allow the boy to live amongst his people.

Such goodness was immediately undone when one night, the boy was possessed with fits and fever. His tortured soul had become a portal of Hell. His body had been contorted and twisted, and his skin had become blackened and lacerated with boils and pustules spewing sickening green fluid. His eyes had bulged until they chanced flying from their sockets, and his pupils turned to view his possessed soul, leaving bloodied white orbs to stare blindly toward the heavens. Black and viperous was his tongue as he licked his parched and cracked lips. Giant flies had gathered around his putrefying body, working their way into his nostrils and feasting upon the poison that had oozed from his rotting tongue. Death would have been a blessing for the boy, yet the Holy Spirit had also entered the boy's body to do battle with the forces of Satan.

Long did the battle ensue. Three full days and nights and the boy's agony persisted. Healers and holy men were brought in to try to ease his suffering. The Zil-at had ordered scribes to sit by the boy's bed to record the seer's ravings and the dialogue between the forces of good and evil. Most of his ravings were unintelligible, but some were spoken sweetly and with such clarity as could only be thought to be Divine warnings from the Holy Spirit. Several of those prophesies were so alarming as to cause great angst amongst all who surrounded the boy.

Herewith, I inscribe Vannozzo's warnings, as told to me by Sebastiano.

Happily, do I fly upon the wings of the eagle; to lead his great and fearful army against his loyal children.

Hungerly, do I feast upon the flesh of the father, who cast aside his own flesh, in favor of Moneta's golden purse.

The boy shall divert the Great Eagle from its intended prey and bring it to roost upon the Sacred Mountains to claim its prize.

Useless are the actions of the innocent in raising a hand against the Eagle, for the innocent shall be consumed in fire and the Ark will sail upon a sea of obscurity and sink into oblivion before father can begat son.

The Chosen shall be found. Their light will be extinguished in a raging blaze, and their hope will sputter and dim as the candle burns itself out.

The echo of the Chosen Ones will resound in the halls beneath the Earth for one thousand years, until it bursts forth and fills the land with beauty again.

With those final words, Vannozzo, my son, who was called Vani-ri-Sandak, had surrendered to the forces of good and evil. His body lay motionless, and his eyes returned to an empty stare. The scribes had been sent to the Council chamber, and the healer and holy man were left behind to clean and sanctify the body. The Zil-at and the Council acted swiftly and began to enact evacuation plans for the aged and the very young, to hidden strongholds deep within the heart of the mountains. All others, men and women, all capable of defending the hidden kingdom, were mobilized and made ready for war. Scouts were sent out to the north, to the south, to the hills in the east and the plains in the west, searching for signs of movement of any large force. With hopes for salvation, Salvatore was dispatched north to Verona, where His Holiness, Pope Lucius, having already infuriated the Emperor, had decided to turn his attention to Church matters. He had chosen not to confront Barbarossa but had left the Emperor to do whatever he pleased within Italy. Salvatore had been armed with the golden medallion given to him by His Holiness Alexander, along with the Pope's sworn oath to send troops to support Curtun in its hour of need. The Zil-at had trusted in the word of the leader of God's Holy Church, but Alexander was dead—and so was his promise.

The plight of the Taurisi was never heard, nor the request for aid, nor Alexander's promise of assistance, for Lucius would not even grant audience to Salvatore. With a wave of his hand, the Pope had guaranteed the doom of the Taurisi people. Salvatore had return to Curtun with the devastating word that help would not be coming from the north, but only broken promises and insincere prayers from the Roman pope. Such betrayal was a crushing blow to Tarquin, one from which he would never recover. It was but one of many betrayals that spelled doom for the Taurisi of the Hidden Realm.

A day after my son's spirit had left this earth, a grizzly scene at the deathbed of Vani-ri-Sandak was discovered, as attendants found the badly mutilated and dishonored bodies of the healer and the priest cast about the room. Their disgust had been overshadowed by their fright at seeing an empty bed where once lay the writhing body of the young seer. The Zil-at and the Captain of the Guard were immediately notified, and a full search for the body was conducted. What manner of heinous deviltry was afoot? None could accept that the boy, in a state of demonic possession, had been returned from the dead and had wreaked such havoc, simply disappearing into thin air. Every corner of the realm was searched, yet no body was discovered. Sebastiano was quickly dispatched to Rusellae, hoping to either find the boy or to warn us of the pending doom that had been prophesied.

I was sickened by his reports, and I mourned for my lost son, yet my own visions were still fresh in my mind. I confessed to him my innocent complicity with the evils that were about to befall our people. My rantings were too much for his gentle soul, and he stared icily at me for several moments, searching for words to say that would somehow bring comfort to either of us. No words were to be found. He simply warned that if the boy had survived and had somehow managed to escape the sentries at the perimeter of his kingdom, he would be intent upon returning to Stigliano with evil designs and a blackened heart.

The boy had been imbued with Satan's supernatural powers and had been given his mission by his demonic masters, to destroy all traces of the Children of Noah. He wailed at his blindness to the evil that was festering within the boy and cursed the day he had taken him back to Curtun against the protests of Nikos. Only Nikos had been wise enough to see that death should have been the only salvation for Vannozzo. His words stung like a thousand wasps, so bitter was their truth. I remember to this day the look in his eyes as we bid our final goodbye. Cursed is my soul for my betrayal of an innocent people—all those whom I loved.

We made ready for the onslaught of the imperial troops, standing ready with weapons recently fabricated for the King of Naples, and gathering supplies and livestock into the cavernous subterranean vaults under Stigliano. What we did not know was Vannozzo had, indeed, been resurrected by the powers of evil for their unholy cause, had had managed to steal several items of great worth and had made his escape through the southern borders of the hidden realm. In addition to the two attendants whom he had left torn to pieces around his deathbed, he had managed to savagely eliminate several guards and sentries posted along the border. He wandered through the hills and valleys, forests and jagged cliffs, that helped to shroud Curtun in secrecy, seeking his way back to Cortona.

Having seen the carnage that had been perpetrated upon the guards at the border, Sebastiano immediately set out to track the boy, intending to destroy him before he could do further harm. It was not long before he had picked up the boy's trail, and Sebastiano was convinced the trail was heading toward Stigliano. After several days had passed, he caught up with him in Sodo on the outskirts of Cortona. Unfortunately, the boy had wandered into the camp of an imperial scouting party, and with all the persuasive powers of Hell, had been able to convince the leader of the guards that he was in possession of knowledge that would help His Imperial Highness to reawaken the power and the glory of the ancient Roman Empire.

With him he had brought the keys to a hidden kingdom that had lain dormant for centuries awaiting the rightful Emperor to return and claim the full power of Augustus. The boy had revealed an ancient relic, wrapped in a faded cloth, a bejeweled dagger, and several gold coins of ancient origin. The power of Satan had protected the boy, for though most of the guards would have gladly slit his throat and taken the treasure for themselves, their captain had sensed the importance of the boy's tale and had decided to bring him to the imperial camp for an official deposition.

Quickly they rode west, and Sebastiano had kept pace with the group, keeping a reasonable distance so as not to arouse suspicion. Opportunity had finally presented itself and Sebastiano was able to sneak into the enemy camp and attempt to murder the boy while slumber had overtaken the group, but his plan was thwarted by the distant howling of a wolf that woke the guards. He was seized by the soldiers, being taken for a thief, and was about to have his throat slit when Vannozzo threw himself upon the captain and pleaded with him to refrain from taking Sebastiano's life. He had told the captain that he knew the would-be assassin to be a prince of the Hidden Realm, identifying him as Tarchon, son of Tarquin, Zil-at of the Taurisi. Seldom were those names spoken outside of the Hidden Realm, and never in the vicinity of the enemy.

With hatred in his eyes, Tarchon looked at the boy and saw his own cousin maliciously, and without a hint of remorse, condemn an entire people to annihilation. All he wanted to do was to free himself from the iron grip of his captors just long enough to rip the throat from the boy whom he had rescued from the claws of death. Steel and dagger could not pierce Tarchon's heart any deeper than the wicked betrayal of his cousin's son. His hands were tightly bound behind his back, and a noose was placed around his neck, the end of which was tied to the saddle of the captain's steed. His feet were bound but kept loose enough so he could walk behind the horses. Never could he lose his footings in the baked clay of Le Crete, for to slip and fall would cause his aching body to be dragged along the ground and the noose to tighten around his neck and to painfully snuff out his life. Only once did the company stop, and only to water the horses and allow the men to relieve themselves. By midmorning of the following day, they had reached the encampment at the eastern wall of Monteriggioni, just as the Emperor and his army were about to travel the final two leagues to the fortified walls of Siena.

The Emperor had planned to enter the city and punish the members of the Council and the heads of each of the leading families for their disloyalty and their aggression toward His loyal subjects outside of the contrada of Siena. In truth, the Emperor had been licking his wounds, which had been festering ever since his defeat at Legnano and his humiliation at the foot of His Holiness, Alexander in Venice. The refusal of Lucius to meet his demands only infuriated the Emperor more, and loyal Siena was to be the whipping post for his imperial rage. Barbarossa's plans had been suddenly foiled though, for the good citizens of Siena, knowing the vengeance of their sovereign lord and master, had refused to open their mighty gates and offer admittance into the city.

Such insulting and disloyal action only caused the Emperor to become more enraged, and he refused to meet with any of the emissaries who were brave enough to show their face upon the wall. Barbarossa had not anticipated such disloyalty and had not brought with him his mighty siege engines. Knowing Old Siena's weakness of not having a fresh water supply within its fortified walls, the Emperor mistakenly decided to lay siege to the city and surrounded the outer walls with his army. He had intended to force its people to open her mighty gates and to throw themselves at his imperial feet to beg for mercy and forgiveness. Had he kept himself informed of the prosperity of his Sienese subjects, he might have known that the city that was famous for its lack of fresh water had, with considerable cost and perseverance, managed to locate the elusive underground stream called Diana. Its pure water had recently been gushing forth from Fontebranda well within the city walls. All the planning, the engineering, the financing that I put into that water project paid great dividends during those dark days of the imperial siege. Yet, as strong and self-sufficient as they had initially appeared, with time, the strangled supply of food was the Emperor's greatest weapon. Supplies were depleted within a few short weeks. While Frederick impatiently waited, his anger never diminished.

Again, I was called upon by the Council to attempt to negotiate a peaceful remedy to the situation with young King Henry. Using my pigeons, I was able to keep communications open with my agents within the walls, and it was thus that I learned of the desperate plight of my fellow citizens. I had hoped the close relationship that I had enjoyed with Henry since his first trip to Siena had survived the years of campaigning with his father. Though always weary of the potential doom his father would bring into Italy, I could not help but like Henry. Though the gods had given him beauty, strength, and courage, Athena had bestowed upon him an abundance of wisdom to temper his taste for war that Mars had given him. He was a man secure in his own abilities and was less prone to fits of thoughtless rage and petty jealousies. Though he was loyal to his father, his intellect had allowed him to see through the thinly veiled attempts of the lords of the mountains to move the power and the vengeance of the Emperor against his loyal subjects. I had come to respect the young king, in spite of his father, and my friendship had not escaped the notice of the Council.

Ever ready to turn a service to a profit, I agreed to travel up to the imperial camp, and to seek a meeting with Henry, and plead on behalf of the citizens of Siena. I confess that profit was not my only motive, for I wished to find some sort of solution to this very incendiary situation, one that would satisfy Barbarossa and send him and his army back beyond the safety of the Alps. No further south did I want to see his ravenous army travel, for Stigliano was but a day's march, and her virtues, I knew, were not strong enough to withstand his rapacious appetite. Foolishly I thought that there remained a chance to alter the course of Fate by satisfying Barbarosa with enough gold and accolades, and to ease his wrath enough to send him back to his northern kingdom, fully compensated for his troubles.

As I approached the Imperial campground, I bore witness to a most disturbing sight. The advance guard and most of the Imperial forces had abandoned their positions around the city walls and had formed into columns to move north away from Siena. The Emperor had lost patience with his recalcitrant subjects and had turned his army and his attention toward some easier prey. Henry had been left behind, his forces greatly reduced, to wait out the siege, and to exact punishment upon the Sienese when they had capitulated. Though I was relieved to learn the Emperor had placed himself at the head of his retreating army, I had somehow known the vengeful Barbarossa was not heading north to leave his subjects in peace, but rather heading east to fulfill a prophesy.

Henry was unavailable to give any audience until the remaining army had been repositioned, in small blockade units, posted at each of the gates and entryways into the city. It was two days before I was summoned to the royal campaign tent. Henry was seated at a large table and surrounding him stood several of his military advisors. The table was covered with maps and architectural drawings of Siena and her mighty walls. It was evident Henry had been planning a major offensive in order to alleviate what had become a long and drawn-out stalemate. I knelt before my sovereign lord and kissed his royal hand with all due respect. Laughingly he rose me to my feet and enveloped me in a friendly embrace, saying to me in a most jovial manner, "Welcome, my most dear and loyal Corsair. I trust you are sleeping soundly within the secure walls of the many castles that you have seemed to accumulate."

My response to my lord was conciliatory though framed in an equally jovial tone. "Though my walls are strong, my lord, sleep continues to evade your humble servant, because of the many disturbances over the past several years that continue to ruin our quiet Tuscan nights. The howling of the wolves from the mountains to the south and west, and the screams of the hawks from the north and along the Arno, disturb the slumber of innocent men. The curses and poisonous lies that have been laid upon the sacred hills of Sena Vita have caused her most loyal citizens to wither upon the vine of prosperity in the eyes of His Most Beloved and Imperial Majesty. Our citizens, though strong and determined enough to rise to any challenge brought upon them from our brother Tuscans, even strong enough to stand against the venomous plotting of the envious lords of the mountains, are mortally wounded and paralyzed with fear at the displeasure and the wrath of His Imperial Majesty. Such cries and prayers for forgiveness have kept this loyal servant awake for so many nights now."

"Wise is the Council to enlist our dear friend to sue for peace with the son of the Great Frederick. Tell me, Giovanni, why have you come forth from your castle to the south, and why have you risked your life to treat with an angry tyrant who, like a serpent, is squeezing the life from your beloved city."

"I come to Siena," said I, "with the utmost love and respect for my emperor, uncaring of the risks to my own person, in the hopes I might plead a most just case for the Sienese people, who have caused no offense to their sovereign lord, but to close their doors to his unjustified wrath until such time as his anger has subsided enough to allow his loyal subjects to welcome him properly, with all due respect, into the heart of their fair city. Most regrettably I have come too late to throw myself at the mercy of the Great Frederick, for though I had looked long upon the hour in which I might have cast my eyes once again upon his most glorious face, I was most disappointed to merely capture a glimpse of his war horse's backside."

Henry's tone changed to one of measured caution. "Fortunate for you, I dare say, my friend, for his anger still burns hot, and his countenance has become less pleasing than his horse's arse. Your silken words would have, most assuredly, fallen on deaf ears if, in fact, you were even allowed to live beyond the first moment you approached the environs of our camp. My father has become very much distracted over the past few days, and for some strange reason, whether through a malady in constitution or some devilish persuasion upon his mind, he has turned his attention eastward. With him, he has taken his army and has left me to deal with your people. He has also taken with him a boy who was brought into camp by scouts from the east, and who, by some strange power, has gained the confidence of my father, enough to cause him to remove his mighty force away from the original source of his anger. This boy has conveyed to my father many secret things and has produced enough evidence to corroborate his fantastic tale of a hidden kingdom, ancient and wealthy beyond imagining, living in the hills to the east, very close to your own city of birth, Giovanni Pecci da Cortona. The boy, in fact, claims to be your son."

My heart began to pound, and I feared I would suffocate for lack of breath. For several long moments I held my tongue. Then speaking most deliberately I confessed to Henry, "My son, he of whom you speak, has always suffered from a malady of the mind in which he hears voices and sees visions. His malady has, I believe, been brought on by a demonic possession, against which I was hoping to buy a cure. I had arranged for my cousin to take the boy to the monastery on Mount Athos, where, I had hoped, the boy's fate would be determined by those most learned scholars. I had lost all contact from them for several years and had presumed them dead. Communications with the scholars at the monastery revealed that the boy had never arrived, and investigation along the route that they were to take had revealed no traces of their existence. Long have I grieved for the loss of my son and my cousin. And now you speak of this boy, who, for me, has returned from the dead, leading an army against some phantom empire. This is too much for the mind of a mortal man to comprehend. I beg of you, my dear lord, to tell me more of this strange visitation."

Henry spoke to me of the cunning self-assuredness of the boy, and his ability to manipulate the guards into taking him into the imperial encampment, his powers of persuasion that allowed him to gain the very ear of the Holy Roman Emperor, and the poisonous words with which this demon had filled that imperial ear. Such superhuman powers of persuasion could only have been given by Satan, himself, for such venomous words had in short order caused the Emperor's moral spirit to rot and his temperament to be clouded with such an evil fog as to erase any remnant of logic or reasoning. Barbarossa's wrath and his petty spitefulness had been turned to greed, and he had been blindfolded to his remarkable wisdom and his shrewdness that had always been his mainstay. Not long did it take him to organize his retainers to march eastward across the Val 'di Chiana toward the forested mountains to the north of Cortona.

The king's story was so incredulous to me—that the mighty Barbarossa could be persuaded by a delusionary boy to redirect his anger from the already suffering Sienese and focus his greed upon an innocent and legendary folk. How could such things happen upon the words of a mere boy? I did not need to speak the words in my heart for I had known the answer all along. I had seen the results of this deceitful betrayal in my visions. I had refused to accept those visions for what they were. I could not bring myself to see the true meaning of those horrible sights, until that very moment. In an instant, I had relived each of those terrible visions, and as a curtain had been lifted from my eyes, I had witnessed all the events that had taken place and were about to unfold.

"You question, as did I, how such madness could be brought, so convincingly, to His Imperial Highness, by a mere boy? Such audacity could possibly have been set aside as the ramblings of a lunatic, if not for the capture of an assassin who had been stalking the boy. It seems that the boy, in order to avoid his capture and ultimate death at the hands of his assailant, had allowed himself to be taken in by our scouting party, and with devilish tongue had ingratiated himself with the captain of the party. The assailant was eventually captured while trying to murder the boy, and should have been instantly put to death, but for the boy's pleading to save his life. Such a valuable hostage would be most appreciated by the Emperor, the guards were told. By saving the man's life, the boy had been able to corroborate his story and to hand over to my father a potential key to this hidden kingdom. With several days of interrogation, and with prodding from the boy himself, our men were able to verify the assailant was the son of the leader, someone known as the Zil-at. Perhaps you know of this Zil-at, or of his son, one whom the boy kept referring to as Tarchon?"

I fell to my knees and cursed Thee, Almighty God in Heaven, for allowing such horrors to unfold. Reason should have told me that Your Divineness, through the Holy Spirit, had given me ample warning of what was to come. It was I who chose to ignore those warnings, and worse, to intentionally keep hidden my son's part in this evil plot, from my own flesh and blood. It was I who was responsible for the destruction of an innocent race. I had had more than enough time and opportunities and counsel to eliminate Satan's pawn from this earth. It was I who allowed Satan to win the battle against the Holy Spirit, and it was I who would have to bear the burden of guilt for all eternity.

I threw myself at Henry's feet and begged him to help me stop the butchery that was about to take place. I told him of my visions and the horrendous outcome that I had seen for my people. He lifted me to my feet and, with a quiet and resolute voice, caused me to face the reality of the situation.

"What is about to happen cannot be stopped by mortal man, for this war has been waged from time immemorial and will persist for all eternity. We are but pawns in this epic saga. Your part has been predestined, as evidenced by your visions. How could you do anything different to change the outcome, lest you prove the prophetic words of the Holy Spirit to be false? We cannot begin to understand the workings of the Celestial Beings, even if we are given the gifts to hear their words or see their intentions. We must accept our roles as vessels of their Holy, or un-holy, intent, and do whatever is necessary to survive, and to protect our people in the known world. The fate of the hill people is in God's hands, not in yours or mine. Have you not considered, by using Satan's tools for himself, God has turned your son's betrayal and my father's wrath away from the starvation and eventual slaughter of the Sienese people? He has bought you and the Sienese time to negotiate a solution to this dreadful stalemate. Lives saved must come at the cost of lives lost. If what you say is true, the Taurisi have had ample time to prepare for their destiny. If God has chosen for them to survive, He will provide them with a way. For the moment, Siena has been saved from annihilation."

The logic of Henry's words was a source of strength for me. His example and his logic helped me to focus upon what I needed to do to save the Sienese people. His sage wisdom, for one so young, was immeasurable in resolving the siege. Within a few days of seeing the armies of the Emperor ride to the east, Henry had allowed me to enter the city walls and to speak directly with the Council, bringing terms for the reconciliation of a sovereign and his subjects. Conditions within the city had deteriorated and food supplies had all but been exhausted. Petty crime had become rampant, and many corpses had been left dangling on makeshift gibbets throughout the piazze in every contrada. Not all those hanging were of lowly means, for I had recognized the bloated and blackened faces of many disreputable merchants and bankers, who most likely had taken advantage of their neighbors one time too many.

Ditches had been dug in the green space behind my palazzo to receive the hundreds of bodies of those who were not strong enough to endure the hardships of a lengthy blockade, and later, great bonfires were made in the campo to consume the bodies of the felons and thieves who had been hung. The anger of the citizenry had gone from simmer to boil, and the Council members had become targets of vigilante violence. Those who remained were more than ready to accept whatever terms would be offered to end the ordeal. I had convinced them a deal could be made with King Henry, on behalf of his father, Frederick, for he was a wise and just man, one with sympathies for his loyal subjects, and one who had seen through the veiled misrepresentations of the great territorial nobles.

At this same time, Barbarossa had marched east and had enlisted additional soldiers from towns and villages, having swelled his ranks to twelve thousand men. At the head of his army, to the left of His Magnificence, was Vannozzo, wearing a gold breastplate and a scarlet cloak, the stolen aquila of ancient Rome held high above his black war horse. Never far did he distance himself from the Emperor but held his confidence and council both day and night. Sebastiano had been marched most of the way, neck and hands yoked as if some beast of burden. But for his strength and determination he would have perished along the way and saved himself the horror of witnessing the destruction of his kingdom.

As the valley gave way to foothills and the paths became small and treacherous, the lines of foot soldiers were forced to thin and follow the mounted knights. Barbarossa held back to the rear of the mounted forces, keeping his protection from attack from the front and from the rear. Vannozzo led the way along with the captain of the guards, with assured confidence and zeal, through rocky crag and wooded gully. Many times, the unsure steeds and their warrior riders tumbled and fell, most to their deaths, sending alarming screams throughout the hills. Surprise would not be their advantage, nor would open fields allow for the full force and might of a large-scale attack. The terrain was unknown to them, and the defenders had the advantage of stealth and deadly determination.

The Taurisi would fight for their very existence, and to the death. Their honor, and their final struggle against unsurmountable odds will be sung for years to come. Valiantly did the Zil-at's people, both men and women, and even children, defend their kingdom and their lives, but too great and experienced at war were the Emperor's troops. Though many knights and foot soldiers perished in those sacred hills, the fate of the mighty Taurisi nation was sealed. The imperial forces gained access to the Hidden City and surrounded the Zil-at's palace. Tarchon was brought before the gates of the palace and offered as a peace offering in exchange for a complete surrender of the royal court and the remaining Taurisi forces.

Knowing the treachery of the Emperor, the Zil-at refused to negotiate. The Emperor then caused his army to hack away at the surrounding forest and to pile the trees against the mighty walls of the keep. All the captured Taurisi, including women and children, were then tied to those trees and put to the torch. Seeing no more use for the prince of the Taurisi, the Emperor motioned to Vannozzo, who strode up to his cousin, lifted his golden dagger, and severed his beautiful head. With a smirk of satisfaction, he cast it into the fires of Hell. So high did the flames soar as they enveloped the entire palace, turning it into an enormous blast furnace. The screams of the children of Noah will haunt the sacred hills of Curtun for all eternity.

The Emperor then ordered his men to scour the kingdom and to butcher all survivors and burn every dwelling. The city was stripped of all food stuff and supplies and the rest set to the torch. Within three days' time, as the ashes turned cold and the smoke continued to rise from the dead heaps, Vannozzo had led the Emperor and his bodyguard down into the bowels of the cavernous armory and through to the sacred resting place of the Taurisi. I was relieved to learn later that the sacred bodies of my ancestors, including those of my father and grandfather, had been removed several years earlier and buried under a secret and newly consecrated hill. Most of the stored treasure had been removed as well, but the incredible armory, which had been accumulated over a millennium, was strewn throughout three enormous vaults. Anything of value was taken, the rest left behind to succumb to the ravages of time. Every passage was sealed up, and any evidence of the Taurisi was obliterated.

The Emperor was not satisfied with mere weapons of ancient wars, and as he was promised gold and treasure beyond imagining, he had turned upon Vannozzo and threatened to bury him alive amongst the charred ruins. The boy, still quick-witted and confident, led the imperial troops to two auxiliary sites where treasures and stock of food had been secreted away in anticipation of this invasion. Satisfied with his conquest, the Emperor decided to take his booty directly back to Germany, leaving his son, Henry, to bring order to his rebellious Italian lands. Vannozzo's usefulness to the Emperor had run its course, and the demonic powers with which the boy had held the Holy Roman Emperor had diminished. As promised, Barbarossa declared Vannozzo Zil-at of the Taurisi, and as such, caused him to be buried alive in the last storage vault, amongst the ancient texts and useless artifacts of his deceased people. The hills fell silent as the last boulders were rolled into the opening of the storage vault, and his screams had faded away.

All this would have been lost to me had it not been for one very brave and resourceful boy named Ari, who, undiscovered, in the secret places of Curtun, had witnessed these events and had miraculously survived the carnage. He was found wandering in the northernmost fields of Cortona and was brought to me to testify with such agonizing detail all he had witnessed.

The slaughter of the Taurisi has been too much for Giovanni to bare. He has sat motionless, staring through the frosted glass of the window toward the hills to the west. The sun is setting, and the shadows grow long. He sits in utter silence, refusing to take any nourishment, and refusing any comfort. My heart breaks for him, and for the lost people of the hills. I grieve at all that he lost. He suffers mightily. I have known over the many years of the burden that he had carried, and its heavy weight upon his conscience, and yet, I had never guessed its enormity. I was moved to tears as he revealed the horrors that he had locked away in his heart, and which had plagued him through all these many years. Merciful God in Heaven show pity on him, for he has lost so much. Has he not already paid a heavy price for his bad choices? Has he not suffered enough?

I cannot bring him out of his solitude. He sits and stares into nothingness. Perhaps he fears his next journey. Perhaps this has all been too much for him and he merely awaits his death. Death may be a comfort to him if it ends his internal struggle. But he has not completed his task, and the fate that awaits him after death may be far worse than the hell he has been forced to endure in his spiritual journeys.

For now, I just wait.

Dear God in Heaven, what have I done? How could I have been so blind not to see the outcome of my inaction? I had received all the warnings, yet I heeded them not. The evil voices in my mind have tricked me into believing that what my heart was seeing was false. Never did I force myself to seek the true vision, for the false one was more palatable to me. What truths will You show me now? Who will You send to guide me now?

There, upon the banks of the river, I see the image of the fair Tarquinia. Oh God! Please do not force me to look upon her loving face, for in her sorrowful eyes, I will surely see the misery I have caused. Spare me this ordeal, for I know that I shall surely perish with her spoken disappointment.

All hail the mighty Sandak, pec-ii of a lost tribe. What troubles thee so? Have thou not attained all that thou had set out to attain? Art thou not pleased with thy success? Speak, mighty Master of the Ark of Rusellae!

I cannot speak, dear lady, for I know not what to say.

Strange that one with such a gifted tongue, who so eloquently spills forth his life's story, with such precise detail, for the sake of his rotten soul, has no words for the one who awakened thee to thine own true self.

Many words need spill forth from my tongue, my lady, but shame and regret have kept my lips still.

Speak then from thy mind's eye, from one pec-ii to another. Speak to me, Sandak, of your misery.

With all I have, and all I hold most dear, I beg of thee, most beloved Tarquinia, to forgive me for my failures and for the breech of my sworn oaths and duties to you, to the Zil-at, and to all the Taurisi who have perished from this world. Long have I carried my own disappointment within my heart. No peace have I enjoyed in my life because of the horrid secret I was forced to carry. The knowledge that my failure has caused the destruction of Curtun and the Taurisi has eaten away at my soul and has driven me to forsake any good that I have left in me. I have lost my humanity for what I have done, and what I had failed to do.

The doom of the Taurisi is not your responsibility, pec-ii. Our doom was foretold many times; our fate has always been in God's hands. Your failure has no weight upon our end. Curtun was destined to die. You were merely the instrument through which God has carried out his Master Plan. No, your failure has been in the nurturing of the seeds of the Children of Noah. You were entrusted with their care. You were entrusted with the hopes of our people for a survival of the Etrusci culture. You were to raise our sons and daughters as Taurisi—to keep our culture alive. The blood still flows, but the spirit has died. You were our only hope, and because of your greed, you failed us.

The wrath of the Taurisi people, living or dead, is upon you for your failure. What has been done shall never be undone. The kingdom of Crano is no more, and never will be. Though you may absolve yourself of all your worldly possessions, you will never be able to bring back what once was. Etruria, which was given into your hands, shall be lost for a thousand years. Perhaps, in time, new shoots shall spring forth from buried roots, but it shall never stem from thy doing.

God's judgement awaits you, Sandak. Go before Him with the knowledge that the Taurisi's judgement has already been given.

Chapter Seven
Deceit

XXIV

From the Ashes, a New Path Taken

I force myself to look deeply into the eyes of the image that reflects upon me from the looking glass, and I see the rotted soul of the man I have allowed myself to become. I am a rudderless ship upon a tempestuous sea, abandoning all goodness and hope for salvation, adrift and off course. My moral compass has been lost, and the only beacon in my life is the gold coin. I have gained great power and wealth and yet I have lost all traces of goodness in my heart.

The destruction of Curtun was a turning point in my life, one that destroyed all hopes for redemption of my soul. I became a man consumed with hatred. I cursed Thee, Lord, for allowing such misery to be suffered by an innocent people. I cursed the holy men for prohibiting us from questioning your plan. I cursed Barbarossa for his actions and Lucius for his inactions. I cursed Satan for using my own son as his instrument of death and destruction, and I cursed my own visions, for being warned and not having the courage to try to prevent the tragedy.

Malice and greed and contempt filled all the holes in my spirit. My heart was soaked in avarice and lust, and I cast aside my faith in the greater good, willing to replaced it with the worship of a golden idol. And yet, I was wise enough to realize that survival depended upon cleverness and deceit while working within the established order of the spiritual and the secular world. I had found it sport to lie, cheat, deceive, and swindle, to gain what I wanted. I lived to profit at the cost of another's misery. All this I had done while wearing a mask of innocence and indifference.

So it was when the Council asked me to negotiate a peace settlement with Barbarossa's son, King Henry. I had been conflicted by my old friendship with Henry and my immense hatred for his father. It did not take me long to realize that I needed to don my mask and begin to weave a web of feigned loyalty to the son of the Emperor, and to use that friendship for my own purposes. I was determined that no future transaction, whether big or small, would ever be made without it being a benefit to me.

I met with Henry on several separate occasions and was able to litigate successfully for the Sienese commune against the malicious scheming of the Ardengheschi and the Guglieschi. More important for me, I used my advantage to turn Henry's punishments toward the lords of Orvieto, swaying Henry's opinions of the lords and his sympathies toward the commune. Offering my services to him, as one who knew the strengths and weaknesses of the Council and one who had so much to lose in this absurd standoff, I convinced the King that his Sienese subjects were loyal to the Emperor and loyal to their King. I argued that they had only feared of their unjust punishment, which had cloaked their good reason and had placed a locked gate and a strong wall between themselves and their beloved sovereign. I convinced Henry that an open and honest dialogue between the Council and a reasonable and just king could produce favorable results for everyone. Our only hope for salvation was having Henry reconcile with the Council, end the siege, and restore order within the city before the Emperor and his army could return.

As it was, the Emperor never returned to Siena, but took his blood money and his pride and headed back to the safety of his German kingdoms. In Verona, he made one last attempt to meet with Lucius, offering to buy Henry's co-emperorship with his bloody treasure. For once, Lucius could not be bought, and he arrogantly turned down Barbarossa's offer. Enraged, Barbarossa announced his intention to marry his son Henry to Constance of Sicily, uniting the Holy Roman Empire with the Kingdom of Sicily and surrounding the Papal Kingdom. Lucius would have none of that, and he quickly called together a synod to excommunicate Frederick. The Emperor then cursed Lucius and marched his army north. He also left behind a group of loyal clergymen to forestall the proceedings, and before he and his army made the foothills of the mighty Alps, Lucius developed a strange fever and died. The eagle had struck, though none could prove his guilt, and the world was, once again, thrown into chaos.

At Siena, Henry was enraged when he learned of the Emperor's play against Lucius. His loyalty to his father and his emperor demanded that his life and his choices were never really his while the Emperor lived. Even so, he had felt betrayed by his father, who had never even discussed the possibility with him. Of course, he would never openly show his displeasure with his father, but our closeness during our negotiations made it apparent that Henry had been upset with the dramatic change in his father's behavior.

Seeing a golden opportunity to drive a wedge between the King and the Emperor, I played upon his insecurities, offering a way to showcase his superior governing skills to his subjects and to his father. I built a solid case against our enemies and presented a convincing defense for the innocence of the citizens of Siena. Henry was so moved by the plight of the Sienese, who had been subjected to great injustices by the scheming lords and the malicious neighboring communes, that he decided to end the siege.

In a formal statement, he recognized the injustice that had been brought upon his loyal subjects and promised to treat them fairly and justly as long as they proved their loyalty to their king and to their emperor. I was asked to carry the terms of surrender to the council. In exchange for their freedom, the citizens agreed to give up all land that they had taken or usurped belonging to the heritage of Countess Matilda and to the margravate of Tuscany, which through birth right had belonged to Frederick. They were required to swear an oath of fealty to Henry, recognizing him as their lord and king and recognizing his absolute imperial rights. They had to promise never to summon together any army without their lord's consent, and they had to agree to restore the lands that they had illegally seized. They would submit themselves to imperial decree regarding such lands and holdings, and in return, Frederick and Henry would grant the Commune the right to elect its own consuls and to coin its own money. This would become most beneficial to my future operation in the caverns of Stigliano. He would also grant them jurisdiction over the city and its contado and over the vassals of the Bishop of Siena. In addition, he granted the

Council the right to tax those under its rule, and in return, the Council would have to pay a fixed tribute every Eastertide to the imperial treasury at S. Miniato al Tedesco.

In retribution for their malicious efforts, Henry commanded the Ardengheschi and the Guglieschi to tear down their fortresses at Lucignano, and the Count of Orvieto to renounce his claim to the castle at Radicofani. As recompense for my services and oath of loyalty to the imperial throne, I was granted full rights to that property. With this one document, I was able to secure for Siena, and myself, control over the Via Francegena north to the borders of Florentine territory and south to the outskirts of Viterbo. A peaceful trading route was assured with the strength of well-fortified strongholds under the jurisdiction of the commune. The Council gladly accepted the terms of peace, and the gates were opened wide to a beloved king. The city had been saved, though at great cost, and the love between Henry and his subjects had been restored, at least for a brief time. Siena, under the protection of her sovereign, had lived through the ordeal and had continued to grow strong and wealthy in the good graces of the emperors. Curtun, however, had suffered a different fate.

Emboldened by the benefits of the peace treaty, Siena continued to flex her muscles and was ever testing her boundaries, especially when the imperial armies were far away. It had not taken long for her hunger for wealth and territory to become insatiable again. The insidious hatred and envy of her enemies was ever present, and it would continue to stain her verdant soil red.

During these troubled times, I had turned all my attention and energy toward expanding my own empire to be greater than the commune that I had so often come to save. My survival had depended upon strength and cunning and being wealthier and more powerful than the sum of my rivals. My standing as a leading citizen helped to secure lucrative contracts for myself, and to play a leading role in the governance of the contrada. I had learned much from Giancarlo about business and politics, especially about the value of information discovered and accumulated on friends as well as enemies. Never would I hesitate to use any bit of secret knowledge, an embarrassing transgression, an illegal transaction, a mortal sin. Anything that could be used against a rival, I never hesitated to use to bend them to my will.

As a member of the Council, I had always directed the laws to be written or enforced, keeping my own interests first and foremost. I became adept in using the other councilmen and the consuls to my own advantage, never hesitating to bribe or swindle when the need arose. No shame nor conscience had I, for my faith and empathy toward humanity had been obliterated. Fear of my God and His everlasting retribution had easily been ignored, for those who had once played upon my conscience were all gone. No longer did I have the counsel of my father or the Zil-at of Curtun, nor that of the Patriarch of Grado. Long dead was His Holiness Alexander and my saintly brother Galgano. Gone too were Sebastiano and Salvatore, and even my uncle, the great Giancarlo Manenti, though I dare say that he, more than any of them, would have been pleased with the deals I had so aptly put together. As great as he had seemed to me in my youth, I can proudly say that my business skills had far exceeded his. I had bested the great Giancarlo Manenti. I have won the contest. Yet, at what price? My chains are too heavy and draw the life from me. My soul has been so blackened with sin that it rots and decays to the point where even Satan may refuse to accept it.

My sons have grown into manhood and have done well for themselves, save, of course, for my first, the source of much of my torment. I am pleased with the other's success and their independence. And yet it saddens me now that they are so distant. As they have advanced in age, they seek not to emulate their father or share in his enterprises but have less and less to do with me. The fault lies solely upon my shoulders, for though they have always been good sons, and I, most regrettably, have never been a good father. Nikos was more of a father to my own sons than I. He had never allowed ambition and greed to overshadow the love and compassion that he held within his heart. I had learned nothing from the broken relationship between my father and myself, nor did I care for anything except that which benefited me.

My one true friend and confidant, my only sense of conscience, was, and has always been, Nikos. And yet, very rarely had I heeded his council, unless it was of benefit to me. Never did I learn from his compassion or allow his love to help me find a more noble and empathetic path in this life. Nay, throughout these many years, the only guide from whom I readily accepted any kind of counsel was Enrico, whose wealth and power had grown even greater than I could have imagined. Throughout his long and successful life, he had been forced to rebuild his family fortune several times; however, Fortuna had been especially kind to him under the dogeship of Sebastiano Ziani. His vast financial empire had spread throughout the Eastern Empire, had dominated the Adriatic, and had stretched throughout the West. His influence had been felt in every major city on the continent, and even throughout the empires and caliphates on the African coast. His enterprises were of a great benefit to me, and for many years we had profited together on many endeavors.

Fortune always seemed to smile on Enrico, and yet Fortune can be fickle. She always collects her price. With Enrico, as his power and fortune grew, his sight diminished. It saddens me that his years were ended in darkness, and yet his life could not have been brighter. Oh, how I laugh at the stories that now are being told about the great crusader. Many speak of how he had been blinded by the angry Emperor Comnenus and his Greek physicians, who inserted glass shards into his eyes for defending his Venetian countrymen. Others claim with certainty that the Greek seers and philosophers had begged the Emperor not to let the ambassador go unharmed for they had seen the great harm the aged man would perpetrate upon the empire. Such stories are mere fantasy and rubbish, for I know the truth about my dear friend Enrico Dandolo, Doge of Venice, destroyer of empires. I was with him, and it was I who saved him and brought him back to the safety of his family and his republic.

Now I must tell you of the web of seduction and deceit that Fate had spun about me, holding me spellbound in the treacherous world of the di Conti. Far greater and more deadly than the web of the black widow, her trap had wound its tendrils around popes and emperors, kings and queens, lords and ladies. We were all bound together with the same string, and throughout this cursed web, like several spiders, ran the di Conti. I do not make this confession to shift my blame to others. The blame for my actions lays firmly at my feet. My Lord and my God has been with me always, and He will judge me, as only He has the right to do. I merely open myself to you, so that you will understand the circumstances that drew me from the righteous path and led me to a path of eternal damnation.

The di Conti have touched my life from the earliest days of my youth. Ugolino was the first, and then his uncle Lotario, and later, his uncle Paolo Scolari. All have influenced the way in which I have viewed the world, and to what depths I would sink my own morals into the fetid mud. I had never thought to emulate them, as I did with my dear friend Enrico or my uncle Giancarlo, but had I been a better man, I would have used their immorality as a model of what I should not become. I dare say, I admired their cunning, their ruthlessness, and their drive to succeed, for, in their own ways, each has attained greatness, even though their notoriety may survive as a bane to mankind, rather than a boon.

Of Ugolino and Lotario, I have already said much; of Paolo Scolari, I will tell more. But first, let me speak of the events that catapulted the di Conti into the highest offices in Christendom, begun by Barbarossa in Verona. The Emperor and his army had not traveled far from Verona when Lucius died, and the Throne of Saint Peter was vacant. It seems so evident today that the cunning Emperor had left his German cardinals behind in Verona, anticipating a new election that would favor a secret supporter of his, an archpriest by the name of Paolo Scolari, who happened to be the uncle of Lotario di Conti. Barbarossa had arranged to have Scolari's name presented for pope, and once elected, the animosity between the Emperor and the pope would finally be at an end. Alas, the Emperor's plans were foiled when the council of assembled cardinals selected Umberto Crivelli, the Archbishop of Milan, someone I had known for many years.

Crivelli was known to be a man of questionable lineage and tastes, being a Milanese, who had a remarkable ambition and an ego to match. He also had a deep hatred of the Emperor. I had been introduced to Crivelli early in my career by Ugolino's uncle Lotario while the younger Crivelli was serving on the curia under Alexander. The young prelate had developed a fondness for certain exotic items and services that I was most happy to supply for him, never questioning nor judging, but always making detailed notes in my journal, just like Giancarlo, hoping that, at some future time, such information would be of benefit to me. Crivelli seemed to have a rather close connection with Ugolino, both of whom seemed to share the same tastes and ambitions, and hatreds for Barbarossa. Crivelli would never forget the Emperor's cruelty toward the Milanese nor the humiliation and disgrace suffered by his family during the Emperor's brutal sieges. Hatred of Barbarossa had become a common thread that bound the three of us together.

Crivelli had risen rapidly through the ranks of the church, championed by the di Conti and Segni of Anagni, and eventually was elevated to archbishop by Alexander. He remained a good friend and most benevolent client and was a source of much information and many lucrative contracts throughout the final years of his life. Crivelli accepted the papal tiara and the name Urban III from the Council that Lucius had assembled in Verona when that Pope had thought to excommunicate the Emperor. Barbarossa had wasted no time in trying to have Henry crowned co-emperor, but Urban would have none of that. The new Pope would never capitulate to the demands of his sworn enemy. Urban would rather see the murderous scoundrel burn in the flames of Hell for all eternity. He knew his refusal would infuriate the Emperor, but he felt confident in the papal army and the League of Northern States and was assured that his destiny was to rid the world of that German devil and all the vermin who supported him.

Siena had to balance upon a wire with this pope, as had I, even though we had had a special relationship for years, because of the oath of loyalty sworn to the Emperor and his son, Henry. It was fortuitous for us all that Urban had been raised as a businessman, and that his true appetite was nourished by his increasing desire for wealth and power. Because of his shrewdness, he would never sever the ties to the ones who controlled the wealth on the continent.

Urban fought against everything the Emperor had tried to accomplish, and finally caused such blind anger in Barbarossa that he ordered Henry to lay siege to Verona and trap Urban within its walls. He then proceeded to occupy all the surrounding Papal territories. Henry was not as kind to Verona as he was to Siena, and the siege was long and harsh. Conditions within the city walls became intolerable, and the Pope and his bishops had to face the realization that none of the monarchs upon whom he had counted for support were going to send relief. Urban called a council of all the cardinals trapped with him in the city to discuss the excommunication of both the Emperor and his son, but the German cardinals and a few of their supporters had voted in solidarity to back their emperor and to sue for peace. Urban was forced to sign an agreement stating he would acquiesce to the Emperor's demands if Henry lifted the siege. Henry showed great humanity and diplomacy in sparing the Veronese the punishment that might have been metered out by his father as he withdrew his forces from the city. However, once the siege was lifted, Urban reconvened his council and continued the excommunication proceedings. The citizens of Verona wanted no cause for Barbarossa's wrath and drove the Pope and his council from the city.

Again, the talons of the eagle had proven to be long and deadly, and while the papal congregation was upon the road to Ferrara, they intercepted an imperial emissary bringing news to King Henry of the fall of Hattin to the Muslim Saladin. It was said that upon hearing of the disaster, Urban collapsed in a fit and was dead within three days. I question Fate and coincidence that the life of my friend Crivelli had been cut short by mere words, and that the murderous Barbarossa did not have his own hand in ending the very brief reign of Urban III, as he had done so with most of his enemies.

Again, the chair of Saint Peter was vacant. Urban's chancellor, a wise, old, man named Alberto de Morro, was quickly elected and took the name of Gregory VIII. I knew Morro to be a good and holy man, a man of simplicity, austerity, and prayer, one concerned with the spirit more than with the purse. I had known, even then, that my soul was beyond redemption, and that the good shepherd could not offer me spiritual leadership nor financial benefit. He would only cause trouble to our world of commerce and finance. His focus was to reform the Church and to assure her safety by improving relations with the Emperor. He had made very few friends in the business world and fewer friends in the Church, for most had coveted worldly goods over heavenly promises. Shortly after his elevation he sent shockwaves throughout the Papal States by writing a conciliatory letter to Frederick and naming Henry Emperor-Elect. He also issued encyclicals on the behavior of the clergy, claiming the disasters in the Holy Land were God's punishment against Christians and the Church for their sinful and hedonistic ways. In his religious fanaticism, he issued edicts against excesses, gambling, sex, and games amongst the clergy. He also moved to condemn the Jews and the Italian bankers, whom he considered to be mortal sinners.

His draconian measures would prove to be his undoing, for such hysteria is never good for business, especially if it is against the bankers. There was resentment and whispers amongst the wealthier merchants and some of the princes of the Church, who believed that Gregory, if left unchecked, would bring business to ruin. I had sided with Paolo Scolari, who had harbored ill feelings because of his missed opportunity to rule the church, his nephew Lotario, and Lotario's nephew, Ugolino, and a small group of cardinals. The shared opinion was that the old man's days were numbered, and perhaps his prayers to stand before God with an unsoiled soul might soon be answered.

The whispers had quieted down when, in late summer, word reached Rome that Jerusalem had finally fallen to Saladin. Gregory had quickly brokered a peace agreement between Genoa and Pisa so their fleets could transport a crusading army to Jerusalem, but before he could finalize his plans, he was dead. He had only occupied Saint Peter's seat for fifty-five days, before his prayers had been answered, and he was called to Heaven.

So it was that within six years of Alexander's death, the Church had lost three more popes. The world, as always, was in turmoil, the imperium was still at odds with the papacy, the Eastern Empire was at war with itself and the West, the Kingdom of Sicily continued to expand northward, and Richard and Phillip Augustus continued to battle over territory on the continent. The Muslim plague was continuing to spread like wildfire, and the Holy Land had been consumed.

Of course, such wars and skirmishes keep the arms dealers in business, and supplies are always needed for the troops. Production, shipping, and transport of these necessities had become a large part of my business. Stigliano had become the industrial center of Tuscany. Not only were we producing iron and steel for weapons, chain mail had become the standard issue for the knights and the crusading armies. Production of the mail soon outpaced my wool production. How ironic it was that the vestments of war became more important than the vestments of peace. I still imported large shipments of

Leinster wool and continued to produce the finest scarlet wool for the princes of the Church. With a steady stream of workers coming to Stigliano from far and wide, I was able to drain the swampy lands from the foothills of the Colline Metallifere to the banks of the River Merse. In that reclaimed land I had cultivated wheat and grain, which when harvested was ground in the wind and water-powered mills that Gontarz had constructed for me along the Merse. The Commune of Siena had grown strong, with thousands of mouths to feed, and by sitting on the Council, I was able to set the price for certain food stock, which helped to fatten my purse. I also made a goodly profit by importing salt from the ancient mines in Trapani, and occasionally, I was able to secure shipments of spices from Constantinople through my Venetian connections. Those rare shipments were most profitable, for the wealthy in the courts of Phillip Augustus and of Henry II, and some of the smaller principalities, were willing to pay handsomely for such exotic treasures.

On occasion, I would arrange to call upon these courts myself in order to keep the personal relationships strong between myself and my clients. On each of those trips, I would bring my son Paolo, for companionship and as my guard, and Pietro would bring young Francesco to accompany us. Paolo and Francesco had become very close, the elder being exceedingly protective of the young boy. I had always tried to keep my distance from Francesco, though it had become increasingly difficult as the boy grew older and our resemblances became more evident. Pietro had developed an unfair disliking for the boy, yet he continued to bring him on these trips, as a means of entertainment for the ladies at court. In all our travels throughout Aquitaine and the French countryside, Francesco had picked up the songs and verses of the travelling troubadours and had become quite proficient on the lute. Pietro viewed the boy as his ticket into the romantic courts of queens, especially Eleanor, princesses, duchesses, and marchesi alike. It so pained me to see Francesco being used in the same fashion as a gypsy would use a trained monkey to collect coins from an attentive crowd, but I was hardly in a position to step in or criticize. I was no more of a father to my own children than Pietro was to his. Pietro's treatment of Francesco also bothered Paolo, much more than it had bothered anyone else, and over the years, Paolo had become more protective of his brother. The bond that had been forged between the two would never be broken, save in death, and the brotherly love between the two would shine as a beacon when all else seemed dark.

It was during those long years of turmoil, of building and traveling, that I became more entwined with the di Conti of Anagni. That was when I first began my secret operations for coining money. I had no difficulty convincing myself that it was my negotiating genius that had led to Henry's great generosity in allowing Siena to mint her own coin. It was only right, I had reasoned, that I should take advantage of the situation and produce my own supply of Sienese coins. After all, I had controlled most of the heavy metal mining and smelting operation in the region, and had the raw materials needed to produce mass quantities of coin. Plus, I had solidified my control over the Council. I had clearly seen the potential for profit with this illicit operation. More to my benefit, a refugee from Curtun by the name of Zed-lith was an alchemist who was well versed in the ancient sciences of alloy and metallurgy. He would prove invaluable to me as I established my counterfeiting operation.

The Council, at the same time, had made plans to issue a new Sienese coin and had sought my advice on the logistics of producing mass quantities of these coins. My colleagues had been aware of my close friendship with Enrico Dandolo, and of his success in introducing a new coin into the Venetian and Eastern marketplaces. The gold hyperpyron of the Eastern Empire had been debased so often by the puppet emperors in Constantinople that the markets were crying out for a more stable form of currency. Venice and its merchants were suffering from the political unrest throughout the Eastern Empire, and after Enrico had been elected doge, he decided to set a new standard of value in the world and to bring stability to all commercial markets. He began by minting a new half-penny that he called the bianco, even though it had only a five percent silver content. It was only valued at half of what the standard Veronese penny was at the time, but it was easy to produce and became widely used in a very short period.

Enrico was brilliant in starting out small and slowly, though it was not very long until he began to produce the quartarolo, which contains no precious metals at all. I thought this to be a real mark of genius. It was only worth a quarter penny, but it has become, by far, the most used coin in all the world. And yet, Enrico had known that it was impractical for large commercial transactions to use such minor coinage, so he created his masterpiece, the grosso, which is weighted at 2.2 grams of the purest silver. Similar to the Byzantine gold coin, which depicts Saint Andrew grasping a cross on the front and Christ enthroned on the back, the grosso depicts Enrico himself and St. Mark grasping the saint's banner on the front and an enthroned Christ on the back. His coins have become the standard currency in Eastern trade due in part to their acceptability and purity, and due to the ever-increasing counterfeiting and debasing of the imperial coinage.

I was able to study and learn under the Master, to drink from the font of his knowledge and his courage, and to benefit from his benevolent friendship. For this reason, the Council sought my advice on the subject, and I proposed that the commune establish a formal commission to formalize their plan to produce Siena's first coins. I generously offered to donate my time and energy to lead a commission in developing the plans. I assured the Council that the commission's deliberations and recommendations, and the actual minting of our first coin, could be executed within a year's time. I was quite successful in stacking this commission with other Council members who were of like mind to myself. At the same time, I secretly began constructing my own counterfeit operation in the subterranean caverns of my castle.

I had long abandoned any hope for my mortal soul and had forsaken any thought or care for God's plan. I was determined that my fate was to be of my own making, and should God deem to have other plans for me, then so be it! Enrico, as successful as he was, had a strong sense of divine purpose and a fear of heavenly retribution. Always in his heart and in his mines-eye were the prophesies of Malachy. Such predictions were always a source of comfort and strength for him and enforced his resolve to live his life to the fullest, for the glory of himself and his God. Often. We would talk about the visions that were visited upon me throughout my life, and of the prophesies that had been written upon the pages of history, the authenticity and accuracy of some, and the absurdity and deceptiveness of others. He had found them all to be equally genuine and important, upon which he relied heavily for guidance with everything he did.

He was not a superstitious man, but I had come to observe over the years that he was a very spiritual man. And yet, as a Dandolo, he was also a very practical man. He was most generous with his time and his wisdom and was most instrumental in showing me the workings of international monetary trade. I was deeply saddened when I had to leave my friend in Venice, for I had known that at his advanced age, I most likely would never see him again. And yet, that amazing man had much more to give to his republic and to the world, before he was called to judgement in the Kingdom of Heaven.

Following my trip to Venice, I prepared and presented my plan to the Council. The beauty of Enrico's style of coins was that they were costly to produce but would be more difficult to counterfeit. I therefore recommended that the new Sienese currency should be more like that issued by the Count of Champagne and Provins, a small silver penny called the provisino or denier. Twelve of them made a shilling, and 240 of them made a pound. Such coinage was the standard currency of the Champagne fairs and had, at one time, been used throughout Europe. I strongly recommended we proceed with caution and implement strict controls over the process to ensure long-lasting success. I insisted I would personally oversee the entire operation, at least in the beginning, and maintain the strictest security. Only the finest craftsmen would be allowed to produce the coinage in a specially designed factory, which I would have built, maintain, and lease to the commune. The entire operation would be open to inspection by third-party metallurgists under the jurisdiction of the commune. Little did the Council know, my own factory within the bowels of Stigliano were already in full production, with Zed-lith overseeing that covert operation. Through further negotiations, I was contracted to supply the silver needed, and feigning impartiality, I allowed the Council to negotiate the price. It was easy to make substantial profits when I owned the raw materials, for I simply had to wet the beaks of my fellow Council members when discussing price.

As I had been secretly minting coin, and Siena was still debating plans for her own coin, Henry of England had decided to produce his own currency, including his sterling silver Brit. That, however, had not been as popular on the mainland and had not adversely affected my counterfeit business in the early years. The Council was anxious to get their denaro produced and placed into circulation, but they stayed true to the plan and proceeded with all the caution I had advised. I had entered into these murky waters by producing a sizable amount of debased provisinos, which were a blend of impure silver and copper that Zed-lith had masterfully crafted to resemble the real provisino. The coins were easily produced, validating our process, and were circulated with great success at the following year's fairs in Champagne.

By the end of that fair season, Siena began production of her own Sienese denaro of silver, a solidus, equivalent to twenty-four denari, and a libra, equal to one hundred solidii. I had already begun to ship massive quantities of counterfeit Sienese coins to my banking agents in and around Champagne. Though my coins were made with baser materials, they were so similar in appearance to the real issue that it would take an expert to tell the difference. My plan was not to flood the market with these counterfeit coins, nor to cause financial upheaval as was done with the eastern imperial coinage, but rather to slowly release them in small quantity to smaller merchant operations, such as my dear friend Pietro and his associates.

I would utilize my coins during the settlement sessions at the end of each fair, only when the Count's guards were sufficiently distracted from their duty, and only when I was sure not to draw the attention of his cruel and swift justice. The good Count was not misguided in his mistrust of the Sienese bankers, or as he called us, the corsari. Never had I dreamt that this counterfeit operation would become such a major part of my enterprises or deliver such great profit to my coffers. The French so aptly accuse the cunning Italians of loving *guadagniernne grosamente*, or big profits. I revel in that accusation. I see no shame in it.

After Phillip returned from the crusades and learned of the ingenuity of the Italian corsari, he decided to get in on the action by minting his own counterfeit currency. The French king was not as wise nor as cunning as the Italians and foolishly flooded the market with his worthless coins. Luckily, I caught wind of his schemes through my agents in Paris and was able to shut down that part of the operation before the market was thrown into turmoil. That was when I turned my attention to the clergy, and further to the east.

Gregory had died and the few cardinals who were with him in Pisa had quickly gathered to stave off the ambitions of the Archpriest Scolari by electing Teobaldo of Ostia to be pope. Another timid man, very similar to the late pope, he looked more toward reformation than to the preservation of authority of the Holy See. Scolari was furious that he had once again been outmaneuvered by the cardinals and visited secretly with the Pope-elect in his chambers. Shortly thereafter, Teobaldo renounced his election and headed back to Ostia. The stunned cardinals could do nothing but to hold another election, at which time Paolo Scolari was elected and took the name Clement III.

I had very little business dealings with Scolari prior to his elevation, but Fortune's Wheel would turn in my favor as my direct partnership with Ugolino and my indirect partnership with his uncle Lotario provided me with a direct link to the new pope. Though I had always maintained the title of Banker to the Pope, which had been given to me by Alexander, I found it difficult to build a lasting connection with the curia because the tenures of the popes had been so short, beginning with the death of my friend Lucius.

With Scolari as pope, my future suddenly seemed much brighter. Scolari was a man of action and opinion. He did not seek to reform his church, nor did he keep his head in the clouds, praying for salvation. No, he was well accustomed to the finer things that wealth and power had brought him, and I doubt he had any remorse for the life of excess and debauchery that he so enjoyed. He was shrewd and intelligent, and he saw that it would take a strong leader to right the wrongs that had been handed down to him by his ineffectual predecessors. He had foreseen that the Latin Kingdom and the Holy Land would eventually fall to the Muslim armies of Saladin, and that all of Christendom was in peril of being consumed, unless a stronger force prevailed. He had inherited trouble with the Commune of Rome and most of all he wanted to resolve, once and for all, the animosity between the papacy and the imperium. Christ's Church was in desperate need of a strong leader, and he knew that he was the man to lead.

Immediately after ascending to the Chair of Saint Peter, Clement negotiated a peace treaty between Pisa and Genoa and called for his crusade against Saladin and the Muslim armies. Negotiations with Barbarossa took longer, but in the end an agreement was reached that formalized the position of the Papal States within the Imperium, guaranteeing peaceful co-existence between pope and emperor. Clement had agreed to crown Frederick's son Henry as co-emperor. More importantly, when Clement launched the third major crusade against the East, the Christian world went to war, and very lucrative contracts began coming my way.

So persuasive was Clement regarding the perils facing the Christian world that he caused the great kings of Europe to set aside their differences and to pick up the Cross and lead their crusading armies to victory over the heathens. Young Richard had just been made King of England upon the death of Henry. Young Philip Augustus of France, a host of dukes, counts, princes, and even Barbarossa, himself, led their armies to do battle upon the sacred soil of the Holy Land. Frederick had aged poorly and had been so plagued with the sins of his many heinous crimes that perhaps he needed to find forgiveness and salvation in that holy cause. But his eternal pardon was justly denied to him, for he never reached that holy destination. Instead, he fulfilled his destiny by being thrown from his war horse while crossing the Calycadnus River. He drowned in those shallow waters amid the piss and shit of a thousand battle steeds. Praise be to God, for the tortured souls of the Taurisi were avenged. Barbarossa was no more. May his soul be consumed by the fiery waters of Hell for all eternity. Often, I hear the haunting words of the great Zil-at speaking the prophesy of his beloved Tarquinia:

The eagle will devour all in his path before he meets his end in a watery grave, and yet he will fail to destroy us. We are saved so long as the Seer's Son is Master of the Ark.

Young King Henry was marching his army south toward Sicily to defend his wife's claim to the throne when news reached him of his father's inglorious demise. He immediately sent emissaries to Rome to petition Clement to crown him emperor, but the Pope would not grant audience to the emissaries. Some say the Pope delayed fulfilling the promise made to Frederick because he did not trust Henry. Others say the delay was due to the Pope's failing health. I am of the latter opinion for it was confirmed to me by Ugolino that Clement was cut down so early in his reign by the fevers of syphilis, which he had contracted during his long life of excess and wild debauchery. Either way, Henry was furious and continued his march southward to claim all that was rightfully his. He planned to deal with the Pope in his own way, and then he would take the Kingdom of Sicily for his own. Within a few days, Henry's army reached the outskirts of Rome, but by then Clement was already dead. Giancinto Bobo was elected as Celestine III, and fearing a siege of the city, he immediately crowned Henry Holy Roman Emperor.

Celestine's seven years as pope were a disaster, for the man could not make any decisions nor show any authority in matters requiring action of any kind. I judge the man not on his effect on world politics, but rather upon the hurt that he did to my business. All those lucrative contracts that had been negotiated for me by Ugolino and Lotario were held in abeyance and never fulfilled. Payments for goods delivered were curtailed, causing me to suffer great loss. Pleadings and petitions fell upon deaf ears, and my acquaintances in the curia were of no help. Luckily for me, the profits lost with my dealings with the clergy were found in the contracts to supply arms to Henry for his Sicilian campaign. Again, my friendship with the new emperor had paid off for his campaign was long and his need for financing and supplies was great. He had, inadvertently, opened another market for my counterfeit coin.

XXV

Of Innocence and Culpability

Let me now tell you of the later years of my life, the years that have been dominated by the di Conti of Segni. All the days of those years were filled with darkness, for the light of the Holy Spirit had forsaken me. The Seer's Son was truly blind. The visions that had plagued and comforted me in the past had abandoned me, even though I had tried everything in my power to bring them back to me. I had consulted theologians and spirituals, all learned in the sciences of the preternatural world. I had sought out fellow seers and psychics, necromancers and sorcerers, and had even consorted with the witch folk who still reside in the hills and forests. I had visited with mystics and holy men and had spent a tremendous sum of money buying indulgences and financing great houses dedicated to God.

With the help of a mystic who had been brought to Venice from the far kingdoms of the Orient, I eventually learned to turn inward to seek that which had been stolen from me. Nikos had always assisted me as best as he could with concoctions and potions, and elixirs and incantations. Neither witch nor mystic nor magic spell could help me in my quest. Over time, I was guided in a most unholy direction, as I sought comfort from those who had delighted in my total corruption—the cardinal deacon, Ugolino, and his uncle Lotario. I speak familiarly of these men for they have been a part of me for most of my life. Like the branches of the wisteria, Fate has caused our lives to intertwine, growing ever stronger to overcome any obstacle that impedes growth toward the sun's golden light. Foul was their counsel, and yet, most willingly did I accept it, and eagerly did I follow them down a crooked path. I do not profess innocence in the corrupt dealings of my later life, but rather I confess my culpability in the sins that have been committed against God and mankind.

Lotario di Conti of Segni had been mentored well by his uncle, Clement III. He had lived a long and successful life since first I saw him at the palace of the Abbot of Montalcino. It was he who had rescued his nephew Ugolino from the clutches of that animal Bernardo, and it was he who metered out his own form of punishment by feeding that villain to the hogs. How happy both uncle and nephew had been to watch the beast devoured amid the piss and shit of the frenzied pigs. Such sights are repugnant to most men, yet I have learned over the years that they bring great satisfaction to men such as these. They are not loathed to the screams of men's agony, but rather revel in such music. I have never comprehended this, and yet I do have the propensity to turn a blind eye to such behavior. My greatest fault was that I found it easy to cast my lot with these men. I reasoned that friendship would be of great benefit to me. It was easy for me to justify that my tolerance for Lotario was in payment for the many favors he had granted me in youth, and my closeness to Ugolino may have stemmed from a sense of guilt for abandoning him at the abbey, with the monster. But in truth, it was merely need and greed that forged our bonds, for in all things we had used each other.

The benefits of rank and privilege had never been wasted upon either Lotario or Ugolino, for each, in his own way, had managed to overcome adversity and to rise within the sacred halls of the church. Lotario was a most learned man and had attended the great university in Paris in his youth. Clement III brought him to Rome and made him cardinal deacon of SS Sergio and Bacco. During this time, I was expanding my business with the curia of Rome, and through my connections with Lotario, I had a direct link with the Pope and his curia. Great was the affection between the Pope and the Cardinal Deacon, and there was much talk that Clement wanted to establish a dynasty and have Lotario occupy Saint Peter's chair upon Clement's death. How scandalous was the notion that the keys to Christ's church could be conveyed by any other means than through the intersession of the Holy Spirit at a duly convened conference of the cardinals.

Such politics and gossip did not concern me. My only concerns were the lucrative contracts that I was able to secure from His Holiness. Clement was head of Christ's Church, but also secular ruler over the Papal States, and thus had always needed money to pay his troops and purchase arms to fight against his many enemies. Most willingly would I provide the arms that he desperately needed, and through my connections with the Jews of Rome, I was able to bankroll his holy, and his not-so-holy, wars. Acting in the capacity of Papal Banker, I was able to borrow great sums of money from the Jewish moneylenders, at usurious interest rates that only the Jews could charge, for their souls are already barred from entering the Gates of Heaven. I would then make an interest-free loan to the papal treasury but charge a hefty fee for my services. The Pope, always desperate for money, was more than willing to concede the difference between the Sienese banker and the Jew, forgiving the service charge as a cost of doing business. Not all popes saw it this way, but such was the special relationships I had developed with di Conti.

When Giacinto Bobo was elected Celestine III upon the death of Clement, Lotario was furious, as all the promises given to him by his loving uncle had been buried along with the pontiff. The cardinals who had gathered in Rome were a fickle bunch, and as frightened as they were of Henry, whose army had been encamped on the outskirts of the city for several weeks, they were more frightened to allow the seat of Peter to be handed down to Lotario. The wisdom of the day was to appease the angry king and maintain the traditions that had been handed down for a thousand years. As fearful as they had been of di Conti and his supporters, the cardinals had allowed the Holy Spirit to guide them and elected Bobo. Lotario never forgot the insult of this betrayal. For seven long years he had to endure the ineptitude of Celestine. The Pope had crowned Henry emperor and then spent the remainder of his days fighting against him.

It is my belief that Henry took great delight in frustrating the Pope at every opportunity. Henry's battles with Trancred to claim the throne of Sicily continued for several years, and the Pope refused to take sides in the conflict. He antagonized the Pope further by taking captive Richard, the king of England, as the Lionhearted was returning from his successful victories against the Muslims. Celestine was duty-bound to protect the young king, but in this he failed miserably. Though I cared little for the sons of Henry of England, Richard was the best of the brood, and he had proven himself worthy of his father's crown.

Though Henry was our emperor and we had all sworn loyalty to him, it was clear that he had overstepped the laws of good government and had cast dishonor upon his imperium. No good was to come from such a move, but only to raise the ire of the kingdoms in Europe. With Trancred's death, Henry was able to extend his empire to the southernmost reaches of Italy. He had even tried to consolidate the German and Italian kingdoms under one hereditary kingdom and wrest total control of the Papal States from Celestine. Opposition by France and the northern city states hindered his plans, but Fate put an end to them when Henry VI, Holy Roman Emperor, King of Germany and Italy and the Kingdom of Sicily, mysteriously died during a revolt of his subjects in Sicily.

It is widely believed he had contracted malaria in Messina, but it has long been whispered that the Empress Constance, having suffered greatly at the hands of her husband, Henry, had plotted to have him drugged and imprisoned in his own castle in Catania. There she slowly administered poison into his food and caused him to die a slow and agonizing death. Such was the end of my friend and my king. Time had proven that that royal apple had not fallen far from the imperial tree. The absolute power that resides within the imperial crown had taken command of its bearer and had obliterated all hope of a fair and just and enlightened leader of men.

Celestine's papacy had become a disaster. He was at war with Philip of France over an annulment that he refused to grant to the king. He had forsaken Richard of England by failing to negotiate a reasonable ransom for his release from Henry. He had aggravated the Commune of Rome with his mishandling of so many political affairs. And he had allowed his adversary to completely encircle his own kingdom. Realizing that things were only getting worse, and frustrated with his own ineptitude, Celestine gathered his cardinals together and proposed to vacate the chair in favor of his chancellor, Giovanni di Salerno. Lotario and his supporters had had enough of

Celestine and had forced him to withdraw his plan. Di Conti had waited long enough. He was determined that the chair would be his, and within a few days, the Pope was dead. The cardinals convened to elect a new pope, and after much controversy, political in-fighting, and physical threats, Lotario di Conti of Segni was finally elected pope. Ironically, he took the name of Innocent III.

Of the young Ugolino di Conti, I have already spoken. He, above all others, has been with me the longest. Throughout my life, he has always been in the background, tempering my hardness with acts of feigned kindness and acts of pure evil. Just as Enrico Dandolo had been my mentor in the business world, Ugolino di Conti has always been that negative force that has led me to my own moral destruction. I truly believe that God has set us on our individual paths toward our own destiny, and that He has given us free choice to stay upon the path of righteousness or to divert our noble purpose toward the path of wickedness. He allows many temptations to be placed before us to test our resolve and our worthiness. Though we may receive the help of others as we struggle on our individual paths, we are truly alone in our mission, and must be responsible for our own salvation or damnation. One man upon one path, for good or for evil.

Yet, there are times when the path of one man runs too close to another and may on occasion converge or intersect at various points. Such, it has been with Ugolino and me. From the first time our paths first crossed so many years ago at the abbey of Sant' Antimo, we have continued to meet simultaneously at the same crossroads where God has tested each of us, and each of us has failed Him. Whether on His holy mission to retrieve the Prophesies or working with His Holiness Alexander in Venice or in Rome, or dealing with the Cistercian Brotherhood during the building of the Abbey of San Galgano, or with the horrible influence he exerted over my son Francesco, we have always found ourselves tossed together, working not for the betterment of our souls and the greater glory of God, but for the enrichment of our mortal status and our personal treasuries.

By the time Lotario had become pope, Ugolino and I had already been working as silent partners through five different pontificates. We had watched as Holy Fathers came and went, and all the time we had done whatever was necessary to build a strong and lasting commercial empire. We, like most of the other successful businessmen, knew that success and longevity could only be obtained through a network of cooperation and alliances made below the table. As any wise fisherman will tell you, it is a durable net, with many individual and sturdy strands, that holds the biggest catch. Should one or two of those strands fail, a good net can easily be mended, and the fishing always continues. The popes know this, though they feign holiness and concern only for Heaven's reward. The emperors know this, as do the royals who sit upon their individual thrones of state. But each of these have their eyes upon one, solitary goal, their own vainglorious accomplishments and posterity. They are all blind to the real power behind the wealth and fortune of this world.

I had learned early of this awesome power as I grew to manhood with my uncle Giancarlo, even more so with my association with Enrico Dandolo, and always, with my secret association with Ugolino and the di Conti. Close did we hold the ear, and the purse, of Innocent III, and through Ugolino I was able to advance my business and to raise my status in the consortium of international trade. It was Ugolino who had convinced me to abandon my pledge to keep the spiritual fires of the Taurisi burning within the bowels of the Ark and to turn the hearts and minds of Curtun's best away from their ancient heritage and to seek prosperity in their new home under the guidance of their savior. Over a short span of time I was able to mold the best of the Chosen Ones into a small army of acolytes, well versed in the business dealings of my nefarious enterprises, fiercely loyal to me, and no other. They originally numbered twelve, and I called them my apostles.

I established each in a different banking center, providing them with new identities and proper Christian names. Each accepted the name of an apostle and the surname of di Stigliano. In all matters legal and illegal, they have represented me well, and have acted as lieutenants of my organization. Over the years, they have grown wealthy and powerful, yet all have remained loyal to me and to what I have built. The rest who have stayed behind in the confines of Tuscany have continued their loyalty to me and have proven to be of great benefit to my enterprise. The Chosen Ones have grown and prospered.

I have saved the children of Noah as I was commanded to do. Their lives have been enriched and their need to cling to the old ways has lessened with each passing day. How quickly and easily the horrors of the past are wiped away and supplanted with a new and promising life. The cloud of ancient teachings and traditions gives way to hope and new ideas; the present obliterates the past. All are now working for the success of Stigliano, for within her subterranean caverns and behind her mighty walls, her glistening tower and growing number of factories, the pride of the Taurisi people is ever strong.

And though I have done all in my power to protect my people, Tarquinia's hope and promise of the new Russelae has slowly died. As my life comes to an end, I mourn for her loss. Ah! Too late and ineffective are my tears. Her words still hang heavy upon my heart. Would that I had only opened my eyes sooner to my own dereliction of duty, I may have foreseen that my detour from the true path would forever close the book on those I was charged to protect and nourish. Voracity has driven me, and avarice has steered my course. And yet, for the Taurisi, the fair lady will say that I have done nothing.

Ugolino continued to advance within the church, and was most helpful, for a large fee, to secure many contracts for delivery of arms and supplies. We had expanded my counterfeiting operations, and with the blessing of Innocent and his nephew, and supplied the papal treasury with a steady supply of counterfeit coin used to pay the many bribes and ransoms the church had been forced to negotiate. Innocent had no moral conscience to forbid him from swindling an adversary by using counterfeit currency, and I had sufficiently buried my conscience and supplied our pope with all the debased coin he needed. My forges have never slept nor have my artisans been unemployed. They have turned out enormous quantities of counterfeit currency now being circulated at the fairs of Champagne and in markets throughout the trading world. When Innocent declared another Holy War upon Saladin in the Holy Land and the Muslims in Spain, both wars abroad returned great profits to Stigliano.

During these times I had to conduct my relationships with extreme caution for the animosity between the Pope and Emperor Henry had grown strong. Though I still had to show affection and loyalty to my emperor, for I had been bound by oath, I had also sworn loyalty to Innocent, as Banker to the Pope. Henry was supposedly my friend and the di Conti were my partners, and yet I had been secretly supplying arms to both. Further complicating my business, Innocent continued to battle with the Commune of Rome, many of whose members, including the Jews of that city, had been intricately involved in my Italian operation. Yet, Innocent was clever, and Fate had seemed to favor him, as Death had visited the young emperor, and a short time later, his murderous empress, and Innocent was able to gain custody of Henry's only son, Frederick II. The Pope had won by eliminating the imperial threat becoming Regent of Sicily, thus ensuring the security of the Italian Peninsula.

As I contemplate Henry's life and death, I must take pause and recognize the special bond that had been shared between my emperor and myself. Though I had grown to detest his father, Barbarossa, may he rot in the fires of Hell for all eternity, I do readily admit I had a close affinity to the young Henry, showing more loyalty to this royal than to any other. In youth, I daresay I would call him friend, and in business, so different was he to his father, for he was always true to his word. And yet I was not blindly loyal to him, for whenever I have found myself having to choose between two masters, I would always choose the one who benefited me the most. Such is business; such is the only way to success.

Still, I look upon his untimely death with a sense of melancholy, for though his governance over his dissatisfied subjects, particularly after he had ascended the imperial throne, had caused him to harden his persona, I do believe that basically he was a good and honorable man. He certainly did not deserve to end his reign in such an inglorious manner. Men may have said that the royal apple did not stray far from the imperial tree, using as example his constant struggle for power with the Holy Father. In fairness, I believe he fought to protect what he thought was his by right. Some may say he was a tyrannical and cruel ruler who caused much misery to his subjects in the south, and to that I somewhat agree. However, I would judge him guilty of neglect rather than of hostility. His empire was too great, and the problems that he had inherited from his father were too exhausting. It was impossible to hold so vast an empire together, impossible even for the great Caesars of antiquity.

And though these German emperors have managed to hold tight the reins of power over some of the northern Italian states for short intervals, it has always proven difficult to govern the brigands and thieves who control the southern shores of Italy. Sicily is a wild place, full of wild and devious cutthroats, and can never be governed from afar. Henry's initial indifference, together with the excessive cruelty of his German minions, had caused the Sicilians to revolt. Even the pleading of his wife, Constance, in favor of her people, had fallen on deaf ears, and the turmoil eventually forced Henry to travel south. Instead of being met by a loving and loyal wife, Henry was met with treachery, and the Empress had her husband locked within the thick walls of her castle. I have heard that Henry was being maneuvered into signing a peace agreement with the rebels, but no such document was ever signed because the young and virile Henry had unexpectantly died.

Was it malaria, as some say, that claimed his young life, or was it poison administered by his deceiving wife, as those in higher spheres have whispered? Only God knows the truth, for shortly after being convinced by Innocent to relinquish the burdens of regency over the four-year-old Frederick, Constance was called to stand judgement before Almighty God. Was that malaria or was that divine retribution? Who is to say? Innocent had become Regent of Sicily and southern Italy, and the son of Henry VI was given into the hands of his archenemy, Innocent III.

With the death of Henry, the world was again transformed. Gone was the counterbalance of power between pope and emperor. Gone was the need to choose sides. At this point in my life, the di Conti pope, Innocent III, had become the master of the world. I cannot underestimate how much of a positive effect the death of our emperor had upon my business, or upon the fate of the Commune of Siena. With his death, all sworn oaths of loyalty to the Emperor had ended. Siena had realized that her protections were now at an end, and so were the restrictions that were clearly spelled out in the oath. Her only chance for survival was to act quickly and to forcefully expand her territory and weaken her jealous neighbors.

She immediately secured the commune against any future tyranny of empire by declaring autonomous self-rule. A massive reorganization of the governing body was undertaken, and in the year of our Lord 1199, we hired our first podesta, a man from Lucca, to replace the consuls. I had secured a seat on the committee whose job it was to interview and hire the podesta. I knew full well the real concern for objectivity, for I had lived with and fought against all the leading families and power bases within the city. Yet I was not blind to the naivete that this system of governance would work on such a short-term and rotational basis. Though not in agreement with the original concept, I had made my desire known that I was to be a part of the selection process, making sure that the selected candidate would succeed in his assigned tasks but would not be so successful that he would be asked to repeat a second term. I planned to see how well the new government worked before inserting myself more prominently into the governing of the city.

There was much to be done and many challenges for a new government to meet, and of course, the old guard was still in place, behind the scenes. Many who had sat on the Council were from the older aristocratic families, but many had been replaced by newly established wealthy merchant-bankers. Included in our ranks were the Salimbeni, the Tolomei, the Buonsignori, the Malavolti, and the Cacciaconti. Though not of noble birth, we had come to be known as the grandi, and I had come to be viewed as their leader.

The new government struggled during the first year of its infancy. I had worked behind the scenes to make sure the foreign podesta was not too successful in his governance. So easy it was for me to mold the young man to my will. The furnaces of Voltuma had never cooled, as a steady stream of counterfeit coin flowed from my factories to the pockets and purses of men and women in every empire and kingdom. Legitimate coin was likewise minted for the commune under much stricter guidelines and security. The Papal Banker was kept very busy. Business was very good.

By the end of that first term, I had convinced the Council to seek a native son to fill the position of podesta, for of course, only a Sienesi could effectively govern the Sienese. The following year, 1200, the Council elected the son of one of my friends and partners, Filippo d'Orlando Malavolti, who had proven to be most accepting of my guidance and direction. Unfortunately, he lacked the skills necessary to lead the wealthiest state in Tuscany. His ineptitude, particularly in handling the Council, created problems that would continue for many years, and which pitted the grandi against the popolo in a most destructive way. His term failed miserably, and it caused the Council to enact a law prohibiting any such future power to be placed in the hands of a native son.

My plans to control the Council had failed, and my desire to openly run the government had cooled. A strong leader was again brought in from the outside just as Siena was finding herself being threatened once again by its neighbors. In order to counter the threat, the Commune began a massive campaign to increase her boundaries. Within the year Montipulciano and Montalcino were subjugated to Siena. I had turned my attention back to what I had done best. My factories were busy again supplying the commune with armaments, and all the great lords, the Cacciaconti, the Ardengheschi, and even Aldobrandeschi were subjugated. Through peace treaties, they were all forced to pay tribute annually to the City of the Virgin.

It was at this time that Perugia, ever aggressive toward her neighbors to the west, had waged war with Assisi, which ultimately led to young Francisco being captured in battle and held as a prisoner of war. He remained in prison for close to a year before being ransomed for a large sum of money. Pietro had originally refused to pay the ransom, which had resulted in Francesco's extended imprisonment and had almost cost the boy his life. But for young Paolo's pleading and my stepping up with the ransom, the entire sum of which was paid in counterfeit coin and delivered by Paolo, young Francesco would have died in that Perugian dungeon. This was not the first, nor the last time that Pietro had neglected his duties as a father, nor was it the first or last time that Francesco had tested the limits of a son.

XXVI

The Sons of The Father

Permit me, Dear Lord, to find the courage to speak of my adult sons, for of the host of individuals against whom I have sinned, I dare say that I have sinned most grievously against my own flesh and blood. Four sons were given to me by my wife, Anna Soarzi. Two have survived: Paolo and Matteo, and two are no longer on this earth. The youngest, Giuseppe had been murdered by the eldest, Vannozzo. Of them, I will say no more. Of the two who have survived, the eldest, Paolo, though I have always held a greater love for him than any of the others, has turned his back on me in my darkest and final hours. Matteo has always remained loyal to me and has worked with me in all my endeavors, learning the trade and becoming the businessman I had always hoped for each of my sons. He has learned the compromises one must make in order to be successful and accepts without questioning, the price for such success. To him will be awarded the full benefits associated with wealth and power.

Paolo, my second son, and the one who is dearest in my heart, had given me his devotion until he was old and wise enough to see that I had become a lost soul. He had followed me down many paths, always trying to sway me toward a better place, never giving up hope that someday I would come to my senses and seek the true path out of the darkness. I believe in my heart that he still holds that hope and still prays for my salvation. Would that I could see his face once again and let him hear my confession, to see that I have found the path out of my misery. Oh, if I could only hold him once again and tell him that I love him and that I am sorry for all that I have done!

I cannot think of Paolo without thinking of Giovanni, the son given to me by Dona Pica, he who has come to be called Francesco. Paolo and Francesco had grown up together and had become inseparable. Nothing on the earth save death itself could part them, and thus it is that only one remains. I lament over the loss of Paolo's affection, yet I grieve at the death of Giovanni. Too many I have given much, and yet to these, whom I owe so much, I have given so little. One was born out of false love, and one was born out of lustful sin. One has forever been protecting all that is good and battling against the evils of this world, and the other being called into God's service to challenge His mighty church in his own humble way. What reward have they received for their service and devotion? One has gained the enmity of God's shepherd on Earth, and the other, driven to live in squalor and denied the chance to fulfill his holy charge. Both were equally deserving of my love and attention, and yet both were deprived of that which was needed most.

Forgive me, my sons, for a lifetime of hurt and neglect. You were brought into this world in spite of my weaknesses and blessed by the Holy Spirit with the strength and sacred purpose to fulfil God's mission of peace for the salvation of Man. Both of you had found the strength that I had lacked to avoid Satan's temptations, and to stay your courses on the true paths toward salvation.

Paolo, my dearest son, how I have disappointed thee? You have become, as I was to my father, a distant stranger. You have shunned all the trappings that I was more than willing to lay before your feet. My father had offered me his wisdom, his strength, his integrity, and his love, all of which I had so foolishly pushed aside, for they had become obstacles upon the wicked path that I had chosen to follow. Heaven had granted you the wisdom to pick up all my father's offerings that I had cast aside so blindly. I chose to chart my own course toward riches, fame and glory, and you chose to steer clear of my destructive wake. Who now is the richer? Who now is the better man? I am but an empty husk, weighed down with golden chains and I rot from within. I have lived a much longer life and have accomplished more than most men. I have traveled the world and have seen everything, yet I have done so with blinded eyes.

My accomplishments mean nothing to me now as I approach my final hours. They will mean less than nothing as I stand before my God and await His final judgement. I beg thee to forgive this old fool. You were wise to see that power and glory must come at a heavy price. My only wish is that I may see you one more time before I pass from this earth and hear your spoken words. I pray that you ease my suffering and say that you know me for who I am, that you love me in spite of my inability to show you love, and that you forgive me.

Giovanni, my son, I beg thee to hear my prayers. Francesco, forgive me for forcing you to live a lie, and for speaking so little with you when you were a young child accompanying us on our business trips. How I made every effort to avoid you, not because I had lacked affection for you, but because your very presence always brought forth the shame and the guilt that I had stored within my heart. Your beauty and your goodness were a constant reminder of the qualities I had destroyed in your dear mother and a reminder of the incurable hurt that I had brought unto her. It was not your fault, beloved son, but ours alone to bear. Forgive me for holding my tongue when you were made to perform for the Queen and her ladies at Ombrone, or when Pietro raised his fist to you or treated you badly. I still cannot understand why I lacked the courage to end the folly we suffered for so many years. Quite possibly it was the guilt for what I had done, and not an absence of love for you, the victim of my actions.

As for Pietro, I must accept the fact that he had always known you were my son. How could he not? You are a mirror image of your brother, who is a mirror image of myself as a youth. I can only believe that Pietro kept up the charade because it benefited him in all ways. Pietro was my friend, though I treated him poorly, and he for many years showed great loyalty to me, or rather to my position. But he was no fool. How it must have irked him to hear the petty gossip of the ladies of the French court, or to be forced to look upon your sweet face and see the image of his friend, the one who hurt him most deeply, staring back at him. For too long we all hid behind our masks and played out our parts in this cruel tragedy. Perhaps you in your heavenly seat can see clearer than this seer's son. Perhaps you know in your saintly state that which I never had the courage to tell you, that I did love you, and I did set my hand to provide for you all that you had needed in this life. Has God Almighty whispered in your ear the reason for such torment of his devoted servants? Is there any good to come from our struggles?

Know that, throughout your life, I was always in the background, standing at the ready to lend support for everything you did. Paolo, your devoted brother, would fiercely defend and protect you, as he did for me even as a young child, and though he would never take from me any help for himself, he would, out of necessity, accept any aid that would bring comfort to you. Covertly I did offer my services to you as you tried to find your way in the world, always hoping that you would succeed in your mission. I had done all that I was allowed to do to aid our dear Paolo in his quest to serve and to protect you. And yet I failed you when it was most important.

I did not see, and therefore did not protect you from the evils perpetrated by my partner, Ugolino. For all my shortfalls, I beg your forgiveness. You were an incredible individual, a true gift from God. Though you were born out of sin and had to endure the hardships of a bastard son, you were able to raise yourself to be the confessor of popes and kings and sultans. Your courage was only strengthened by your simplicity and your naivete, and through it all, you have become a beacon whose blinding light has shown the wickedness of the world in all its ugliness. Your goodness continues to shame me, for I am the greatest sinner, and not worthy of your forgiveness. Yet, it is your forgiveness I seek, as well as your posthumous understanding of my motives and my actions.

I devoted little time to you, dear Paolo, when you were a child. I was too busy nurturing my business. Of that, I have already written. Little care did I have for the most important people in my life. I was blind to those things that should have been most important for the betterment of my soul. I concentrated more on those things that were most beneficial to my purse. Such a fool, and in spite of the pleading to the contrary of Nikos, I was more than willing to relinquish my fatherly duties to him. Although, I must confess to you, my dear son, that I did you a greater service, for Nikos has always amazed me in his capacity to love and to nourish. He was more a father to you than ever I could be.

Was it not he who trained you how to defend yourself against your tormentor who, through my own blindness, had nearly caused your premature death? Was it not Nikos who gave you your first blade and taught you to wield it with such deadly accuracy? Was it not he who taught you to love and respect your fellow man, and to stay true to the path of righteousness? It was Nikos who had always found a way to bring us closer together, and it was always to Nikos you would run, seeking solace when I would inevitably disappoint you. What better gift could I have given you than to remove myself from your upbringing? My intent was never to harm you, but to keep you safe from those demons that had constantly plagued me. Know that I have always held you in the highest regard, even though I showed you little affection. At that time, it was completely beyond my capabilities. I have always harbored great pride in all that you have done for yourself and for others. You have lived your life in complete opposition to mine, and yet you have accumulated a greater treasure of love and happiness than ever I could have hoped to buy with my stockpile of gold.

How well I remember that day when you saved me in the wood near Assisi? How brave and fearless was my young Leoncello, how protective and selfless? It amazes me to this day that one so young could muster such courage, and charge with wild fury and conviction into a maelstrom, totally unconcerned for your own safety. I question not your motives, for I know that you did it out of love and concern for me, and for that I am eternally grateful. It amazes me still to look back upon that day when I was restored to my senses and I beheld you cradling your brother, Giovanni. You showed such love and compassion and did not hesitate to show me how love and gentleness was supposed to be between family. How simply you had shown me, that in the one moment you could face Hell's fury and plunge your dagger into the heart of a murderous brigand without remorse, and in the next, with those same young hands, you could cradle and soothe a crying babe with loving caresses. How utterly amazing you were to me.

And yet, I made no attempt to learn from my young son the art of connecting so totally with another human being. It is so apparent to me now that we are all born with the wisdom derived from the Tree of Knowledge, and in our infant innocence we are more open to that which comes natural to us. It is only as we age that we forget the knowledge and bury our innocence and our willingness to connect with others. For me, there had been too many horrors at too early an age that caused me to bury that knowledge and trust into the deepest recesses of my soul. In truth, I had nothing to give, though I tried in my own way to make up for my shortfall.

You were with me on many of my trading missions for I had wanted you to become like me. I was always impressed with your abilities to learn our trade, and I had felt it only natural you would one day become my partner and successor. You hurt me deeply when you matured and saw me for who I was. Deeper was the hurt that you did not like what you saw, and that you chose to separate yourself from me and all that I had created. I cannot blame you now, but as I watched you slowly pulling away, I had grown jealous of the relationship you had forged with your brother, Giovanni. Your shared spirit had grown faster than your physical bodies, and it was not long before you found a new purpose to replace your apprenticeship with me.

Whether by personal choice or by Divine intervention, you and Giovanni had become inseparable. Though there were many years between you and your brother, you never left his side, always there to protect him from danger. He would follow you wherever you led, and he spoke incessantly about everything under the sun. Even when we joked about how Francesco could talk the birds out of the trees or tame the wildest of beasts with his stories, you always found the need to defend him. You were always so patient with him, even though he was so jovial and mischievous, for he would always get you two into trouble. You still found the time to watch over the boy, even though I demanded much of you as my apprentice.

Regrettably, I chose to believe in those early years that you were unaware that Giovanni was your half-brother, and yet I remember so clearly the quizzical look upon your face when you first looked at the baby in your arms, and then stared directly into my guilty eyes. Was I the only one blind to the obvious on that day? And yet, my sin did not repel you but only strengthened your resolve and your love and affection for your brother. You must have sensed even then that Francesco's life would be difficult. I remember how thrilled you were when Pietro allowed Francesco to accompany us to Champagne. You never tired of his questions. You always encouraged him to be himself, and you were always there to console him when Pietro had become overbearing, as oft times he would do. Believe me that it was most difficult for me to hold my tongue when he was intentionally cruel to the boy, but a father, even a false one, does have a right to discipline his son, and as long as I had relinquished the title of father and all rights that come with the title, I had been forced to remain silent.

You had no such restriction on you, and though you did not openly defy Pietro, nor did you ever entice Giovanni to stand against him. You were always able to divert Pietro's anger away from his son. It is to your own credit that Pietro always held you in high regard. In fact, he cared for you more than he cared for Francesco, and he always commented to me on how fine a boy you were. It was his trust in you that enabled you, and to some small degree, me, to provide your brother with the support and guidance that he so desperately needed as he searched for his own path.

Had I only been stronger or more aware of the evil that lurked close by, when Pietro sent Giovanni to San Galgano to be educated by the Cistercian monks. Lucius III had already canonized Galgano, elevating him to sainthood before I had even completed the small chapel at Montesiepi that holds his holy remains. Clement then wasted no time in capitalizing on the good name and works of the Saint from Montesiepi. I was called upon to finance the building of a magnificent church to honor the saint and his holy deeds. He had envisioned the church and the abbey to be a great center of learning and devotion to rival the great Sant'Antimo, and he enlisted the help of Bernard of Clairveaux's Cistercian monks to build and to reside in the abbey. Of course, the funds generated from this new holy center would flow directly back into the papal coffers, and he set his nephew Lotario to oversee the entire operation.

Lotario brought in Ugolino to oversee the governance of the complex. I was expected to contribute the lion's share of the funds needed to build, for which I did receive a percentage of the profits. Forgive me, Brother Galgano, for I had not set myself to capitalize upon your name and deeds, but rather only to be recompensed for my investment in the project. We had done this all when my partnership with the di Contis was growing strong. It was just another avenue to make a profit.

By the time Giovanni was old enough to be schooled, the monks had established a new chapter house that was fully sanctioned by the Pope, himself. As I had been heavily involved with the building of this center, I convinced Pietro to send Francesco to these Cistercian monks for a formal education. This order was renowned for their knowledge of medicine and law, especially Roman law, which in our business has been most helpful when dealing with the curia and the Roman institutions. Pietro accepted my advice, having decided that it would be most beneficial to him to have Francesco educated under the watchful eyes of the di Conti. Little did I know how low and despicable the di Conti would turn out to be, but in those earlier times my eyes were still clouded by the success and resourcefulness of my partners, and I could not see the poison that had been bubbling beneath their fair appearances.

I did not heed your warnings, dear Paolo, nor listen to your accusation of the misery being suffered by your brother. God in Heaven! How can you allow such things to happen to ones so innocent and so young—and by one of your own servants? How unjust is it that such vile devils can prevail behind a mask so fair? Are the sins of the father doomed to be repeated by the son? Did Francesco ever have a chance to reclaim his stolen innocence? Verily, I believe he had tried, and yet we now know he was never quite the same after he was finally free of that place.

No distance is too great to separate us from the evil that torments us, and so it was that Francesco could never free himself from the influence of his tormentor. I know too well the damage to my soul that I had suffered, and I also bore witness to the damage that the young Ugolino had suffered at the hands of that demon Bernardo. Only Death could save us, and the satisfaction to see while we lived that justice had been served. What comfort was there for Francesco? Where is his justice? His demon still lives and breathes and tends his holy flock—a wolf in sheep's vestments? It is no wonder the young man had cast away all of the trappings in this world and had sought the protective embrace of the Lord.

Francesco had endured his education for just over two years when the mysterious death of Celestine had elevated Lotario to pope. The scoundrel had become Innocent III. Whether it was God's will or Lotario's own purpose and pride, Innocent was determined to set aright all the wrongs of the world. Through edicts and excommunications, with pen and with sword, no sovereign was left untouched by this most powerful man. His Holy Crusade had been diverted through mishap and greed, especially on the part of the merchants of Venice, which had led to the sacking of Rome's greatest adversary, Constantinople. Of this Holy Crusade, much has been written, and men will speak of such brave, and such cowardly deeds, of noble causes and petty jealousies, and of heralded courage and unsurpassed greed. I leave such writings to the critics and the historians.

For your edification, dear Paolo, I wish to record here that the culmination of Innocent's pontificate, the Holy Crusade of 1203, which he launched against the Muslims in the Holy Land, was his greatest disappointment. Though the arrow never hit its mark, the unintended consequences of the diversion enabled the crusaders to establish the Latin Empire in Constantinople, reopen trading routes, and secure for the Republic of Venice the title of Sovereign of the Seven Seas. Our commercial consortium, bankers and corsairi alike, owe a tremendous debt of gratitude to those brave crusaders who risked their lives to keep the arteries of trade flowing. Songs will be sung of the valiant Enrico Dandolo, Doge of Venice, Admiral of God's Fleet, one hundred years old and totally blind, who led his forces over the great walls of the Eastern Capitol.

Much had happened in the world during Innocent's papacy, and my partnerships with the di Conti flourished. Innocent eventually made Ugolino Bishop of Ostia, and then appointed Fra Vernaccio to oversee the abbey. But Ugolino, as I was to learn much later, never took his eye off his precious Francesco, nor did he abandon his desire to possess the young boy's mind and body. Pietro sent for Francesco after two years of education at San Galgano, finding him of greater value on his business trips. It was during this time, with my eyes blinded by greed, that I lost my two sons. The truth of the matter is that I had abandoned them. Francesco had been lost in his own world of spiritual and mental agony, and you, dear Paolo, had forsaken the life that had been offered to you, and had chosen to travel with your brother and to protect him at all costs.

Through some of those years you persisted, unsuccessfully, to steer him from his disastrous path of self-destruction, yet, in the end, I believe you simply resolved to follow him. Francesco, even at a very young age, had always had the ability to charm, to entertain, to lead, and to convince others to follow. That was why Pietro brought him along on our business trips. Francesco was an asset for Pietro to use, whether he entertained with his lute or told some fantastic story or sang the love songs of the wandering troubadours. Whenever Francesco accompanied Pietro to court, increased sales were guaranteed. He was the darling of all the ladies, and the young men flocked to his lead. He was even crowned Lord of the Feast in the Compagnia dei Tripudianti.

Yet behind that mask of frivolity cried a deeply disturbed young man. I need not tell you this, Paolo, for you were always there to see this firsthand. You were always there to help him. Know this, that Francesco's anguish was evident to most who knew him, even to me, his own, true father. Heavy is my burden that forces me to confess my complicity in my own son's agony. Grateful am I that you were there to protect him. Even when the charade was finally ended, that fateful day of the trial that would forever sever the ties between Pietro and your brother, and forever poison the relationship between Pietro and myself, you stood by Giovanni's side and comforted him. After he had renounced Pietro in front of the Bishop of Assisi, telling the entire town that Pietro was not his father, you stood by him, and after he had stripped himself naked and had laid all of his worldly belongings at Pietro's feet, relinquishing all familial claims, you stood by him. And even after he had been sheltered by the Bishop and later by Ugolino, you did not abandon your brother. It was you who had freed him from the clutches of the demon and brought him to the safety of my father's farm in Cortona.

Little did you know that I had to pay a large ransom to the Bishop to secure Giovanni's release into your custody. This I did most secretively so as not to damage my relationship with the di Conti and their friends. It was with Nikos' help that I was able to provide the funds needed for you to support your brother during his troubling times. So often I had to create diversions that would turn Ugolino's attention from searching for the boy, for as strange as it may seem, his obsession was very powerful and most unseemly and unnatural. I regret that I did not possess the courage to snuff the life from that venomous snake, for my murderous deed would have saved the agony of my son and prevented all the evil that has been hatched from his wicked heart.

But Ugolino was a shrewd and patient man and knowing that the object of his affection had been closely guarded by my son, he chose to wait for the right moment to reclaim that which he considered to be his own. I should have been able to see that there was more to his obsession than mere physical attraction. Had my eyes been opened to the truth, I would have known that Ugolino had longed to possess Francesco's soul. What evil spell had been cast upon the two to bind them so tightly, only Satan knows. The reason for this to happen to such a gentle and loving youth is for only God to know. The spell was strong, and its poison had eaten away at each of them for the remainder of their lives.

My Francesco would suffer, both physically and mentally, for the short time he walked amongst us, and Ugolino still rots upon the Throne of Saint Peter, continuing to deteriorate from the acid of guilt and fear of God's final judgement. The cost of your holy plan, Lord, was too high, and you placed too heavy a burden upon the shoulders of one so young and fragile. Was the course upon which we imperfect mortals sail altered significantly by the pain and suffering of my son? Forgive me for questioning Thy wisdom, and forgive this old man for grieving, too late, for his lost son.

Little did you know the efforts I had to make to mend the relationships that had been shattered because of that trial. Within a year, I had arranged to bring you out of hiding and buy you admittance to Assisi, though far from a normal life would the two of you live. Too proud were you to come to me for support, and too stubborn were you to accept my help when I offered it through Nikos. Instead, you stuck by your brother as he gave away all that came to him, even when he dressed himself in the rags of the beggar and leper. You followed him when he went from house to house, village to village, begging for brick and mortar in order to restore the small chapels that I had arranged to transfer unto his conservatorship.

Did you know that I wept when I heard from Nikos of your anguish and agony over Giovanni's apparent loss of mind and senses when he began to experience Heavenly visitations in the chapel of San Damiano? You should have known that such visions and visitations are not uncommon for the children of Noah, and the curse of the pec-ii is upon you, as well as your brother. The sight is such a powerful tool, and yet it can be so easily misapplied or misunderstood. Visions come to us in riddles and are never easy to understand. Never should we question that Francesco had heard the word of God; however, I believe that he mistook the meaning of God's command to "go and restore my house, which you see, is in ruins." We, who have dealt in the spirit world, know that God is not interested in the physical world, but the true meaning of his command was that Francesco shine a beacon upon the evils of the Holy Church, and show the world that the true wealth of humanity is measured in love and kindness to each other while we live upon this earth. His task was arduous and seemingly impossible, and yet, here I sit, Master of the World of Finance, confessing my sins for all to see, and begging forgiveness from those whom I have wronged. Through the life and death of my son Francesco, the Seer's eyes are finally opened.

Bless you, Paolo, for keeping Francesco safe, and helping him to achieve the task that was set for him by the Holy Spirit. I marvel at your steadfastness and I honor your loyalty and your courage to never abandon your brother, even though you faced the wrath of the most powerful men in this world. Certainly, you have risked death from the many who would see all that your brother had stood for obliterated from this earth. I am shamed by your humility and your goodness, for unlike your father, you have held yourself protectively in the background, and have allowed your brother to shine in God's Holy Light. You held him up when he needed your strength and you gave him love when he needed that most. I wish we could have kept him safe, together you and I, here in Siena. Oh, but the world would be a worse place for not having his guiding light to shine upon it. Happy was I when you finally brought my son to Siena so that I might see you both again, and yet utterly disappointed was I to learn that our physicians could not remedy his ailments. It grieved me deeply to hear he had found no comfort at the farm in Cortona, and that he had passed from this earth in the same manner as my dear brother Galgano, stripped of his worldly possessions and laid naked upon the earth, wrapped in the loving arms of those most dear to him. I continue to grieve, for I was not there to witness the passing of my son nor to comfort you in your terrible loss.

Since your brother's death, we have done much to see that Francesco's life and his mission is truly honored, that his spirit lives on to carry the guiding light that was given to him by the Holy Spirit, and that his tortured soul has finally found peace in the land of his forefathers. We have battled His Holiness Gregory IX, the treacherous Ugolino di Conti, for your brother's remains to be interred in the chapel in the Church of San Francesco, which I have commissioned to be built on my land in Cortona. It is only fitting that a descendent of Crano should be brought to his ancestral home. Together we must fight to protect his good name and his remains. Although I am most grateful to His Holiness for recently elevating our dear son and brother to sainthood, I am fearful that his obsession has never abated and that his guilt will cause him to stop at nothing to gain complete possession of everything Francesco had tried to do. I beseech you, Paolo, to come to Stigliano and take from these aged shoulders the burden of protecting your brother in death, as you had done in life, from those who would profit on his memory and his good name. I leave behind all my worldly possessions and hope that you will use whatever is needed to accomplish this. Give as you see fit to give, just as your brother gave all that he had to give.

Our dear Francesco's accomplishments are many and his deeds and his love and his wisdom will be sung by millions until the end of time. And yet your love and your support, given to your brother most freely and without need or desire for recompense, will remain obscured to all but a few. Know that I appreciate all that you have done and be assured of my love and admiration.

XXVII

The Final Chapter

I have no more to give, Nikos. My time is over, and though I have highlighted the major events in my life, there were so many more ways in which I chose to sin. My sins are too many to list and we have not enough parchment to contain them all. Heavy and dark are those sins, as black as the ink that sits upon the vellum, and it has been too painful to bring forth all such frailties. Yet I have done so with honesty and hope that my spirit may be cleansed, and this heavy weight might be lessened before I make my final journey to stand before God. I fear God, Nikos. I fear his vengeance. I do not want to die—not before I try to make things right. Yet die I must. I fear my final visitation.

The Holy Spirit has given me seven days to confess my sins, and lo, I see that seven has not been enough. No more spiritual guidance shall help me. I am doomed. Forgive me, dearest Nikos, for putting you through my agony. I shall make my last journey, knowing that you sit here beside me. Your love and your loyalty have always kept me anchored in this world and you have nourished my spirit even when I chose to starve it.

Continue to record all I have to say, loving scribe, until I have no more life in me. Pray for my soul, Nikos, and tell my sons that I died loving you all. All that remains, I leave to the three of you to do whatever you wish. Do not do as I have done. But then, you never did. Watch over our sons, for they are yours as much as they are mine. Gather up these writings—my true confession—and let them read of my life and my death. Ask them to pray for me.

Hold me as I sleep, brother.

I, Nikos Koniates, most faithful and loving servant, partner, and friend of the great Giovanni Bartolomeo Pecci da Cortona, will most humbly and with great honor transcribe from his sweet but parched lips his final words and his thoughts, for as long as he still has breath and voice. It is my master's wish to complete this confession before he is taken from this earth, and to leave this document to his eldest surviving son, Paolo, in the hopes that with revelation and understanding might come forgiveness and salvation. I have sent for you, dear Paolo, with the hope that you may return before this final chapter is closed, and that you might, upon reading this journal, come to know the one who has always been your loving father, and who lives and breathes with such labor and pain, only to chance hearing your voice and seeing your face one more time, and to tell you, himself, how true is his love for you. I have prayed to the Queen of Heaven, and all the angels and saints, that you arrive in time. But time has run out.

Giovanni rests, conserving what little energy he has left, awaiting his final journey. But he has finished, as best he could, the task that was given to him. As promised, I will record his final words and complete his obituary.

How long must I endure this? My body and my soul are being torn asunder, and with each nightly visitation, Satan has claimed another piece of my soul. I am but a shell of a man. Like the withered and dried-up husk that clings stubbornly to the vine when winter's frozen wind exerts its mighty force, and yet persuades it not. I have no more to give.

I still live. I still breathe. Though arms and legs have failed me in their use, my dying spirit yet has hope enough to give me what little strength is left to me, so that I may complete this task that God set for me, and through which, the Holy Spirit has been my guide. My hands are useless, but my protectors have spared my tongue. Fortuna has also given me my companion, Nikos. Dear Nikos, you who have given to me your undying love and affection since early youth. You have stood by me unfailingly through the sunniest days of my life as well as through my darkest nights. Upon this final journey of my life, dear Nikos, you are carrying me within your loving arms and have taken up my quill for me. You shall be my voice for those who may read this. From you, I have hidden nothing, for you have been with me always and you know, all too well, my strengths and my weaknesses. I have seen you sit, with tender and loving eyes, with arms wrapped about my feet, as I sailed upon the spectral seas and heard the thoughts of angels and demons. Lift then my quill, my beloved Nikos, and mark upon the vellum my final words and confession.

My time upon the earth is at an end. The Holy Spirit has revealed the path upon which I must travel when I shed this fragile shell. I see it clearly now. The battle for my immortal soul is almost over here. I begin my trial of purification in Purgatory, knowing that, for as long as it may take, my soul will finally be cleansed of the poison that has consumed every morsel of goodness I may have been gifted at birth.

See there, Nikos, by the fire. My guide has come to escort my soul. Pray that my eyes do not deceive me. It is my Father, or rather, the shade of my Father. Look! See how sorrowful he appears. Why does he weep so? Father, I am here! See, it is I, Giovanni. What troubles you so? Have you come to bear me upon your shoulders like you did when I was a boy? Oh, how I loved you as I wrapped my arms around your strong neck and together, we explored everything you so patiently had to show me. Are you not pleased to see me again? Are you to share more guidance with me? I listened to you, Father. Let me tell you now, what I was never able to tell you whilst you walked upon this earth. Pity me in my hour of death and hear how truly sorry I am that I never was given the chance to hear your dying words or to tell you how much I loved and respected you. You left me before I had the chance to open myself to you, before I had the chance to tell you that you were right. You were always right. I was too blind to see. The seer's son could never see.

Why do you stare at me so? Know that I have agonized over these many years for not being at your side when you joined with the shades of your ancestors. I was not there to hear your final words of warning, and yet, those sacred words that you so entrusted to my dear cousin were only to fall upon deafened ears and a heart of stone. Your warnings were not enough to open my eyes or to melt the ice that had shrouded my spirit. I heeded your warnings, not. I have failed you, Father, as I have failed my people. I have failed all those whom I tried to love. If only I could travel back to my earliest days, and speak to the innocent young Giovanni, and somehow change his worldly path. If only such counsel had moved that boy onto a poorer and more obscure path, had robbed him of the wealth and power he would accumulate at the cost of others. How many innocent lives would have been spared? How many souls would have remained in this world? I pray thee, gentle spirit, do not look upon me with such disdain.

Nikos! Save me from this horrid sight. Chase this demon from my hearth.

Wait, spirit. Do not leave me. Father! Come back!

Lo, who are these shades who accompany you? Oh! Merciful God. I see the agony that you have chosen to foist upon me. I see you, Giancarlo, and you, Sebastiano. Tarquin and sweet Tarquinia, and gentle Salvatore. Why do you stare at me thus? The host of shades who stand around you, I know them all, and have oft named them friend and brother in times past. And Mother?

What grieves thee? Have I been such a disappointment to all of you that you would stare at me so? Why do you point at me and judge me so harshly? I did what I could! Nay, I did more than most men would! I have paid for my sins with an extended life upon this wicked world. Such prolonged agony I have been forced to endure. My torment has always been the gift to see what could happen and to be powerless to affect any change, to relive every misstep I have taken along the paths I have chosen for myself. Your judgement, as harsh as it may be, is a tiny drop of water compared to the deluge of wrath that awaits me in the Courts of God's Kingdom.

Why does this spectral host grow more numerous? Countless are its numbers. Are these all the souls who, through my stubborn blindness and greed, have been brought to ruin? Merciful Lord, have I no sympathetic spirits to guide me through my purgation? Holy Father, Blessed Alexander, I see thee in the corner. You who have always loved and trusted in me, will you not let me hold onto your velvet robe whilst you plead my case before thy Master? Or you, Blessed Galgano, friend and brother! You were always my protector. Take up thy sacred sword and help me pass through the army of wicked demons that await my tortured soul. Ah, my sweet Genevieve, and poor Anna, always so miserable. Why do you weep so? And, ah, my Dona Pica, you who have brought such goodness into the world. I did what I could to protect our son. I beg you to release me from your curse. Will not any of you stand by me to lessen my burden?

Nikos, Nikos, the fire fades! The shadows are melting away. Wait! Wait!

Will none reach out to help this sinner? I am alone. The Holy Spirit has abandoned me. I am alone. Where is Paolo? Where is my son? Look! A spark remains. The embers glow. They hiss and crack and spit at me. They tell me what to expect. I see a face in the dark. I know that face. It is mine! Nay, it is not my ghost. It is Francesco! Blessed Francesco. I see thee. Have you come to guide me? Gentle Francesco, I am not ready to go. I must see Paolo. Where is Paolo? Paolo, why have you not come?

I can wait no longer. My fate calls me. Nikos take my love and share it with my sons for I have no need of it in the next world. Francesco reaches out to me. I feel the waters of Devine reckoning enveloping me. I am being swept away. Reach, Francesco! Further! I cannot reach your hand. Cast me your rope.

Francesco! Save me! The waters are dark and cold. I am drowning. My life is floating away. Take my hand. Where are you?

Ah! I am too weak, and your grasp is too strong. Loosen your grip, my son, you are hurting me!..............Vannozzo?

Ω

These are the final words of Giovanni Bartolomeo Pecci da Cortona, also called Sandak, Last Pec-ii of the Taurisi.

May his soul find peace, Amen.

Author's Notes & Acknowledgments

Thank you for sharing this story with me. This is the first in a series of novels concerning the ancient line of Pecci whose earliest histories I have traced to twelfth century Tuscany. This is a historic fantasy novel. Although many of the people, places, and events mentioned in this story have a historic basis, the memoir is being dictated by a fictitious person. The views of the main character and his interaction with actual historic figures is pure fiction. Even though Giovanni has told his story almost eight hundred years ago, it is as if he has journeyed through the mists of time to make his confession directly to me.

The story of Giovanni had grown out of an earlier idea for a book about Giovanni's son Paolo. As I started to write that story, I began to develop the character of Giovanni, more as a basis for establishing the ancient lineage of Paolo. As I expanded on what was supposed to be a minor part of Paolo's story, I began to realize that Giovanni's story was becoming more compelling and needed to stand on its own. Thus, *Confessions of A Corsair* was born.

The second novel in the Pecci Chronicles series, titled *Of Sinners and Saints,* will chronicle the lives of Paolo and his half brother Francesco. It is my intention to produce a series of books dealing with the generations of Pecci members who, since the twelfth century, have helped to govern both church and state, and who have made important contributions right up to the twentieth century, culminating with the reign of the Pecci pope, Leo XIII.

Giovanni's story has always been with me, though it had been buried deep within my sub-consciousness. The seeds of his story began to germinate about twenty-five years ago. Perhaps, as it had been foretold by the lady Tarquinia, new shoots from a long-dormant vine would someday spring forth and the story of the Taurisi would be told. That awakening took place when I was forty years old.

I had been having some health issues which, it had been determined, were the result of stress. Choosing holistic remedies over drugs, I threw myself back into painting (such a wonderful therapy) and also began to meditate. Through the combination of art and meditation I learned to get in touch with my inner self. I sought self-awareness through vision and journeying. Over many months I found my inner voice and saw drastic changes in my life.

I listened to the ancient voices within me as I meditated, and my dreams were shrouded in the mists of ancient times and faraway places – sometimes so vivid and so real as to stay with me for weeks at a time. My painting style began to change as I tried to convey my dreams and visions onto the canvas. Italian dreamscapes with recurring themes – starry skies, cypress trees, dark foreboding woods, olive groves and vineyards, ancient stone buildings – began to replace the still- life which I had been painting. Though I had never been to Italy, nor ever had a desire to travel there, I was morphing into an Italian – and an ancient one at that!

I began to learn the language, began reading any book I could find on Italy, embracing an entire cultural shift. Finally, I convinced my wife to travel with me to the place that was calling to me. On our first trip we ended in Siena. I don't know why I chose Siena, but when we arrived there, I instantly felt that I was home. Every place was familiar to me and I marvel at that familiarity with every return trip. With over a dozen trips back, we have never ended our journey of re-discovery.

As we began our travels, I began my own personal journey, tracing the Pecci line back into history. From the histories of Pope Leo XIII, my research took me from the small town of Carpineto-Romano south of Rome, back to Florence and Siena of the sixteenth century. From there I delved deeper into Siena and the century of the Black Plague, and beyond that to the thirteenth and twelfth century of the Crusades. I finally was drawn to twelfth century Cortona where I happened upon a reference to a wealthy merchant banker by the name of Paolo Pecci. It is this Paolo, I strongly believe, who has held his lantern high to illuminate my path back in time. It is Paolo who I have connected with, and it is Paolo who is calling to me to tell this story.

I have researched for more than ten years, examining texts and original documents, pouring over old maps and drawings, and consuming a myriad of books, both fiction and non-fiction. For this series I owe a great deal to the works of Brother William Kieefer, S.M. and Rev. James J. McGovern, D.D. concerning the history of Pope Leo XIII, to Rupert Matthews, *The Popes,* Charles Eliot Norton's *Historical Studies of Church-Building in the Middle Ages,* Paul Lacroix's *Manners, Customs, and Dress During the Middle Ages and During the Renaissance Period,* Schevill's *Siena the History of a Mediaeval Commune,* Douglas' *A History of Siena,* Giovanni Antonio Pecci's many volumes on the history of Siena, the Commune, and the Novesci rule, Jonathan Phillips book T*he Fourth Crusade and the Sack of Constantinople*, and Thomas F. Madden's *Enrico Dandolo & the Rise of Venice.* I would also like to thank Pope Pius II, whose *Commentaries* has lent a medieval voice and point of view to Giovanni, and to my story. I also wish to acknowledge a great debt to Andrea Borracelli, current owner of Poggiarello Stigliano, who has, over many years, provided me with source material and incredible stories of the history of the Pecci Castle. Giovanni may be a fictitious character but the castle at Stigliano is real and it continues to give up exciting secrets from the past.

www.ingramcontent.com/pod-product-compliance
Lightning Source LLC
Chambersburg PA
CBHW030419310726
48979CB00009B/1527/J